Weller Browning is a professional musician, linguist and writer. She had a difficult childhood, which helped to form the nucleus of this story. Weller Browning has two children and she loves cats and dogs. She enjoys learning languages and writing her books. As a child, she was dyslexic but was always creating stories in her mind. Weller Browning lives in an old mining cottage in South Wales.

To my sons, Rory and Phil, for all their help and constant encouragement. And to Sammy, my Springer Cross, who listened to every word.

Weller Browning

WILD MARJORAM

AUSTIN MACAULEY PUBLISHERS

LONDON * CAMBRIDGE * NEW YORK * SHARJAH

A CIP catalogue record for this title is available from the British Library.

ISBN 9781528998147 (Paperback)
ISBN 9781528998154 (ePub e-book)

www.austinmacauley.com

First Published 2021
Austin Macauley Publishers Ltd®
1 Canada Square
Canary Wharf
London
E14 5AA

My gratitude to Sergeant Gary Humphreys of Swansea Central Police Station, and to Mrs Rhisian Davies and her daughter, who helped me so generously with their advice. Thanks also to Rory for all his dedicated help and to Phil for his unstinting support.

Saturday, 9th May 1981

I heard him say, "I know she's dying," and I heard her groan. Then the front door slammed.

But how can you hear a door slam shut in a dream?

I stirred uneasily under the duvet, the old fear pressing in on me, my mind searching for the dying woman. It was the same nightmare that had haunted me since childhood—the same voice, the same words, the same man with a gun, hiding in the dark background of my bedroom, a man without a face, and the same loud thud as the door shut. Each night I reached out to touch the woman who was dying, but I never felt her. I never saw her. I only heard her groaning. By dawn, the man with the gun had always gone.

The nightmare became intermittent when I married Richard. It had been comforting to lie beside his strong body, his arms round me, protecting me, his voice soothing when I woke with a cry; but the protection had been withdrawn when my marriage ended and the Decree Nisi had dropped through the letterbox.

Slowly, I opened my eyes. It was ten past six, and a pale light was slanting through the half-open blinds at the bedroom window. I lay back against the pillows thinking over the past twelve months. Even before the divorce, Richard had sold our flat over my head and I had found myself homeless, the second time my home had been snatched away from me. The second time my life had fallen apart.

On 18th April 1980, I left London and took the train to Norwich. Carrying two suitcases, I found a B&B near the station. The talkative landlady found me sullen and uncommunicative. Nine days later, on a miserable rainy Saturday afternoon, which exactly mirrored the twilight world of my wretchedness and failure, I moved into a rented ground-floor flat in Norwich.

My eyes followed the streaks of pale sunshine flitting through the dirty, slanting blinds. I had been in the flat for nearly two weeks, sunk in misery, shutting myself away. In a piercing moment of disgust, I pulled myself up, repelled by the grubby blue and white spotted paper on the walls. It was as if I were seeing the room for the first time with its horrible paper, dirty window and badly hung blind. What the *hell* was I doing in this flat, on my own, by myself? *How many ways are there to say you're alone, divorced, twenty-nine and your life is over?*

In the morning light, the dream was blurred and insubstantial. I got up stiffly, made some coffee and opened the kitchen door to let in some fresh air. Leaning against the door-frame and drinking my coffee, I looked round the dirty yard with its two dented dustbins. God, what a dump! If I were going to stay here, it would have to be brightened up. Flowers. Lots of flowers. I would have to find a garden centre. There was a chill in the air and I put both hands round the hot mug. Sipping the coffee, I knew that the past was a dangerous place, a place of guns and murder. I had known, with an unshakeable certainty from the age of sixteen, that one day the man with the gun would step out of the shadows and shoot me.

The past was confusing. The terrible things that had happened were hidden deep in my mind, but sometimes a sound, a word, a sudden shaft of light would activate a spasm of memory. There would be a glimpse of blood spreading over flagstones, or a woman dying on a rug, and the smell of lavender leaves would fill my throat and choke me.

I walked round the flat and, despite the grubby wallpaper, the old Victorian furniture and the damaged bath with the enamel flaking off, I could see the place was roomy and had its merits. The house was detached and double-fronted. There was a small hall with a cracked mirror on the wall above a wobbly three-legged half-moon hall table. The sitting room and kitchen were on one side of the house, and the two bedrooms and bathroom on the other.

Depression and loss of self-esteem seemed to have blinded me to my surroundings. Well, I wasn't blind any longer. What this flat needed was a good airing and a complete make-over by a good builder. I might not know where I was going in my life, but I decided, *definitely* decided, I wasn't going to live with this wallpaper any longer. It was as if I'd been sleep-walking in a dark tunnel of despair and now I wanted the sun back in my life. I pulled on some jeans and a defiant red shirt and went and picked up the post and the *Eastern Daily Press*.

The post made depressing reading. The bank statements reminded me that my current account held only what was left of the money I had earned while working as a legal secretary at Inner Temple in London. *That* would not last long.

There was also a savings account which contained my share of the money from the sale of the London flat, but I was determined not to stealth-steal from that. I had hopes of using it one day to buy a house in Norfolk, where property was less expensive than in London.

The second letter was from Mr Leonard Carless-Adams, the solicitor who had drawn up the terms for letting the flat. Carless-Adams wrote that Captain Ronald Dalton, who owned the house, was offering to sell me the freehold of the property for a very reasonable sum because he wanted a quick sale. There was one proviso: Dalton wanted to stay on as a tenant in the upper flat. If that were agreed then the sale could go through quickly. He added that Captain Dalton was offering to pay a year's rent in advance and thereafter every quarter starting immediately. Carless-Adams suggested I should meet my own solicitor to start the searches and arrange for a survey so that exchange of contracts could take place.

He wrote, "May I suggest Parr, Parr and Bretherton, the solicitors who work next door to Sellick's Estate Agency in Norwich? I personally know both Mr Sellick and Mr Bretherton. Parr, Parr and Bretherton undertook searches for this property only three months ago, so Mr Bretherton will be up to date with all the details."

I had no experience of buying and selling. Richard had seen to all the details of our flat in London, but this was an opportunity I couldn't miss. I looked up Parr, Parr and Bretherton in Yellow Pages, and at nine o'clock I rang and made an appointment to see Mr Bretherton on Friday 15th May at 10am.

Then I turned to Situations Vacant in the EDP. I would have to find a job.

There were two vacancies for legal secretaries and half-a-dozen for office clerks, but I didn't want to work in an office or have anything more to do with solicitors and barristers. Richard was a solicitor at Harries and Watling, and I had worked for Sir Selwyn Freeman as his legal secretary for eleven years at Inner Temple. I had prepared his briefs, liaised with police and probation officers, looked after our clients and managed the office.

And I had loved every minute, loved being part of the team and working with Selwyn. Perhaps Richard had been right when he said the work at Inner Temple had been more exciting than my marriage. Richard was thirteen years older than I, unimaginative and jealous, a big man, his thick brown hair falling over a wide forehead. He had resented my success and friendship with Selwyn. I thought of Selwyn's fury when I told him I was leaving.

"You're a bloody fool, Paula, you're throwing everything away! Dammit, girl, you're throwing *me* away! You can't do it. I won't let you."

But my heart and body were sick, so I slipped quietly away to Norwich which represented summer-holiday happiness with my parents. And I desperately needed to touch some of that elusive golden quality.

A part-time job caught my eye: estate agent for a Retirement Homes project. The agents offering the job were Sellick's of Norwich. Carless-Adams had mentioned Sellick's. The job was in Swaffham, but had a Norwich phone number. I looked Swaffham up on the map. It was about twenty miles west of the city.

I was sixteen when I applied for my first job. I had been through a difficult year. My father had walked out of the house on the day my mother died in May 1967. I never saw him again. Our home was sold quickly and I stayed with a friend. Then one day, I witnessed a murder. A man, standing in the shadows of the room, had shot a woman. I never saw his face. I had run away. I was ill for weeks. It was during that time that the nightmares started.

I was awakened one night by the sounds of a woman groaning. In the flickering shadows of the dying night-light, I saw the curtains move. The silhouette of a man holding a gun stepped forward. He had no face, just a curved line for eyebrows. I heard him say "I know she's dying." I heard the bullets cross the room. Then the woman groaned again. I lay there paralysed with fear. I told no-one about the man with the gun, or about the woman who was dying.

Over the months and years, the memory of the murder had disappeared into a secret corner of my mind. It only reappeared when sunlight dazzled me, or shadows moved in the evening light. Then I would be overcome with terror, unable to explain why I was frightened.

In the summer holidays in 1968, I received a brochure through the post. It was about a law firm in Inner Temple. A covering type-written letter gave details of jobs being offered by the firm. A teacher at school had tried to help me in those dark days. I thought she had sent me the article. I applied to Inner Temple and was accepted as a very junior clerk in August. I went to evening classes and worked hard at shorthand, typing and law. In two years I became personal secretary to Sir Selwyn Freeman. I married Richard when I was eighteen. We divorced eleven years later. It doesn't take many words to describe a life.

At nine o'clock, I telephoned the Norwich number. It would do no harm to enquire about the job at the Retirement Homes, and a part-time job would give me time to look for a more permanent position. An appointment was made with a Mr Inglis at Sellick's Estates Head Office in Norwich for nine o'clock on Thursday, 14 May. The receptionist said I should send a CV before the interview.

Apart from the bank statements and the solicitor's letter, there were three leaflets about properties in Damgate Lane. They came from an estate agent in Acle, a village not far from Norwich. From the day I had moved into the flat, leaflets about properties in Damgate Lane had dropped through the letterbox. I had thrown them impatiently into the bin. I felt my frustration rising. I phoned the agents. A woman's voice said a man had rung and told them to send me the leaflets.

"What man?" My voice was sharp.

The woman on the phone asked round the office and came back. "He didn't give a name, just said you were interested in properties in Damgate Lane."

"Well, I'm *not* interested and please stop sending the leaflets."

This was not the time to remember Damgate Lane and the past.

But Damgate Lane and the memories would not go away.

July 1962

It's the school holidays. As usual, we're staying in Yorkstone Cottage in Damgate Lane in Acle, near Norwich. It's a hot summery day and I've wandered into the garden with my notebook. My mother calls me over and I sit on a low stool beside her while she's painting. She explains how the morning heat haze has altered the shape and colours of the dahlias growing against a low red-brick wall.

As I write and illustrate my story, I listen to her in the stray way that young children do as they carelessly absorb information from their parents. Mum holds out her hand and I give her my story about a boy who has lost his identity. She reads the first part, commenting in her usual brusque manner. "You observe well, Kindchen, you have a good eye for character and plot, that's your strength. But here...and here, see? The sketch is too fussy, too messy. Draw with the minimum of lines and sketch the features more sharply. Your plot is good and exciting."

Fussy, messy! Harsh words for an eleven-year-old. The final words are lost in my tears. I run into the kitchen. Dad gives me a hug and a tall glass of orange juice. "Don't worry, honey, Marjorie's under the illusion that honesty is a virtue. I'm leaving in an hour for Paris, so you've just time to read me your story."

13

Later, he kisses me goodbye and says he'll be back in three days. "I like the ideas you have about the boy, and the drawings are great. Have it finished for me by the time I get back. In the meantime, look after your mum while I'm away."

Unfettered admiration from Dad and the closest scrutiny from Mum, nothing in between to cling to. I wander back into the garden and sit down, fingering Mum's painting brushes. She tells me, as she always tells me, to stop touching the brushes.

"Why is Dad going away again?"

"Business."

"Business" is always the answer. Mum sounds tired. She's writing and illustrating another book on gardening, and the editor is getting impatient. I watch her drawing the summer mist into the canvas, the background blurred behind the starry petals and pompoms, but after a while I go back to my story. Dad has promised to take Bobby and me on a Broads cruiser when he gets back.

Summer holidays at Yorkstone Cottage were forever associated with Bobby, a black and white springer spaniel who lived in Brownleas with his owner, Mrs Anna Lacey. Brownleas was a red-brick cottage lying over the hedge at the bottom of our garden. Every day at ten in the morning Bobby would come leaping joyfully through a hole in the hedge. There was always a smile in his golden eyes and a tennis ball in his mouth and together we would explore the fields and the nearby Broad. They were happy days until the stranger walked into our garden and died.

Amongst the post was a handbill from a builder. The first thing I noticed was the name: *Jolley and Merryweather*. They sounded an attractive duo. I started thinking that if I were buying the house then I would be in a position to have it decorated. The ghastly mahogany furniture, the dirty old cooker, the wallpaper and that flaking bath just had to go. I phoned and Mr Jolley said he could come round in the afternoon and price the work.

When I was young and we lived in Ealing, our builder was called Mr Isaac Badger. I was mesmerised by his amazing woollen jumpers with their brightly coloured interlinking circles. He moved in shimmering rings. Dad had got on well with Mr Badger. "He always sees the job as a whole, not as separate issues."

I had added Isaac Badger to my sketches. On the odd occasions that I look through my sketch-books, the people from the past leap out of the pages and I hear my mother's voice as she worked to improve my technique.

"Soften the shadows under the cheeks." She would take my pencil. "See, *Liebling*, like this. Look for the irregularities in the features. Note how people balance themselves through their backs and shoulders, and look at the eyes of an older woman, how the lines age the face, while in a man they increase his gravitas. And this one where the neck has fallen in, stretch the ligaments more."

In a few lines, I would see at once what she meant. If I didn't have a sketch-book with me, I used an invisible pencil on an invisible pad. Just the act of sketching sealed the subject in my mind. Over the years, sketching had become compulsive.

You could have mistaken Jolley for a businessman: blue suit, blue tie, smart brown shoes, a forthright manner. He explained he usually supervised the work moving between different sites. "Though I can turn my hand to anything."

He had lived in North Wales and London, he said, but had settled in Norwich. "The business was failing when I bought it and now I've built up a good team. I'll give you a good price if you give us the job."

He looked at his clipboard. "Let me get this straight. You want a new bathroom, and a new kitchen with new kitchen units, new fridge, new washing and drying machines, a new cooker and a new kitchen floor; all the wallpaper off in all rooms and the walls painted; double-glazing throughout and new light fittings and blinds." He looked at me. "That right?" I nodded. "And you want the whole thing done ASAP. That right?" I nodded again.

Mr Jolley pulled some paper away from the wall. "Um, plaster looks okay." He went into the kitchen and opened the cupboard door. "The boiler's old, you'll need to replace it soon." He pointed to the meter. "That's new, looks like the owner rewired the place, that'll save a bit."

Jolley kept consulting a book which had a lot of prices in it. I watched anxiously as he wrote figures down on his clipboard. He drew a sketch of the kitchen. "You should limit yourself to two hanging cupboards, here, and there, and three floor units so we can fit the clothes washer and dryer in. If nothing nasty turns up, we *might* do the job in about ten days. At the moment I've got two other jobs on the go. I'm hoping to finish one on the other side of Norwich by the middle of next week. Until then, I'll have to share the team out to cover your work, but I'll give you a good price." He looked up, his left eyebrow raised. "You may want upstairs done later, so it'll be to my advantage to give you a reasonable quote now."

He showed me the figures on his clipboard. I could see there wouldn't be much left in my current account. The "year in advance" rent from Captain Dalton was suddenly very attractive.

"You say you can do it in ten days? When can you start?"

"I'll bring a couple of men in on Monday and Tuesday, the 18th and 19th. They'll start pulling everything out of the kitchen and stripping the walls. Then, let's see, ok then, on Wednesday the 20th, I'll be able to take two men off other jobs to come and work here."

I could either accept it or get another quote and that would take time, and though I missed Mr Badger's brightly circled jumpers I rather liked Mr Jolley. So I agreed to his price as long as he started Monday week.

I asked him how he had pulled the business round.

"My father was a builder. Every job's different and that's interesting."

Jolley was in his late fifties, grey hair combed straight back and watchful dark blue eyes behind brown-rimmed spectacles. His nose wrinkled as he looked at the carpets and furniture. "Are you keeping all this old stuff?" He pulled a clump of horsehair out of the decaying armchair. I assured him everything would go including the carpet. "It'll be messy living here with everything going on," he said.

"I'll be out at work all day."

I didn't tell him I hadn't got the job, or even the house, yet. "You can get rid of everything except the bed, the bedside table, the wardrobe, the dolls house and the chair in the spare room. Oh, and the kettle, the television and my radio. If you leave the flat in a reasonable state for the evenings, I'll manage. And when you get to the guest room, I'll move back into my present bedroom when the new furniture comes."

He opened the door to the guest room. "What about those packing crates?" He looked surprised at the dolls house. "It's big, isn't it!" I told him my father had built it for me. "He did a good job!" Jolley responded.

I hadn't yet unpacked the two large crates that had followed me from London. I didn't want their contents sullied by the flat. The wardrobe was quite decent and I'd decided to keep it. "Perhaps you can work round them when you decorate the room?"

"No probs!"

He got some sample books out of his van and I chose the kitchen and bathroom, and I was firm. "No bath! I want a large American shower."

"You've got to have a bath," he objected. "A house needs a bath."

But I insisted. I wanted a large shower. The flat was so dingy it had left me feeling dirty, inwardly as well as physically. I wanted to experience fresh water surging over me, cleansing me, healing me.

Mr Jolley raised his eyebrow whimsically. "Well, you know your own mind, I suppose." But he doubted it. "I'm thinking you might find it difficult to sell the flat if you don't have a bath."

"I'm not selling," I said defiantly.

He shrugged and I could hear the unspoken *On your own head be it!* "Now then, what colour paint are you wanting?"

I chose ivory. Ivory everywhere. And then came the light fittings and blinds. I kept everything simple to save money. I began hoping, *seriously* hoping, I would get the job at Sellick's.

I had bought a second-hand television when I first moved in. The evening news was stark. The recently reformed Red Army Faction had assassinated the head of a German bank. Kidnappings and murders by a splinter group of the left-wing terrorist organisation had been carried out in London, Stockholm, and West Berlin. Sometimes a finger would be amputated and mailed to the victim's family with threats of further violence, or a body would be dumped in the street.

Equally vicious was a right-wing neo-Nazi group calling itself the *Sons of Hermann* with bases in West Berlin, Paris, London, Stockholm, and East Anglia. The newsreader said they were responsible for several bombings. The police had also reported a surge in people buying Nazi memorabilia. "At the same time," the newsreader added, "a series of planned marches against nuclear weapons took place in London and West Berlin today. Five policemen were injured in London, as well as two of the protestors. In West Berlin, violence escalated when a policeman was shot."

It was all so depressing. Two world wars and there was still violence for Causes. I turned over to a play on another channel. Two unhappy lovers were so determined to share their emotional tantrums with the public that I had to turn their miserable lives off the air and put the radio on instead.

It was after ten when the doorbell rang. I slipped into my zig-zag flip-flops and walked slowly down the entrance hall. It had rained on and off most of the day and the sky had darkened. I approached the door with trepidation, half-expecting to see Richard or Selwyn confronting me, arguing with me to return.

A stranger stood on the doorstep.

"Sorry to disturb you, ma'am, but perhaps you can help me?" He was of medium height, early fifties. The edge of a red and brown woollen scarf showed neatly under the narrow brown fur collar of his short black overcoat. It had started raining again and a sharpening wind was fluttering the leaves of the bamboo in the front garden.

"It's late, after ten. What do you want?"

"I'm making door to door enquiries, asking if anyone's seen this man." He held up a photograph of a man wearing a blue and white striped tee-shirt with a gold-linked chain round his neck; his short brown hair was parted in the centre and combed to the sides.

"And *you* are?"

He held up his ID card: *Ram Setna, Private Investigator.*

I looked back at the photograph. There was something vaguely familiar. "What's his name?"

"John Millar."

"Is he in some kind of trouble?"

"No, but his parents are very concerned for him."

"Well, I've only just moved in. I don't know anyone locally."

"Perhaps you saw him or spoke to him when you were out shopping?"

"I would have remembered. I'm sorry, I've never seen him."

His eyebrows went up at my brusque tone. "Two people noticed him looking at your house."

"Well, this flat was to let until recently. There was a sign in the garden, but like I said, I don't know him."

"Anyone else live here?"

"The owner lives upstairs, but I don't know if he's in."

"I'll ring the bell anyway." Setna turned and walked round the side of the house to the door leading to the upstairs flat. I heard him ringing the bell and I waited until he came back towards me. "No luck!" he called out. I watched him go down the path. The street lamp lit up the drizzling rain as he closed the garden gate. He turned and walked on down the street.

That night, I didn't dream of the woman who was dying. Instead, the dream started at the end of the nightmare with the front door banging to and fro. In the dark blur of sleep, I saw Ram Setna standing on the doorstep. I heard him say, "You know I'm dead, the man in the flat killed me."

With a sickening jerk, I woke, my heart hammering unevenly. I pulled myself up, hugging my knees. It was two o'clock in the morning. *You know I'm dead.* I could see his face staring at me through the darkness. How could I *know* he was dead? I thought a *woman* was dying.

I huddled the duvet round my shoulders and dozed uneasily. At seven in the morning, I was exhausted. A migraine was throbbing behind my left temple and I had cramp in my leg.

Sunday, 10th May 1981

I spent the morning going round the flat, measuring for new furniture. I felt more confident now that I was going to buy the flat. I had taken some aspirins earlier hoping they would stop the migraine getting worse. I took another couple before I went to a garden centre on the outskirts of Norwich. My mother had written and illustrated many books, including *English Flowers, European Flowers and Shrubs*, and *Garden Designs from the Sixteenth to the Twentieth Century in Europe*. In that strange osmosis that takes place between children and parents, she had imbued me with her knowledge and love for blooms and colour, shape and design.

When I was six, my mother asked my father to construct a wheel to help me learn the names of the colours. He made one from matches and painted each match a different colour. The twenty-four matches were placed in a circle and held together with a wire attached to a piece of wood on the back in such a way that I could rotate the wheel. My mother called it the Wheel of Truth, because colour influenced everything she did. "Without light," she once told me, "there would be no colour, and without colour the world would die." The Wheel went everywhere with me. It reminded me of sunshine, flowers, and summer holidays in our cottage in Acle.

The first thing I ordered at the garden centre were two black dustbins. Then I got thoroughly carried away and bought planters, ceramic pots, a wooden table and two chairs, a yellow parasol and lots and lots of plants including some climbing roses. And I didn't stop there. I added bags of compost, gardening gloves, a strong garden brush, watering can, trowel and secateurs. Under a bush I found two large old scullery sinks and added them to my order. I was determined to turn that unloved yard into a place of loving colour.

The assistant offered me some lavender bushes at a special discount, pushing one of the plants towards me. "They grow well in the soil round here and have a lovely scent."

I stepped back, feeling the familiar pricking at the back of my throat. I refused the offer firmly.

I told him to deliver the plants and pots on the 20th of the month. "The yard where the plants are going will have a skip, but the builders have promised to get it straight by Wednesday the 20th. And please make sure you water the plants in the meantime."

I wrote out the cheque. I hadn't realised how expensive plants were. Then I worried how much it would cost to have the yard cleaned.

Monday, 11th May 1981

I drove to Jarrolds, a big department store in Norwich, and ordered a large three-seater sofa, two coffee tables and two armchairs for the sitting room. These were to be delivered on Wednesday, 27th May. Then I went into the carpet department and settled on a carpet with colourful squares which could be laid on Tuesday 26th. I wondered if I were a fool to be making a home for myself in such a tired old flat.

That night, I was exhausted and the migraine was worse. I made some hot soup, took some tablets and went to bed. Sometime in the night the man with the gun stepped out of the shadows and I heard his weapon discharge across the room. I heard the woman groan. I struggled to wake up. I switched the light on and the shooting stopped. I searched every corner of the room, but there was no-one there. I kept the light on for the rest of the night.

Tuesday, 12th May 1981

At seven o'clock, I stirred uneasily. I had been dozing on and off most of the night. Finally I got up, took a couple of aspirins for the migraine, and then washed and dressed. I was putting the kettle on when the doorbell rang and I heard the rattle of milk bottles.

A man in a white coat and cap stood on the doorstep. He was brisk. "Jack at the corner shop said you'd just moved in so I thought you'd like your milk delivered." He smiled, holding out a pint. "I came yesterday, but you weren't in. I'm Gerry Scott and I'll bring your milk every day, and fresh eggs, bread, bacon, yogurts, the lot! You name it, I'll get it. I settle accounts on Tuesdays in this street."

Great salesmanship! I drink a lot of tea and coffee so I told him, okay, I'd start with a pint of milk, eggs, bread and a pack of yogurts. Then I gave him my order for the rest of the week.

"Good, that makes you eligible for this week's promotion!" He gave me a large oblong box filled with a selection of plain and chocolate biscuits from a well-known brand. My father had bought them every week as a treat during the summer holidays in Acle.

I laughed. "They remind me of school holidays. How much are they?"

"Nothing. Like I said, they're a promotion we're pushing this week." He put everything on the doorstep. Resting his back against the door-frame, he wrote my order down. "Come up from London, then?"

I nodded.

"On holiday?"

"No, I've got a job. How much do I owe you?" I was in no mood for gossiping. We settled the weekly sum and he looked up at the top flat.

"Anyone living up there?"

I froze, remembering the private investigator and my nightmare. "I don't think anyone's in."

"No worries, I'll ring anyway!"

Setna had said that as well.

Gerry closed his account book. "You on your own?"

"At the moment."

He picked the bottles up, but before I could take them, the postman arrived and handed me the mail. He nodded sourly and left without a word.

Gerry snorted. "He's a barrel of fun, for sure!"

On top of the mail was a postcard. It was a photo of Norwich Cathedral.

I turned it over. My name and address were written on the right-hand side in an even script. On the left were the words: *Why did you come to Norwich?* It was unsigned.

"Good news?" Scott asked.

I forced a smile. I didn't know what to make of it. I took the milk bottles he was offering me with a nod.

"OK then, I'll try the flat upstairs," he said.

I was about to shut the door when I saw Gerry close the wooden garden gate and climb into his milk float. He waved. "Nobody in!"

I took everything into the kitchen. Damn! *More* leaflets about Damgate Lane properties! I threw them in the bin.

After I made some coffee, I found my sketchbook and began drawing the milkman standing by his float near the street lamp opposite the garden gate. It had become a ritual to recall the people I met, but the anonymity of the white coat and cap obscured the man, and I recalled him only as slim, thin-faced, moderate height, a crisply spoken Cockney voice and a little intrusive. I thought he may have been in the forces. His walk had reminded me of my father.

I wondered if I'd been too forthcoming about myself. Lonely people are often indiscreet, their loneliness reaching out to strangers.

And then there was the postcard. *Why did you come to Norwich?* Perhaps it was a joke. Someone knowing something I didn't know. At first I wanted to destroy it, but finally I put the card in my shoulder-bag, made some tea and took more aspirins for the migraine.

I was taking the rubbish out to the dented dustbin in the yard when I caught a glimpse of a figure moving in the kitchen. I rushed back indoors. There was no-one in the kitchen, but the bedroom door was ajar. I ran over and pushed it wide open, but the attack came from behind. I was thumped on the back, bundled into the room and the door was slammed shut behind me. I fell awkwardly and banged my head and shoulder against the frame of the bed. It took me a moment to gather my wits. I realised, even as I fell, that my attacker could have killed me. I had felt the strength in his arms. I was sure it was a man.

I got up slowly. I had a cut on my forehead and an aching shoulder. It had been foolish to tackle the intruder on my own, but anger had proved stronger than prudence. Going round the flat, I found the front door open. His escape route. Then I found the means of entry, the window in the guest room was swinging to and fro. I had left it open on the latch to air the room. The window looked out onto the front garden and was hidden from the road by the thick fronds of the swaying bamboo. I closed the window firmly, but on a final look round the flat, I found nothing had been disturbed.

I went into the bathroom, washed my face and covered the cut with a plaster. Then I rang the local police to report what had happened. I was surprised how quickly PC Wayland arrived. I answered all his questions and he left to make house to house enquiries. He came back later to tell me there had been no burglaries locally. I should ring the station if I remembered anything useful.

I held back from telling him about the postcard with its threatening message. For how could PC Wayland know the answer to *Why did you come to Norwich?* when I had no idea what the question meant?

After PC Wayland left, I sat down at the lift-up flap that served as an inadequate breakfast bar. I could feel the migraine throbbing. I pushed aside the cold chicken salad I had made for lunch and made some tea instead.

The intruder had awakened memories, including two burglaries at our flat in West Kensington. Both times, the burglar had been disturbed by neighbours.

And now an intruder, here, in Norwich. The only expensive thing I owned was a Crux Gemmata which had belonged to my mother. The medieval Cross was decorated with small diamonds and rubies. It was a gift from a Frau Lang for the help Mum had given her in the war. I usually kept the Cross in my shoulder bag, but last night I had put it under my pillow hoping it would exorcise the faceless man with the gun. Unhappily, it had no effect on my nightmare. With an exclamation, I ran into the bedroom. The Cross was still under the pillow. Perhaps I had disturbed the man before he had time to search the room. Tonight, I thought, I would place my revolver there as well.

I went into the sitting room and sat in the horrible brown armchair with its bulging seams of horsehair stuffing. The postcard and the attack had upset me.

I needed to rally myself, to look back and remember who I was before the divorce.

In April 1980, I still had a husband, a large flat in London and a great job as a senior legal secretary. And then the blow had fallen. Without preamble, Richard had said he wanted a divorce. His voice had risen. "I've met someone else and I want to marry her. I want to lead a normal life."

A *normal* life? And then the bombshell. "She's pregnant, we're going to have a child."

It was strange how 'she' had remained an anonymous figure, but out of that nebulous cloud a shape had formed in my mind of a large full-hipped young woman with big boobs, spaniel eyes and saccharine lips called Sheila. She had come to Harries & Watling straight from university. And Richard had barely mentioned her. I had seen her once on a quick visit to the office.

Then came Richard's fractious tone again, his voice high and spiteful. "It was *you* who always said wait until we could afford to start a family. You never listened to *me*. I wanted children, but you already had your own family, your *pals* in Inner Temple."

What *rubbish*, I thought. Another barbed arrow: "The trouble with you, Paula, is that you get more satisfaction from your job than I can give you. We lost touch years ago, but you were so busy you didn't even notice."

True? Well, perhaps, a little, but we'd *both* agreed to wait until Richard got his partnership before starting a family. The trouble was it was taking longer than we'd planned. Richard still wasn't a partner at forty-two. I admitted I hadn't noticed all this dissatisfaction creeping in, but looking at him, I could see how much he'd changed. He seemed older, petulant, his lips drawn into a thin obstinate line, a deep furrow between his dark eyes.

Older and furrowed, but attractive enough to start a new life with a young woman. "I can't talk with you anymore," he said. "It's been a long time since you were interested in what *I* do or what *I* think. It's always been about *you*. You and bloody Selwyn Freeman."

And Richard had slammed the door and left me standing speechless in the middle of the lounge. Richard had never liked Selwyn. The chemistry between them was sour. According to Richard, Selwyn was an egocentric bore. According to Selwyn, Richard was old and tired at forty, without ambition, and what, in God's name, had I ever seen in him?

I should have picked up on all these signs. I should have noticed our lives drifting apart, just as the intimacy in our marriage had drifted away, but I knew from years of working in Chambers, that there are two sides to every marriage break-down. Whatever the rights and wrongs, the flat was sold and I was given half the proceeds. After a short stay in hospital, I left Richard and London with an aching heart and an emptiness for the wasted years.

From that moment, all the old anxieties came flooding back, and so did the nightmares and the man with the gun.

I felt restless and insecure after the attempted robbery. I checked the flat again, closed all the windows and locked the front and kitchen doors. My "drawbridge mentality" was being fostered by fear. I looked up a locksmith in Yellow Pages and Mr John Watson agreed to come before ten the next morning.

That night, the old dream returned. I saw the curtains move, heard the bullets screech across the room. There was blood on the floor. I heard myself screaming behind a door, but *which* door, *which* room, *which* house?

Wednesday, 13th May 1981

The locksmith came at ten and went through the flat suggesting what should be done. He gave me a price for the work and said he could come back on Thursday about six in the evening. It wasn't cheap, but the advice was good.

"You young women, you should take care and think about security, see?" I wasn't offended, he was right. I would feel much better when it was all done. He stretched himself into his raincoat. "Terrible weather, hope the summer's better when it comes. OK. Tomorrow evening then!"

I spent the entire day in Norwich ordering cutlery, crockery, a kettle (to replace the old damaged kettle the landlord had left), and four Clarice Cliff mugs and coffee jug. Clarice Cliff was out of my price range, but these were seconds with minor blemishes occurring during production, cutting the price from the impossible to the just possible. As I held the coffee jug, I was overcome by a wave of emotion. I remembered how everything had been sold, including the Clarice Cliff, when Mum died. Mum had loved her Clarice Cliff.

"Is there anything else?" the assistant asked briskly.

"A microwave!" I said. The assistant explained how efficient the oven was. Richard had refused to have a microwave because he enjoyed cooking. He prepared everything and simmered, boiled, poached and braised. He was very good, the meals were delicious. I had done nothing in the kitchen, except help with the clearing up. I had liked having a man in the kitchen. Now I was on my own and bereft of cooking skills. The new microwave had been created for people just like me. I had everything packed up and taken down to my car.

In the afternoon, I spent more money buying sheets and pillows for the new beds. I told the saleswoman everything was to be delivered on Tuesday 26th. I kept hoping to God I would get the job at Sellick's.

In the darkness of the night, the man with the gun moved out from behind the curtain. I was sure he was going to shoot the dying woman. I screamed to him to stop. With an enormous effort, I pulled myself up and ran across the room to put myself between the gun and the woman. When I woke, I was lying huddled on the floor by the bed, cold, crying and scared out of my wits.

Thursday, 14th May 1981

By seven-thirty in the morning I had washed and dressed. I chose a straight black skirt, white shirt and dark blue jacket with a discreet Celtic gold brooch for the lapel, black tights and high blue wedge shoes. I put enough make-up on to hide the injuries to my forehead. I arrived at Sellick's head office in Norwich just before nine and was interviewed by Jim Inglis, slightly built, South African accent. His heavily-lined forehead, receding hairline, arched eyebrows and tired blue pin-striped suit made him look older than his sixty odd years. I sat opposite him at his table in the main office.

Inglis was holding the CV I had posted earlier in the week. He told me he'd been working for Mr Sellick for over thirty years. "And the business has been going since 1947, in London first, and then here in Norwich. We run a tight ship, Mrs James, everyone pulls their weight, and that makes Sellick's a successful estate agency. But the job we're advertising isn't in Norwich, it's in Swaffham."

He looked at me intently through his dark-rimmed spectacles. "You'll be selling new buildings to people of retirement age. Most of the time, you'll be on your own in the office. Of course," he continued, "it's a bonus that you're older. Pensioners are put off by doing business with people as young as their grandchildren." I began to feel my age. "You admit, in your CV, that you've no experience in real estate. Why do you think you can handle this job?"

"Well, I'm used to working on my own. I'm good with people and very organised, but, of course, I shall need your help and advice."

He liked my modesty. "Yes, yes, you'll need advice." He glanced again at my CV. "But why aren't you looking for secretarial work? You're very well qualified, and the solicitors next door need a legal secretary. Are you sure you wouldn't be happier in that field?"

"Absolutely sure." Confidence shone out of me. "My life has changed. I want to do something *different*." He looked unimpressed. I reminded myself that I really needed this job. I reeled off my good business traits. "And I live alone, there are no family commitments, so I can work all kinds of hours. But what exactly *is* the job in Swaffham?"

Inglis jumped at the chance to explain. "The Retirement Homes project is Mr Sellick's own idea. He's in the process of constructing over three hundred flats and bungalows on a site just outside Swaffham. The properties are being built for retired folk in good or reasonable health. The site is to be known as Dunham Village." He wagged his finger at me. "I want to stress that the Village is for people who still enjoy an active social life. They're not coming to a nursing home and you'll have to bear this in mind when you talk with your clients."

The finger dropped. "The job in Swaffham starts on Monday 25th, still more than a week away. Why not spend the day here and see how you get on? It will give us an idea of your suitability for the job. And, if I *may* suggest," he gave a dry cough, "a little *less* make-up would be advisable."

I suppressed my fury at his comment, concentrating on how much I needed the job. I pointed out that the 25th was a bank holiday. He was not slow to expose my ignorance. "We do very good business on bank holidays."

He got up and led the way across the room to where a woman in her forties was sitting next to a vacant table.

"This is Mrs Paula James, Corrie. She's new to real estate, so help her all you can."

"I'll look after you, Paula, don' you worry." Corrie had a strong Norfolk accent. She pointed to the leaflets on my table. "Read all that stuff and go through the paperwork in the top drawer. You'll need to know what to do if you get a client. Oh yeah, and tell the punters there's a solicitor's firm next door. That helps us, as well as helping them."

I told her I would be seeing Mr Bretherton in the morning about a property I was buying. "Though I thought they only paired estate offices and solicitors in Scotland."

Corrie grimaced. "Dunno about that, but Sellick insisted on it." She pointed to the drawer. "You'll find a name holder in there. Can you type? Good, type your name and slip it in the holder and put it on your table."

I typed my name on the electric typewriter and displayed my identity. I looked round the office. It was a large room with a sensible dark brown carpet, gaudy chandeliers and some good paintings and prints on the walls. Corrie didn't think much of them. Her nose wrinkled. "I don't like paintings with shapes, anyone can paint shapes. I like dancers, ballet dancers, showing me what I could never be, well, not with these legs, but it's nice to dream."

There were five women and two men working in the office apart from Inglis. Corrie told me their names: Sue, Lorna, Cathy, Martin and Ken. "Martin Spencer's going down to the Thetford branch next week. That's promotion. Of course, it's all right if your uncle's someone." She sniffed. "We've all been gone down to Swaffham to help out till Sellick choose a permanent agent again."

"Again?"

"The last one didn't suit, she didn't get on with Pat Heals. Pat? She manage the Retirement Homes. Sellick think a lot of her."

Corrie pointed to a woman in her early thirties who was crossing the room to Inglis's table. "Tha's Brenda Crossley, Sellick's personal secretary. Sellick like big boobs, so you're OK, Paula!"

Thanks, Corrie! Brenda had watchful eyes, her well-formed breasts almost popping out of her low-cut blouse. Inglis was all over her.

Brenda swept past us, files filling her arms, her grey eyes flicking me up and down, her beaky nose in the air. I heard the door bang as she disappeared into the back.

I asked Corrie what lay behind the door.

"Brenda's office and Pat Heals' room. Then there's Sally, she's Accounts, and some cupboards where the stock's kept. The kitchen and loos, and of course, the stairs leadin' up to Sellick's flat. I wanted to speak to Sellick about Ted, my old man. Inglis wouldn't listen, but Pat catch me just as I go up the stairs. I tell her I want to ask Mr Sellick if Ted could work here, but she send me back to my table."

"What does Ted do?"

"It doesn't matter what you do, anyone can learn this job. Ted speak well, better than what I do, and he know the city, but if you really want to know, he work in a furniture store. About two year ago, he hurt his back, some of that stuff's heavy to carry, and working here'd suit him much better."

"Well, this job was vacant," I pointed out. Of course, I was glad it had been offered to me, but Corrie's story made me feel uncomfortable. "Who was here before I came?"

"French woman, didn't want to talk to rubbish like me. Called herself Renée Tournai." Corrie's chin went up as she lengthened her vowels. She brought her chin down. "We get a lot of foreigners who want to buy places in Norwich. I always thought that was why Sellick brought her in. I used to watch her cosying up to him. Pat didn't like that. She's pleased Renée's gone. Renée was sent down to Swaffham as well, but she was only there a couple of days when Audrey Simpson wasn't well, but Simpson say Renée had her nose in everything. Anyway, Renée was only back here for a week before she was dismissed. Inglis say she went back to France. And now you're here. D'you speak foreign languages?"

"Well, a bit." I hesitated. "German and French."

She humped her shoulders up. "Well, maybe tha's why. Ted don' speak no foreign muck." She looked at me. "Sellick going to give you the job in Swaffham?"

"I don't know."

"Any one of us could do the job, so why's he askin' people who know damn all about selling property?" Her gaze was hostile. "There's more money in working at the Retirement Homes, too."

"Perhaps he wants a new face, a new way of looking at the problems."

She shrugged.

The place was suddenly busy as several clients came through the door. I kept my head down and started reading and writing out notes on a pad of A4 paper. Corrie gave me a street guide.

"You'll need it when you take the punters up the city."

Corrie was short and plain-looking with a full face, short brown hair and a straight cut fringe. She was such a down to earth person, I wondered how she got on with her clients. A moment later, a couple walked over to her table and she stood up and greeted them. I listened to the conversation while surreptitiously going through some pamphlets. Corrie knew her job and did it well.

Then I was delighted to have my own clients, a Mr and Mrs Luis Guarda. Mrs Guarda was a businesswoman, a director in a firm selling farm machinery. She listed what she wanted: a big kitchen, five bedrooms and a *really* large garden for two Labradors, four young children and a husband. In that order. I looked through the files and found three five-bedroom houses with generous gardens. I made appointments at two of the houses. The last property was empty and I took the keys with me.

We went in the Guardas' Land Rover. Luis Guarda was a courier escorting tourists round the great cities in Spain. They fell in love with the empty house.

"I'm away, on and off, for six months of the year," Luis told me. "So it's important Rita has the house she wants. We've already sold our property so we'll start putting things in motion."

I was elated.

Corrie smiled. "You done well, Paula, maybe you got the knack."

A dark-haired petite woman came into the office. Jim Inglis hurried across and whispered something to her and they both came over to my table.

Inglis said, "This is Mrs Patricia Heals who's managing the project at Swaffham."

"I hear you've already made a sale." She spoke with a London accent and her oddly tilted eyebrows lifted like horns. "You've done well." She swept regally through the office and disappeared through the back door before I could respond.

Corrie leaned over. "Pat's sharp with her tongue. An' she's nervy 'cos she's put a truckload of money into the Retirement Homes. She's a friend of Mr Conrad's daughter. Conrad died this year. He was a jeweller and he put a *lot* of money in as well. Pat's husband, Lawrie, got a job here because Sellick knew his parents when he was in Pretoria in South Africa. Although Lawrie work mainly in the Acle branch. I heard they got some good cottages for sale in Damgate Lane. You might've done better to look there first."

But Damgate Lane was not where I wanted to live.

"Pat and Lawrie married 'bout seven years ago, but they separated lately. Lawrie want Pat to go back with him to South Africa, but Pat won't go now Sellick put her in charge of the Retirement Homes." Corrie lowered her head. "There's Sellick now with Stella Linsey, Conrad's daughter. Sellick like comin' round, makin' sure we're workin' hard. If he had a whip he'd crack it, just to watch us jump!"

I caught a glimpse of a broad-shouldered, thickset man with white hair, talking to a pretty woman with a spoilt expression. There was a short lunch break for Corrie and me at one o'clock, and we went over to the *Norwich Fish and Chippery* opposite the estate office. While we were having coffee, I took my sketchbook out of my shoulder bag and made a quick sketch of Patricia Heals.

Corrie leaned over. "Tha's really good. You got that look about her." She struggled to explain. "You know, clever, hard and that 'come hither' she give Sellick! And the eyebrows, you done them really well."

Corrie put her hand on my arm. "Can you draw me?"

With a few lines, I sketched her sitting at the table, catching the full round face, the thick brown fringe touching the even brows, the hazel-flecked eyes and small mouth above an attractive cleft chin.

"You have really nice eyes," I said as I signed the sketch and passed the book over to her. Corrie was overcome.

"Can I have it?" she asked diffidently.

"Course you can!" I eased the page out and gave it to her. I would sketch it again when I got home.

"It's ever so different from a photo," she said. I nodded. Why is the intimacy of a portrait such a surprise to the sitter? "What's the D in the middle?" she asked.

"Denby. Paula Denby James. You can frame it, if you like."

She looked taken aback. "I've never seen myself in a frame." She looked up. "Ted'll be ever so pleased. Thank you, Paula. I didn't know I looked like that. No-one's ever said I had nice eyes."

I thought Ted should have told her. I finished with a drawing of Jim Inglis with his grey arching eyebrows and stress-lined forehead and widow's peak. Corrie nodded. "Jim had lots of hair when he first come, but he worry too much an' he's losing his hair, just like Ted."

I mentioned that Inglis spoke with a South African accent.

"He met Doug Sellick in South Africa. I dunno what they did. After the war, Jim work for Sellick in the London office, and then he come here."

She stared at the sketch I had given her. "You're ever so clever, Paula." She looked up, her forehead wrinkled. "You don' have to work in a dull office like me."

I hesitated. "It's not as simple as that, Corrie. Life isn't simple, is it?"

Corrie agreed cheerfully. "You can bloody say that again!"

At the end of the day, Inglis came over. "You've done well, Mrs James. Mr Sellick wants you to work here next week and if you do well, he'll see you next Friday at noon to discuss the position at Swaffham. Can you do that?"

I thought it was a good idea; a portmanteau of opportunity to earn money, see what the work was really like and a chance to get away from the flat and the builders.

"Very well, you'd better go to Sally in Accounts. She'll take your details and tell you your salary. You'll be here from Monday to Thursday, from nine until six, and Friday till twelve."

I drove home feeling a lot happier, glad to have the chance to earn some money. The locksmith had said he would be at the flat about six. He was waiting in his car round the side of the house. I apologised for being late and said I had just got a job and it had all been a bit hectic.

"A job, eh? You'll be able to pay me then!"

I smiled dutifully. Watson was a short, untidy looking man, but his appearance belied his work, for he was neat and efficient.

"You'll be safe and secure with my locks. Now, I've put triple safety locks on both doors, but seeing as you're having the windows replaced, what I've done is screw the windows shut. You won't be able to open them, but you'll be safe and secure. It'll be a determined bugger who'll break into the flat with these locks."

I told him the new windows would be put in within two weeks. I thanked him as I wrote out the cheque and said it was worth every penny to feel safe.

I had put the post on the hall table when I came home. Damn, two more leaflets for Damgate Lane. And the Decree Absolute. My elation became depression. I had almost forgotten about the final piece of paper. It told me what I didn't want to recognise, the rebuttal, the rejection of *me*, the failure and the stark finality. In the cracked mirror in the hall, I looked at my reflection: thick honey-blonde hair, a generous mouth, pale complexion and dark blue eyes beneath raised brows. The fractured glass picked out the fear in my eyes, fear of being on my own, fear of the man with the gun who haunted my sleepless nights and fear of the blood-stained knife twisting in the sunlight.

Friday, 15th May 1981

Mr Bretherton was a quietly spoken elderly man with a reassuring manner. "Mr Carless-Adams has already been in touch and I'll be happy to act for you. You say you're working next door at Sellick's Agency? Good! We have an arrangement with Mr Sellick that his employees get a discount for any property they sell or buy if the client acts through us, so I'll see that a discount is reflected in my fee."

I began to feel things were looking up. Bretherton explained that he had conducted the searches for Captain Dalton's property only three months earlier.

"Mr Carless-Adams has explained that you're renting the ground floor apartment from Captain Dalton. Are you applying for a mortgage or buying the house outright?"

I confessed I had been unsure at first. "But the offer is very good, and as I have the money in an account, I've decided to go ahead and purchase the whole property."

"Very well then, I'll submit the searches again."

After a discussion on fixtures and fittings, stamp duty and references, I gave him the addresses of Sir Selwyn Freeman and Jane Donovan.

"Good. I'll register the Change of Title at the Land Registry, and when completion takes place, we'll meet again, when you must pay the outstanding sum owing. At that point, you'll receive the deeds to the building." He showed me a contract, and I wrote out the cheque for the deposit. "And I shall need your signature here…and here…and there."

I asked why the house hadn't sold before. Bretherton shrugged. "The buyers dropped out at the last moment. I understand Captain Dalton was very upset."

"But why is Captain Dalton offering *me* the opportunity to buy the house?" I hesitated. "And why hasn't it been put back on the market?"

Bretherton spread out his hands. "I understand the captain wants someone reliable." He looked at his file. "Mr Carless-Adams has kindly sent copies of Captain Dalton's file round with copies of your earlier references." He looked up with a smile. "Mr Carless-Adams has told me that you're Marjorie Denby's daughter. She came to see me in, yes, it was in Easter 1966, the year before she died. She wanted me to prepare her will. Afterwards, I took her next door to introduce her to Mr Sellick, an old friend. Mrs Denby was a redoubtable lady. Yes, indeed."

But I had never seen my mother's will.

"Captain Dalton is in Australia at the moment," Bretherton went on, "but Mr Carless-Adams has assured me that all forms have been signed by him, and as we have worked together in the past, I feel sure all will go ahead smoothly."

"That sounds very good," I said, "but just now you mentioned my mother's will. Could you give me a copy?"

He leaned forward, pressed a number on his phone and spoke to his secretary. A few minutes later, a smartly dressed middle-aged woman came into the room. She told us that the will Mr Bretherton had prepared had been destroyed, and added, "I understand Mrs Denby made a new will with a solicitor in London."

Bretherton rose to his feet. "Your mother wasn't well towards the end of her life. People often change their wills at such times. I'm sorry not to be more helpful."

We shook hands. "I'll be in touch as soon as I have news," he said.

A shaft of sunlight burst through the open window as I turned to leave, and the room was divided sharply into light and dark. A breeze fluttered the curtains and I stood, frozen, waiting for the sound of gunfire, but almost at once the sunlight faded and the room resumed its grey appearance. I turned on my heel and hurried out.

Saturday, 16th May 1981

By Saturday morning, the remnants of the migraine had gone. About ten in the morning, I had a surprise phone call from Jane Donovan. Jane was a solicitor who worked with Richard at Harries and Watling. I hadn't seen her since I left London. The familiar crisp tones informed me she was coming up to Norwich next week. She suggested we could meet for lunch. I was taken aback. I wasn't sure I wanted to resume contact with the past.

"I'm having the flat decorated. You could come Saturday fortnight. On the 30th, that is." It sounded ungracious.

"Great, I'll ring you when I'm in Norwich." She hadn't noticed, or perhaps had ignored, the negative tone. I gave her my address, but before she rang off she said a man, ex-army, had been enquiring about me at the office.

I felt a stab of fear. "What did he say?"

"Gwen spoke with him. You remember Gwen at reception? Dark-hair, good organiser, no imagination? The man seemed to think you worked at the office."

"At Harries and Watling, you mean?"

"Harries, Watling and *James*, darling."

So Richard was now a partner. Presumably, I was no longer holding him back. "I can't imagine who it can be," I said slowly. "Did Gwen give him my address?"

"Of course not, darling, she doesn't have it." There was a pause. "Does Richard know where you are?"

"No!" The break had been complete.

"Well, I'm glad you know about the ex-army man in case he turns up on your doorstep. I didn't see him myself, but Gwen said he was good-looking. And then, if someone's determined to find you, they'll find a way. See you last Saturday in the month then!" And she rang off.

Later, I wondered how Jane had got my phone number. What had she said? *If someone's determined to find you, they'll find a way.* It was disconcerting and a little worrying.

In the evening, I put the telly on and watched riots taking place in cities up and down the country. The arguments on both sides were aired with passion but little content. Nothing had changed down the years. Depressed, I turned to a crime drama.

I must have dozed off. I was opening a door. A man was coming towards me. There were no features on his face, just a curved line across his brow. In his hand, a pistol. The sound of gunfire was all round me. I screamed and woke to knocking and ringing on the front door mixed with gunshots coming from the television. I stumbled to my feet, the dream more vivid than the present, my heart a racing irregular beat. I turned the television off and blundered out into the hall. I opened the door, keeping the chain on. Two men stood outside.

"Is everything all right, miss? We heard someone screaming."

It was after ten. It had been raining hard all evening. I could smell the damp muskiness rising from the grass in the dark. "It was the TV. Who are you? What do you want?"

The older man held up a warrant card. "DCI Quinn and this is DS Penry. And you are Mrs Paula James?"

I had kept my married name. Richard was unfaithful, not I, and my marriage had been important to me.

Quinn was wearing a grey raincoat with a turned-up collar. He looked tired. "Have you seen this man? I'm sorry, the photo may upset you."

I drew back. It was the face of the private investigator who had asked questions about the man who had disappeared. Setna had been shot between the eyes. I closed the door, took a deep breath, put the hall and porch lights on, released the chain and let the men into the hall. I didn't invite them into the sitting room. I wanted them to leave quickly.

"That's better," Quinn said. "Now then, what can you tell us about him?"

"Why are you questioning me?"

"A neighbour saw you speaking with him on Saturday evening. He'd been to all the houses in the street."

I was brief. "There's nothing I can tell you. He asked questions about a young man who was missing. He said he was a private investigator. His name was Ram Setna."

"Setna had a diary," Penry said. The DS was young, dark-haired, well-dressed, and had a slight Welsh accent. "Your name is in it and under your name Setna wrote…" He looked at his notebook. "*She knows something. Go back tomorrow.*"

"I don't know why he wrote that," I said quickly. "He had a photo of…now who was it? Oh yes, John Millar. He asked me if I'd seen him."

"And had you?"

"No."

Penry wanted to know where I worked.

I told him where I would be working and where I had worked before I came to Norwich. He would find out anyway.

"You had a burglary recently," Quinn said.

I looked at him nonplussed. "Nothing was taken."

"I was told you were attacked."

"I was pushed from behind, nothing serious."

He was trying to find a connection between Setna's death and my intruder.

As they turned to leave, Quinn asked me if my husband knew where I was.

"No, we're divorced," I replied.

And then they left. I went into the sitting room and poured myself a brandy. I hoped it would kill the picture of Setna's face with the hole between his eyes. I sat down holding the glass tightly. Setna's photo had triggered one of my memory flashes:

It's night-time.
There are women in gowns and men in evening dress.
A shot.
A young man falling.
My mother running along the pavement.

The memory-spike disappeared and I drank the brandy quickly, my heart racing, as it always did when these turbulent glimpses from the past flashed through my mind.

Before I went to bed, I took the pistol out of my shoulder-bag, checked the ammunition and put the weapon under my pillow. The picture of the dead man had unnerved me. I wondered if Setna's death was a warning, like the postcard.

Sunday, 17th May 1981

DCI Quinn and DS Penry came back at nine in the morning and questioned me further. Patiently, I went over everything again: Setna had shown me the photo. I hadn't recognised the man. And I *really* didn't know any more.

Quinn then asked me about my time in Inner Temple. "You worked for Sir Selwyn Freeman, right?" He was thinking this through. "So what are you doing in Norwich?"

I wanted to scream, *I ran away from Freeman, from Richard, from everyone!* But adults can't admit to simple truths like that, and women are labelled "hysterical" if they scream, so I shrugged and said I'd wanted a change.

"But why Norwich?" he persisted.

My voice was flat. I didn't want Quinn connecting me with things that had happened in the past. "Oh, I don't know, just somewhere to come, that's all."

Quinn wasn't satisfied. He had a persistent manner and a distrustful look in his grey eyes. He pushed his lower lip forward. "I'm wondering if there's a connection between your work in Inner Temple and this murder in Norwich."

I could see now where this was going. My answer was robust. "I worked for Sir Selwyn as a secretary. I was never involved with criminals."

Penry, bright and suspicious. "The connection may be there, but you may not be aware of it."

I thought, *That's really clever of you.*

I went back over some of the cases Selwyn had recently covered. A kidnapping. Two family murders. Fraud. "As I said, I was never in contact with the criminals."

Quinn hadn't given up. "You said Setna was a Private Investigator?"

"*He* said he was a PI. He showed me his licence."

Penry interrupted. "Setna was an undercover police officer. I've read his notes. He was sure you knew something."

"Well, I wasn't to know he was a policeman," I snapped. "I didn't tell him anything, because I don't *know* anything."

Quinn wasn't reassured. He asked me again why I had come to Norwich. I was becoming exasperated. "It was somewhere away from London."

They were turning to leave when Penry said quietly, "It'll be good to get home, sir." He smiled at me. "We've just got back from Belfast, but we came straight here when we heard Setna had been shot."

I watched them walk down the path to their car. Penry had mentioned Belfast deliberately. I was even more alarmed that he said they'd come straight to me on hearing Setna was dead. Why should one sentence in Setna's notebook bring them hurrying to my front door?

That night I dreamt that Setna was ringing the bell to the upstairs flat. There was no reply. He came round the side of the house to my front door. "Quinn knows where you live now," he said.

As he walked down the path, a shot rang out and he fell forward, shot in the back. I struggled to break through the shifting shadows of sleep. "But he was shot between the eyes," I whispered to the room.

I pulled myself up, hugging my knees as I did when I was a child. I remembered feeling uneasy when Setna showed me the photo of John Millar. There had been a pricking at memory, something about the gold-linked chain, but it had not been sufficient to trigger a spike.

I shivered in the cold night air. It was twenty past four. I stayed awake and watched the damp early morning light filter mistily through the half-opened window.

Monday, 18th May 1981

Mr Jolley dropped in with Len at eight in the morning. I was disappointed to see only one man from his team, and Len must have been in his sixties. I wrote down Sellick's number for them and told them I had ordered pots and plants that would be delivered on Wednesday.

"The yard needs a good clean. Could someone do that and let me know what it will cost?"

Len opened the kitchen door. A skip was already there. "Pots, you say? You want a heap of pots to brighten this dull space. No need to worry, Mrs James, we'll see to everything."

I left for work as Len began stripping the paper off the walls. The day went slowly at the Agency. Martin had gone down to the Thetford branch and Corrie and the others were out most of the time. I went out only once, to a flat in central Norwich. The elderly client I was accompanying showed little interest in the small apartment.

When I got home, Len had gone and everything was neat and tidy. I made some tea. I couldn't wait for the furniture to come so that I could sit, civilised and graceful, on a sofa in the sitting room. I shared the spare room with the mean single bed and the battered cane chair and wardrobe Dalton had left. The two packing cases from our London flat were up against the wall beside the dolls house. The boxes contained memories, and I *needed* the memories from my childhood, for there were things I had to sort out from those troublesome years.

That night I didn't dream of the man with the gun, instead I dreamt about my mother. I was twelve years old and Mum was painting the reeds fringing the

River Bure at Acle. I woke with a jolt and a picture came into my mind of a hot summer day and my mother painting at the cottage.

1963

Mum is making a preliminary sketch of a clump of wild thyme for a book on medicinal plants. I'm sitting on a garden chair beside her and she has leaned back to look at the painting. "The bees love this plant, it's full of goodness." She smiles. "I gave you some thyme honey when you had that irritating cough last November, remember?" And then she adds, "Mrs Kent has told me you want to join a clay pigeon shooting club."

Startled, I sit up straight. I'm not expecting the shooting club to pop up like that. I wanted to prepare the ground first. Josie Kent is my best friend at school. She has an older brother, Clifton, who shoots at the club. He's eighteen, with dark curly hair and soft brown eyes, and I'm madly in love with him. Josie is really good at shooting, and she told me to ask my mother to let me join. But I'm sure Mum will never agree.

"It's the shooting club in Apswood Drive," I say sulkily. "I didn't think you would let me learn to shoot."

"You shouldn't decide what people think," Mum replies tartly. "Actually, it will be good for you to learn how to handle a weapon. I've booked you in for twelve lessons at the same time as Josie. You need a fine eye, a steady hand and self-discipline to shoot well. Let's see how you get on."

I had got on very well, but Josie was always better. She wanted to shoot for England in the Olympics and practised every day. Clifton went on to university and I never saw him again.

Wednesday, 20th May 1981

Before I left on Wednesday morning, Jolley came and told me he could only spare three men to do the job. "That'll be Len, Nick and Fred. They're all good. You'll be pleased with the result."

I hoped I would be. When I got home that evening, Len had washed the yard down revealing some attractive grey flagstones to accommodate the pots and plants that had been delivered in the morning. He asked me where everything should go. Walking round the yard, I showed him what I wanted.

He grunted. "You should've bought a wheelbarrow."

He was right. I should have bought a wheelbarrow. Nick and Fred joined us in the yard and helped Len move the two deep sinks and ceramic pots to the exact place where I wanted them, and Len filled them with compost. He had installed an outside tap that morning so that I could water the garden easily. I told Len I would plant everything over the weekend, and I gave him a couple of pounds to share with Nick and Fred at the local pub.

Friday, 22nd May 1981

The week at Sellick's had gone quickly. In the end I sold a house and two flats. Property was expensive in central Norwich. I began to feel I'd had a good deal from Captain Dalton. At 12 o'clock, Jim Inglis took me up to Sellick's office on the first floor. There was a short introduction and then Inglis left, closing the door reverently. *Creep*, I thought.

I stood by the door and glanced round the room. It was dominated by a mirror in a magnificent gilded frame above an ornate fireplace. A large table covered in green leather stood commandingly in the centre of the room. Standing against the opposite wall was a beautiful rosewood cabinet. All were symbols of perceived power, reinforced by the building's Corinthian pillars, Norfolk red bricks, and the thickly carpeted floor, redolent of Victorian England.

I was astonished to see a framed sketch in charcoal of Sellick on the wall by the window. It had been drawn by my mother. Although she was known as a painter of gardens and plants, my mother did occasionally paint Dad and me and local celebrities. Her simple clear strokes had cleverly captured the power and attraction of her subject, an attraction that belied Sellick's square head, heavy brows, thick nose and uncompromising chin and squat neck. Sellick had scarcely aged since the sketch was made, his silvery-grey hair still brushed back off his face.

Before I could ask him about the sketch, Sellick waved at me to sit down.

"I've been watching you," he began abruptly. "I phoned your last boss, whasisname…" He pushed some papers round on his table and found my CV. "Ah yes, Freeman, that's it, Sir Selwyn Freeman." He looked up. "Now let's see, he says you'll be wasting your talents and your time working for me. Looking at your CV, I'd say he has a point, although you need plenty of talent and determination to work in real estate." He leaned back. "You had a good job, why did you give it up?" He slammed the CV down on the table. "Damn silly thing to do."

For a moment, I was consumed with rage. I didn't need a fat man to comment on my fractured life. I replied slowly, dampening the anger in my voice by spacing out the words. "My marriage had fallen apart. I'm divorced. It changed everything."

His response was caustic. "That's what's wrong with women, letting emotions get in the way of earning brass. How do I know you won't do it again?"

"Do what again?"

"Give up the job."

"I'm skint," I said promptly. "I *need* the brass!"

His thin lips almost flickered into a smile. "Aye, well, we'll see. As I said, I've been watching you. You're good with people. And sensible. That's rarer than you think, sensible."

He leaned back in his comfortable green leather armchair. "But you've spoken to Jim Inglis and you know you're not here for a job in this office. The Retirement Homes project, that's what you'll be doing. Jim tells me you're well organised and you're good at working on your own, but in Swaffham you'll have to sell bungalows and apartments to folk who are retired. You'll have to push the boundaries and convince them that Dunham Village is the only place they want to settle in. And I'm offering a lot. Three hundred properties at different prices, some reasonable, some expensive and some really special. I've put in a medical centre, a community hall and a shop, a bowling green and croquet lawn, bike lanes and allotments."

Bike lanes and allotments! I repeated the words aloud.

Sellick was earnest. "Allotments, yes, because the British love growing things, and I've included bike lanes for the exercise. *And,*" he paused, "I've built a magnificent golf course. That's what'll pull 'em, a golf course on their doorsteps."

Jim Inglis hadn't mentioned the golf course, an incredible omission. Sellick said the Americans were starting retirement communities. "And I want to be the first to build 'em in this country, and a golf course will attract buyers."

"But if people are in good health," I objected, "why should they sell up and move away from their families and friends?"

He was aggressive. "You think like that because you're young. You don't know what it is to feel tired, to have to cope when arthritis steals into your bones and cripples your fingers, and the older you get, the harder it is. The children grow up, leave home, the house is too big, parents begin to think of downsizing;

they're tired of battling with life, the struggle's grown too uneven. I'm giving 'em an alternative, an *active* life and good security. I'm giving 'em Dunham Village, which has everything they want!"

"American ideas don't always translate well in Britain," I argued, "but if you're a pioneer in the field and it catches on, you could be onto a winner."

Sellick leaned forward, his face puckering, his stubby forefinger banging on the rich green leather. "Pioneer, eh? I like that. My father's family are descended from Boers. *They* were pioneers! And you're right, you've got to think 'different' these days, you've got to *believe* in 'different'. My village gives older people their independence and there are security staff on duty day and night all year round. What do they say today? Security 7/52, that's it!"

He leaned back. "Let me tell you a little about the history of the place. There are two Dunhams near Swaffham, Little Dunham and Great Dunham, and I've incorporated both of 'em into the complex and called it Dunham Village. And I've linked the place into its historical past by absorbing the Nelson Obelisk, St Margaret's Church, and the American wartime aerodrome."

He pushed a thick brochure over the table towards me. "It's all in there. Read it and you'll know as much as I do. I've interviewed a lot of people for this job, fools most of 'em, and none of 'em convinced me they could do the job as if they believed in it or had a future in it."

Sellick looked at me earnestly. "I like the way you question things and stand up for yourself, and you were successful in your last job." He leaned forward. "I'll tell you something, Mrs James, success is a state of mind. Your old boss tells me you work hard. He wants you back, but I hope you'll stay and work for me." He leaned back having made his point. "If I've convinced you, and if you want the job, you can arrange the days with Patricia Heals. She's put money into this project and she knows everything about the scheme. At the moment it's only part-time work, just four mornings." The salary was paid by the hour; it was certainly not generous.

"Less than you earned before, eh?"

A hell of a lot less.

"Well, it's more than I offered the others who applied, but if you do well, I'll double it after the first month. As I said, you shouldn't have given up the good job."

"Maybe, but as you're offering me so few hours, I'll have to look for another part-time job."

Sellick grunted. "Let's see how it goes, but I want you to have this job for a special reason. You see, I know quite a lot about *you*, Mrs James." He smiled suddenly and I felt the charm in the man. "You're Marjorie Jeffries' daughter! I met her years ago, during the war and while she was in Acle, she sketched me." He pointed to the charcoal sketch. "Is that what you call a cartoon?"

I smiled. "A kind one."

Sellick grunted. "I'm offering you this job, not just because you're Marjorie's daughter, but because Freeman writes that you're a good manager. I've been waiting for the right person to take over the Retirement Homes project in Swaffham when Mrs Heals leaves to start a similar scheme in Wales, and later in Yorkshire." He leaned back. "I think we could work well together, but you've got to learn the ropes from the bottom.

"Now, let me tell you something about myself. My father sent me out to South Africa when I was seventeen and I had to stand on my own feet. When I ran out of money I joined a fair as a boxer and took on anyone who wanted a fight." That explained the nose. "When I was nineteen my father arranged for me to study engineering and metallurgy at the Mechanics Institution in Manchester, the greatest industrial city in the UK. In '37 I went back to South Africa determined to make myself rich.

"That's when I met Cedric Conrad—that's right, the man who owned all those jewellery shops. We were lucky. Conrad knew about diamond mining. There had been heavy rainfall for two weeks which led to a landslide at an old mine near Pretoria. Everyone thought it had been worked out, but Conrad went a mile out and started digging in towards the old seam. It was then we found the minerals. They'd been washed to the top because of the landslide. We both brought back a decent fortune in diamonds.

"Then the war came. I became a civil servant because of my knowledge of South Africa and its industrial diamonds. When the war ended I went into the estate business. After Apartheid I cut my links with South Africa and concentrated on building properties in the UK. I've made mistakes, I admit that, but *now!*" He banged the table with his fist. "*Now* I'm on to a winner."

"You've led an interesting life, Mr Sellick. Do you keep in touch with people in South Africa?"

"Christmas cards and so forth. Nadia sees to that." He jerked his thumb towards a photo on his table showing a middle-aged woman wearing a beautiful diamond necklace. "Nadia's from the Orange Free State."

An Afrikaner, fair hair set in waves framing a stern face. Not a wife who would easily forgive a matrimonial misdemeanour. I wondered how much money Sellick, or his wife, had put into the project. Despite all the talk about diamonds, Corrie had implied he was dependent on the support of a lot of people.

Sellick got up. "Let me show you what I've been doing."

We walked over to the wall where a large map hung over the rosewood cabinet. Its title was printed on the top: *Retirement Homes Project, Swaffham.*

"In a small way, I'm continuing the Boer tradition," Sellick said. "The Dunham Village I've created allows people to migrate to new holdings, giving them control over their lives and new motivation. I want you to understand I've sunk a lot of money into this idea."

No mention of Mr Conrad's contribution.

"I've made it a local community effort and money's come from banks, local business and from ordinary folk who know me. I want this project to succeed, dammit it's *gotta* succeed. Now let me show you what we've done. The golf course was laid down first and I employed the best course-architect for the job. It's a full eighteen holes with a club-house and a practice putting-green, and I'm betting it'll draw the customers in."

The flats and bungalows were being built round the course. A block of buildings had been enclosed in a red line. "Those properties are Pat's, you don't touch 'em," Sellick said.

We went back to his table. "Once the golf course was laid down, and that took a life-time and a half, then the builders started on the houses. That was in May last year. There have been problems; flooding, people objecting, but at last the project's taking shape. Now I want the properties sold quickly and efficiently. Fifty have been completed, but it's going slowly, too damn slowly, and I'm bleeding money.

"It's taken me years just to negotiate with the council, with farmers, with every bloody man and woman who thought they could squeeze money out of me. Now I want bright young people, intelligent, inquisitive people, to work for me, people like you, Mrs James. In Swaffham, you'll be on your own. You must keep exact records and follow up the financial arrangements so that sales go through smoothly. And you have to get on well with people. All the buildings have to be finished within the next few months."

Sellick walked over to the wide window overlooking the High Street. "This is an important year for me." He turned. "I'm standing for mayor again and I don't want any disasters."

"But you need to make the project attractive to people. How have you advertised the scheme—locally, nationally, internationally?"

He looked hard at me. "Mmm, I like people who think beyond their remit, I'm beginning to think I'm right about you!"

He pressed a button on his table and Pat Heals popped into the room like a witch in a pantomime. She must have been listening outside the door. Sellick greeted her with a nod.

"Pat, I've offered the job to Mrs James."

I was surprised he hadn't consulted her first. She nodded. "We met, briefly, in the week."

Patricia Heals was in her early forties, a petite figure dressed in a dark green business suit nipped in at the waist, neat-featured, make-up discreet, smooth dark hair styled like a close-fitting cap. Her pointed chin gave her an elfin look, but it was her eyes that gave her away, green suspicious eyes under her plucked, upward-tilted eyebrows.

"You're in charge of advertising, Pat. Where did you send the adverts?"

She was momentarily flustered. "I, well, I sent them out to all the newspapers in East Anglia. You have to build these things up gradually."

I interrupted her brutally. "With a scheme like this, you have to fling the net wide. Mr Sellick said it was a *new* idea. Well, you have to keep attacking the public, get them used to the concept until it begins to feel familiar."

Sellick nodded approvingly. "Sounds good to me. Give a copy of the advert file to Mrs James, Pat. Let's see what she makes of it."

The Witch's high heels bit into the deep-piled red and brown patterned carpet. Sellick's eyes followed her neat tucked-in behind, then he turned back, stabbing his finger at me. "I want people queuing up to buy my retirement homes and if you've got ideas, *any* ideas, I want to know about 'em. And I'll be watching how you do. If you're as talented as your mother, we'll get on well. And remember this, every property you sell you get a bonus, a *generous* bonus. Understood?"

I recognised that Sellick saw only his own parameters and expected me to be equally focussed on his scheme.

I went down the stairs suffused in the glow of Sellick's ideas. Heals was waiting for me at my table. She was brisk. "Here's the file with the adverts. You know the work is part-time." She put her head to one side and looked up at me. "You're sure this is what you want?"

She was as underwhelmed by me as Sellick was impressed. "Right then, I've made a timetable."

My name had been pencilled in for Monday, Tuesday, Thursday and Friday mornings, 9 am to 2 pm.

"I work in Swaffham most afternoons. You won't be needed Wednesdays and someone else takes over for the weekends, though occasionally you may be asked to stand in." Her tilted eyebrows lifted like horns. "I read your resumé. Why *exactly* are you looking for work in this field?"

I shrugged. "My life has taken a different direction. A part-time job will give me time to sort out what I really want to do."

"So this is just a convenience job for you, is that it?" Her voice was unfriendly.

"It may be the job I settle on," I replied coolly.

"We'll see! You'll have to work damn hard in Swaffham to make sales. You'll be part of a team although you're mainly on your own in the sales office. You can't sell the block of buildings enclosed in the red line or deal with those clients, but you may sell any other property. When a client wants to put a deposit down on a flat or bungalow you must fill in this solicitor/deposit form and add details of the property. The clients then take the form to their solicitor who will liaise with you.

"And you need to be practical and helpful. The clients must feel the agent has all the answers to their questions. And enter every client's name into the diary you'll find on the table, including the date and time of any phone calls."

She looked up sharply. "You may think your mother's friendship with Mr Sellick will give you a certain protection, but he'll fire you immediately if you don't measure up to the job." She really didn't like me. Perhaps she saw me as a threat to her relationship with the big man, or maybe I'd been too aggressive about the advertisements.

"I'm looking forward to the challenge," I replied evenly.

"Perhaps! You have a lot to learn before you can take over the Retirement Homes project." She added drily, "You're not the first to have that promise. In the meantime, read my notes and this booklet." She put some folded pieces of

A4 paper and the booklet on the table. "Study the layout of the different properties in Dunham Village, you'll have to answer lots of questions from the clients so read the booklet thoroughly and then follow my instructions exactly."

Jawohl, mein Kommandant!

I was told to clear my table and report to the Swaffham office on Monday the 25th at 9 am.

To celebrate getting the job, I had lunch with Corrie.

"Sellick interviewed at least fifteen people before you," Corrie said. "It's like he was waiting for you, the way you got the job."

It was disturbing the way she put it. "Most of them were just kids out of school, and Sellick's got no time for 'em; there were some who'd worked in agencies, but he wasn't interested. Maybe you just fitted the bill, knowin' German and French, like."

She poured out coffee for both of us. "I've known Sellick since I was a kid. His mum come from Norwich but his dad's South African. He was a builder an' made a truck-load of money, but he was mean with it. He send Sellick out to South Africa when he was only a kid. Doug know my mum and was sweet on her, but his dad wasn't having none of it. There's a lot of money riding on the Swaffham project and it's getting on his nerves. In the 1970s he build this big estate in Lincolnshire, but he lost a packet, thousands and thousands, and he let a lot of people down."

Corrie waved her fork, pierced with mash and sausage, as she explained. "Them two years were the wettest on record. The builders didn't put in a good drainage system, and you gotta do that in the Fens, but they did it on the cheap, and what with the floods an' all, it was a disaster. He's only able to do this Swaffham thing because Mr Conrad, the jeweller, back him.

"Mr Conrad was a big name round here, he was mayor once, but he died in January. Sudden like. Sellick's hoping his widow and daughter will carry on. A lot of local firms have backed him, but now Mr Conrad's dead they're gettin' jittery, too."

Again, the Swaffham job didn't look so secure. Corrie accompanied me to the carpark at the back of the agency. "You done well, Paula. Pat Heals don't like you, but you can deal with that."

I asked her why Pat shouldn't like me.

Corrie snapped, "You're young, good-looking and confident. Pat don't like competition."

She limped over to her old blue Ford and I waved as she drove away.

Young. Good-looking. Confident.

I was surprised how good the words made me feel. I got into the small red second-hand Fiat I had recently bought. Before driving off, I sat for a moment thinking things over. *It's like he was waiting for you.*

I spent some of the afternoon in the local library reading up about the Swaffham Retirement Homes scheme. Sellick had bought the site of an old aerodrome used by the Americans during the war, together with a lot of the surrounding farmland. It had taken him over ten years to set the whole thing up, to raise the money and purchase the land from the council, the farmers and the Americans.

The prospectus was well set-out, the aims clearly presented. Sellick had wanted to create a community for the active-elderly. Dunham Village would sequester its inhabitants from the noisy side of city life, people would be of a similar age with similar needs and interests. Sellick had arranged for a doctor to be on site every morning, and there was a social hall for dances, bingo, bridge, concerts, whatever was wanted.

Swaffham was also ideally placed. Norwich was under an hour's bus ride away, and buses would stop at the Village every two hours. On the way to the car park I bought a book about Swaffham and its famous pedlar and his dog.

I got home and opened the door. A flat in the builders' hands is stripped of warmth and character. It smells of wet plaster, wet floors and general mess. Earlier, I'd learned that water had been seeping through the wall from the flat above and the plaster had to be stripped off the walls in the hall and both bedrooms. Mr Jolley obtained a key from the solicitor, Carless-Adams, for the upstairs flat. Jolley's team, to their credit, had left the bathroom, the kitchen and the spare room habitable every evening although the flat had echoed eerily.

But tonight, I could see my flat was taking shape. All the dirty blue-spotted paper had gone, exposing where running water had stained the bedroom walls and the hallway. The leak had been fixed, new damp-proofing had been injected, the walls skimmed and new windows put in. The flagstones in the kitchen were now in place and new units, beautiful in light oak, had been fitted. A studio dishwasher sat comfortably on top of one of the kitchen units. The horrible old cooker would be taken out in the morning and a new gas oven put in.

Jolley walked round the flat with me. "We'll get the shower in tomorrow morning and finish the tiling after that. Fred's started painting gloss on all the

48

woodwork, so be careful where you put your hands. With a bit of luck, we'll be finished by noon on Wednesday."

I said I hoped his locks were as good as Mr Watson's.

"Huh!" Jolley replied. "D'you know your Mr Watson came round and checked up on our locks when you were out at work? He said you'd had a burglar and he wanted to make sure everything was safe and secure. His words, not mine."

"I had no idea. I'll phone him later to thank him."

Jolley looked at me quizzically. "Most workmen wouldn't give a damn."

"He knew I was frightened. He was really nice and I was grateful for his thoughtfulness."

Jolley smiled. "You'll be pleased to know our locks passed muster. Well now, how's the job going?"

"I start at Swaffham on Monday. It's going to be a new experience."

"You'll be fine," Jolley said. "You're good with people. Len told me!"

I laughed. "Len's been really helpful."

I reminded Jolley that the carpet was coming on Tuesday morning, and some of the new furniture would arrive on Tuesday afternoon and Wednesday.

In the evening, I decided to look through the advertising file. It held basic information. There was no pull, no razzmatazz. Dunham Village would need a vigorous advertising campaign to quell the doubts raised from the Lincoln build and to make it attractive to elderly people, a segment of the population most set in its ways. I knew I could do a lot better, but I needed to find out more about Dunham Village and the selling side before I started writing a text for advertisements. I found myself looking forward to starting the job on Monday. That night, I read the book about the pedlar and his faithful dog.

Saturday, 23rd May 1981

Every weekday I was up early so that I could wash, get dressed and have breakfast before Mr Jolley's men arrived. Saturday was no different. As usual, I picked up the post and glanced through the EDP. Inside the pages was a circular from Jarrolds, the big Norwich store. It was advertising a special sale of fridge-freezers and furniture.

There was a letter from Sellick's Estate Agency confirming my appointment and salary as his agent in Swaffham. And there were two postcards. One of them showed the picture of a shop with *Norwich Art Gallery* engraved over the window. On the back I was invited, by name, to attend a *Wine and View Evening* the following Wednesday. The writing was flowing and quite unlike the other postcard and was signed *Peter Schiffer*. I slipped the card into my jacket pocket, wondering how Schiffer knew my name and address and my connection with art.

The other postcard was illustrated with tall Corinthian pillars supporting an ornate building with the legend *Pforzheim* written beneath. Bemused, I turned the postcard over: *We know you came to Norwich to meet Denby. Give us the Pforzheim miniatures, Mrs James, or you'll end up dead like Setna.*

With a bullet between my eyes.

I stared at the card. *Pforzheim!* A memory rose in my mind and I heard my mother shouting the word at my father. I burrowed into my shoulder-bag and compared the writing of both postcards. It was the same, but there was no telephone number, no address, no way of getting in touch. It was all so anonymous, so threatening, so personal.

We know you came to Norwich to meet Denby.

I was nineteen when the police came to our flat in West Kensington and told me my father had died in a train crash outside Paris. Someone was playing a horrible joke.

The postcard had shaken me. *If someone's determined to find you, they'll find a way.* Jane had said that. And there was Corrie's strange comment: *It's like Sellick was waiting for you.* Disturbing words spinning a web inside my head. I put the postcards in my bag where I couldn't see them or think about them.

The doorbell rang and I quickly thrust the rest of the post into the drawer of the wonky hall table. Mr Jolley had arrived with his men and the new shower.

"If nothing goes wrong, you should have your first shower tonight." Jolley liked to presage his opening statement with a hint of Olympian doom. "And we'll be working on the spare room today as well." I was glad I would be back in the larger bedroom.

I left the flat and drove into Norwich, my mind fixed on the postcards, wondering again how the art gallery people knew my name, knew where I lived. I drove into a car park in the centre of Norwich. Shopping was an analgesic and I needed to replace Dalton's small beds with two large beds. Whether I would live long enough to enjoy a large bed was another matter.

I bought the beds and two small cabinets, some more linen and candles, and a bin for the kitchen. Then I went to the Assembly House in Norwich and treated myself to a light lunch and a glass of white wine. I enjoyed the elegant room and service, a far cry from microwaved meals in my flat. I caught fragments of conversation between a well-dressed man and his attractive companion at the next table.

"…explosion at RAF Marham."

"A plane."

"…hijacked."

"Fatalities."

I heard nothing more as I walked to the door. RAF Marham is an airfield not far from Norwich. Whatever had happened would be on the news later that evening.

On the way back to the carpark, I saw a painting in the window of a shop across the road. I stopped abruptly and the man walking behind trod on my heel. I steadied myself against a shop window and heard his muttered remark as he passed me. "Silly woman!"

The heel of my shoe felt broken. Feeling down gingerly, I decided I would manage, but he'd laddered my tights and scraped the skin on my heel. He should have apologised instead of insulting me. I felt for the card I had earlier slipped into my pocket. The same flamboyant lettering on the card was repeated in the inscription above the window: *Norwich Art Gallery.*

I crossed the road and stood in front of the large window. A painting had been placed on an easel. A card beside it displayed the words, *Wild Marjoram, from an original painting by MJ Jeffries.* The original oil painting had hung on my bedroom wall when I was a child.

Wild Marjoram's reddish stems and tufted pinky-purple flowers stood out vividly against an ivory green background. Why do paintings have such a passionate response from some people, while others pass by untouched by their colours and design? *Wild Marjoram* had been part of a series of books on wild flowers and garden designs which my mother had written and illustrated in the 1950s, including *Wild Thyme, Lucerne, The Guelder-Rose, Fox-and-Cubs* and *Blackthorn.* They had made my mother a household name. Large audiences had listened to her on radio when she talked about her interest in gardens and painting. Taking a deep breath I opened the door and went inside.

It was a big gallery with two long rooms filled with paintings and some small tables and chairs. There was a pleasant hum from the twenty or so people wandering round. I went straight to the window and tried to reach over the easel to get to the print.

"Just a moment, miss, that's only for display, it's not for sale." A young man wearing a loose brown velvet jacket, stretched over my shoulder and lifted the picture off the easel. Hesitating a moment, he looked round the shop. "I'll get Mr Schiffer. He'll know what to do."

Schiffer's name was on the card in my pocket. The young man led the way to a group standing round a painting called *Unstill Centre* by Gillian Ayres, a work I know well. A man was facing the painting illustrating subject matter and emotional impact in abstract art.

Velvet Jacket eased his way through the group and gave the picture to the lecturer who turned and made his way towards me. I came forward, my hand outstretched.

"I didn't realise the gallery belongs to you, Mr Schiffer."

The name had meant nothing to me on the card, but I instantly recognised the narrow high-boned saturnine face confronting me. Schiffer had put on a little weight over the years, but his thick grey-streaked hair was still brushed back from an attractively haggard face with dark narrow eyes and a cleft chin; it was his reaction to me that was strange though.

He stood quite still, his face blank, his hands by his side. Three women who had followed him stared at me coldly. Ignoring them I smiled uncertainly, letting my hand drop. "I met you years ago when I was a little girl." Of course, it was easier for me to recognise Schiffer, than for him to equate a 29-year-old woman with a five-year-old child. "I'm Paula James, Paula Denby before I was married. You knew my mother, Marjorie J Jeffries. She painted *Wild Marjoram*, the picture in your window."

His face relaxed. "Of course, of course." He clasped my hand warmly and led me over to the window. "When did you say we met?"

"You were sitting on the patio with my parents at Yorkstone Cottage in Damgate Lane." I faltered as flagstones stained with blood flashed across my brain. I laughed nervously. "Yes, yes, you were talking about a young artist…" I hesitated. "Lejeune. Pierre Lejeune, that's it."

He looked astonished. "Unfortunately, Lejeune didn't live up to his early promise. It's amazing you should remember."

I cursed myself. I should have kept my weird and wonderful memory to myself. "It's called 'flash-bulb' memory. You triggered the memory of Lejeune, that's all."

"Remarkable!" was Schiffer's dry reply. "Yes indeed, I met Marjorie many times at the cottage. I remember your father. Digsby? Dogsby?"

"Denby, Eric Denby," I corrected him clearly.

He nodded. "It's flattering you remember me after all this time." He turned and brought the three women into the conversation. "This is Marjorie J Jeffries' daughter, Paula. I know you're interested in the Ackert/Jeffries canvases, Madge, now you can ask Mrs James all about her mother."

The eldest woman, American with a blue rinse, smiled as we shook hands. "This is very unexpected. I'm Mrs Falcon Conway, Madge to my friends. Do you have any of your mother's canvases?"

"No, that's why I rushed over when I saw *Wild Marjoram* in the window. When it was painted, and the plates had been made for the book, my mother hung *Wild Marjoram* on a wall in my bedroom. She said it would protect me from evil. It was my fifth birthday. I used to think I could smell the herbs as I fell asleep."

The slight figure beside Madge came forward. "Ailie Schmidt," she announced, her voice high with a South African lilt. "That's a really lovely personal story, it brings the picture to life."

The third woman offered her hand. "And I'm Bette Bergen. Did you know there's a huge resurgence of interest in your mother's paintings from the time when she was known as Ackert through to her adopted name of Jeffries? The canvases are selling very well right now."

I was used to hearing my mother called MJ Jeffries in the UK, though her married name was Denby. In Europe, she was still called MJ Ackert, her maiden name.

"But that's not why we're here," Madge interrupted. "We're trying to get Mr Schiffer to bring his collection of MJ Jeffries paintings to Virginia and put them on display in our museum." She pointed to a row of paintings in an alcove. "Paintings like those."

Schiffer nodded as he turned into the recess. "These are part of my personal collection of Jeffries' work. From the age of fifteen Jeffries was commissioned to paint portraits, that's thirty-five years of producing great works."

I was astonished. I had no idea my mother had painted portraits. The side room had canvases from Mum's *Flower Collection,* but also a painting of two men in uniform sitting at easels set out on yellow flagstones. The stones had formed the patio outside the front door of Yorkstone Cottage. The date on the painting was 1942. I said I'd never seen it before.

Schiffer raised his eyebrows. "Well, Marjorie gave art classes to wounded soldiers between 1940 and '46 in Yorkstone Cottage in Acle. The courses were set up by the Government. In fact there were several artists in East Anglia offering similar programmes, and writers, musicians and sculptors were all giving classes as well. The men in this picture are Ken Purley and Charlie Gardiner. I knew them. They'd had a rough time in North Africa. Painting, like music, is therapeutic, and the Broads are a wonderful environment to ease the pain of broken minds and bodies. Marjorie used her garden and the staithe near Riverside Inn for her painting groups. The river's called—"

"The Bure," I said mechanically.

He nodded. "We had some very good meals there, even though it was war-time." He smiled at the tall American. "You should add the village of Acle to your itinerary, Madge, it was there before the Romans came. The Riverside Inn serves very good meals, and there's a church with a Saxon round tower which you won't find in America. Add the windmill and wherries and you'll find a picturesque place."

Bette laughed. "Well, that's true, we don't have many Saxon towers in Virginia!"

Ailie asked me what the name Acle meant.

I told her it was a clearing in an oak forest. "All the trees were cut down so that Elizabeth 1st could build warships to fight the dastardly Spaniards. The Riverside Inn's been near the bridge over the Bure for over a hundred years."

"That's real history," Bette said, and Madge added that they'd be sure to visit the village. "And we'll have a meal at the inn as well."

Schiffer smiled. "Good, Marjorie loved going there." He walked along the side room and stood in front of a painting. "This is what I wanted to show you, Mrs James."

I recalled that he had said Paula Denby earlier. Schiffer moved to one side and revealed a sketch executed in pencil, charcoal, and watercolour. It was a painting of two young boys. It was signed MJ Ackert, Bremen, 1938.

I moved forward and stood in front of the painting. For an instant I had an overwhelming impression of laughter and love. I faltered. "I've seen this painting before."

Schiffer was dismissive. "*The Brothers* hasn't been on public display since the 1960s."

Madge's drawling accent cut into his reply. "It's such a bee-utiful painting, Mr Schiffer. How did you get hold of it?"

Schiffer frowned. "It came on the market soon after Jeffries' death."

"I read somewhere that Jeffries was very fond of her cousins," Madge said.

Mum had never spoken about any cousins.

Schiffer turned to me. "Their names were Curt and Marcus Ackert and, as Mrs Conway says, your mother was fond of the boys." His voice was without expression.

I stared at the teenagers. They must have been about fifteen and seventeen. Schiffer identified Curt, dark-haired, sitting on a brown wooden-slatted garden chair, his arm thrown across the back; and Marcus, younger, blond, his hand on his brother's shoulder, half-leaning down to talk to him. There was energy flowing from the sketch, an intensity of vigour, rhythm and light. On the left was a flowering cherry tree, the top branches picked out in sunlight. The painting was balanced by shadowy shrubs filling the space behind the boys. My finger followed the pencilled outline of the side of a house on the right, the dull yellow-brown stone tempered by the reflection of the sun, the gentler water-colours softening the pencil and charcoal figures. Jeffries' treatment of chiaroscuro was never harsh.

I pointed some of this out. Schiffer asked if I painted.

"I sketch a little." I stepped forward. "It's such an intimate portrait. The onlooker is drawn into that very moment in their lives."

The brushwork on the cherry tree had the same energy that had lifted all of Jeffries' flower designs and reminded me of the cherry tree in our garden in Ealing and the little bird we had rescued lying near the birdbath.

"You say the boys were sketched in 1938 in Bremen, but my mother never spoke about any cousins, or about Bremen. Where exactly was this painted?"

"In your mother's garden in Bremen."

I was stunned. I couldn't understand why there were so many gaps in my life, why so much had been kept from me.

"They're good-looking young men," I said slowly. "Where are they now?"

"Dead. In the war."

I glanced at Schiffer nervously.

"Did you know them?"

"Only briefly."

I tried to imagine what the smiling boys had been like and how they had died—from gunfire…in a burning tank…or shot down, their broken bodies filled with shrapnel, the friendly young faces twisted in death. Friend or foe, death is the same enemy. I was filled with sadness that I had grown up never knowing about them.

"When I was young, my mother only painted plants and flowers, except for the occasional portrait of some local people, and me and Dad, of course." I pointed to the signature. "I knew her maiden name was Ackert, and that she later adopted her stepfather's name, Jeffries, but I didn't know she lived in Bremen. When was she known for painting portraits?"

Madge broke in excitedly. "Jeffries started painting when she was very young. Such a precocious talent! She was Marjorie J Ackert then. We have some of her work in America. Film stars, celebrities, politicians."

"I never knew," I said helplessly. "Do you have any?"

"If only! But we have three of her paintings in our museum in Virginia. One is of a local politician, but the other two are quite mysterious. One shows an elderly woman standing outside a cottage with a windmill in the background. It's signed MJ Jeffries, Acle, Norwich, 1951. And the other is earlier, 1940, at a place in Wales, spelt R.H.Y.L.L with a woman standing next to a Welsh dresser. And that's signed MJ Jeffries as well. We know nothing about the subjects and that's why we're here, acting as art detectives. We were hoping Mr Schiffer could help us, unless of course *you* know who they are." The inference being that, as Jeffries' daughter, I must know all about them. "Look, I have photos of both paintings."

They were pen and ink sketches with an ink wash and soft colours. Both women were in their fifties. The first was wearing a red and blue head-scarf and a dark blue dress under an old winter coat. Her features were strong and care-worn. "I don't think she's English," I said hesitantly.

"But it says Norwich," Madge pointed out.

I shook my head. The second portrait showed a much happier woman, black hair like Irish hair, wide dark blue eyes. "I'm sorry, I wish I knew who they are but, as I said, my mother never talked about her earlier work."

"Of course, the photos don't do the work justice." Madge began, but Schiffer interrupted her sharply.

"I'm coming over to the States in the fall. You could show me the paintings then."

Madge was delighted. "You've got my phone number, Mr Schiffer, give me a bell and all will be arranged, and I hope you'll consider my suggestion about bringing your collection for us to see."

Schiffer smiled distantly. I said urgently, "If these are examples of her work, I would love to see more." I looked at him. "How can I find out about her portraits? Do they ever turn up in auctions?"

"The portraits? Seldom, and you're lucky if you find an original painting of her early flower designs. I go all over the country, and abroad, to buy any Jeffries that come on the market." He gestured to Madge. "That's what Mrs Conway and her friends are doing." He pointed to a large painting of mixed dahlias. "I bought the *Dahlias* in Paris last year."

I told them I had watched Mum painting the flowers on a lazy summer day a long time ago in the garden at Yorkstone Cottage. I explained that she had prepared the canvas earlier and mixed her own paints. The flowers had burst across the canvas in tumbling yellows, pinks and reds, exploding in tight pompom clusters or looping layers of petals, the densely packed canvas vibrant in the hazy sunshine.

"You're lucky to have such memories," Schiffer said. "And you'll agree that, although the *Flower Collection* and *The Brothers* are very different subjects, the brushwork and the use of space on the canvases are very similar. The brushwork is a painter's signature. It may develop, but it never really changes." He stepped back. "See how every petal, every unique cluster is different in every detail, quivering with life, it's quite amazing."

It was extraordinary how much of that long-ago day was crowding into my mind: summer holidays, Mum's paints laid out meticulously by her painting-bag, the carafe of water, the flowers carefully prepared for their metamorphosis onto canvas—and always the powerful aroma from the tall dark-purple lavender bushes leading to the garden gate. Memories are burned into the mind through sight and sound and smell.

"Why did she stop painting portraits?" I asked.

There was a moment of silence. Madge looked sideways at Schiffer.

"If you know something," I said impatiently, "tell me."

Madge raised her shoulders. "I thought you'd know. It was because of the Nazi connection. *Personally*," she breathed heavily on the word, "I never believed it."

"Believed *what*?"

Schiffer took up the story. "Marjorie's father was a Nazi. It was in the thirties, a politically unstable time. Nazis and Communists were forever marching in rallies, banners flying, fighting and killing each other. And always there were rumours, about Ackert and Marjorie."

"And wasn't there a young man she ran off with?" Bette interrupted. "He was a Nazi and her lover. And didn't they say she murdered him, and that was why she was arrested."

I was dumbfounded. "You're saying my mother, my *mother*, was a *Nazi* and she *murdered* someone?"

Schiffer was annoyed. "Nothing was ever proved. In fact, I *know* Marjorie detested the Nazis. She risked her life trying to get her fellow artists out of Germany. In my opinion, she became so traumatised by the war she nearly gave up painting altogether."

I seized on his earlier words. "I don't understand. She was either a Nazi or she wasn't."

"It was a long time ago, Mrs James. 1933 to 1945 was a complex and difficult time for Anglo-Germans. And of course, it wasn't until much later that people read of her courage, but by then, the damage had been done. After the war, the great and the good decided to have their portraits painted by a younger generation of talented painters. The old guard sometimes has to step aside. Despite everything, but especially because Marjorie was an inspired artist, she retrieved her reputation and built up a huge following for her flower canvases. The British love their gardens and plants. My advice is forget the past, Mrs James."

I had no intention of forgetting the past. After the revelations about Nazis, murder and lovers, I wanted to learn everything I could about my mother. The trouble was, none of it bore any relation to the woman I had known as my mum.

I turned to Madge. "You said she ran away with someone who was murdered. This is the first I've heard of it. Who was murdered?"

Schiffer stepped forward. "Your mother didn't murder anyone."

Madge ignored him. "I'm surprised you don't know more about your mother. She was very famous, you know."

Schiffer turned to me, saying he wanted to discuss business.

Madge took her dismissal with good grace. "There's a coffee shop next door, perhaps you can join us when you're free again?"

With a nod, Madge and her friends went to the end of the gallery, and Schiffer and I began walking back to the front of the shop.

He was abrupt. "Jeffries made a name for herself in Germany." He still assumed I knew everything about her. "Her portraits commanded the greatest admiration and financial reward."

Financial reward! We had never been rich. Not poor, but never rich. I realised Schiffer was watching me and I stammered. "Of course, but, well, I suppose I…well, I only saw her through a child's eyes. I don't know anything about her life in Germany. What was she like in those early years?"

He thought for a moment, his brows drawn down. That haggard look was very attractive, but I was startled by the harshness in his voice. "I loved her. She was beautiful, and she always portrayed the truth as she saw it." There was something in the tone, a veneration and a darkness.

"Did you sit for her?" It was a shot in the dark, but Schiffer's bone structure and dark narrow attractive eyes would be easy to draw. For a moment, I thought I had actually sketched him. I could see the pad and charcoal pencil in my hand, but the faint touch of memory slipped away as Schiffer went on. "Yes, yes, there is a portrait, and of course, we kept in touch."

"I'd love to see the painting, it might help me understand my mother."

He laughed without humour. "She was a difficult woman to understand."

I made a frontal attack. "Please show me the painting. You see, I only knew her as a keen gardener who wrote and illustrated books about plants."

He glanced at me sharply. "Several portraits were hidden." I looked at him uncomprehendingly. "She never told you?" I shook my head. "They'll come to light, they always do." That curt sound again. "All right then, come this way and I'll show you."

He turned to his assistant who had been listening avidly. "Jordan, wrap *Wild Marjoram* for Mrs James, then look after the shop. I'll be upstairs for a few moments."

I followed Schiffer upstairs to his flat on the first floor. The lounge was L-shaped, the decor and furnishings simple. Despite the minimalist effect, there was an air of warmth and repose from the magnificent red and green woven Persian carpet, the dark-red leather suite and two small coffee tables, one with a blue porcelain vase containing yellow roses. Two bookcases filled with volumes on art and history covered one wall and a baby grand stood against the other wall.

We walked down the room and turned into the L-shaped recess. I stopped and steadied myself against the leather sofa. For the first time I understood what my mother had meant by the mediocre and the brilliant, for I was swept away by perfection. Flawless. Immaculate.

On the wall facing me was a full-length watercolour of a young man and woman. It was signed *MJ Ackert 1937 Berlin*. I stood absorbing the scene, oblivious to everything round me. The picture was alive with movement and bold colours. The clothes and the atmosphere breathed the thirties. Schiffer was instantly recognisable—slim-hipped, early twenties, his thick dark hair combed straight back, full lower lip and lean face. A woman was seated at a small round table with two wine glasses and an opened bottle of red wine. The table was on the pavement outside a bistro called *Der Rosengarten*. The sign was decorated with trailing leaves and tiny rosebuds.

Schiffer wore a tight-waisted blue jacket and the wide-flared trousers of the time, with an open-neck blue shirt and a red neck-scarf. He was in love. There was passion in the way he leaned towards his lover offering her three red roses, his lips parted, as if he were about to speak.

The woman was young. She was reading a menu, ignoring her courtier, her face tilted to one side, the wide brim of her light-green hat shading the soft contour of her cheek. She was wearing white buttoned gloves and a green and blue silk dress which clung to her body. There was something provocative and desirable about her. The bold colours in the forefront were softened by the greying bricks of the bistro which filled the space behind the figures. A brown barrel with a rusting metal band stood against the wall. It was filled with red and white roses climbing up the side of the wall. A splash of bright yellow sunshine lay across the table.

If I had been a psychologist, I would have noted the importance of the buttoned gloves and the rusting metal band. Instead, all I saw was the emotional energy sparking between the protagonists. Schiffer loved her, but she was turning away. And why were there three roses?

Schiffer grimaced. "Yes, I loved her, there's never been anyone else." His voice darkened. "The roses? They stood for love, fidelity and truth, two of which Marjorie never understood." The words were bitter. "She never felt the same passion for me. She spread her love too freely. Her name was constantly being linked with Rik van der Vendt and Franz Helmann."

I scarcely recognised my mother in the painting. I only remembered her as rather dumpy, and not at all sensuous or mysterious.

"I hardly recognise her. She was thirty-six when I was born and…well, she looked different. I wish I'd known her when she was younger."

"They were the *best* years." Schiffer was caressing the words. The barriers that protect the reticence of normal behaviour had fallen away. "There was an enchantment about her. She swept me into her life, her arms, her bed. Then she threw me aside, said I'd never be a painter, and she loved someone else."

I wanted to stop this astonishing flagellation of self. I reached out to shake his arm, but he pushed me away. "The young Dutchman had nothing, *nothing* to offer her. She went off with him in that capricious way she had and I was left in the shadows."

All the bile and spite of the past were spewing out of his twisting mouth. "Then the stupid Dutchman gets himself killed and Marjorie's charged with his murder. Of course, *Bergmann* rushes across the border. I don't know how he did it, but he got her out of prison and brought her back to our apartment in Berlin. She collapsed completely, and I looked after her." His face changed. "But then things went sour."

The past had become the present to Schiffer, his voice was rough, the veins in his forehead throbbing, the diatribe so personal I recoiled from him. "And then she chose to abort my child. I'll never understand why she married that fool Denby and kept *his* child."

"Why are you *telling* me this?" It was as if he had struck me. "And anyway, my mother would *never* have had an abortion." *I* was angry now. "She was a devout Catholic. Maybe there was a miscarriage, or the child was adopted. If you loved her, you wouldn't *say* such things."

I didn't want to hear about his lost baby, and it was offensive to be dismissed peremptorily because I was my parents' child.

His hand closed round my arm and I felt the shock of the nervous strength running through the man. Then his face relaxed. He looked subdued, younger, vulnerable. "I'm sorry." He dropped his hand. "I can't believe I said those things."

He sat down on the sofa, his head in his hands. "Standing there, beside you, beside the painting, I wanted you to understand how I felt. Marjorie was wayward. She didn't understand loyalty and devotion. After van der Vendt died, she started an affair with Franz Helmann. I challenged him, but the fool laughed and fired his pistol into the air. I was left looking stupid. All these years I've kept silent, but no-one loved her like I did."

Perhaps Schiffer saw me as some kind of catalyst for this extraordinary outburst. He looked up, his voice suddenly muted. "You're like her, you know, the way you move, the way you speak. I recognised you immediately."

Then you disguised it damn well, I thought savagely. He'd put me in an impossible situation. And I didn't like it.

"It affected me, you standing there beside me." His voice rose. "It's because you're *her* child, Paula. I didn't realise it would affect me so much. I just wanted to shout it all out, make you understand how she broke me." His voice cracked. "But whatever I did, I always loved her. There was never anyone else."

I was overwhelmed. On first seeing Schiffer talking to the group in the shop I had thought he was cold and aloof, a man who transferred his lack of empathy into the dried paint of pictures in order to massage his emotional senses. How wrong I had been!

As if to confirm my poor reading of his character, he reached out and held my hand. "I've never spoken about it to anyone before. Marjorie isn't dead, you know, she lives on in these paintings. Every time I look at them, I feel the magic in her."

He gave a short, ugly laugh and dropped my hand. "Everyone talks about her empathy, but there was another side to Jeffries, a dark and cruel side. Instead of worshiping the brilliant and clever persona she showed the world, they should have queried where her true allegiance lay. There were rumours, *ugly* rumours in the war, just as you heard downstairs."

I stared at him.

"The war changed us." Schiffer shook his head. "It changed everything. War twists everything, Paula, and the truth gets lost. You wanted to know what she was like? I'll tell you. She was a difficult, impossible woman, but *I* knew her, *I* loved her. Without her I simply exist, make a living, do what I can. No-one can touch me now."

His voice had lost its rage. He was resigned, rational. "I was devastated when I heard she died." He looked up. "Does any of this make sense?"

I couldn't answer him. I didn't recognise my mother in anything he'd said. It was all so emotional, so revelatory. At first, I'd thought he was mad. Richard and the pregnant bombshell had been shocking, but this, *this* was something else.

I glanced round. "You've built a successful business, you lecture on the paintings, people respect you, you've made a life for yourself."

"Perhaps, but there's always regret for the lost dream." He cleared his throat. "I'd be grateful if none of this went any further. As you say, I've made a success of my life, despite Marjorie." He got up. "Come, we should go downstairs." The man who was simply existing had returned.

I stopped at the foot of the stairs. "I want to buy one of her portraits. Perhaps *The Brothers*. I don't have any, you see, and it might help me understand her."

There was a curious look on his face. "Have you enough money to buy it?"

"Does everything come down to price?"

He shrugged. "I'll think about it." He led the way back to the painting of my mother's cousins. I was surprised to see Madge and her friends still waiting near the stairs.

Madge raised her eyebrows as she scanned Schiffer's face. "We have to leave soon, but we decided to wait to explain our interest in MJ Jeffries to Mrs James. We've formed a club, you see, to collate all Jeffries' paintings. We issue a magazine every six months in which an aspect of her work and life are discussed. I'd be delighted if you would contribute some articles, Mrs James. If you have any paintings perhaps you would let us exhibit them for a short time in our museum in Virginia. We would take great care of them."

Ailie clasped her hands. "There are thirty-five branches of the club in the USA and Canada, and we're forming branches over here and in South Africa as well. How many portraits do you have? Will you be giving a private showing of her work?"

I'd had no idea there were MJ Jeffries clubs. "I don't have any portraits, that's why I'm interested in these."

Schiffer hesitated, and then said sharply, "All of you, come over here." He seemed to have recovered from his emotional breakdown. "I want you to see this."

It was an oil painting, dated *Bremen, 1931*, and signed *MJ Ackert*. It showed a middle-aged man, clean-shaven, with dark blue eyes, fair hair, a keen intelligent face and a duelling scar across his left cheek. He was sitting in a dark brown leather armchair. On the wall was a portrait of Wagner; to his right, a low table with a pipe resting on a small green and white ceramic plate. The man was looking straight at the painter, who was partially visible in an oak-framed mirror standing on a dressing-table. A smile was lifting the corners of the man's lips. I felt as if I were an interloper overhearing a private conversation.

"Why is she always so self-effacing?" I asked Schiffer slowly.

"A form of titillation or divertissement, if you like."

"Perhaps she was showing a balance between herself and the subject," I suggested. "Everything I've seen today has such a such a *personal* touch. She's much younger in this painting." I looked up. "Who's the man?"

Schiffer stepped back, open disbelief in his eyes. "You don't know?"

I was equally terse. "I don't know."

"Then let me introduce you." He was heavily sarcastic. "This is Dieter Ackert, your grandfather. Marjorie was *very* fond of him. She would have talked with you about him."

I was beginning to feel uncomfortable, more than uncomfortable, distressed. The words rushed out. "I've never seen the painting before."

"That can scarcely be true." Schiffer's tone was unpleasant, and the three women chattered together, their eyes suspicious. "I met Ackert and your mother many times in Bremen. I was *there,* in Bremen, when Ackert was leading a Nazi rally. I saw him and my father shot dead!"

"You say Ackert and your father were *shot*?"

"In Bremen. In 1931."

I was hearing things I'd never heard before. I was a stranger in a world where everyone else belonged.

"I'm sorry your father died, but my mother never talked about her early life." I could see now there might have been reasons for her silence. My voice rose. "There were no photos at home, no portraits, nothing."

Madge said she could see a resemblance between myself and Ackert.

I stared at the portrait. Why do you never see the likeness yourself? "I do recognise something," I stepped forward. "The ring on his finger. My mother had a ring just like that."

Schiffer held up his left hand and I saw the Odala ring. "I inherited my ring from my father. Your mother would have left her rings to you."

They were all looking at me curiously. I decided to bring this bizarre meeting to a close. "There were no rings and no portraits," I said harshly.

Firmly, I led the way back to the counter, trying to retrieve something of normality in my behaviour. "It was nice to meet you all and hear about the clubs. I'm sorry I can't help you."

The trio nodded frostily and Schiffer accompanied me to the front of the art gallery. Jordan was waiting at the counter, the print neatly wrapped with the cord ending in a loop at the top. Flustered, I searched for my purse and cheque book in my shoulder-bag. "I've been rather foolish," I muttered. "I haven't asked the price of *Wild Marjoram*."

Schiffer touched my arm. "The print is my gift to you, a thank-you for your forbearance earlier."

I was disturbed at his generosity, it did not fit in with the man I had spoken with earlier. Jordan handed me the print and I noted his sly smile. I walked with Schiffer to the door.

"You may be interested," he said. "Dales in Holt is auctioning portraits all day next Tuesday, the 26th." He scribbled the address on the back of one of his cards. "Some of your mother's works have appeared in several of their auctions."

At the door he held my hand in both his hands, a gesture I particularly dislike. "I'm glad we've met after all these years, Paula. I want to apologise again for distressing you earlier. It was outrageous. To show I'm forgiven, please come on Wednesday to our Wine and View evening. I'll be giving a small talk on Monet's triptych, *The Water Lilies. I believe you already have an invitation."*

He opened the door and gave me his parting shot. "I'm *absolutely* sure Marjorie will have left her portraits *and* her rings to you." He tapped me on the shoulder. "You must do your best to find them."

I walked quickly away, hating his smug assurance, hating the tapping finger, longing all the while to brush my shoulder clean of his touch. Schiffer seemed to be going to extraordinary lengths to make me produce these non-existent paintings and rings.

In the car, I brushed my shoulder vigorously. As I drove out of the carpark I tried to come to terms with having a grandfather who had been a Nazi. Of course, Schiffer and the American woman may have been speaking half-truths. It had been embarrassing to admit I knew nothing about Ackert and his Nazi links. I wondered why all these things were happening to me since I had come to Norwich.

My mind wandered back to Schiffer. *I didn't know it would affect me so much.* It reminded me again of Corrie. *It's like Sellick was waiting for you, the way you got the job.*

I had told the truth when I said there were no photos or portraits of Mum's family in the house. My mother had never mentioned Peter Schiffer or her other lovers. It had been awkward when Schiffer blurted out about the abortion. I wished he hadn't said that.

As I turned into Eversley Road, I wondered how my name had got onto Schiffer's mailing list. And twice he had called me "Paula". I began to think *Wild Marjoram* had been placed deliberately in the window. But no-one could have known I would be passing the shop on that particular day. Unless I were being followed. Which was ridiculous. I recalled Schiffer's voice as he said, *Whatever I did, I still love her.* The words were disturbing. I found everything about Schiffer disturbing. As I opened the front door to my flat, I had the uncomfortable feeling that, behind the façade of surprise, Schiffer had been expecting me all the time.

I was relieved that Mr Jolley and his men had left by the time I got home. I went straight to the bathroom. The room and the shower were a poem in grey and white. I moved on to the kitchen which was now complete, with grey flagstones on the floor. My microwave and kettle were standing comfortably on the worktop. The new oven and the units were all in place. I moved on to my newly-painted bedroom. The bed, table and lamp, and the disintegrating cane chair, sole survivors of Captain Dalton's ugly Victorian furniture, had been moved from the guest room into my room. The dolls house, the crates and the wardrobe had been left in the guest room for the decorators to "work round". No new furniture yet, that was coming on Wednesday.

I heated some mushroom soup in the microwave and took the Clarice Cliff mug back to the bedroom. The ugly broken blind had gone and a pale blue venetian blind and dark blue curtains were in its place. I unwrapped *Wild Marjoram* and put it on the bed.

In Schiffer's gallery, the print had been whisked away before I could touch it. But this was no print. It was a canvas, the vibrant colours glowing on the uneven texture as if the paint had just been brushed across the surface. I stepped forward tremulously and stretched out my hand to touch the chip on the left-hand upper corner of the frame. When I was eight, I had been throwing a small hard ball at the wall in my bedroom and it had damaged the corner. I was overwhelmed. This was *my* *Wild Marjoram.* The picture Mum had painted to protect me from evil. Perhaps it had come back into my hands to fulfil my Mum's wishes in these new and disturbing times.

When my mother died and the house was sold, *Wild Marjoram* had been left behind. The estate agent had said my mother's death was tragic, but it hadn't stopped him making me clear everything out within a week of her passing. The new owners were anxious to move in "like yesterday". In the painful rush of collecting my possessions, the painting had been overlooked. How had it found its way to Norwich? It added to the strangeness of the day.

I sat on the cheap chair with its broken bits of cane, facing the painting, remembering how Amy, my mother's friend, had helped me empty the house. Amy was anxious not to have a lot of "children's junk" in her home, so I had taken my clothes, my schoolbooks, my sketchbooks, a little bear with a singed ear, my mother's painting-bag and the duvet and fleece from my bed. To Amy's consternation, I insisted on taking my dolls house. I remembered the day so clearly.

"But it's so big," Amy says, frowning.

"I know, I know, but it's my dearest, dearest thing! Mama made all the clothes for the family, and she painted their portraits. Please, please, Amy, let me keep it."

"Stop blathering, child, let me think!"

Amy can be sharp. I have never thought of her as loving. The agent, who is watching us, says it can go on the fire in the garden. At the sight of my horrified face, Amy steps forward.

"It's so big," she says again. "What have you got in it?"

I am anxious to tell her. "All the house dolls and their toys and the furniture and the garden tools..."

"That's enough! Let me think." After a moment she asks me if there is a wheelbarrow. I find it at the bottom of the garden. With the estate agent's help, the house is lifted across the wheelbarrow and taken to the car. It just fits into the boot.

"I should have got the removal men to drive it home," Amy says acidly.

"I'm sorry, I'm sorry, but I can't live without it."

I try to explain it's a link with Mum, but Amy tells me to stop being obsequious. "I don't want to hear another word about the wretched thing. Now then, have a last look round. Have you got everything? The house has been sold and new people will be moving in over the weekend. You know you won't be able to go back after today."

The harsh words reinforce my misery. I'm being stripped of everything in my life, my home, my mother, my father and the familiar possessions I had shared with them. I burst into tears and stumble into the car. Amy sighs. "It's not an easy time for me either, Paula. We've both lost a dear friend." She passes me a box of tissues. *"There's a lot to arrange and nothing is straightforward. Dry your tears, Paula, you must be a brave girl and help me all you can."*

I frowned as I remembered that first night in Amy's house. I lay in a strange bed, cuddling the little bear under the duvet and the fleecy blanket decorated with running horses. My mother had brought the duvets with her from Germany. Mum had not liked sheets and blankets.

I cried myself to sleep every night. I stayed only a short time with Amy before I had to move on again. Then I married Richard and he insisted the dolls house was put into the spare room in our flat in West Kensington. Now it was in another spare room under the builders' rough brown sheet.

I sipped my soup and sat looking at *Wild Marjoram* and suddenly a memory-spike pierced my brain: My mother shouting, shouting at my father, *"The paintings, the paintings!"* And then another word, *"Pforzheim!"* Then my memory crashed. I went into the kitchen and poured myself a whisky with unsteady hands. God! What was happening to me? It seemed inconceivable that Schiffer hadn't recognised *Wild Marjoram* as an original painting. The picture had unlocked the memory of my mother's anger. I found the postcard in my shoulder-bag and studied the picture of a large Greek-looking building with the legend *Heimatmuseum Pforzheim*.

It was frustrating not to move the memory forward. These prickings from the past were unnerving.

I switched the radio on. The newsreader was describing an attack at RAF Marham by a group calling itself the *Sons of Hermann* who had tried to hijack a plane. Three men had died in a bomb blast and four others were injured. After the news there was a soap with the airwaves overflowing with the family's squabbles. I kept the radio on as background to my thoughts. I didn't trust Schiffer. I wondered if my mother had really loved him. I didn't believe she'd had an abortion.

The unfolding drama on the radio penetrated my thoughts. A man was going mad. I turned the radio off, grateful I could rid myself of the unwholesome story with the turn of a switch. If only life were as simple.

Before I went to bed, I stepped into the grey and white shower and let the hot cleansing water wash away the fears that haunted me. That night I put *Wild Marjoram* on the windowsill where I could see it before I fell asleep. I hoped it would become my protective guardian again.

Deep in the shadows of sleep, I dreamt that I walked down the hall and opened the front door. The moonlight lit up a young man. It was the man with the gold chain in Setna's photo. Millar was standing on the doorstep saying, *Why don't you tell them who I am?*

My voice echoed eerily round the darkened porch. *But I only saw you for a moment before the trial collapsed.*

Abruptly, I sat up in bed, fully awake, my heart pounding, I began filling in the gaps in my memory.

A room full of people.

Paintings everywhere.

The man in the photograph talking to my mother.

The gold chain.

A shot in the night.

My mother running.

Everyone running.

Then the short pulse of memory faded. I felt disoriented. I hated these memory-spikes pricking at a moment in the past. They left me feeling incomplete and very frightened.

It was two o'clock. I switched on the bedside lamp and watched it illuminate the galloping horses on the blanket on my bed. *You know who I am*, he'd said on the doorstep. The wheels were turning in the space where memory was stored. Of course, the *trial!*

Selwyn had been prosecuting counsel. And it was James Mitchell, not John Millar. Mitchell had been an agent in Criminal Intelligence, CI2. He'd been acting undercover. Selwyn Freeman had explained how WATID, the War Treasure Investigating Department, and CI2, were involved in a world-wide search for paintings plundered by the Nazis and allied soldiers from the occupied countries during and after the war. Although the war had been over for more than three decades there were still active Intelligence units in America, the UK and all the European countries, including Germany and Austria.

Mitchell had been brought in because the body of an ex-soldier had been found in a half-sunk cruiser in one of the small fishing Broads comprising Martham Pits near Great Yarmouth. The man had been murdered, but hidden in his clothing was a miniature portrait of one of the English royal family. It had been lost during the war.

Selwyn's hobby and passion was collecting miniatures. He had shown me a photograph of the portrait in an art magazine. It was of Princess Victoria, Prince Philip's grandmother, who had married Prince Louis of Battenburg. It had been painted on ivory by Reginald Easton and had been on display in Berlin in 1938 in a Fine Art exhibition. After that, all knowledge of its whereabouts had been lost until it turned up in a watery grave thirty-six years after the war had ended. James Mitchell had been assigned to investigate how the ex-soldier had acquired the miniature.

It was during that time that I saw Mitchell silhouetted in the corridor as he was leaving Selwyn's chambers. I never spoke to him. Selwyn had briefly mentioned his visit, but I didn't hear of him again until Ram Setna turned up on my doorstep with a photograph and a false name. But I should have remembered the gold chain.

Sunday, 24th May 1981

After breakfast, I decided to sort out the pots in the yard. May was keeping cold. It had rained all night, but now the sky was clearing and there was even a hint of warmth. I put on some jeans, an old blue cotton shirt and sandals, and wrapped a square silk kerchief round my head. It was the first time I had ever prepared a garden by myself. Of course, this was only a tiny patch compared to my mother's splendid garden in Ealing.

I had asked Len to arrange the pots in groups. Colours feed on colour and they should be bunched together so that plants can explode in brilliance and shape.

I put the azalea, pansies, tulips and dahlias in the pots, and the hydrangea in one of the deep old sinks. I filled the other sink with larkspur, sweet pea and more pansies as house-guests. A small bamboo went into a large wooden planter. I was hoping it would spread its delicate leaves and cover the dull grey house bricks. In another planter, I put the climbing rose against the bathroom wall. Len had thoughtfully put in two large hooks for hanging baskets. I filled them with trailing lobelia frothing over the edges, creeping aubretia and drooping pansies. The washed flagstones were a beautiful backcloth to the flowers, and the new dustbins were discreetly hidden behind the wooden planters. The dustbins were painted with A and B and the number of the house. There was never anything in Dustbin B.

I made a coffee and sat on a wooden chair beside the square garden table, and as I looked round the yard, it occurred to me that Mr Siskin would have praised me for creating a space for a garden. Mr Siskin had played an important part in my young life. As my mother constantly reminded me, he was a famous landscape gardener, a renowned member of the RHS, and a Master of Horticulture. A certificate of his achievements had hung on the wall in his lounge in Lintwhite Villa. Mum told me once that Mr Siskin shared her passion for wide borders filled with blooms.

I hadn't thought about Mr Siskin and his family for years. He belonged to a happier time when I was a schoolgirl and played with Mr Siskin's daughters, a time before there were guns and bloodshed in my life. If it had been warmer and sunnier I would have opened the yellow parasol. It was then I realised this was no longer a yard. It was handsome enough to be called a "courtyard". From a neighbouring garden the haunting music of *Chariots of Fire* floated softly over the heady, perfumed air.

When I finished the coffee I swept the flagstones, tidied the pots a little this way and that, and finally washed and cleaned the tools and put them in the cupboard under the stairs. One day, I told myself, I would buy a small tool shed. I felt pleasantly tired and decided I would go out for Sunday lunch. I had a shower and changed into a skirt and blouse and high-heeled sandals.

Schiffer's mention of Acle and the inn near the bridge over the River Bure had reminded me of summer holiday treats with my parents. I got in the car and made my way to the A47, then onto the A1064. I passed the Fishley Carrs woodland and continued up the Old Road until I came to Acle Bridge and the inn. As I drew into the car park I immediately recognised the thatched dome on the roof of the building and its strange, overlapping pantiles.

Hesitantly, I walked past the beautiful flint wall into the hundred-year-old restaurant. It had changed very little since the fifties when I had gone there with my parents. I ordered a meal: dover sole with a green salad and a gin and tonic. Then I eased my feet out of my shoes, as I always do when I relax, and enjoyed my drink while the food was cooking.

With my glass in my hand, I looked casually round the room. A young couple was sitting close together, nuzzling each other like puppies. Two businessmen, their briefcases on the unoccupied chairs, were talking heatedly over a roast chicken dinner. I saw a man in a dark suit stand up, his back towards me, talking to his companion. Then he turned abruptly and walked past me.

My mind flipped between dark and light like the shutters of a camera. The man in the dark suit was Mitchell, the CI2 agent Setna had been looking for. And Mitchell was walking out of my dreams and into the daylight. I sat, numb, unable to distinguish dreams from reality.

The waiter came over with my order. I clutched his sleeve. "That man, the man in the dark suit who's just left, do you know him, his name, *anything?*"

The waiter removed my hand ungently. "Never seen him before, madam, but that gentleman seemed to know him." He pointed across the room. Mitchell's companion was wiping the table with a napkin. I slipped on my shoes and went over.

"I'm sorry to disturb you," I began. "Why…it's Mr Schiffer!" The rich intonation reached out to me.

"Won't you sit down, Mrs James? Some wine?" He seemed unsurprised to see me. There was no recall of our earlier meeting. A waiter whipped away the wet tablecloth and placed a clean napkin and a fresh wine glass on the table.

I sat down slowly as if I really were in a dream. This was more than coincidence. Again, I wondered if I were being followed. The waiter asked if he should bring my lunch over. Schiffer nodded. "Yes, yes, of course." He turned to me. "The food here is delicious."

With an effort, I smiled. "I thought I recognised the man you were speaking with earlier. Unfortunately, I've forgotten his name." I didn't want to reveal more about Mitchell than I had to.

Schiffer shrugged. "He was a stranger. The room was full earlier. He asked to sit at my table and I agreed. We exchanged a few words. Then he left."

"He seemed upset."

"A glass of wine was accidentally knocked over. You say you know him?"

"Vaguely, but I would like to get in touch with him."

"Well, Mrs James, *if* I should meet him, I will tell him." Schiffer was smooth. His use of my married name was a further closure on yesterday's uninhibited outburst.

I asked him if he often came to the inn.

"From time to time. They have a good chef. French, you know. Will you be having a sweet?"

"I prefer coffee." Schiffer ordered coffee for two. I told him he had given me an oil painting and not a print of *Wild Marjoram*.

He leaned back. "I blame young Jordan. He's been selling Jeffries' prints very successfully over the last two weeks." He smiled. "Well, you wanted an original painting and I'm glad you have that one."

Why was he lying? Jordan had shown him the painting.

"How did you get hold of it, Mr Schiffer?"

"I bought it at an auction in London."

I pointed out that it was curious it should be displayed in his window on the day I was in Norwich.

"It's been on display all week." He was dismissive and refused to be drawn further.

"I'm working in Sellick's head office in Norwich," I persisted. "He has some good paintings on the walls. Do you or Dales provide them?"

He looked up, his eyes glinting. "I was right, you do have a good eye. Yes, I provide the paintings for all Sellick's offices in East Anglia and London. Clients often buy them. In fact, three were bought last week, so it's a good arrangement for both of us."

Then he harked back to Jeffries' early portraits. "Have you searched for them in your flat?"

"Mr Schiffer, I brought very little with me when I left London and definitely no portraits." I stopped, suddenly alert. "There was an intruder in my flat recently. If someone is floating the idea that I have these portraits, that might explain the burglary."

Schiffer leaned forward, excitement widening his eyes. "You're saying someone broke into your flat?"

I was terse. "Did you instigate it, Mr Schiffer?"

He laughed aloud. "You're not afraid to ask the awkward question, are you! Marjorie was like that. She could be so intrusive, rude even. She wasn't a woman to take lightly, and I can see you're of a similar ilk. But to answer your question, no, Mrs James, I don't burgle houses. I pay for what I want."

He paused, his finger lightly tapping the glass of wine he was holding. "I don't want any enmity between us, Paula, but there are things we have to discuss. Some cartoons, painted in Berlin before the war, are missing. They were drawn by a well-known artist, one of Marjorie's friends. The cartoons are clever. They poke wicked fun at prominent figures in the Nazi political world. There are about fifty. The last I heard was that Marjorie had them. I want those sketches. Now, I'm willing to offer a generous sum of money for them."

"How generous?"

His breath quickened. "So, you *do* have them! I'll give you a hundred for each sketch." He was watching me. "And I'll be equally generous with any portrait you, er, may find."

"Mr Schiffer, I have neither portraits nor sketches." I decided to open up the conversation. "A lot of strange things have been happening to me since I came to Norwich. Perhaps if I knew more about the past, I might understand the present better. Could you tell me about my grandfather, Dieter Ackert?"

Schiffer frowned, and I pencilled in the harsh line between his eyes on my invisible sketchbook.

He seemed reluctant at first to talk. "I don't know if it will help, but I'll tell you what I can. I first met Ackert and your mother when I was fifteen. In 1931 I was in Germany, visiting my father for the New Year celebrations. Dieter Ackert, Jürgen Bergmann and my father were old school friends. They'd fought side by side in the Great War. My parents were divorced and I lived in London with my mother and English stepfather."

He was silent for a moment. "Your grandfather was a remarkable man. He influenced everyone he came in touch with. Words cannot describe his manner, the way he spoke, the quality of his leadership. Charismatic is what you'd say today."

From his wallet, Schiffer took out a folded section of a faded German newspaper with a photograph of Dieter Ackert and Adler Schiffer.

"They were young when they died," I said quietly.

"The epitaph of the Great War."

"You say you met Ackert in Bremen?"

"Everything began in Bremen." Schiffer began speaking more freely. "Jürgen Bergmann, Dieter Ackert and my father were war heroes. What they said, what they did, mattered. My father told me they joined the Nazi Party as a protest against the inertia of the Weimar Republic." He raised his shoulders. "They were difficult, confusing times and, personally, I don't think they would have remained Nazis. Everything centred on the march Ackert had organised in February in Bremen. As I told you, Ackert and my father were shot dead. Only Bergmann survived the chaos of the march.

"In February 1931, Marjorie was fifteen, beautiful and a talented young painter and I fell in love with her. Jürgen Bergmann and I stood beside her at the funeral for Ackert and my father. A Dutchman, Rik van der Vendt, stood with us. He'd finished painting Ackert's portrait only a few days before the march. I admit I never liked him. After the funeral I had to return to London. I met up with Marjorie again in Berlin in 1935. It was then we became lovers."

I listened breathlessly as he described Berlin, a city full of sensuality and self-indulgence, filled with Strauss's waltzes, men in uniform and women in beautiful dresses.

Schiffer went on, "Marjorie was in great demand to paint portraits of the great and famous, but she had a wicked imp inside her. She called it her English gremlin. I loved that side of her, spiteful and playful. I knew she would make a name for herself in Europe. Then stupidly, she ran off with van der Vendt and got herself in the newspapers for the wrong reasons. In 1938, Marjorie's mother married an English attaché in Berlin, a Maurice Jeffries. Marjorie took his name and the family left Germany soon after."

Leaning forward, Schiffer said, "You want to know about your mother, what kind of person she was and how it was between Marjorie and me?"

I nodded, transfixed by his intensity.

"Marjorie could be so obstinate, so entrenched in her views. And volatile. My God, she was volatile! People saw the successful, dynamic force that was MJ Ackert. They seldom saw the real woman, fitful, harsh and capricious. And let me be honest, it was love and hate, sweet and sour, between us."

I was disturbed by his remarks. I waited while he lit a cigarette. "In 1937, we joined the Bruderbund. Hitler had outlawed the Bund after three Bruderbunder were murdered by the Nazis. There were no trials, just the death sentence and the axe. So Marjorie, Bergmann and I formed our own secret group within the Brotherhood. We called it *Der Ritterorden*, the Order of Knights. We were young and idealistic, but we could all see what was coming, and that's when we swore allegiance to Arminius."

I smiled. "The German warrior who destroyed three Roman Legions and shamed Augustus."

Schiffer nodded. "We could have done with Arminius in 1939. Well, the *Ritterorden* made a pact: whatever happened, our conscience and moral values would guide us through the coming war." He poured out more wine. "The *Ritterorden* helped many artists, scientists, and writers to escape from Nazi Germany before and during the war."

"And you were part of that?"

A rueful shake of the head. "In 1939, I was celebrating gaining my Masters at Oxford. I drank too much and was in a car crash and my left lung was damaged. When I recovered, I was appointed onto the Commission for the Safe-keeping of Art, or *CoSA*. It was of national importance, and was one of the most successful enterprises of the war. I'm proud of what we achieved. We emptied the museums and galleries in London and all the major cities, and hid the paintings and artefacts in caves in Wales and Scotland. It was a busy time, but I still managed to see Marjorie. By that time, she was giving lessons to injured service men and women at the cottage in Acle, and here, by the Riverside Inn.

"After the war, the pictures were returned to the galleries by the *CoSA* team, and in 1947, I started my gallery in Norwich. It was then Marjorie asked me to search for news about her cousins. I visited her in Yorkstone Cottage and told her the boys had died in a Russian labour camp in 1954. It may have been then, Paula, that you saw me, but Marjorie refused to believe me. She'd just heard a rumour that the boys had been returned to East Berlin."

He looked up, his eyes hard. "It was a lie. Terrible things happen in war. Images become too stark, too poignant." His voice rose. "Marjorie wasn't perfect, you know. I wanted to marry her, but she fell in love with the young Englishman. Not your father. This Englishman was much cleverer than Denby."

Angrily, I interrupted him, "Who was he?"

Schiffer frowned. "You ask too many questions, Paula, that's all in the forgotten past. You're missing the *real* truth. Marjorie's paintings are important. We need to have the whole archive of her work. She was a prolific artist and painted the most significant people in Western Europe before and during the war. She was an astute political observer and she portrayed the social history of her time. Those works need to be shown in public. If you know where those early missing portraits are you must tell me."

"But I don't know anything about missing portraits!"

He frowned, watching me. "She could have hidden them."

I shrugged. "It's much more likely she disposed of them. Did you know she was unwell before she died and she found it difficult to hold her pencils and brushes? My father walked out of our lives the very day she died. There were no portraits in the house when it was sold."

"Could she have put them in a bank? Do you have any keys?"

Amy and the little keys! Too small to be safe deposit keys. "No keys," I said firmly, "and no deposit boxes."

Schiffer grunted, disappointed. "Then they must be somewhere else."

"How many paintings are we talking about?"

"Maybe twenty."

"But where do these paintings come from?"

"Some were lost in the war, others pilfered, some changed hands and the new owners never declared the deal, and some she kept back, perhaps to put on the market at a future date. Some of those portraits depicted very controversial figures." Schiffer looked at me, the frown creased deeply between his questioning eyes.

I stood up. "I know nothing about any early works." The conversation was over. "I'm glad we talked, Mr Schiffer, and if you *should* meet the man who shared your table, please let him know I'd like to see him."

I drove back home thinking about the conversation with Schiffer. When I was fifteen, my mother told me she'd given Dad's cache of stolen miniatures to a friend to look after. She had never mentioned anything about early portraits or cartoons. No paintings of any sort had been found in Amy's house after her death. Perhaps the intruder at our flat in West Kensington, and at my flat in Norwich, were actually searching for these nebulous works of art. Perhaps, a hideous thought, the faceless man with the gun was looking for them.

My mind veered back to Schiffer. He was shrewd, clever and manipulative. I was disturbed by the summary of his relationship with my mother: *love and hate, sweet and sour.* The love and devotion she had inspired in him were hidden behind the malice in his dark voice.

Monday, 25ᵗʰ May 1981

Swaffham is a pretty market town with some beautiful Georgian houses and a rotunda in a large square. I drove through the town and arrived at the wrought-iron gates of Dunham Village at eight-thirty in the morning. On the right of the gates was a bungalow. A man dressed in a guard's uniform was standing outside. I stopped and introduced myself as the new estate-agent. The guard, "Call me George!" ticked me off on his clipboard and gave me a printed card with my name attached to a red ribbon which I put round my neck.

"What's it like working here?" I asked.

"Sure you want to know? OK then. Well, the last woman kept asking questions and Mrs Heals sacked her. Then she sacked the French woman because she was argumentative. And the man before them was always late and he lost his job as well."

I was taken aback. Corrie had mentioned Renée Tournai and Audrey Simpson, but nothing about the man who was always late. George pointed out the carpark behind the sales house and wished me luck with a wry smile.

I had arrived early in order to look round the site. Opposite the sales house was a community hall and the supervisor's house. A supervisor and security guards were on duty night and day throughout the year. Security was what Dunham Village was all about. Going further, I found myself on a huge building site. Houses were sprouting up in groups and I began to get an impression of how it would look when it was finished. The setting of the golf course was superb.

My sales office was in the lounge of the first bungalow that had been built. It had been decorated blandly in magnolia and had dark red curtains at the windows. On a table were a telephone, a large brown leather appointments diary, a square glass ash-tray and a half-open box of tissues. It stood opposite a fire-place with a simple stone surround.

The table had three drawers on the left and one on the right. In the top left-hand drawer were forms for the purchasers to fill in, the second drawer contained files with the names of clients who had already paid deposits for their properties. I put the A4 list of instructions Heals had given me the bottom drawer with some empty files, brown envelopes, a stapler, a paper-punch and a list of all the properties that had been sold. In the right-hand drawer were a cash-box and a paying-in book with my name and "Sellick's Agency" on the cover. Facing my chair were two chairs on the other side of the table. Under the table was a cane waste paper bin.

A Paisley-patterned fabric sofa stood under the wide window beside a long low glass table with pamphlets, brochures and yesterday's local and national papers. My first task was to gather up the old papers and arrange Monday's papers attractively on the glass table. I put the old papers in a bin in the kitchen.

On the wall behind the table was a large map of the Retirement Homes development. Properties that had been sold had little flags with the number of the building and initials of the buyers and sellers: PH, AS, LH, and MS.

Pat Heals' red-lined block of properties contained a mixture of flats on three floors and bungalows. These were buildings I couldn't sell or get a bonus for. To one side of the map were long rows of wooden racks screwed to the wall with hooks holding keys to properties that had been completed.

I had picked up the post and a bottle of milk on the doorstep when I came in, and I was pleased—no, I was *delighted*—to find the kitchen was equipped with a small, clean fridge, a kettle, some pink and blue mugs, a jar of ground coffee and a packet of tea-bags in a cupboard. I had put the kettle on, a ritual of love, and hung my coat on a hook on the back of the kitchen door, when I heard someone come into the sales room. I had been told to keep the front door open as an invitation to passing clients.

I went back into the office as an attractive woman walked up to my table. She moved like a model, head high, shoulders back, swinging from the hips. She was wearing a red linen summer coat with wide shoulder pads, a pleated silk Emanuel dress in cream, and high slim court shoes in beige. Her Gucci handbag was styled in rose and brown. She was the sulky, attractive woman I'd seen in the Norwich estate office talking to Doug Sellick.

There was no greeting. She faced me, the petulant expression deepening. "Have you seen my mother?"

I was brusque. "I've only just arrived. I haven't seen anyone."

She looked round the room. "Where's Mrs Heals?"

"She'll be here this afternoon."

She nodded and swept out of the room, almost knocking into a man coming through the doorway.

I watched him step nimbly to one side. He came up to me with a rueful smile. "I thought Eris had brushed my sleeve."

"Eris?"

"The goddess of strife and discontent!" The lines round his eyes crinkled as he smiled.

I laughed. "The goddess is looking for her mother." I signalled to him to sit down at my table. "How can I help you?"

He was older than I had first thought, casually but well-dressed, his thick light-brown hair parted at the side.

"I got your letter, so I've come along to settle up the final sum." He peered at the name tag round my neck and frowned. "I understood Rowene would be here."

"I'm Paula James, her replacement." I answered smartly. "This is my first day here and you're my first client."

He seemed satisfied. "Well, let me give you this first."

It was a typed letter from the Retirement Homes Project, signed by Renée Tournai, informing Mr Thomas Cameron that the flat would be ready on Monday 25th, in the afternoon, and requesting him to come to the Village to settle the final details at 9.30 in the morning.

I asked him if he would like to see the property first. To my surprise, it was the first time he'd been in Swaffham. We drove round in a golf buggy and I was surprised to see the flat was already furnished, the armchairs looking well-lived in.

Cameron's manner was confident. "It's all Dad's things, they were delivered on Saturday. Everything had to be auctioned after the house-clearance, but we kept these back. Dad's been staying with us, but the wife's found it, well, a bit difficult." He paused, and the problem of an unwanted elderly parent hung in the air.

Back in the office, I asked Cameron how he'd chosen the flat. He frowned. "From the brochure *The Helpline* sent with the advertisement."

Heals hadn't mentioned a helpline. I asked him if he had the advertisement with him. He shook his head impatiently.

I opened the middle drawer of the table. Cameron's file held the details of the property, the deposit and final payment to the solicitor. I handed him the two forms he had to sign.

"More forms!" But Cameron had already begun to fill them in with the details of his father: address, next of kin, doctor, bank, and the number of the recently purchased bungalow. On the second form, he ticked off cleaning and laundry that were among the services offered at an extra cost. I asked him if he was satisfied with the arrangements.

He nodded as he swept his signature along the bottom of the form. "Yes, *The Helpline* did a thorough job."

"*The Helpline*?" I echoed.

"The umbrella organisation that offers legal, financial and medical assistance. All the paperwork was done through them." He frowned. "You've been properly briefed, I hope?"

"Of course, but as I explained, this is my first day and I hadn't realised how complex everything would be." I smiled weakly. "I'm having to learn as I go along." I let the impression lie that I wasn't very bright.

Cameron handed me a cheque. "You'll manage," he said coolly. He was giving nothing away.

I stapled the receipt onto the top copies of the forms and gave them to Cameron. Then I entered details of the cheque, and the time of Cameron's visit, into the table diary. I sat back and ran my eyes over the forms he had just filled in.

"You've come from Aylesbury!" I was startled. I had understood that Pat Heals' advert had only come out in East Anglia. I asked if Aylesbury didn't have its own nursing homes.

"Well, yes." He looked rattled. "But this isn't a nursing home, it's a *new* idea, isn't it?"

"Of course!" I looked up. "It's just that I see your father is eighty-two. Will he be able to manage on his own?"

"He's very independent," Cameron snapped. He looked at me sharply. "Rowene was *very* helpful, there was none of this questioning."

"I'm sorry if I've annoyed you, Mr Cameron. As I said, it's my first day."

He was sarcastic. "Well, I hope you'll see a second day. Now there's no problem in Father moving in this afternoon, is there?"

"Of course not, I hope he'll be very happy here."

But I had not expected such a pragmatic attitude. Aylesbury is a long way from Swaffham. Was he just dumping his elderly father here? Tentatively, I asked where he had read the advertisement about the Retirement Homes.

"In the paper." He was brusque, his voice hard. "Any *more* questions?"

I gave him the keys to his father's flat. "This is my big moment, Mr Cameron." I was trying to heal the breach between us. "These are the first keys I'm giving a client."

He nodded curtly, put the keys in his pocket and left. I had a nasty feeling he was going to complain to Pat Heals about my poor handling of his interview.

I glanced through his file again after he had left. This was Cameron's first visit. There had been no telephone calls or appointments, except for today, and MS had initialled it. I knew Martin Spencer worked some afternoon shifts at the sales house. There was no mention of Rowene. Next to his appointment, I wrote that Mr Cameron had settled up the final sums and now had the keys to Mr Louis Cameron's flat.

Cameron's attitude had been odd, but it only reinforced the strangeness of my appointment. Sellick had made a big fuss about recruiting an agent for Dunham Village, but the only reason I was here was to show people round the site and collect money for the services. Nothing more. A sixteen-year-old could do the job. I hoped the work would soon become more challenging. I wrote a shorthand summary of Cameron's interview in a notebook in my bag. I might need to quote what had been said.

I opened the bottom drawer and took out the pieces of A4 paper Pat Heals had given me and read them through. They contained very precise instructions and were written in a neat round hand:

The top drawer holds all the forms that the purchaser must fill in with details of the occupier, including information about address, bank, doctor, solicitor and next of kin. The second sheet has all the details about the property that has been purchased, together with the services we are offering, such as golf fees, laundry etc. Every part must be filled in. When completed, both forms must be signed, and the agent will give the top copies to the client, while the second copies are placed in the client's file and put in the middle drawer on the left. All transactions must be recorded in the diary on the table, with the name, the time of sale and details of the cheque.

The name and address of the clients' solicitor, and the amount of the deposit for the property, must be noted on the form headed Solicitor/Deposit. The client then takes that form to their solicitor, and the solicitor will liaise with the estate agent.

The cheques covering the amenities must be put in the cash box beside the paying-in book. These must be kept in the upper drawer on the right of the table. The properties within the red lines are to be sold only by Patricia Heals. Your initials must be written on the flags when a deposit is put down on a property, and when that property is finally sold, it must be recorded in the diary. All sales must be entered in the client's file, as well as in the table diary.

Heals had added that it was part of my duties to go to the bank in Swaffham at the end of every morning to pay in all cheques and cash.

I went over to the map on the wall. The builders had been busy and a mixture of forty bungalows and apartments had been added to those already completed. Another twenty had their foundations in. Perhaps Sellick had trebled their wages in the hope of getting the complex completed quickly. Nine properties had been sold by AS, Audrey Simpson, during February, March and April. A few by LH, Lawrie Heals, and MS, Martin Spencer. CS, Corrie Smiley had sold four flats. Pat's initials were against a further twelve flags. All were within her red lines.

I pulled one of the flags out. Under the name Denning was the imprint of another name. It was hard to make it out. Possible *Slur…Stur?…ss. Sturgess*, or maybe the double 's' was an 'n'. I looked at a couple more. One flag was unused, but a name, *Johns*, had been written over *Standard* on the next flag. There were six more 'spoilt' flags. The remaining flags had names of recent sales. I didn't remember seeing a Sturgess or a Johns on the A4 sheets. There were no records of the sales of the eight properties that had changed hands so quickly. Perhaps Heals kept a separate log for that block of houses. The properties could only have been sold in March or April and then quickly resold.

My job as a legal secretary had made me careful and cautious. I took out the file with Cameron's details and this time I studied it. The bank was a well-known name on the high street. Cameron and his father shared the same solicitor, the same doctor, the same address. I wondered where the father had lived before he moved in with his son and disgruntled daughter-in-law. It was strange that Cameron was happy to leave his father in a retirement home so many miles from Aylesbury. Of course, age is deceptive and Cameron senior might be a frolicking octogenarian, but perhaps I should have questioned his son more robustly.

I also entered the names of the owners I had tried to decipher on the flags, people who had stayed for such a mysteriously short time in Dunham Village. Why had Sturgeon/Sturgess, Standard/Johns, Wright, Dean/Bradley, Wilkinson and the others come and gone so quickly? Death, if it were death, must have been very sudden. Had eleven years of dealing with criminals made me suspicious of even innocent facts? I decided it would be circumspect to keep my own copy of any sales I made in case any doubts about the elderly clients should arise. So I wrote down all the details Mr Cameron had entered on the forms into my notebook.

I walked back to the map on the wall. I began to appreciate Sellick's concern. No wonder money was haemorrhaging out of his bank account.

I had just replaced the file in the middle drawer when a couple knocked on the open door. They hesitated apologetically on the threshold before stepping into the room. "Is this where we come if we want to see the bungalows?"

A small robin-like woman waved her hand. I gestured to her to come over to the sofa where the brochures and the Purchaser's Information Pack—the PIP—were laid out on the table. They introduced themselves as Mr and Mrs Lionel Redding.

Mrs Redding was cheerful in a long red dress and green woollen coat. Her husband was a quiet, almost bald, clean-shaven man, with careful eyes and heavy lines down to his chin.

"This retirement community sounds a *wonderful* idea. Our family is in Australia." Mrs Redding peeked up at her husband. "We went out there and stayed with our son, his wife and the grandchildren, but we didn't like the spiders and snakes!"

The Robin hurried on breathlessly. "This is ideal, *everything* we want, no worry about maintenance or security. We're not sick, we're still pretty active, we don't want a nursing home, and the golf course is fantastic!"

And that just about summed up the attraction of the scheme. I asked them if they had received a letter from the Retirement Homes. No letter. I persisted, "Did you hear about the scheme or read about it?"

Mrs Redding laughed. She had small dark eyes and quick, pecky movements. "Oh no, dear, we live just outside Swaffham. We've been watching the golf course taking shape and the buildings going up."

Her husband nodded. "It's a good use of the old wartime aerodrome and if we like what we see we'll put our house on the market."

His wife broke in, "And that's why we've come to see the flats."

I took them round the Village in a golf buggy. They liked one of the upper flats overlooking the golf course. I advised them to put in an offer quickly. Back at the sales office, I wrote their names and the time they had arrived down in the brown leather-bound table diary, and then I added some shorthand notes in my own notebook.

As the Reddings left, two men came into the room. The older man was walking heavily with a stick, his left arm hanging by his side. His companion introduced himself as Neil Dermott. "This is my uncle, Edward Dermott. We saw an advert and someone sent us this letter and a brochure, like that one on the table. My uncle's had a stroke and he feels this is the right place to enjoy his retirement."

Apart from the date, the letter was the same as Cameron's. I put it to one side as Edward Dermott sat down. "The stroke came out of the blue. My own doctor wasn't much help so Neil took me down to London. To Harley Street. I saw some big-wig there. He was thorough, I'll say that for him. He said I've got hypertension and..." He turned to his nephew. "What did he call it?"

"Hemiparesis."

Dermott grunted. "Yeah, that's it. I'm sixty-four. I've built up a good business, but now this doctor says if I don't stop, I could get a massive second stroke and my mind could be affected. I don't want that, so Neil's taking over the business while I get quietly on with what's left of my life."

The business was in general haulage and storage with multi-unit facilities in warehouses in all the principal cities in Scotland and the north of England.

The warehouse business had its main offices in Glasgow. How often would Neil come to visit his sick uncle?

"You must have worked hard to achieve so much," I said appreciatively.

He nodded. "Yeah, me and the wife, we worked all hours. Nora died last year. Cancer. *That* was sudden, too. Well, I've had a good run and there's only Neil and me left now." He pointed at the brochure on my table. "Neil heard about the scheme first, and when I saw the details of the golf course I thought, right, this is the place for me, and the doctor says exercise will be good. Anyway, I've put aside enough to see I'm well looked after. I've chosen the flat from the brochure, contracts have been exchanged, so we've come to settle up the golf fees and bits and bobs and look round the place."

Despite the talk of stroke and hypertension, Dermott's speech was only slightly slurred. His nephew sat stolidly beside him, his mouth half-open in a fixed smile, his eyes meditating on his stomach. One of Selwyn's witnesses had spent his entire interrogation in the dock looking down at his navel. Selwyn had called him 'a study in omphaloskepsis'.

I asked Neil if he had the Information Pack and he nodded. He took out a cheque book and I saw the transaction was to be made through a private account. From what Edward had said, his business must be worth a great deal. I watched Edward sit back. He had mentally handed everything over to his nephew. I thought he'd given up too soon.

The Dermotts had decided on a ground-floor flat overlooking the golf course. Edward nodded. "The furniture's being delivered early tomorrow, so I'll move into the flat in the afternoon. We're staying at the Pedlar Hotel in Swaffham. Neil'll give you the phone number."

I went and got the keys to the apartment and wished Edward Dermott a happy retirement. He nodded at Neil and said he'd wait for him outside. Neil had filled in the forms and was now writing out the phone number of the Pedlar Hotel in case I needed to get in touch. Before Neil left, I asked him if he had the letter sent by the agency. In silence, he searched his inner jacket pocket and handed it over to me.

"Oh, and do you have the advertisement?" I asked briskly.

Neil looked closely at my name-tag. "I was expecting someone else."

"I've just joined the team," I explained.

"That's not what I meant," he said.

I asked him how he had heard of the Retirement Homes in Norfolk. He got up abruptly. "Through the ad in the paper," he mumbled and joined his uncle outside the sales house. I watched them walk round to the carpark. I wished I'd asked him about *The Helpline*.

I began tidying up. It was then I noticed a business card on the floor. I picked it up and saw a small folded piece of newspaper under the table. I opened the piece of paper first. It was an advertisement for Dunham Village from a local paper in Glasgow. Neil had dropped it. The name of the newspaper was placed just above the article.

Dunham Village is a new idea, a retirement homes complex for elderly or retired people who are mobile and in reasonably good health. It is not a nursing home. Dunham Village offers the prospective purchaser a great social life in a safe and secure environment with a choice of sports, on-site medical centre, shop, community hall, and frequent bus services into the centre of Swaffham, to King's Lynn, and to Norwich.

Dunham Village is a market town, a place of dreams, where, like the famous pedlar and his dog, you may find your own kind of treasure through enjoyment of resources in the Village or improvement in your health. There is a great selection of individual bungalows and apartments at attractive prices built round a magnificent golf course constructed by Erik Maroc. If you are interested in these retirement homes please telephone us on 0603 717239

If you are satisfied then we can arrange for you to meet our representative who will answer all your questions. Our team in The Helpline are sensitive to the difficulties you are experiencing, but we are sure we have the right answers for you. Ring us if you have any questions.

The advertisement Heals had placed in the local press was in the file. That advert was exactly the same as the one I was holding, except that it contained only the first paragraph and the telephone number of the sales office. There was no mention of "right answers" to difficulties being experienced, or *The Helpline.*

I picked up the phone and rang the number in Dermott's advertisement. It was a recorded message asking me to leave my name and telephone number and my reason for calling. I put the phone down quickly. Then I looked at the business card I had found on the floor. It had a caption *The Helpline.* Beneath were the words *memento nobis.* On the back was a list:

House-Clearing
Auctions
Legal and Medical Advice
Finance

The card must have fallen out of Neil Dermott's pocket with the newspaper advertisement. I turned it over. *The Helpline.* This must be the umbrella organisation Thomas Cameron had talked about. *Memento nobis.* Remember us. It had a sinister ring. There was no address, no phone number, no names.

I entered everything into my notebook and the table diary, filed away the papers and put the cheque in the box in the top drawer. I thought it strange that Neil Dermott had said someone had sent him the brochure about the Retirement Homes. Heals had focussed her advertising campaign on East Anglia so how had Cameron and Dermott got in touch with Heals?

I opened my shoulder-bag and slipped the card into the envelope with the letters and the advertisement. MS's initials were on the little flag over Dermott's bungalow. Still no generous bonus for me.

Three couples wandered in, asked some questions, then went round the Village and left without showing any interest. A thickset man popped in about one in the afternoon, announcing himself as he strode through the doorway.

"Good to meet you. I'm Hal Goodison and I've come for the keys. Number 80. That's it. Next to the golf course."

He walked quickly over to the wall. "Final touches today and I'm moving in tomorrow. See, my name's on the flag." He came over to my table, flamboyant, assured, with deep-set grey eyes and ugly sandy-coloured patches on his bald scalp. "I've been waiting nearly a year for this bungalow. I put down a deposit before they even started building."

He leaned forward, breathing over me. "So now it's just the final cheque. You'll find the forms I filled in for Mrs Heals in that drawer."

He leaned right over the table and pulled out the middle drawer. "Check my file, you'll see it's up to date." He sat down on the chair opposite. "I like to be sure about things."

I glanced through the file. "Everything seems to be in order."

"Everything *is* in order," he replied drily, and wrote out the cheque for the amenities and membership of the golf club. I gave him the two top copies and a receipt which he folded neatly, pressing the fold hard with his thumb-nail before putting it carefully in his wallet.

"I sold my house in London over a year ago," Goodison said, "and I've been renting a flat in Norwich till I could move in here."

"You're a Londoner! I didn't know Dunham Village had been advertised in the capital."

"It wasn't. I heard about it from Mrs Heals. We were friends when she worked in London. She told me about Dunham Village and the golf course." His voice turned ugly. "You're very full of questions for an employee, Mrs James."

I flushed at his rudeness. "I'm learning my job as I work, Mr Goodison, and that means I have to ask questions."

"I thought your job was to sell the properties, not chat up the clients. That's how the last agent got herself sacked."

I controlled my anger. "Mr Sellick has asked me to write advertising copy for Dunham Village, so I have to learn all I can. That means I have to ask questions." I braced myself. "Tell me, Mr Goodison, have you been approached by someone called Rowene at the Retirement Homes?"

He frowned. "You mean a call girl?"

I was taken aback. "No! Someone who works here."

"Never heard of her."

As I put his cheque in the top drawer, I wondered if Goodison could have a financial interest in the project. A couple came hesitantly into the room and Goodison turned and marched out angrily.

The Murrays were in their seventies, lived in Surrey and had a daughter in Norwich. No letters, no *Helpline*, no Rowene. They just wanted to look round. They came back and said they'd return later in the week with their daughter.

Over the phone, I arranged further appointments for a Mrs Summerhayes on Wednesday, and for Paul and Wendy Smith on Thursday and entered their names in the leather diary. Then I started filling in the paying-in book.

"Typical!" A shout came from the doorway. It was Hal Goodison. "You talked so much you forgot what your job is. You're like the others. Totally incompetent."

I stared at him. "The keys!" he snarled. "I've had to come back because you forgot to give me the keys to my bungalow. I ought to report you."

I went over to the key-rack and found the keys for number 80. I kept my voice low. "I'm sorry for the confusion. It's my first day and not everything has gone as planned."

He slipped the keys into his pocket. "First day, eh? Oh well, no harm done."

To my relief, he turned and left the room and I locked up. Pat Heals would be arriving any minute and I did *not* want to tell her about my first day as an estate agent. I was sure Cameron and Goodison were waiting to tell her how badly I had done.

I waved to George as I drove through the iron gates. Finally, I went to the bank in Swaffham. Then I headed home.

In Norwich, I stopped at the Central Library and looked up directories for nursing homes in Aylesbury and Glasgow. Both cities had several nursing homes and private hospitals, but neither had a social complex for active people from fifty plus. I closed the directories and made a couple of entries in my notebook.

When I got home, I asked Mr Jolley to hang *Wild Marjoram* on my bedroom wall. I knew exactly where all the new furniture was going and I wanted the painting to face my bed. He asked me why I had bought it.

"The owner of an art gallery gave it to me. Apparently, he knew my mother. Mum painted *Wild Marjoram* to act as a shield to protect me. It must have been sold after she died and ended up here in Norwich."

"I'd never have thought a painting could protect you." Jolley measured the wall and marked the places with a pencil. "My wife wouldn't think it unusual though, she believes more herbs should be used in medicine."

As he checked the spirit level and laid out his tools, I began to draw him in my sketchbook. Idly, I marked out the preliminary proportions and found his left shoulder was higher than the right one. A lot of blemishes reveal themselves when sketching.

Lazily, I asked him what had happened. He turned. "Happened?"

"To your shoulder." He frowned, and I explained that he held his left shoulder slightly higher and closer to his neck.

"I didn't think it noticed." He was suddenly quiet.

"I've been sketching you. I do it all the time," I explained. Now *I* was on the defensive.

"Show me!"

He took my book, looked at the unfinished work and then flipped through the rest of the book.

"You're very good," he said slowly. "Your people are alive." He went back to the drawing I was making of him. "You've caught the way I stand exactly." He handed me the book. "I didn't think it was noticeable."

I reassured him. "It isn't to most people. It's just that when you sketch someone, the pencil records everything, the way you stand and move and fit into the measurements I've made."

He smiled ruefully. "I was injured in an accident. Years ago. It affected my neck and shoulder. I hope you can't read my mind as well as you can draw. Was your mother as knowledgeable?"

Now it was my turn to look surprised.

He pointed to *Wild Marjoram.* "Enid, my wife, has a similar sketch of some herbs. She told me the painter was Marjorie J Jeffries and that you're Jeffries' daughter." I didn't see how she could possibly have known, but Jolley went on, "My wife knows a lot about plants, they're part of her job."

I was mystified. It didn't explain anything.

"Enid cultivates herbs. She grows marjoram, but the plant doesn't like the cold. You have to pamper marjoram, she says. Worth it, though, makes meat taste a treat. Enid would like this picture. If you ever think of selling it, let me know."

I told Jolley I would never sell the painting. Afterwards, I walked with him into the courtyard. "It was just a dirty yard when I came, but I've transformed it by the magic of plants. I call it a courtyard now."

He told me he'd made a sketch of the yard, naming the plants. "Enid will be interested," he explained. He seemed to have recovered from my observations on his shoulder.

Tuesday, 26th May 1981

I had my usual briefing with Mr Jolley before I left for work. The flat would definitely be finished by Wednesday at noon. I reminded him the carpet would be laid today, and the new beds should come as well as the cutlery, crockery, sheets, duvets and blankets.

"No probs, we'll see to everything."

The sky was filled with a persistent drizzle and it was chilly enough to be February. I was worried I had dressed too casually on Monday, so I decided to look business-like in a straight blue skirt with a plain white blouse, a loose-swinging dark-blue jacket and court shoes with high heels. I like to walk tall. I arrived early at the Retirement Homes office. The first thing I did was ring the carpet department to confirm my carpet would be laid today.

A Norfolk voice replied, "No worries, Mrs James, they're now comin'."

The linen and cutlery were already in the van, she said, and the beds would be delivered before midday.

I picked up the milk, the post, the newspapers, and went into the kitchen to make a mug of coffee so that I could at least start the day fortified. I was bringing the pink mug into the sales-office when an elderly woman carrying a large paisley fabric bag wandered into the room.

I had a fleeting impression that I had seen her before. My client was a short plump woman with narrow cheekbones above hollow cheeks, a sallow complexion, hazel-green eyes and thick wavy white hair unfashionably dressed in a roll at the back of her head.

Most of all, I was struck by the all-pervading colour of brown: brown coat, brown leather gloves, brown shoes with silver buckles, brown close-fitting cloche hat with three brightly-coloured duck quills on the left side. I was irresistibly reminded of Alfreda, a lop-eared rabbit a school friend had loved, and I mentally named her "Brown Rabbit". A pink daisy-flowered chiffon scarf floating round her neck lightened the sombre effect.

As she sat down, I saw five large, round, shank ceramic buttons on her coat. Each was decorated with an English garden flower: rose, pansy, daffodil, iris, lupin. They reminded me of my mother's work.

"That coffee smells delicious!" She smiled and took off her leather gloves and laid them carefully on the table. A diamond ring glittered above her wedding ring. I gave her my coffee and gestured to her to sit down.

She snuggled into the chair. "It's so nice to talk with you," she said cheerfully. I hadn't said a word, but I understood the sentiment. I sat down opposite, thinking I should start the business-talk rolling.

"Are you thinking of buying a bungalow?"

"Oh, no, dear, I have a very nice house of my own."

"You're here for someone else then?" I probed gently.

She leaned forward confidentially. "They're trying to *make* me sell my house, dear. They want the *money*, you see, *and* the diamonds. The *Pretoria* Diamonds. My husband was a diamond expert and helped the government in the war, but he died recently. I have a daughter. She married Peter Linsey and Peter needs *lots* of money. So Stella took me to a doctor in Harley Street who said I was incompetent to manage my affairs, and now she's taking steps to take out a Power of Attorney. The doctor said I was *Non compos mentis*. Do *you* think I'm senile?"

I leaned back, overwhelmed at receiving such intimate confidences. "I don't think you should be telling me this," I began awkwardly.

"But we're already old friends," she responded warmly. "Daughters are so like their mothers, aren't they, although my daughter has taken after her father, a determined and ruthless man. Did I tell you he killed the man I loved? With an axe!"

I began to think that her daughter could be right. "And the really terrible thing is," my companion continued, "they'll kill my rabbit and tortoises if I move here." She looked disconsolate. "I love my rabbit and talk to him every day."

I concentrated on her last sentence. "My friend, Josie, had a rabbit called Alfreda. Her fur was as soft as cashmere and Alfreda used to sit on Josie's shoulder while she was doing her homework. We used to tell Alfreda everything about school and she always listened very carefully, not like adults who only hear half of what children say."

My visitor, I could not call her a client, clapped her hands delightedly.

"How *lovely* to meet a fellow admirer of rabbits. But what I *really* wanted to say…" She turned and stiffened as a woman strode into the room.

The goddess Eris had returned with anger in her walk. Brown Rabbit leaned forward. "Don't tell her I said anything, will you?" There was fear in her eyes.

I stood up as the angry woman reached the table. "So *this* is where you are, Mother, I've been looking everywhere for you."

Brown Rabbit tittered nervously. "I've been having a cup of coffee with this young lady while I was waiting for *you*, Stella."

Stella's voice was hard. "I told you to wait outside while I was talking to the supervisor." She turned to me. "You said Mrs Heals would be here today."

I was anxious to lower the heat. "I'm sorry if I misled you, but Mrs Heals only works here in the afternoons."

She nodded impatiently. "All right, all right, but you shouldn't be speaking with my mother. She's an elderly woman who doesn't know what she's saying *but*, as we're both here, you can take us round this bungalow."

She moved quickly towards the kitchen. I did all the sales patter, but Stella wasn't listening. She looked into each room cursorily and moved on without a word. Her anger went everywhere with her.

"It'll do," she said at the end. "You have other flats like this?"

I told her there were several similar in size. Her mother was never consulted. I tried to bring her into the conversation, but Stella always cut me short. Brown Rabbit had become a nonentity, a shadow in the background. As we made our way back to my table, I asked Stella to choose a property from the map on the wall. She pointed to the house divided into three flats nearest the supervisor's house.

"The ground-floor flat will be best and Miss Farrell can keep an eye on her." She turned to me briskly. "My mother will move into the flat within the month."

Execution day was approaching for the rabbit and tortoises. I wondered if I would ever get used to dealing with unpleasant people like Goodison and Stella.

I gave her the forms and when all the details were completed and receipts given, I offered them a cup of coffee. Stella looked up, eyes steely blue. "No coffee." The words shot out like bullets.

Silently, I put the copies in a file I had made out in her name. The cheque was signed and handed over. I stood up to shake hands, but Stella turned away, her padded shoulders swinging aggressively as she held her mother tightly by the elbow, steering her towards the door. I thought that would be the last time I would see Brown Rabbit and the beautiful ceramic buttons.

The name on the form was Mrs Gillian Conrad. She lived in Unthank Road, an area with fine Victorian and Edwardian houses. As I wrote my initials on the little flag on the map, the elation I should have felt was muted. Gillian Conrad was an unhappy woman who didn't want to leave her home and her garden pets. I filed everything away before writing up the details in the table diary and then in my own notebook. It was only when I was writing the name 'Conrad' that I remembered Corrie Smiley saying, "Conrad put a lot of money into Sellick's scheme."

I had made an appointment the previous day to meet Miss Margaret Farrell, the supervisor of the Retirement Homes. I left a notice on the table informing any clients who might come that I would be back shortly. Farrell had her own bungalow, which was also her office. She had been a matron in a big hospital in London before 'matron' became 'clinical nurse manager' in the late sixties.

Margaret Farrell laughed as we shook hands and talked about her role as supervisor. "Call me Meg. I'm adviser, friend, manager and shock-absorber when problems arise. My front door is always open and everyone calls me Matron. I think they find it comforting. So many of them live in the past, don't they!"

Patronising or practical? At least she hadn't called the elderly "old dears". She took turns as supervisor with a Mrs Irene Browne who worked nights. "Irene takes over when I can't be here, and I do the same for her."

Meg Farrell was attractive in a big sort of way. Short fair hair swept back in a wave, searching light-blue eyes, full-bosomed, she had a nurse's confident manner. She passed me a mug of coffee. "Obviously, there's a long way to go before we're full," she said in a light Highland accent, "but when the builders finish the next two blocks, I'm sure they'll start selling quickly. Mr Sellick's had a lot of ups and downs with the farmers and the council, but the snags are being sorted. He told me you'll do well. The last woman was dismissed by Pat Heals for being nosey and argumentative, but I'm sure that won't happen to you."

It sounded like a quiet warning. She was interrupted by a young man hurrying into the room. He held back when he saw me. "Sorry Matron, didn't know you had company."

"That's all right. Tim, this is Mrs James. She's working in the sales office now." His name was Tim Harvey and Farrell didn't sound too enthusiastic about him.

"Nice to meet you." His eyes smiled as they skimmed over me. He had tight curly fair hair and an inquisitive face. He turned to Meg. "Dr Roberts asked me to tell you Mrs Whisby's not well."

She made a note on a pad by the telephone on the low table by her chair. "When did Doctor see her?"

"This morning surgery. He's given me a prescription for her. He wants you to look in on her this evening. I'd better get going. I've still got a dozen prescriptions to see to."

He nodded to me before leaving the room. "Is he the chemist?" I asked.

"Good heavens, no! He was reading pharmacy at Bath, but was sent down in his third year. Cannabis, I think. Now he works for Bradley the chemist in Swaffham. He says he'll go back to uni one day and get his degree, but I don't see him doing that. Success or failure, it's all in the mind. Tim's become something of a dogsbody." She stood up, smoothing her dress. "Now let me take you round to the surgery and introduce you to Dr Roberts."

The medical centre was impressive with a bright and welcoming reception area, a consulting room, physio department, a minor surgery room and a nurse on duty all day. It was better equipped than many urban centres. Roberts was a distinguished-looking man in his late fifties with bold, hooded eyes and wavy brown hair, greying at the temples. His brown-striped, double-breasted suit showed a man concerned with appearance. After the introductions, I told Roberts I would like to make an appointment. I hadn't registered with anyone since I came to Norwich.

"Any problems?"

"Migraine. I understand there are new treatments and it's ages since I've seen anyone about it."

"Make an appointment. Hopefully, I'll be able to help you."

I saw the receptionist on the way out, made an appointment for Friday morning at nine and returned to the sales office. As I walked into the room, I gasped and cringed against the wall. A gust of wind had flicked the red curtains out like the crack of a shot and the faceless man with the gun stepped out of the shadows, his hand raised, the gun pointing at my head. As the curtains swung back, the man with no features disappeared.

In the shock of the moment, I slid down the wall to the floor, my breath suspended in fear. Seconds like hours passed, then I heard myself breathing again, but I could not control the trembling in my legs. For the first time I had caught a half-glimpse of a face; but fear had shut down the memory spike. As I struggled to my feet, I told myself fiercely that I didn't *want* to remember. Let memory lie dormant, let the cloistered peace of amnesia keep me safe. Every time I saw the man with the gun, I was engulfed with panic, and now the images from my nightmares were springing out of the darkness into the bright light of day. First Mitchell, and now the man with the gun.

I shuddered as I closed the window. It was a quarter to two. In my head I heard the words, *I have to get away.* If Patricia Heals came early and found I'd left, too bad. The words echoed furiously in my head. *I have to get away.* I picked up the paying-in book, locked the door of the sales office and ran to the carpark behind the house. Acknowledging the guard with a muted wave I drove through the decorated iron gates, headed into Swaffham, deposited the cheques in the bank and sped home.

I arrived back to be greeted by Mr Jolley in the hall. "The carpet's down and Len's hoovered it." The carpet spread out before me, beautiful in its manifold-coloured squares. "They came at ten and everything else came as well. The kitchen things are in the kitchen, and the linen's on the bed in the spare room."

What a wonderful husband he must be, I thought. The warmth and colour from the carpet wrapped themselves round me. After Jolley had left, I felt restless, no longer at ease in my own company, fearful lest the faceless man appeared again. I heated up some soup for lunch and listened to the radio. There was a talk on nineteenth-century paintings. Schiffer had mentioned my mother's paintings had been auctioned at Dales. I decided to drive out of Norwich along the Holt Road and see the place for myself.

The ambiance in the auction rooms was pleasant and reassuring. My father had taken me to auctions when I was a child and I had enjoyed the studied nonchalance in the bidding and the occasional flurry of excitement.

The rooms were large. One was given over to furniture, another to arts and crafts, jewellery and nostalgia from the glitzy twenties and thirties; but this Tuesday afternoon the main room was being used to auction nineteen and twentieth-century paintings and prints.

There must have been over seventy people wandering round examining the exhibits. I was drawn to a print by Andrew Wyeth. A girl was lying on her front in a field, her back towards the onlooker, her face turned away. The field was large with a steep rise up to two houses, one gabled, the other formless in the distance. The girl had raised herself up onto her hands as she gazed at the houses, but she seemed unable to move forward. I was absorbed by the mysterious locked-in element which reflected my own life.

The painter's insight was disturbing and I moved on down the room. There were no works by my mother on display, but as I approached the end of the room a painting by Chirico stepped out of its frame. I stood hypnotised by the dreamlike quality of the large empty piazza. On one side of the courtyard was a tall building with small square windows and tall arches forming a colonnade. A man with no features was walking out of the shadows of the building towards me, his arm raised. I saw the gun and heard the shot. The room spun round as I stumbled back against a chair.

I am standing by a door,
A woman is groaning.
She is lying on the floor
Her blouse is stained with blood.
Amy! Amy is dying.
At last I know her name.
Amy must be the woman in my dreams.

I was back in the auction house, but my mind was fixed in the past.

"It was Amy," I said aloud. "The man in Chirico's painting shot Amy."

I looked up and my eyes widened with alarm. Peter Schiffer was helping me to my feet. A woman came forward whispering her concern, a glass of water in her hand. I took it and thanked her.

"You're as white as a ghost!" Schiffer said. "Lower your head, you'll feel better in a minute." Then he offered to find my friend.

"Friend?" I gasped.

"Amy. You called her name."

"Amy's not here."

My brain said, *Amy's dead.*

I forced myself to look up. The picture was back in its frame. I was safe. Schiffer followed my gaze.

"Ah, Chirico, was that it?"

I shuddered. "The faceless man! He had a gun. I heard the shot."

"The man has no weapon," Schiffer said. "He's pointing towards something, that's all."

But I had seen the gun and heard the shot. Schiffer's dismissal of my fears annoyed me. And I was angry that I had fainted and shown weakness. I turned to him. "I'm surprised to see you here, Mr Schiffer."

He smiled. "I'm here, as I presume you are, because Dales are holding an auction of some exciting prints and paintings. In fact, I recommended you to come. I was standing across the room when I saw you looking at the Chirico."

Chirico's use of light and shade, the melancholy of the haunted square and the figure advancing towards me, had affected me deeply. I got unsteadily to my feet and told Schiffer I'd been foolish and had had no lunch or breakfast, an excuse for fainting.

We walked through the building, his over-familiar arm helping me out through the door and into the carpark. I felt better when I got in the car and drove away. All I wanted was to get home. I needed to explore the curious image in the Chirico painting and the man in my dreams. I needed to know I wasn't going mad. When I had told Richard about my nightmares and violent memories, he had dismissed them.

"They're a fantasy of your imagination, distorted figments you keep dreaming up." He had added, "It's attention-seeking. You should practise it on Freeman instead of me."

But Chirico's painting had made the dream and the threat of violence tangible. After fifteen years of pricking glimpses of a woman lying dead, I now knew that woman was Amy and the sudden inexplicable spikes of memory were based on an action that had really taken place in the past.

The man with the gun had shot Amy. I had *seen* him shoot her. I had stood by the door and seen his shadow against the wall. At last I accepted that the man with the gun was real.

That night I knew something in my brain had moved. The faceless man in Chirico's picture had released a trigger and the shutter that had blocked my memory had opened a little. I had feared the past. The past was a place of guns and murder, but now, *now* I wanted to know more. I wanted to retrieve what had been lost.

I kept a small photo of my father in the drawer of the bedside table. It showed a confident man with grey eyes, a straight nose, wide mouth and light-brown hair. When he smiled, the smile had reached his eyes. I remembered him as an attractive man of medium height. He told me he would have liked to be taller; I had thought he was perfect. I never heard him raise his voice, until the last two weeks of my mother's life. The shutter in my mind opened wider.

We were a normal happy family, or so I thought, but everything changed in the two weeks before my mother died. There were arguments, angry words, threats. It seemed to be all about some small paintings Mum had found.

Sunday, 28th May 1967

I am standing behind the conservatory door, clutching a tea-tray. I can hear Dad shouting as I watch through the glass panel. He is walking up and down the room. His face is red and angry. "Don't be a fool, Marjorie, give me the miniatures. And then I'll go, I'll disappear." His voice rises. "You should never have touched them."

"The miniatures you stole are in a safe place where you'll never find them." Mum sounds as if she's crying.

"I risked my life for them, and the medals. You had no right to interfere."

"And Stan!" The interruption comes harshly. "Perhaps he's sold some of the medallions, and that's how they know."

"Stan wouldn't do that, he's loyal to me."

"Greed makes traitors of the best of friends, Erich. The Pforzheim miniatures must be worth thousands now. No wonder your erstwhile friends are pursuing you. Stan, or someone he's confided in, has told them where you hid them. Everyone now knows I found them and removed them."

I am not prepared for what happens next.

Like a snake uncoiling, Dad springs to his feet and pulls Mum up out of her chair. "Where are they?" he screams, shaking her.

Mum's lips are clenched like a blood-line in her pale face as he pushes her back in the chair. She reaches over the table and picks up her Cross and its long golden chain. Her voice is muted. "The past is always pressing on our heels. There's no escape, Erich. Bremen is part of my past and Pforzheim is part of yours." She looks up at him sideways. "The war tainted all of us. We can redeem ourselves in some small part by saving the miniatures."

He leans against the wall, his lips pulled down. "I say the blood's on your hands, not mine."

She says nothing as the heavy chain slips through her fingers.

"Give me the miniatures, Marjorie. I swear I'll keep them safe."

"They are safe, where you and your criminal friends will never find them." She looks up. "I can at least save them for posterity."

The word infuriates him. "Damn posterity! I'm warning you, Marjorie, The Auctioneers are no longer a group you can reason with. There's a new accountant and he's ruthless. He'll enjoy torturing Paula to make you speak."

She says nothing. Dad comes to the door, his hand on the handle as he turns to her. "I'll find the miniatures, Marjorie. Pray hard I find them before the Auctioneers do."

He flings the door wide, almost knocking the tray from my hand as he storms out of the room. The ferocity of their argument has frightened me. I wait until the front door bangs shut. It always sticks unless it's closed firmly.

I creep into the conservatory and put the tray down on the table. I've made a pot of tea with Mum's favourite herbal tea called Melissa, which means 'honeybee'. I love the name, but hate the taste. Mum's been ill for over a year. She says she can't feel her fingers and her brushes and pencils keep dropping from her hand. Mum thinks she has cancer. The doctor says it's flu.

"What are these miniatures, Mum? Why are they so important?"

Mum is holding the gold Cross in her hand. "You heard? I see. Yes, we both said bad things in anger." The heavy chain of the Cross falls through her fingers. "Choices have to be made in life and sometimes, if something is truly important, then a stand must be made, whatever the cost. I have made my stand."

She takes the tea I have poured out. "Listen to me, Schätzchen, and forget that ugly scene. I was going to talk with you when your school exams were over, but I can't leave it any longer. I'm sure I have cancer in the lungs, that's why there's so much of this horrible mucus. I've spoken to Father Petrie and he's helping me. Don't cry, darling, I just wish I had more time to sort things out for you."

I kneel beside her, holding her hand tightly, not wishing to let her go. She smiles faintly.

"As I think you overheard, your father and his friends stole some famous paintings during the war. After the war they sold them to greedy, contemptible people, but Erich also stole medallions and some beautiful miniature paintings. He hid the miniatures under the shed at the bottom of the garden. But Erich was not so clever, because I found the bag in which he hid them. They're worth thousands of pounds. Erich has told me he was part of a gang calling themselves The Auctioneers, desperate, ruthless men. Now they've driven him out of the gang and they're hunting him for the miniatures and medallions he stole in Pforzheim.

"Well, Liebchen, when I found the miniatures, I wanted to take them to the British Museum. They would know what to do with them, but I'm too ill and your father won't help me. I'm not asking you to do it now, Paula, it's much too dangerous and The Auctioneers are watching every move we make. At the moment, the miniatures are in a safe place with an old friend. When you're older, my friend will give you the little paintings and you can go to the Museum with them."

She pulls herself up. "I know you love your father, but you mustn't tell him you know about the Pforzheim miniatures. It's our secret, Liebchen. From now on, Paula, hidden eyes will be watching you. It's a dangerous world and you'll have to be very careful."

I think she's talking about the Cold War, and I don't believe Dad's as bad as she's making out, but I promise to be careful to please her. Then I help her get into bed and find an extra blanket in the wardrobe because she's feeling cold. Mum is convinced she has cancer, but I'm desperate to make her listen to me.

"The doctor says it's flu, and you're going to get better, Mum, and live to be a very old lady with lots of grandchildren."

She smiles faintly, then dozes off, so I get my books and sit beside her revising German, the next exam. Later, when she wakes, I offer to make more tea. The Honeybee is all gone so I make a pot of Indian tea and put some custard creams on a plate. We enjoy the tea together, and I decide it's a good time to ask her about the Rhine trip. I asked a whole year ago, but she refused to discuss it then.

"I'd love to see the castles on the Rhine," I begin cautiously, but her response is swift and hard.

"No! We will not be going there. We've talked about this before, Paula. Why don't you listen to me!" I lower my head mutinously, and she goes on more quietly. "It's difficult for you to understand, but the past is too near, too terrible, and I don't want it to harm you." She reaches out and holds my hand. "Perhaps…when you're older, Paula. Yes, when you're older, then we'll cruise down the Rhine." She pauses. "When it's safer."

I smile uncertainly. It isn't dangerous to go abroad. Lots of my school friends have been to France and West Germany. I pour out some more tea and, to please her, I ask her about the Cross.

"A dear friend gave it to me. She was a chemist, but when the Nazis came to power, she refused to work for them. I helped her and in return she gave me her Crux Gemmata."

I ask her why she speaks in German when she runs the chain through her hands. She looks at me oddly. "You're sometimes so perceptive, Paula, it may not be wise to ask so many questions. But I'll try to answer this one. English, like German, is a logical language, but the rhythms are different. The rhythm of the German words is warm and familiar, and sometimes I need to hear them."

"Tell me about your names," I say. "Marjorie Johanna."

Her smile reaches her eyes, smoky blue eyes like Norfolk skies misty after rain. "Marjorie is my mother's name, but my father insisted on Johanna for the second name, instead of Joan, my grandmother's name, but he always called me Hanna."

I ask her to talk to me about her father. "I don't know anything about him or your mother."

She is suddenly agitated. "I don't want to talk about them, the past is too painful. One day, one day…" The Cross falls on the bed and I pick it up and ask why it's so elaborately carved.

Mum's face lightens. "It's a mediæval Latin Cross. The vine is said to depict the Tree of Life." She takes it from me and turns it over. "The back is really strange. It doesn't have the usual engraving of Christ on the Cross with Mary kneeling beneath Him."

She gives me the Cross and I take it uncertainly. Christ is hanging from the Cross, but all round is darkness, a darkness split by a blood-red moon. I shudder. "It's really spooky. Why do you like looking at it? The front with the vine is much prettier."

"Never turn away from the truth because it's unpleasant or doesn't suit you, Paula. The red moon and the sudden darkness that fell over the light of that day show what happens when an evil deed is done and the truth is hidden. Just like the evil deed your father has done and the truth he has hidden from us all these years." She points to the bottom of the icon. "Nor are you the sort of person to be seduced by thirty pieces of silver."

The tiny coins are strewn round the foot of the Cross, the edges of each one picked out in red from the light of the bleeding moon.

"I hope not," I say tremulously. "I hope nothing like that day happens where we live."

She smiles faintly and takes the Cross from my hand. "See how the blood from the moon creeps insidiously into each silver coin. That is how betrayal begins, like a slow poison that steals away your life."

I stare at her. "Who betrayed you, Mum?"

She looks at me so strangely. "The man I loved betrayed me." Her eyes are dark, her lips drawn back. "How could I have known he was part of a conspiracy?" Her voice trembles. "Many people disappeared in the war, in that terrible conflict. So many families have never been able to lay their children to rest." She pauses. "Love blinds you, Paula."

I've never heard my mother's voice so low and hard. Love and love's betrayal sound terrible. I ask her how you can tell you're in love. "Maybe it's just me," I say. "I mean I don't understand how anyone can be swept of their feet by an emotion."

"So you've got over Josie's brother at last!" Mum smiles at me.

My cheeks burn. "Oh, that wasn't love, I know that now, although at the time it seemed real."

Mum looks at me reflectively. "You're growing up, and you express yourself well. I don't know if anyone can answer that question. You have to be in love to explain love, and yet you can't explain it, because love's emotionally inexplicable."

I ask for an explanation of the emotionally inexplicable. "Well, I'll use my own experience." She lies back against the pillow, her voice soft and husky.

"Love overwhelmed me. It was in the air I breathed, in the sweet smell of flowers, in the hot rays of the sun; love heightened my senses, the pulse of life beat faster. Love embraced me as I lay in the arms of the man I loved."

I stare at my mum, my everyday mum who paints flowers and who isn't at all beautiful, like Marilyn Monroe.

"Is that what happened to you?" I ask breathlessly.

"That's what happened to me."

I hesitate. "It's a bit scary, all that about being overwhelmed. Is it like that for everyone?"

"No, it can be bittersweet, or joyless and sacrificial, but if love really does sweep you off your feet, you will feel the magic of that moment."

"Does it last forever? Or does the magic fade, like it says in the poems?"

"It will last forever, if you both believe in it." I know, without knowing how I know, that her forever-love is not Dad. She stretches out her hand and I hold it tightly. "You'll know when the magic happens to you, Liebchen."

"And the man you loved," I whisper. "What happened?"

"He died." Her voice vibrates harshly. "Thereafter love was only transient."

She drops my hand and begins to crease the duvet nervously between her fingers.

I wonder how you would know a transient love from a force that made your life-pulse beat faster.

The next day, I ask Josie what she thinks about love. "Sex!" she says. "It's all about sex."

Monday, 29th May 1967

Today is Mum's birthday. The German exam is in the afternoon. I want to stay with Mum in the morning, but she is adamant that I must go to school.

"Being with your friends and teacher may make a difference." She is firm. "I want you to do well in your exams and go on to university, so you've got to get good results. And there's something else. I want you to be business-like as you grow older and understand the importance of money."

Then she startles me by telling me she's made a will. "You'll receive the income from the sale of my books and any paintings I leave and—" She waits, enjoying the dramatic moment, "—on your thirtieth birthday, Mr Siskin will tell you a secret!"

I'm taken aback. "Mr Siskin?"

But Mum is serious. "Mr Siskin is the keeper of my memories."

I laugh, I can't understand what she's talking about. "What would Mr Siskin know about your memories?"

"You shouldn't laugh so easily, Paula. Just remember what I'm saying. On your thirtieth birthday Mr Siskin will reveal a secret."

At fifteen, a thirtieth birthday is a very long way away, and her remarks about Mr Siskin are so bizarre I simply dismissed them.

The next moment Mum is suddenly brighter. "Amy will be coming over in the evening as usual, and we'll have a little party to celebrate my birthday."

The doctor is visiting her every day now and I tell him Mum thinks she has cancer.

"I know, but this new strain of flu is pretty virulent, and she's distressed about the arthritis in her fingers. The best way for you to help your mum is to do well in your exams."

I've been sitting with Mum every evening going through my revision, but she's upset, because Tony Hancock is talking about going to Australia. "He must stay in England," she keeps saying. She loves Hancock's Half-Hour.

Amy generally comes over on Friday evenings, but only if Dad isn't here. She can't stand Dad. But she's coming today, because it's Mum's birthday. Mum always looks happier after Amy's visits. They are old school friends from the time when they both studied in Berlin. They came to London in 1938 and Mum went on to teach art and Amy became a math teacher.

I've saved up the money Mum gives me for washing her brushes and other odd jobs and bought her a posy of roses and a box of her favourite pralines. Amy gives her a new lamp with a swivel head, a birthday cake, all fruit and icing that she has made, and three photographs of Mum's prize-winning gardens.

Amy greets Mum in German. "Alles Gute zum Geburtstag, Liebling." Mum is delighted, but she scarcely touches the cake. Father Petrie comes round while Amy's there. He has some of the birthday cake and asks how my German exam has gone. I tell him it went well. Amy asks him about Mum.

"She still refuses to accept she's got flu, but I'm supporting her with God's help."

My father comes home after Amy has gone. I half expect him to look different, all wicked and evil, but he's exactly the same dad I love.

He holds me tightly. "You're the best thing that ever happened to me, darling." He gives me thirty pounds, a fortune, for my birthday on the 6th June. "Now I'm going to see Marjorie. I've come to say I'm sorry for what happened earlier." He looks at me and smiles. "I love Marjorie. I've always loved her, but sometimes your mum can be very obstinate." He opens the Marks & Spencer bag he's carrying and shows me the flowered silk scarf he's bought for Mum's birthday. "What do you think, is it OK?"

"It's lovely. It will match her rose-coloured jacket. You've done really well, Dad."

He looks pleased and goes into the bedroom. I listen outside the door, my heart racing like a runaway engine. I hear the odd word, Mum saying she's afraid. Dad's voice, "I'll see she's all right."

The voices die down. No arguments. Dad smiles when he sees me waiting outside the door. He says they had a good talk and everything's all right. "She's sleeping, better not disturb her until morning."

He kisses me goodbye, saying he'll be back on Monday, then he leaves and I hear the front door slam shut.

I look in on Mum about ten o'clock. She's fallen out of bed, her glass of water upturned on the floor beside the silk scarf. I phone the doctor and she's admitted into hospital. *Mum dies that night from pneumonia, a complication of flu. Amy Eggers stays with me all night. I'm so grateful to her. She's a tall angular woman, very strict, but that night she holds me in her arms and we cry together. Amy makes all the arrangements.*

A week later, when Mum is buried, only Amy, our doctor, Father Petrie and the agent for Mum's paintings stand beside me. Dad never came. After Mum's death, I stay with Amy. I've no idea what I'm going to do now. Mum wanted me to go to university, but I don't feel I can talk to Amy about it. I'm grateful to Amy for giving me a home, but it's a lonely time and I miss my family. I can't see beyond each day.

Amy doesn't want me round the house in the summer holidays, so I spend the mornings with Erica Manning and afternoons with Josie Kent, my best friend. Amy looks tired and anxious, but I put it down to Mum's death.

And then she tells me abruptly she's going away. Tomorrow. For a while. "You're going to stay with Josie."

"But why?" I'm overcome with anxiety. "Where are you going?"

She puts her elbows on the table and holds her head in both hands. "There are problems, difficulties. I can't explain. Not now."

"Does that mean you won't be with me on my birthday?"

She reaches over the table and holds my hand. "Don't cry, Paula, I hope I'll be with you." She's struggling to speak. "But as I'm not sure what's going to happen in the next few days, it might be better to give you your birthday presents now while we have tea."

I look at her, aghast. "Something bad's going to happen!"

"Nothing bad's going to happen, Paula. It's unsettling, I know, but we can still enjoy the rest of the evening."

Amy makes the tea while I get the cups and saucers. She's bought some chocolate-chip cookies, a special treat, and I try to enjoy them for Amy's sake, but my hands are trembling. Amy passes me the canvas bag Mum always used for her paints and brushes.

Among all the painting paraphernalia, there is a velvet box and a velvet pouch. "Marjorie gave them to me on her birthday," Amy says. "She wanted to give them to you on June 6th, but she told us the truth, Paula, she knew she was very ill."

It's shocking that Amy doesn't want to wait a few more days till my actual birthday on the 6th. I open the pouch first and pull out Mum's Crux Gemmata.

I hold it in my hand, tears running down my face. Then I open the small box. It contains two miniatures framed in silver. Amy leans forward. "You were sixteen months old when Marjorie painted this and you were adorable."

A solemn fair-haired little girl wearing a full white dress decorated with cornflowers, looks out of the frame. The girl is sitting on the floor and is almost dwarfed by a large white cat.

"Christopher!" I had forgotten the friendly compliant cat who had died when I was four. Why must everyone you love die and leave you in a lonely place?

I give a cry of joy when Amy gives me the second miniature. Mum painted it last year. I am wearing a green top and shorts and leaning against an iron gate near a pink-flowering cherry plum bush with daffodils and crocuses standing proudly in its shade. I know the date, because a finch is standing on the back of my left hand, the yellow flash on its wings gleaming in the spring sunshine. The bird was injured and we nursed it lovingly back to health. Two weeks later, we released it in the garden and it flew away.

Amy's voice comes back into focus. "You know Marjorie was finding it difficult to hold the brushes, but she was determined to finish this painting."

"I never knew," I say softly.

"Marjorie never said a lot, Paula, but she loved you dearly and she nurtured your talent."

"But she never said I was really good."

"Nonsense, she wouldn't have wasted time helping you if she hadn't believed you had that God-given spark of talent."

But it would have helped me believe in myself. And then Amy does a very un-Amy thing and gives me a big hug, a kiss and her gift, a blue and green shoulder-bag. "It's just what I want!" I'm delighted. Josie Kent has a shoulder-bag. I thought I'd never have one.

"And I know you'll like these."

I take the large box of chocolates and the flowered silk scarf Dad gave Mum on her birthday and put them carefully in my new bag with the two silver miniatures and the Cross. I'm surprised Amy has given me the scarf. I don't know what to say.

Then I ask Amy if Mum has left me her father's Odala ring.

"There were no rings."

As we chat and have tea, I cannot shake off the feeling of dread. "You're not going to die as well, are you, Amy?" I'm tearful again.

She tells me it's just a temporary move, she should be back in two weeks. She takes a box out of the canvas bag with two little keys inside. "Put these on your key-ring. When you're older, I'll tell you what to do with them."

The shafts are beautifully decorated with entwined rosebuds and leaves. Both keys have tiny numbers on them: 5 and 6. The keys are too small to open a door. I hold them uncertainly. Then Amy gives me a watercolour sketch of Mr Siskin. It shows a sturdy middle-aged man in a tweed cap and a brown and red gardening smock, wearing galoshes and leaning on a spade. "It's lovely, just like Mr Siskin!" I exclaim. And then I ask, "What did Mum mean when she said Mr Siskin is the keeper of her memories? I mean, it's such a weird thing to say."

Amy sighs. There are lines on her face I haven't noticed before. "There are things you know nothing about, Paula. Marjorie wanted to protect you." She hesitates. "She asked me to give you one more thing. I disagreed with her, but she was adamant that you should have it."

She goes to her handbag and takes out a revolver in its soft holster and puts it in my hands. "When you're older I'll tell you everything you need to know."

"Tell me now!" I urge her. "What do I need to know?" And all the time I'm weighing the Walther PK revolver in my hand, becoming accustomed to its weight and size.

"These are difficult times, Paula. Marjorie was involved in dangerous things. She was afraid they would affect you when you were older."

Mum said we'd go to the Rhine when it was safer.

Amy's voice rises. "I said you wouldn't understand. It's a lot for a young girl to take in. Anyway," she adds reluctantly, "I have to carry out her wishes. It was her pistol, the one she used in the war."

My eyes light up. "Do you mean she was a spy?"

"It was a long time ago." Amy's voice is like a whisper. "Another life ago!" She seems distracted. "I've already spoken to Mrs Kent. Your gun club will arrange a permit for the gun and will make sure you know how to handle it." She passes Mum's painting bag over to me. "And that's for you, too."

But the revolver still holds my attention.

"Did you have a gun?" I ask idly.

She nods wearily.

"Is it something to do with the paintings?"

Her voice is sharp. "You know about them?"

"I heard Mum and Dad arguing." It's hard to believe it was only a few days ago.

"Your mother died to protect those paintings."

I frown and put the revolver back in its holster and into the painting bag. Mum died of pneumonia. I can't understand why there's so much fuss about the paintings.

We have collected up the tea things and taken them over to the kitchen sink. I ask Amy if my dad really is a wicked man.

Amy runs water into the bowl. "I'll wash and you wipe." She hands me the tea-cloth. "You want to know if your dad is a wicked man. Well, Paula, if you knew the Catholic Collects, you would know that we're all wicked but we can expiate our sins, be redeemed and know we have eternal salvation." I have forgotten what a devout Catholic Amy is. She rinses the bowl and leaves it upside down on the draining board. "Yes, Paula, your father has done bad things, criminal things, and he has small respect for human life, but war does that to a man. I've never liked him, you know that, but he loved Marjorie. Most of all, he's devoted to you. Always remember that."

"But he left us when Mum was dying," I cry.

"I know, I know, dear, but he was in dire trouble with his criminal friends. I know Eric loves you."

But love is not enough.

In the morning I go out early to buy some flowers for Amy as a "Thank You" for looking after me. She's packed, all ready to leave and it's been arranged that Josie's mother will pick me up before lunch.

It's a bright sunny morning and I walk up the path to the front door carrying Amy's favourite flowers, a bunch of red carnations. The front door swings open as I touch it. I step quietly inside. I can hear Amy talking in the lounge. Her voice rises in anger. I reach the lounge door, which is ajar. I look through the narrow opening. A bright burst of morning sun has lit up one side of the room, creating a sharp dividing line between light and shade across the floor.

I see the curtains move. A man is hidden in the shadow of the curtains. No features on his darkened face. His arm is outstretched. I hear the shots. See Amy fall, the pistol spinning from her hand, blood staining her blouse and spilling over the rug. Another shot. Another. And Amy lies still.

Terrified, I stumble out into the street. I run and run. My mind is screaming with fear. The flowers fall from my hand and red petals scatter like drops of *blood across the pavement. I think I hear running steps behind me and bullets hitting the garden walls. I run and run until I collapse at my friend's house.*

Everything changed after that. There was a new name, I cut my hair and stayed with a family who helped me recover and I took my O-Levels at a new school. Amy's murder was never solved. With the passage of time, I had suppressed the memory of her death, but in my conscious mind, the fear never left me. It was always there in the quickening beat of the heart, in the sharp slap of rain against a window, in the billowing of a curtain in the wind, in shafts of light and moving shadows. There were fewer nightmares after my marriage. Until I came to Norwich. Until I was on my own.

The Chirico painting had been a shock. It had forced me to confront the dark shadows of my teenage years. Richard had made me believe the man with the gun was a phantom, but Chirico's painting had shown me the man was real. He had shot Amy and he had tried to shoot me because I had witnessed Amy's murder.

The police had believed the gunman was my father, but I would have recognised him. Despite months of searching, my father was never found. For years I believed he was dead, shot by the same man who had killed Amy, until the police told me, when I was nineteen, that he had been killed in a train accident near Paris.

Wednesday, 27th May 1981

Wednesday was my free day. On the morning radio at breakfast, there was a talk about what constitutes "happiness". The panel suggested that happiness is subjective, but can be linked to time and place.

I thought I'd been happy living with Richard, but Richard had been miserable and was now divorcing me. Someone said that happiness cannot be judged by others, only by oneself. But what are the parameters for judging?

My old shoulder-bag was falling apart so I decided to go to Jarrolds and look at bags. The new shoulder-bag would be an early birthday present. No-one else would be giving me a gift.

I reminded Mr Jolley that more furniture was coming, then I left and drove to Jarrolds. After I had looked round the ground floor, searching for ideas for the flat, I went into the restaurant and had a coffee. It was still early and I was feeling pleasantly relaxed when a silvery voice floated over my shoulder.

"How *lovely* to see you again, dear!"

I turned with a smile and signalled to a waitress for more coffee. Gillian Conrad was alone. She was so much more confident without her pretty, pouting daughter pulling her by the elbow. I pointed to the large buttons on her coat. "I noticed them when we first met. They're beautifully hand-painted."

"Yes, dear. It's nice to have someone admire them."

I explained that my mother had painted flowers. "She once painted a series of *Flowers of the Seasons* for a magazine and your buttons reminded me of them." I smiled, recalling the past. "She wrote books and spoke on the radio about plants and gardening."

Gillian seemed delighted at my interest. She took off her hat with the duck feathers and folded her brown coat neatly, patting it as she put it on the chair with her hat and paisley bag. She was wearing a dark green woollen cardigan over a green and yellow flowered dress with long flared sleeves and a beautifully smocked top. Above her wedding ring was a blue diamond.

"What a *wonderful* story," she said. "You're *so* lucky to have had such a *clever* mother. *Such* a good model for you. My mother was married at seventeen. She was a delicate woman, but there was always a new baby, you see. Most of them died when they were small, and Mother wasn't even thirty when she passed away, but she looked so frail and old. There were no choices in her life. How lucky you are that your mother gave you a love for flowers. And you're quite right, all the buttons are hand-painted."

She was speaking clearly, no sign of the nervous twitter she used when Eris, the angry goddess, was present. "They were painted by a famous artist, MJ Ackert, although in this country she's known as Marjorie J Jeffries. She was your mother. I was sure you would recognise her style of painting, dear."

This was creepy. She had known all along who I was, just like Peter Schiffer. And then I allowed an earlier remark to seep slowly into my brain. It was soon after we had first met in Jarrolds. *But we're already old friends*, she had said. *Daughters are so like their mothers.* And then she had gone on to talk about Stella, and I had not grasped the significance of what had been said. In her strange, odd way she had been telling me we had already met. What a weird, elfish woman! My voice was harsh.

"What do you know about my mother?"

"Marjorie was a friend. Of course, you won't remember me, dear, but many years ago, when you were *very* young, Cedric and I had tea with your dear mother and father in Yorkstone Cottage."

I remember people vividly from the age of four, before then the picture is vague. There had been that second of indecision when I first saw Gillian, but I couldn't recall Cedric at all. I expect, like most men, he had avoided the small child. Gillian pronounced her husband's name as *Ceedric*, but without any affectation.

Gillian poured coffee for both of us. "At the time Marjorie was upset about her cousins. She'd been told they'd died in a POW camp in Russia. Sellick knew the truth, of course. Cedric met Sellick in South Africa."

I had pulled myself together. Gillian knew things about my mother, things I wanted to know. "You said Mr Sellick knew my mother's cousins," I said cautiously.

Gillian was dismissive. "Sellick had his fingers in many pies."

I smiled. "He told me how your husband found the diamonds with him."

"But did he tell you they both joined the South African Nationalist Socialist Party?" She leaned forward confidentially, "The *Nazi* Party to you and me, dear. Very attractive to some people. The salutes, the banners, the rallies! If you'd been there, dear, you'd have been swayed by it."

If I'd been there. The picture she painted drew me into shouts of *Sieg! Sieg Heil!* "*You* were there," I said slowly. "You were part of it."

"You couldn't help it. You were embraced by the excitement, in Pretoria, in Berlin."

"Were you a Nazi?" I asked bluntly.

"Oh no, dear. I prefer the English way of stepping aside and doing nothing. Cedric, of course, was attracted to the ideas, his German ancestry pulled him in that direction. He was born in Hamburg, you know, but Hitler was the stumbling block. Cedric simply didn't like him. And then, he had Jewish friends in the jewellery trade. You know that Marjorie and Elèna, Cedric's niece, helped many clever men and women escape from Germany?" She shook her head, her eyes clouding. "Desperate times, desperate times!"

I sat back, trying to sort out what she was saying.

"Marjorie was very careless with the men she loved," Gillian said suddenly, her voice raised sharply. "Rik van der Vendt, another artist, was so attractive. Byronic, you know. Marjorie was madly in love with Rik and ran off with him.

Then it was all over the radio. She'd been arrested for his murder. Of course, she had a long-standing arrangement with Peter Schiffer. She used him as a safety net when she got into difficulties. The best was Franz Helmann, but Marjorie lost him as well. Finally, she married an Englishman and seemed to settle down when her baby daughter was born. But she was never very good at choosing her lovers." She turned suddenly to the room. "Cedric died after the second stroke!" she announced.

People looked round, shocked at her disclosure. Gillian smiled and waved graciously. Turning back, she ordered more coffee and some pastries, and my mother and her lovers were forgotten. "Of course, Cedric never liked Peter."

"Is that why your husband had a stroke?"

Gillian's wide hazel eyes stared at me. "That's so clever of you, dear. Peter Linsey is Stella's husband, an accountant who works for our firm. His passion is racing cars. He has a friend, Dr Davis Barrow, an engineer who's designed a new car. Or is it a new engine? *So* confusing! Peter wants to sell our firm and pour all our money into Barrow's car. But I will *not* give up my fifty-one percent of the company. Both he and Stella are putting pressure on me to sell. If I do not, they will kill me."

The words were uttered calmly. "Are you sure you know what you're saying?" I stammered. "I mean, have you understood properly?"

"Don't be foolish, Paula. I *may* call you Paula? Peter is obsessed with the racing car and Stella is obsessed with Peter. She believes he loves her, but he loves only her money. Because Stella's older, she's frightened of losing him. Stella hates me because Cedric and I opposed their marriage. We were not invited to the wedding, and there has been discord ever since."

I passed the pastries and Gillian took a strawberry tart. She picked the strawberries off the cream and lemon curd and sank her teeth into the pastry. "Death and love can be so disappointing!" she said, patting her lips with the napkin. I looked at her blankly. "Girls expect too much from love, and expectations can be too high from death." She put her spoon down with a dramatic clink on the saucer. "Peter and Stella will be disappointed when my will is read." She raised her cup daintily. "And now they have Power of Attorney. I suppose it's safer than murder!"

I watched Gillian as she drank her coffee. Apart from the beautifully cut diamond ring, there was no other jewellery, no expensive watch or clothes. Did Cedric's business make enough money to kill for?

113

Gillian changed tack again, her voice suddenly fractious. "Elliot should be here. A young man has been round asking questions." Her mind seemed to be wandering all over the place.

"Another young man?" I asked curiously.

"He talked about the old American air force base, the one Sellick's incorporated into his Dunham Village. He wanted to look at papers my husband had. *I* thought he might be a journalist. Well, of course Cedric had acted on behalf of the council when the Americans first arrived and he became very friendly with them, but I do *not* want the young man to have his papers." She began fidgeting with her bag. "The young man knows something about the Pretoria Diamonds. He may know the truth. I don't trust him."

"The truth?" I repeated.

Gillian drew back, distrust frowning in her eyes. "Well, dear, it's really nothing to do with you. I'm waiting for Elliot, he'll know what to do."

There's nothing like a good old-fashioned snub to put you down.

Gillian leaned back. "Major Denby has a plan. He wants to smuggle the diamonds out of the house and take them to Cedric's old chief in MI5. Of course," she leant forward, "I shouldn't really be telling you all this."

I couldn't believe I'd heard her aright. My father had died when I was nineteen, but Gillian was rushing on. "Cedric was speaking with the Americans only this morning. They'll all be flying back home now the war's over. The young man was watching me last night when I was talking to my blue Shubunkins and their friends, the Lion-heads and Butterfly-tails. The Shubunkins are so beautiful with their pearly scales and they so love swimming in our pool! Sellick's builder constructed it. Did I tell you he served with your father in Pretoria, dear?"

I would have liked to interrupt, but Gillian was sweeping forcefully on. "I will *not* give Sellick more money for his village." She sat back suddenly, her eyes fixed on me. "I knew your father when he was a major, dear. *So* good-looking!" She lowered her voice, "Eric's on a secret mission with Cedric. It's all about the industrial diamonds. Very hush-hush! Of course, Cedric knows *everything* about diamonds! Did you know he went to Heidelberg to study mineralogy? He met Sellick out in South Africa, that's where they worked in the diamond mines."

"And my father was with them?"

114

"Of course! He and his men were guarding Cedric and Sellick. There were plenty of Nazis in South Africa during the war." Gillian's voice faltered. "Cedric admired me and enjoyed my position in society, but he drew the lines. After what happened in Berlin, I was always afraid of what he might do next. The shadow of the axe was always there, you see. Cedric enjoyed that. Before he died, Cedric made the house burglar-proof, but of course, and you'll understand, Paula, if someone's determined to get in, they'll find a way. I said you'd understand."

Why would I understand?

"I wish Mr Smithson would phone." Gillian fidgeted nervously with her cardigan. I drew back, reminded of my mother picking at the duvet before she died.

Gillian put her cup down. "Stella doesn't like me speaking to you about the nasty goings-on." Decisively, she gathered up her possessions in one smooth movement and got to her feet. "You should never have come to Norwich, Paula. Your father cannot help you now."

Astonished, I watched her walk away with her mimsy steps, her head held high, the flowered chiffon scarf floating over her shoulder, a short, plump woman with a silvery voice and a sting in her words.

How much could I believe? Perhaps Stella was right and Gillian didn't know what she was saying. She'd even implied my father was living with her. Which was nonsense. But the words: *You should never have come to Norwich* echoed the message on the postcard.

I was looking round when I noticed a man and woman sitting together at the far end of the room. They were almost hidden by one of those absurdly frothy palm trees, but the angle of the woman's face and shoulder and the close-fitting hair were familiar. The young man was facing her. He was good-looking, his short fair hair parted in the middle, a smile lighting his face as he talked animatedly with her. There was no mistaking the warmth between the pair. Husband? Lover? That elfin look could be very appealing. I wondered fleetingly who was watching over the sales office in Swaffham.

The waitress came up and asked if I had finished. I nodded and paid the bill. As I got up, two middle-aged women came over with resolute tread to claim the table.

I went straight to the furniture department and bought a small square kitchen table with three chairs, and then a light oak gate-legged table and chairs, and a matching bookcase with useful drawers. They were in the sale and would all be delivered in the morning.

Then I went to the bag department. As soon as I saw the dark red leather bag with its bright yellow daffodil motif in the upper corner, I knew it was the shoulder-bag for me. The daffodil was the herald of spring, a sign of hope for the future. There were no dark secrets hiding in the bell-shaped corolla of this daffodil.

It was still early when I got home. Mr Jolley was waiting for me in the hall. The sofa, the armchairs and the nest of tables had arrived. The flat was beginning to look lived in.

I wrote a cheque for the final instalment and found Mr Jolley wasn't charging me for cleaning the yard. He took my cheque with a nod and put it carefully in his wallet. "You're on your own now."

On my own sounded great. I thought it would be a friendly gesture to invite Mr Jolley and his wife to tea. "She might be interested to see the courtyard and it would be really nice to meet her." I smiled. "You'll be my first guests!"

He looked pleased. "Enid will like that. She'll ring and arrange a time to suit."

When he had gone, I went into the spare room and put the old shoulder-bag at the back of the wardrobe. I couldn't throw it away because the bag held love from the dark passages of past pain. By the side of the bed was the large dolls house and along the wall were two wooden crates full of memories from childhood. I opened a crate and took out a shoe box. A toy bear was lying inside wrapped in a small purl and plain blanket I had knitted for him years ago. He had been one of twenty damaged toy bears lying on a counter in the toyshop in Ealing. I could see the row of bears so clearly in my mind.

I am eight years old in a red and white pinafore dress. My mother asks the elderly assistant why the bears are so cheap.

"It's such a shame," the shop manager intervenes warmly. "There was a fire and some of them were burned. If these are not sold by the end of the week, they'll be destroyed."

I'm holding one of the bears close to my heart. One ear is slightly singed. I don't want him to die. His heart is beating with mine. My mother looks down at me. Her short thick light brown hair is held back by a ruby clasp. "We'll keep

this bear," she says firmly. "It's too easy to destroy things." I squeeze her hand.
How well she understands. She strokes the bear's poorly ear.

I remembered the scene so well. I hoped the little bear would like living in my new flat. I wrapped him in his red blanket and put him back in his box and placed it carefully in the wardrobe on top of my mother's painting bag. The wooden crate also held my books. I would put them in the bookcase when it was delivered early in the morning.

In the second crate were my sketching books from years ago. I wished I had my mother's old notebooks. She would often use them to make preliminary sketches of her subjects. I had no idea what had happened to them. Idly, I looked through one of my early stories, the one about the boy who had lost his identity. The story wasn't bad, it wasn't bad at all. And I liked the sketches. I would work on it and finish it.

I wasn't that surprised when I opened an old sketching-pad and saw a drawing of Peter Schiffer at Yorkstone Cottage. I was pleased I'd caught the attractive narrow eyes and strong lower lip, but my mother had been right: the sketch lacked vitality. A pity I had heard it only as a negative comment. With a sigh I closed the book and put it back in the crate with the others. I would go through them later.

On an impulse I opened my new sketchbook. I focussed on Schiffer with my mind's eye, remembering how my invisible pencil had drawn him, and then I started sketching him as I had seen him in his art gallery. My pencil moved purposefully over the paper, the lines clear and unfussy, movement in the turn of the face and the questioning eyes. I put the sketch aside until I had time to colour in the background.

My dolls house, with its close-fitting grey cover, stood against the wall near the side of the guest bed. I eased the cover off. All the curtains were drawn and the roller blinds in the kitchen and upstairs bathroom were pulled down. In my heart I wished I could crawl inside, into the dark, out of sight, away from threatening guns. I made a promise to myself. One day, when I was safe, when everything had been explained, I would open the doors of the dolls house, let light into the windows and revisit my childhood, but now was not the time to unlock Lintwhite Villa.

At twelve o'clock, I sat in my courtyard and listened to Queen on my cassette player, one of the few gifts from Richard that I had kept. I wanted to start making notes about advertising Dunham Village. I opened Pat Heals' folder of advertising material and the notebook in which I had recorded all the transactions at the Retirement Homes.

I had begun to think that people were coming from cities like Glasgow and Aylesbury because there really were no similar places available in the UK. It was annoying that I still didn't know how they had heard about Dunham Village.

In my opinion, the Retirement Homes project was a good workable idea, it just had to be presented well. I glanced through Pat's material again. It was dull and unimaginative.

My theme would be spread between three articles that would show how Sellick had made his dream come true. From the notes I had made when I was in the library I began with the history and development of the project. I wrote quickly and fluently.

Sellick had purchased a discarded wartime American aerodrome from the council. He had then bought some wasteland and woodland and sold farmland inherited from his father and had also bought up some local farms. It had been a massive undertaking involving large contributions from local business, a fundraising campaign for individual donations, and finally a very large sum had been contributed by his wife.

He had kept the memorial stone pillar filled with the names of the American airmen who had perished in the war and had built a Garden of Remembrance round it. The Fransham Obelisk, raised in honour of Nelson, and the historic St. Margaret's Church, had been skilfully incorporated into Sellick's Village, giving it a sense of history. Finally, I added a plan of the nearly three hundred bungalows and flats that were to be built round the magnificent golf course.

I left room for photographs to be added and then I made a jug of hot coffee to accelerate the thinking process and started on the second article, which began with a paragraph on the entrepreneurial spirit in Norfolk as exemplified by Doug Sellick and the growth of his Estate Agency since the war.

In the third article, I gave prominence to the architect of the golf course, Erik Maroc, and to the local building firm owned by Bob Stevens, which was creating Dunham Village. Then I dealt with the different styles of building with a wide variety of prices for active elderly people in a pleasant and restful environment, the role of the community hall, the full-time security, the bowling green, cycle tracks and vegetable plots. At the end of each article, I added the phone numbers of the sales offices in Norwich and Swaffham.

When I had finished, I went indoors and typed out the three articles, after which I drove down to Swaffham, took some photos of the Retirement Homes complex and then went straight to the Swaffham Gazette. The Gazette had its offices in a building off Buttercross Market Place. I was directed to Trish Porter, the editor. Porter was a tall woman, carrying her fifty-odd years well. Everything about her spoke of the 'individual', from the dark green jacket, black velour trousers and blue shirt with wide sleeves, to the beautiful diamante bun ring holding up her thick grey-speckled hair. She was a plain woman, but her dark blue eyes lit up her long face.

She signalled to me to sit down and I explained that I had written some feature articles about the Retirement Homes Project. Would she be interested?

She took the articles and read through them quickly, making notes as she went along. Her voice was crisp. "I've known Doug Sellick over many years and he's sunk his money and reputation into Dunham Village." She had a brisk, terse way of speaking. "He rushed into a similar scheme a few years ago, but the builders and architects he used were second-rate, and a lot of things went wrong with the Lincoln build. Many people lost a lot of money. That's why he's finding Dunham Village hard to sell."

She looked up. "He's lucky to have you. These articles are well written and a good advert for Norfolk. I'll put them in to appear next week on Wednesday, Thursday and Friday. And I'll get in touch with my opposite numbers in the Midlands and see if they're interested." Her smile transformed her face. "Any ideas for more articles? You might consider joining us. I'm looking for someone from outside Norfolk who can cast an unbiased eye over this individual county. Would you be interested?"

"*Very* interested. Would you consider part-time at first?"

"For a short time." She leaned forward. "Look, I'd like to go round Dunham Village and see the place for myself. The Council has had to deal with a lot of objections to Sellick's ideas, and there was some violence. In fact, opposition was strong at one time." Trish looked in her diary. "I can come on Monday 1st June at ten. If I like what I see, I'll bring my crew down later, do interviews and make Dunham Village part of our 'Around East Anglia' Series. That might give it a boost as well. Then we can talk about adding you to our staff, if that's OK?"

I was delighted. I drove to Sellick's Norwich office and left copies of the articles on his secretary's table, adding that the articles would appear in the Swaffham Gazette next week and would be circulated in the Midlands later. In a

PS, I added that the editor of the Gazette had agreed to visit Dunham Village on Monday 1st June at ten and Mr Sellick should be there.

Soon after I got home, Sellick's secretary phoned me. "Sorry I was out when you came. Mr Sellick's read the articles and is very pleased with them. He'll be joining you at Dunham Village on Monday."

I suggested we should get in touch with radio and television as well.

"I'll talk it over with him." Brenda's beaky voice echoed nasally down the line.

At five o'clock, I had tea in my courtyard and took the radio with me. The flowers had their usual effect and I relaxed and felt at ease in their company. The news on the radio was all about the forthcoming wedding of the Prince of Wales and Lady Diana. I was comfortably tired when I went to bed. I looked at the painting on my bedroom wall and hoped it would chase away the man with the gun. *Wild Marjoram* must have cast its aura of Roman happiness for I slept soundly during the night.

Thursday, 28th May 1981

The kitchen table and chairs, and the bookcase with the useful drawers, were delivered and put into place at seven-thirty in the morning. I would see to them properly when I came back home. I put the post in the drawer of the hall-table and left for Swaffham. I arrived early at the sales office, made a coffee and sorted out the newspapers and the post.

There was very little movement in selling the properties during the morning, just two appointments for later in the week and only one couple dropped in to look round the Village. I went over to the map. Heals had sold five more bungalows, and LH and MS had sold four flats. It must be busier in the afternoons and evenings.

I turned as I heard voices at the door. Peter Schiffer and a woman in green overalls were coming in with a short ladder and four parcels wrapped in brown paper that were placed on the floor beside my table.

Schiffer smiled a greeting. "Mr Sellick asked me to suggest some paintings for this room." He waved a languid hand at his assistant. "June, dear, start unwrapping the top three paintings while I look round."

June, middle-aged, short, flushed cheeks and cropped red hair, raised a comical eyebrow at me and unwrapped the pictures painted by local artists. She told me that the top one, which had a sweeping lawn and six peacocks, was a painting of Felbrigg Hall, a country house where her father worked as a gardener. The second canvas illustrated a spacious, long-reaching evening sky above the River Yare in Brundall and the third was a full-length photograph of Donald Judd's sculpture known as *Stack*.

Schiffer began walking up and down the room carrying the short ladder. "It's a good-sized room, quite pleasant, good light, and…*yes!*" He pointed to the wall with his pencil. "The Norfolks will go here, and *there*, on opposite walls, and Judd's *Stack* will face the door."

He was jaunty, flourishing the pencil as he spoke. He marked the places on the wall and turned to me from the top of the ladder. "They'll make a statement, don't you agree?"

I was surprised he wanted my opinion. As directed, June stood each painting on the floor under the pencil marks. I stepped back as Schiffer asked June to hold up the photograph of the Judd sculpture.

"What d'you make of this, Mrs James?"

It showed a three-dimensional cantilevered structure, the stack of twelve green oblong metal boxes appearing to hang in space, their dark shadows foreshortened and reflected on the wall behind. The boxes were equidistant and the depth of green paint differed on each one. I saw it at once as a staircase, the twelfth step showing an ominous mixture of red and green paint.

What was Judd hoping to show? Ambition, equality, nihilism, hope, despair? It didn't matter, because for me the structure had leapt to life. Every day I felt I was climbing steps, just like these, hanging in space, making it difficult to climb from one to the other. I stared at the twelfth step, the top step, with its threatening hint of red. I struggled to understand how I knew I would never reach it, but it would always be a step too high. Perhaps the man with the gun would move out from behind the tin can ladder and shoot me before I could pull myself up to safety. The thought was so frightening I heard myself gasp.

"What are you thinking?" Schiffer was standing behind me, his hand on my elbow. "You find it disturbing, yes?" His voice was low and urgent. "Talk to me. Tell me what you see."

I tried to pull myself together, to curb the breathlessness. "Why did you choose it?"

"I like minimalist art. And you, Paula, what are you seeing?"

I answered him slowly, mesmerised by the construction. "It's a statement. Steps on a stairway. Every day I pull myself up steps like that, steps hanging in space, difficult to reach." I faltered. "There's blood on the twelfth step and blood splattering the wall." I turned to Schiffer, my hand reaching out to him. "How do I know that?"

He shook my arm impatiently. "Did someone die on some stairs?"

But the moment and the frightening memory passed and I looked at the structure again and saw only a green montage of metal boxes. I felt exhausted. "It happens a lot. I get these sudden glimpses into the past, *memory spikes* I call them. They come in the form of moving pictures, or words, and then, suddenly, it all goes and I'm left feeling very frightened." I pointed to the picture. "She said he was shot before he reached the twelfth step, and now I'm afraid he'll shoot me before I can reach it."

"Who's going to shoot you?"

There was a rough edge to Schiffer's voice.

Tersely, inexplicably, I confronted him. "Were you the man with the gun? Did you shoot Amy?"

June stepped back, her mouth wide open as Schiffer recoiled from me. "What *nonsense* are you saying?" But at once, he grew calmer. "No, no, wait a moment. The Chirico painting. You said a man had shot your friend."

I stared past him, my voice a grey monotone. "He shot Amy and the petals fell like drops of blood. I witnessed him shooting her, but I never saw his face. But he saw me." My tone changed. I was becoming hysterical, my hands round my head. "I tell you, he'll shoot me before I can reach the top step."

June ran into the kitchen and returned with a glass of water. She shook my arm. "Sit down, love, drink it slowly."

Schiffer frowned. "We need more than water." He gave June his car keys. "You'll find some brandy in the glove compartment in the van. Make some coffee and add a splash of brandy for Mrs James."

June nodded and Schiffer sat down beside me. "So you never saw the man who shot your friend?"

I was calmer now. "No, but he thinks I did. That's why he haunts my nights and days."

"Did you tell the police?"

"They thought my father had murdered Amy."

"Here, drink this!" June said.

I smiled my thanks, grateful for the warmth and fire which cleared my head. I sat up straight. "I'm sorry," I said. "It was silly to react like that."

"No, no, reaction is *good*. It's what all artists crave. Do you always react so…*intensely* to works of art?"

"You mean in that hysterical way? No, of course not."

"But you fainted at the sight of the Chirico painting and you were overcome just now when you saw Judd's *Stack*."

I struggled to explain such extreme behaviour, not just for Schiffer, but for myself. "It's because they were so *personal*. They both related to what's been happening in my life, things from the past, frightening things, but I've never felt like that before." I hoped to God I never would again.

His face softened. "I wish everyone reacted so spectacularly to good art."

June asked me if I were feeling better.

"I feel really silly," I told her, and thanked her for the water and the coffee.

Schiffer frowned. "We'd better get on. There are two other sales offices to visit. Now let me see!" He put the brandy flask on my table. "The Norfolks will face each other on the side walls and the Judd will face the door." He turned to me. "Believe me it will present a challenge to your clients and put their minds in the right frame for choosing a property."

I tittered dutifully at the pun, but I would make sure I was sitting looking away from *Stack*.

"And this one?" June held up the last parcel.

Schiffer unwrapped it. The small canvas showed the portrait of a young girl. June balanced it on the back of the sofa and Schiffer stepped back. "Now. Tell me what you see."

If Schiffer was expecting another hysterical reaction he was disappointed. I said nothing at first. The girl in the painting was instantly recognisable. She was leaning against a wall near a door, the white lacy blouse and flowers in her hair emphasising her youth. She was looking to the side, towards the artist, one brow raised provocatively, a smile shaping her lips. A lamp by the door picked out a vase of dark purple and bronze chrysanthemums standing against a yellowish coloured wall. The light illuminated the young woman's seductive attractiveness and the awareness in her eyes.

"She's waiting for someone. She has that translucent glow of a woman waiting for her lover." I wondered who had painted her. I didn't recognise the style, but found the signature *R. van der Vendt a*t the bottom on the right. I leaned forward. "Look how he's captured that tantalising angle of the head." I turned to Schiffer. "How long have you had it?"

"It was painted in 1931 in Berlin when Marjorie was fifteen. She gave it to me soon after the war. But you're right, Van der Vendt found the magic in her, the seduction that draws you to her side."

Schiffer's face was set, his eyes dark. "We all went to art college in Berlin— Marjorie, Rik, me and Franz Helmann. I could see, even then, how good Rik was."

June had settled the painting on a pile of cushions on the sofa. She came round and stood beside me. "Who is she?"

"She's Marjorie J Jeffries, my mother." I turned to Schiffer. "Van der Vendt was good. Tell me more about him."

He was suddenly exasperated. "He's not important."

"Just a little," I begged.

He frowned and warned me that it was sometimes better not to know.

But I was persistent. "Oh, very well then." He frowned irritably. "Rik was a braggart and a womaniser. I warned Marjorie, but she wouldn't listen."

June butted in. "Perhaps that's the kind of man she wanted."

Schiffer looked furious. I nudged him quickly with a question. "When did they first meet?"

He shrugged sullenly. "In '31, when Rik was painting Ackert's portrait. Marjorie was about fifteen, I expect he seduced her then, but the strange thing …" the bitchiness suddenly left his voice, "the *really* odd thing is that Rik and Ackert became friends."

The recollection of the strange companionship seemed to leave him bemused. "They were both politically active and neither liked what was going on in Germany—the political assassinations and instability. And then Ackert confided his secret plans for the future to Rik. When I heard about it, I couldn't believe it. Van der Vendt was a *stranger,* and a Dutchman at that."

He was slowing down, wrapped in the fog of his discontent.

"Yes, yes, but what happened *next*?"

Schiffer roused himself. "Rik finished painting Ackert's portrait before the end of February, that was just before Dieter Ackert and my father were shot on the march to the Town Hall. Then in 1937 Rik was commissioned to paint Drexler, who had fought with Ackert in the Great War."

He paused, and took a drink from the brandy flask. "In '37 Drexler was still part of the Nazi hierarchy and Hitler was working on his master plan for Europe. During his sittings, Drexler told Van der Vendt that it was Hitler's intention to use Colign, the Dutch Prime Minister, as a puppet leader after Holland was invaded, and this *despite* Germany's guarantee of neutrality. This so incensed Rik that he dashed off to Groningen, trailing Marjorie behind him, to tell his hot-headed Dutch friends from the University what was going to happen. From what I heard, he then set up meetings with Colign and Mussert, the leader of the Dutch Nazis."

"How did that help?"

Schiffer shrugged. "Rik was naïve. He had decided to discredit Hitler by revealing Ackert's secret plan to the tabloids. He was murdered that night."

"But why should my grandfather's secret have *mattered*? It was six years after his death."

Schiffer's response was swift. "It *mattered* because the Nazis were afraid of Ackert's secret being revealed. They couldn't risk being discredited by the people's hero. It *mattered* enough for someone to shoot Rik and throw his body in the canal and bury the secret for ever."

He looked suddenly distressed and June pushed the brandy towards him. He nodded his thanks. "Someone contacted Jürgen Bergmann, the police commissioner in Bremen. He was Dieter Ackert's oldest friend. He was told Marjorie had been arrested for murder, and if he valued her life he should get down to Groningen at once."

"And then?"

"Well, it was a bit baffling. The Dutch police simply released Marjorie into Jürgen's care. They came straight to Berlin and he left her with me. She was in a terrible state, clinging to me, begging me to stay with her. She was convinced the Dutch were sending an assassin to shoot her. Van der Vendt's death was hushed up. It was a political thing."

"But what if my mother knew Ackert's secret?"

Schiffer was adamant. "She would have told me. Marjorie was never afraid to face the truth. She would have revealed the secret if she had known it. Rik was a ticking bomb waiting to explode in a world of ticking bombs. The Dutch Parliament and the Nazis had to get rid of him. It was as simple as that. No-one was ever charged with Rik's murder. But what I still don't understand is why Marjorie ran off with him. He was unstable, a dreamer."

"Mrs Conrad called him 'Byronic'."

He snorted. "He was a puffed-up braggart. He was always going to end up dead in the canal."

"That's harsh," I retorted. "He was a good painter."

"Well, his work doesn't sell for much today," Schiffer snapped back. "And anyway, after his murder, Marjorie hid the portrait away. She told me she never wanted to see it again. The next I knew she was off again, this time with Franz Helmann. But that liaison didn't go smoothly either. It was off. It was on. It was off again, but I was always there when she came back to me. Marjorie trusted me."

I wished I had known about these people. "Groningen," I said idly. "It's not far from Bremen, is it?"

"Not far."

A windmill turning in the wind near a house of death. Goodness, where did that image spring from? Disturbed, I turned quickly to the painting. It was no longer a portrait of a young girl painted by a little-known artist. The wonderful innocence in that face was now imbued with a deadly history. I desperately wanted the picture. I asked Schiffer if he would sell it to me.

"I've buyers in America who would let me name my price."

Numbers screamed in my head. I was bitter. "Well, I haven't got that sort of money."

"But you *may* have." Schiffer was harking back to the old plea. "Marjorie painted a great deal between 1937 and 1951. Some of those paintings have disappeared. I'm absolutely sure she hid them for the purpose of leaving them to you."

I was blunt. "Not even blackmail can make me give you portraits I don't possess." I turned away. "If I can't have the picture then I don't want it here."

I couldn't bear to look at it every day and not own it. I couldn't bear the thought that other people would look at her.

Schiffer stared at me, frowning. "You really do have a painter's perception." His eyebrow lifted. "Successful parents can be wrong about their offspring, you know. They have no elasticity in judging their children's efforts. You should have persisted with your art." Then he went on, "Last Saturday, in the gallery, you asked if I had a painting I could give you. Well, here it is, the Van der Vendt picture." He breathed deeply. "It's difficult for me to let it go, but you can have it, Paula, because *you* are my link with Marjorie."

He added quickly, "And here are two small early sketches, one of *Wild Marjoram* and the other of the Kafka dahlia you liked. You can see where she changed colours and perspective, but it still has the Jeffries magic. I've put them in a double frame so you can have it on your table."

It was unexpectedly kind of him. Thought had gone into the gift. I put my arms round him, my face against his. He stood immobile, his arms by his side.

June, on the step-ladder, shouted, "I'll start drilling the holes now, ok?" The drill sprang into a blast of ear-splitting cacophony, and the moment passed. The paintings were hung, the nature scenes on the side walls and the photo of *Stack* facing the door. Then the Van der Vendt painting was wrapped in its swaddling layers of soft white tissue and brown-paper covering, and at last Schiffer and June left, leaving *Wild Marjoram* and the *Kafka Dahlia* miniatures on my table.

As soon as Schiffer had driven off, I put the *Daisy* picture in the boot of my car. I couldn't wait to get home and pore over it, bit by bit, seeing her through that moment in history. I didn't believe the part about the brazen braggart, that's exactly what Schiffer *would* say. I hoped there was more to Van der Vendt than seducer and political activist.

It was fortunate that no clients had interrupted the Van der Vendt story, but clients were not rushing to view the flats and houses in Dunham Village. Two couples went round the Village later in the morning. Mr and Mrs Tyler's verdict had been immediate and disagreeable, "Too many bloody rich for neighbours!"

Tyler had a high-arched nose, an opinionated voice and a pushy nature. My next clients, Mr Renfrew and his partner, on the other hand, were pleasant and happy with what they saw. They left to drive into Norwich to see their solicitor about purchasing a bungalow. I hoped I would get a bonus.

The next moment, DCI Quinn walked into the office with his long lanky stride. The tiredness hadn't left his face, but his grey eyes were watchful. He was wearing his raincoat, though the sun was shining and the day was pleasantly warm. No sign of Sergeant Penry.

I gestured to him to sit down. He looked at Judd's montage.

"What's that about then?"

"It's minimalist art. You can see it as a geometric abstraction, or it can conjure up mental pictures, subliminal images that influence the onlooker. If you like, the viewer unconsciously sees another picture within the picture. At least," I added, "that's how I understand it."

Quinn raised his eyebrows. "And what 'other picture' do you see?"

Judd had not had a dramatic effect on Quinn. I decided to brazen it out. "It's quite an emotional one."

We walked over to it and I tried to explain what the picture meant to me. "I don't see twelve tin cans hanging in space. I see a ladder. You can label it ambition, or creativity, or the impossible task." My voice broke suddenly. "Why did Amy have to die?" I turned to Quinn. "Amy was shot. Murdered. Blood was on her blouse and on the rug."

I always saw it in that order: Blood. Blouse. Rug. "I saw him shoot her, but I never saw her killer's face."

Quinn was taken aback. "You're telling me the picture reveals a killing? Who's Amy?"

I told him about Amy's death and the man with the gun in my dreams.

Quinn listened with his head to one side. "I always knew you were involved in some way. Not that I can see the connection with Setna yet, but I will." He pointed to the Judd montage. "Tell me, why do I just see twelve green cans hanging in space?"

"Perhaps the experiences in your life don't respond to that particular piece of art. But that's not why you're here. What is it you really want, Mr Quinn?"

He took out his notebook. "You said you didn't know the man Setna was looking for. Sir Selwyn Freeman, the man you worked for at Inner Temple, knew him."

"I didn't remember the name at first," I answered shortly. I couldn't tell him I'd seen Mitchell in a dream, could I? "We never met, we never spoke. I saw Mitchell briefly, one afternoon, coming out of Sir Selwyn's rooms. Later Sir Selwyn told me Mitchell was working for CI2. I did see him briefly again at the Riverside Inn."

"Why didn't you tell me about Mitchell?"

"I thought CI2 would tell you. Is that why you're here?"

"I came to see Mrs Patricia Heals."

My voice brightened. "Well, Pat works here in the afternoons, she comes in at two."

"Has she spoken with you about her husband?"

"Pat Heals doesn't confide in me, Inspector. I'm the newcomer. I only started work on Monday. Pat has put money into this enterprise and she's close to Mr Sellick. Other than that, I don't know anything."

"But you worked in the main office in Norwich for a week. Did anyone mention Lawrence Heals while you were there?"

He was checking *my* movements? I shrugged. "Someone said he comes from South Africa. He's separated from his wife, and he works at the Acle branch. You might find him there."

"He's not there. His colleagues don't know where he is." He was frowning. "Are you friendly with Mrs Heals?"

I replied quickly. "Mrs Heals doesn't like me. After eleven years of marriage I found my husband didn't like me, either. Look, Inspector," I was conciliatory. "You're barking up the wrong tree. I left London to escape a broken marriage. I need to earn money. I'm lucky to have got this job, and I'd like to keep it. As I said, I'm not involved in anything criminal. If you thought otherwise, you would have arrested me."

"Well, don't leave Norwich. Oh, and what time did you say Mrs Heals would be here?"

"Two o'clock," I repeated curtly.

He picked up his coat. "Your mother was half-German. What was her maiden name?"

The shift in emphasis startled me.

"Ackert." But I pre-empted the next question. "Her father was Dieter Ackert."

"That's right!" he said and marched smartly out of the room.

On the way home, I went as usual to the bank. I was standing in a queue behind a couple, and couldn't help hearing them talking about a woman they had recently met.

"She was younger than that sour-faced old bitch we saw the first time in the sales room."

I frowned. I'd heard that voice before.

"Yeah, an' useless at the job." the man's companion replied.

The man turned slightly and I matched the voice with Tyler's high-arched nose. They were talking about me! It was like a physical blow. I bit my lip and wondered who the sour-faced old bitch had been. They moved up to the counter and I slipped into another queue. Anything to get away from them.

Perhaps Selwyn and Richard had seen me as shallow and sour-faced. Before we parted Richard had accused me of snooping, simply because I'd called in at the office on a Saturday. He shouted that I was "checking up" on him. I had retorted it was nonsense. "I came to take you out for lunch."

129

He went very quiet. "You can be so cold sometimes, really unpleasant." He had put his overcoat on and walked out of the office, leaving me to face the rest of the day alone. It was only later I realised he had gone to his mistress.

And only now did I grasp that his emotionally pointed attacks on me were a cover for the guilt of his own infidelity.

When I got home, I stood the *Daisy* picture on a shelf of my new bookcase. Schiffer had called my mother a ruthless woman. It was hard to reconcile this slight, provocative girl with the rather plump and intimidating woman I remembered as my mother.

In the painting, she was fourteen years younger than I was now. I felt frustrated. Why had Mum never talked about her early life, or her family, or what she did in the war? After a few moments I phoned Mr Jolley and told him I had a new painting. I repeated my invitation to tea. I heard him consulting his wife in the background. He said they could come tomorrow at five.

After lunch I emptied the first crate of my books and arranged them on the shelves of the G-Plan bookcase in the sitting room. I was glad I had all Mum's gardening books, including the *Loddon Blue Lavender* series with its dedication to Henry Siskin.

Finally, I stood a framed photograph of both my parents on a shelf beside one of my mother which I had snapped when I was twelve. I put some bottles of wine and wine-glasses in the drawer with the leaf that pulled down. I began to feel as if I belonged in the flat.

Later that evening, Jane Donovan rang. "I can't manage tomorrow, but would Saturday next week be OK?"

I'd completely forgotten about lunch on Saturday! Eagerly, I agreed to postpone it.

She asked me if I were looking forward to my birthday. I laughed ruefully. "It's just another day."

"Oh no, it isn't. Let's make next Saturday a birthday lunch, Paula, and just to let you know, I'll bring someone with me."

At once, I was uneasy. "Do you mean Richard?"

"Of course not. I thought you'd split up!"

I despised myself for asking the question, but I had to know. "When did you realise he was playing round?"

She was reluctant. "Richard was careful, but the signs were there over the months."

130

"Why didn't you *tell* me?" I cried.

"I hoped it was nothing serious."

"Serious! We're divorced! I've had the Decree Nisi."

"You know he's married again?"

God, that was quick. "It's Sheila, right?" Why did I torture myself by asking?

Jane, an invisible nod. "That's her. And you'd better know now, there's a baby as well."

I put the phone down abruptly. I remembered going to the office to meet Richard for lunch. It was about a year before my marriage ended. Sheila had walked across the room to Richard's table. I could see her clearly—young, passive, big hips, wide eyes, thick lashes, short dark curly hair. It was as if I were sketching her. She hadn't looked at me at all. Richard had been monosyllabic throughout the meal. I had felt rebuffed, and I couldn't understand why. We had left the restaurant together, but mentally and emotionally, we were miles apart. I had stood on the pavement and watched him climb into a taxi, his back stiff. He didn't even look back to wave. Why did it still hurt?

That evening I took the *Daisy* portrait into the kitchen and stood it up against the cheese box on the new table. My mother looked so young, so alive. I wanted to reach out and touch her and tell her I was here. I wished I could have shared everything with her. I wished I could hear her voice telling me I should be doing everything differently.

Friday, 29th May 1981

I was in the sitting room early in the morning having a coffee before leaving for the sales office. It had rained in the night. The air was cool and the tapering leaves of the plants were dripping with bright droplets of rain. May was going out in a cold shudder of drizzly, misty days. It was the anniversary of my mother's death. I let the heavy chain of her Crux Gemmata run through my fingers in memory of the nearly sixteen years we had shared together, and as the beads ran through my fingers the 'slate trough' came lazily into my mind.

Mum had ordered a large trough to hold a miniature rock garden. It was to be used to illustrate a series of books on Alpine Plants. I had been helping to lay the gravel and sand and compost in the trough. She had cried out to me not to disturb the covers over the drainage holes as I busily arranged the broken pieces of Welsh slate to form the scree acting as a background to the plants. The camera began turning in my mind.

May 1964

Mum is sitting in the garden on her grey canvas stool on the yellow flagstones at Yorkstone Cottage. The trough is on a low wide wall and the plants are in little pots standing on the soil ready to be planted. She calls the trough 'Tÿ Blodau', House of Flowers, because she's using Welsh slate.

As usual, she is sketching some preliminary designs. Dad carries out a tray with a covered jug of steaming hot coffee, a cream jug, two mugs and the morning paper.

I'm watching my parents from behind a lavender hedge as they talk on the patio. Mr Siskin's children, Jenni and Suzy, are with me behind the thick-stemmed hedge of Loddon Blue lavender.

Mum looks at the paper and draws in her breath. "Janus is dead!"

Dad frowns and looks at the article. "You mean Sheldon Asquith? Why do you call him Janus?"

"It was his code-name." Reluctantly, she adds that she last saw him three years ago at the Royal Academy Exhibition. "You remember, Erich, that was when we heard Jürgen Bergmann was in West Berlin."

"Ah yes, the day the young man was shot. And Janus?"

"Janus was head of Section 23, Niederlande und Deutschland Abteilung, from 1939 to '42. When Janus was head of operations we lost a lot of agents. And there were rumours about a mole in the Section. That's why it was closed down. Colonel North took over and I was relocated."

"Did you suspect anyone?"

"Everyone was suspect. When Arno was captured, the finger was pointed at him, but I never thought it was Arno. It was Sheldon I distrusted. In the early years, he was sympathetic to Hitler's ideas, but then, like many English people, when war started he 'readjusted' his views. But there was something else that worried me more."

"Go on."

"A man called Hannagan. His name came up when I was attached to a new group investigating Irish militants. They were killing troops, police and civilians here in the UK and Northern Ireland."

"The IRA?"

Mum nods. "He may have been connected with them at one time, but I was told by a trusted friend in Europe that Hannagan was a German agent. He had a companion, a woman. I always wondered if Sheldon, who was Irish, had some connection with Hannagan." She sits back. "I've never understood Irish politics. Foreigners find the lines blurred between Irish and Irish, and Irish and English."

Dad shrugs. "That's civil war for you. But Sheldon wouldn't have kept his job if he'd been involved with militants."

"Were you ever in Ireland?"

"Once. We were sent to Belfast in '43. The IRA had been bomb happy against the security forces. I was glad to leave and get back to fighting the Germans, the real enemy. As a German, you must have found it difficult at times."

"Anglo-German, Erich, and yes, because of my father, some people accused me of being the mole in Section 23."

"What went wrong when Asquith was chief?"

I watch Mum. She's uneasy.

"He was involved in the Stefan Radevsky affair."

"Ah, German painter. Died early in the war."

"Political cartoonist. Brilliant. Escaped into Holland in November '39."

Dad lights two cigarettes with one match while Mum pours out the coffee. He takes a cigarette out of his mouth and gives it to her.

"You're being short and sharp about it, Marjorie, not your usual fluent self. What are you hiding?"

"We all have things to hide, Erich." She waits while Dad pours her out some coffee. "In November 1939, Amy and I were pretending to be tourists in Holland, but actually we were on a mission to get Radevsky out of the country. This is what happened."

From behind the bank of raised lavender hedge with its brightly coloured purple flowers and sharp pointed leaves, I listen spellbound to a story that runs like a thriller as spies and counter-spies converge upon a city called Groningen.

It is November 1939.

In an old house beside a windmill and a canal in Groningen a young man is penned up in a room. He can hear the sails on the windmill creaking as they turn in the cold night air. He sits, facing the door, his long dark overcoat wrapped round him, the belt drawn tightly round his waist, the brim of his grey felt hat pulled down, a suitcase by his side, a flask on the table, a heavy service revolver in his hand pointing at the door. Stefan Radevsky is waiting for Marjorie Ackert and Amy Eggers, agents assigned to get him safely out of the country.

Marjorie and Amy are cycling round the Netherlands as tourists. They chat together as they ride along the wide road to Groningen. The Dutch Gestapo, the

Nederlandsche SS are everywhere. Holland is still, technically, at peace, and tourists and businessmen are enjoying a late Indian summer among the canals and lakes.

The two women cycle past shop windows filled with posters offering vast rewards for information on the whereabouts of Stefan Radevsky. The reward is equal to a year's income for a fisherman in Friesland.

Amy has mapped out their route: Amsterdam to Soest, where they spend a night before moving on to Zwolle. They spend a day in Zwolle looking round the city before cycling on to Drachte for another night's rest. Amy is convinced their cover as tourists has been blown. She tells Marjorie she's seen the same man twice, once in Amsterdam and again in Zwolle. "They've known about us from the beginning!" Her voice is shaking. Marjorie reassures her friend, but she is just as anxious.

They start out early in the morning from Drachte and make good progress to Groningen, where they slip into a small hotel in a side-street near a park.

They sit at a table in the small restaurant in the hotel and Marjorie asks her friend if she recognises anyone. Amy is pale. Her eyes dart nervously round the room. She says she's not sure. They finish their meal and then tell the receptionist they're going out for an evening walk round the city. They leave their suitcases at the hotel. Twenty minutes later they turn into another side-street where a slate-grey BMW saloon is parked by the pavement. The driver, dressed in a German field-grey uniform, gets out of the car and greets them. A gold-linked chain is just visible round his neck under his unbuttoned tunic. "Thank God you're here." Arno Müller shakes hands with the two women. "The police are everywhere. I had to change my route a dozen times." He is tired, and grey lines are etched deep into his face.

He shows them a map and the route they must take. "After a mile turn left and follow the canal. See, I've marked it on the map. The house is the last one before the windmill. It's owned by Willem de Vries. Stefan is there, waiting for you."

He folds the map and gives it to Marjorie. "Destroy it as soon as you can. If all goes well de Vries will show a green light at a downstairs window. You must rap three times, wait, then three times again. Tell de Vries you've come for the parcel and he will let you into the house. If there's no light then make your way immediately to the coast. Hopefully I'll find you on the way. If the light is on you have only twenty minutes to complete your business, then you must leave. I'll be waiting near the house with the car."

Amy is unsure. "Why are you wearing that uniform, Arno?"

He shows her some papers. "I'm on my way to pick up the mayor of Groningen. Now you must go."

But Amy's voice is rough and urgent. "Have you seen the posters? The reward is huge! It's amazing Radevsky's still free!"

"Yes, it's risky." Arno pulls his cap down over his eyes, quickly does the five buttons up on his tunic and turns to Marjorie. "Did Sheldon give you the money?"

She nods, tapping her handbag.

"Good, now you must leave."

Arno gets into the car, but Amy holds his arm through the open window. "Why can't you drive us to the house, Arno?"

"And tell the whole street you're visiting de Vries? The more invisible we are, the greater the chance of success."

Marjorie draws Amy back. "We should be in and out of the house and on our way to the coast before anyone notices anything. Your job is to keep watch at the window while I talk with Stefan."

Arno drives away, but Amy's frowning eyes are following the car. Marjorie takes her friend's arm and they walk briskly down the road, turning right and then left and later taking the path along the canal. Here Marjorie puts a match to the map and scatters the ashes in the water. It's another twenty minutes before they reach the small row of houses beside the mill. A wind has sharpened and they can hear the windmill's sails turning in the night air.

The green light is on in the window and Amy raps three times on the door, and then raps again. It is opened by a surly-faced old man. "Meneer de Vries, we are here to collect the parcel." Amy's voice is soft.

De Vries jerks his thumb towards the stairs and grunts. "Daarboven!"

"Stay by the window, Amy," Marjorie mutters. "Shout if you hear anything."

Marjorie runs quickly up the twelve steps. The door on the right is open and she sees Stefan sitting in a chair by the table, the lamp lighting up the low heavily-beamed room. Stefan looks sullen and ill. Constantly on the run has taken its toll. Stefan knows only the closest of friends can be trusted, and greed is the greatest enemy.

Marjorie kneels beside him, holding him close, shocked at his drawn face, the chalkiness of his skin and the air of defeat. It is as if fear has eaten away his skin. Suddenly, Stefan stands and pulls her up into his arms. "I trust no-one, Marjorie, do you hear? No-one but you." His voice is muffled as he holds her close. Then Marjorie pulls him down onto the chair, calming him as she speaks.

"You trusted the Bruderbund to get you over the border," she says.

"Trust? Every time I move to a safe house the Gestapo follow on my heels. There's no safe house any more. An informant, someone close to us, tells them everything. Did you know Jürgen Bergmann's an Oberst in the Police?"

Marjorie is mollifying. "Jürgen became a policeman in 1923. He was my father's closest friend, and a good friend to me."

Stefan grunts. "You mean the Van der Vendt murder?"

"I was arrested, but Jürgen rushed over from Bremen and talked them into releasing me. He's a Bruderbunder, Stefan, he would never harm us."

But Stefan is sceptical. "Bergmann knows all of us. I say he's a Nazi through and through. Before we left for the border there was a rumour that he's working for the Gestapo. Mein Gott, a Bruderbunder in the Gestapo! They're closing in on us. We'll never get out of this verdammte place alive."

He is becoming more and more agitated. Marjorie is firm. "We will get out, Stefan, but we must move quickly."

He stops her, his hand on her arm. "You tell me to trust our people. Well, hear this: Professor Baumgartner, a Bruderbunder, and Elèna, his student, were escorting me on the train. It was arranged I should leave them at a station before the Dutch border and meet Peeters, but I sensed something was wrong, so I slipped off the train a station earlier. It was a miracle Peeters caught up with me, but he managed to bring me to Groningen in his cart under sacks of knobbly turnips and potatoes. But the police were waiting for Baumgartner and Elèna at the next station and they were questioned through the night. I'm sure Bergmann was involved." He cannot control his nervousness. "Have you got the money to pay our contact?"

She tells him she has the money for the boatman. But Stefan is feverish. He keeps saying the SS are waiting outside the house with their sharpened knives and machine guns.

Marjorie stands up. "There's no-one outside. Leave the suitcase, Stefan, it's too conspicuous. Come, we must go now."

Stefan looks at her, his light-blue eyes sunken in their sockets. "Wait, there's something I must do."

He snaps open the suitcase and takes out a thick bundle of paper. "These were drawn with my heart's blood." He hands them to her. "Take them, all sixty of them. They tell the story of the madmen who have stolen our country and betrayed the German people."

Marjorie puts them in her bag under her revolver. Radevsky is suddenly calm and controlled. "Very well, let's go!"

They are halfway down the stairs when the front door bursts open and plainclothes policemen storm into the room. Amy screams and fires and fires again. The pistol is struck from her hand and she falls as a policeman hits her head with the butt of his revolver.

Firing rapidly, Stefan turns sharply and runs back up the stairs. Marjorie follows him. A policeman stumbles away, clutching his face. Arno runs out of the kitchen and up the stairs.

He snatches hold of Marjorie's coat and drags her down, shouting all the time, "Leave Stefan to me! Get out, get out!"

At the kitchen door, Marjorie turns. Stefan is reaching for the twelfth step, blood is spurting onto the wall from the wound in his throat. Amy is lying unmoving by the window and Arno is sliding helplessly down the stairs as the police surge forward. The harsh noise of gunfire and shouting fills the room.

Marjorie backs into the kitchen. She sidles out of the back door and runs out into the street. She is shaking uncontrollably. She tells herself she should never have left Stefan. She should have stayed beside him as the police charged up the stairs.

A car drives slowly along the road and Arno Müller pulls up beside her. Müller is wounded. There is blood on the steering-wheel and on his clothes. He is swearing in Dutch and says he shot his way out of the house.

"And Stefan?"

"Stefan's dead. Amy and de Vries were dragged out to a police car."

Arno's right hand is a mess of blood, his third finger hanging by the skin. Marjorie ties her handkerchief tightly round the wound. She takes the wheel and drives over the moving shadows of the windmill's rasping sails and takes the road to the coast.

While it's still dark, they make their way to their assignation where Jan Bakker is nervously waiting for them. Marjorie gives him the money and Jan rows them out to the island where they board a low-lying craft. An SAS soldier pulls Marjorie up into the boat and holds the shivering woman in his arms before he reaches down and helps Arno on board. There is a whispered conversation between the soldier and the Dutchman. Then Bakker rows away. The soldier is Captain Denby. He leads the way to the cabin.

"You'll soon be in England," he reassures them, and gives them blankets to put round their shoulders. The ship's captain looks them over and then the MTB creeps quietly out of the inlet and into the North Sea where storm clouds are gathering.

Two weeks later Amy is put on board a Royal Naval ship with members of the exiled Dutch government. The British Embassy has arranged her release. Amy is interrogated by the Security Services when she reaches England, but thereafter Amy never again speaks about her imprisonment in Groningen. It's clear that NDA23 has been infiltrated.

In 1942, Marjorie, Elèna and Arno are escorting their "baggage"—two writers and two chemists—out of Germany. They are going down the Dutch route. Marjorie is lagging behind Elèna and Arno, because Johan Sandor, one of her chemists, has sprained his ankle. Johan says nothing, but he knows his ankle is broken. He dares not tell Marjorie in case she decides to leave him behind.

On reaching Emden, Eléna's group is ambushed. Elèna and Arno hurry their writers, Becher and Frisch, across the street. Marjorie gathers up her two chemists and hides them behind an outbuilding. They have been betrayed. The next moment Elèna raises her weapon and fires. She has seen police and Gestapo creeping up behind Arno who is on her left. Arno and Becher fall under the withering return of fire and Frisch dies in the next blast. Marjorie does nothing as Elèna is captured. Her duty is to keep her two chemists alive. She flees down the side streets with them, and with the help of the Dutch Resistance they are eventually rescued by a corvette and taken to England. Marjorie tells her chief there is a traitor in Section 23. Once again the Section is ripped apart in the search for the mole, but no-one is arrested.

Three weeks have passed since the ambush at Emden and the Code-Room at NDA23 headquarters in Box Hill begins receiving messages from Arno Müller. His regular wireless operator, Olivia Droon, identifies Arno's signal and codes. She's certain it's Müller's touch. Arno explains he was rescued by a group of French saboteurs on his way to the prison and he's remaining with them. He arranges with Major Asquith, CO at Box Hill, that four agents will be dropped by parachute near the woods at Groningen, and then another three the following week at Winschoten, and three weeks later another three at Stadtskanal and so on for six months. These agents are to form the nucleus of a force of saboteurs who will act with the Allies in the coming invasion of Europe.

Six months later, Major Asquith is sitting in his office facing an exhausted Dutchman who has made his way to England. Van Dijk's tired voice holds Sheldon's complete attention. "There was nothing to be seen as we parachuted down, but as soon as we landed the soldiers and police were there, sweeping us up like hay into a hayrick. We were endlessly interrogated, then one by one our agents were taken out and executed. I was lucky. My cousin was one of the prison guards and he got me out. We both got out."

Luuk van Dijk leans forward, his eyes hard. "They all died dropping into the same trap. I hope to God you're not sending any more poor buggers into Holland."

Asquith is appalled. "You were supposed to meet up with Arno Müller. He's been orchestrating the whole damn thing."

Luuk laughs harshly. "You've been 'orchestrating' with Dutch SS Intelligence." He nurses his broken arm. "Arno's probably dead. What a bloody awful mess."

Sheldon Asquith is then quietly moved into a non-active role while Colonel Edgar North closes down NDA23. Everyone is vetted again and dispersed into other units. Many are convinced Arno is working with the Germans, but Marjorie Ackert defends him.

"We worked together," she tells North. "Arno saved my life." She tells the Colonel that Arno has a sister married to an Englishman. "He has an English nephew. Before the war Arno was a salesman in small arms. He's a good agent and he loves this country." She's adamant that Arno isn't the mole in NDA23.

And she's bitter. "No doubt, Colonel, you'll be told I'm the mole because my father was a prominent Nazi. But those who know me have never doubted where my allegiance lies."

I've been playing with Suzy and Jenni and miss the next part of the story. A little later we creep back to our listening post at the Loddon Lavender hedge and I hear my mother saying something about the Radevsky fiasco.

"After that we stuck with the Ritterorden, and did not rely on what was left of the Bruderbund."

139

"Ok. Who were in the Ritterorden?"

"Professor Felix Baumgartner. He divorced his wife and married Elèna, his student. Felix was a psychologist who joined the police. Cedric Conrad and his wife Gillian joined the Ritterorden in Berlin. Conrad is an expert on minerals and precious stones. Peter Schiffer was with us from the beginning. Jürgen Bergmann is my father's oldest friend and a Bruderbunder. He's also a policeman. The writers, Johan Frisch, Marin Becher and Trudi Hartmann, joined us in 1938 and so did the two chemists I got out of Germany. Stefan, Amy and I were in the Bund and the Ritterorden from the beginning."

Dad screws up his face. "You're looking for a traitor? Well, my money's on Schiffer. I've never liked the little toad. Has he asked about the cartoons?"

"He said he'd heard of them when he was in Berlin. Sheldon Asquith thought I had them. My rooms were constantly searched, but the cartoons were never found."

"Well, I'm asking for them now." Dad smiles. "Where are they?"

Mum returns the smile, but it's a secret smile that I recognise. "They're well hidden. No-one will ever know where they are until I die."

"Why didn't you have them published, especially if they would have had such an impact?"

"They would have been ridiculed as forgeries. Stefan had to be alive to present them. That's why he was silenced. But they could damage the neo-Nazis. Even now, Liebling, Europe isn't at peace."

As they get up to go into the house, Dad says, "Europe's never bloody at peace!" His arm is affectionately round Marjorie's shoulders and they are arguing in that happy, non-aggressive way lovers have.

My fingers were wrapped round the chain of the Crux Gemmata. I sometimes wondered how much I actually remembered, or pieced together from different conversations. It was odd how Judd's *Stack* had coloured a lost memory of the Radevsky affair. And that strange moment when my mind opened and told me about the windmill and the house of death.

I could still feel the heat from the sun on my face from that hot day in May. Where have those long hot summers gone? Dad had loved Mum then. You can't mistake genuine affection.

Slowly, I put the crucifix back in its velvet pouch and dropped it into my shoulder-bag.

The doorbell rang. Friday. Payday for the milk. I had the money ready on the hall table, but instead of Gerry Scott on the doorstep, a younger man was writing up the account.

I looked round. "Where's Gerry?"

"Gone back to Cambridge. Stood in for me while I was on holiday. I'm Dan Whitley."

It was funny Scott hadn't mentioned he was leaving. I settled up with Whitley and added more butter and bread to my weekly order. I noticed there was no packet of biscuits.

Dan shook his head. "You can order them, but there's nothing on special promotion. Never has been on them biscuits."

There was a letter amongst the post. Colonel Edgar North was requesting my presence at an official hearing at the Lansbury Hall Hotel in Norwich on Wednesday 10th June at 3.30pm. The hearing concerned an attack on Pforzheim in Germany in 1944, and the theft of paintings from the Pforzheim Museum. As far as I knew, I had no connection with the Pforzheim Museum. My mother had called the name out, years ago, and one of the strange postcards had the word *Pforzheim* on it. I could contribute nothing to Colonel North's hearing.

I was on edge. *Nothing on special promotion.* Then why had Scott said otherwise? And now some kind of court case about something that had happened thirty-seven years ago. Why was it all happening *now*? The past was rearing up and snapping in my face, and I didn't like it.

After a moment, I pulled myself together and went into the bathroom and checked my make-up. I reminded myself I had an appointment with Dr Roberts at 9.00 am at the Retirement Homes. I put the letter from Colonel North in my bag. I simply couldn't deal with the wretched thing now.

Roberts had two surgeries, one in Swaffham in the evenings, and the morning surgeries in the Retirement Homes Village. He took down details of my past illnesses. "How long have you had migraines?"

"A long time, but the attacks have become worse over the last couple of years."

"It may be stress." He asked me what medicine I was taking.

"Aspirin, but that upsets my stomach."

"You may be sensitive to the coating. Aspirin isn't right for everyone. I want you to try these capsules. We've had good results. Take two when the attack starts and two every four hours for four days. If the migraine continues come and see me. Is there anything else?"

I shook my head. Roberts got up and put on his overcoat. "Surprising how chilly it is today. Tim will bring the medicine along later this morning. The sooner you begin the treatment the sooner you'll feel better. In the meantime I suggest a wholesome diet, exercise, and a quiet life."

It was sensible advice. It was not Dr Roberts' fault that he had no idea how unrestful my life had become. Roberts went over to a filing cabinet and took out some medical records for his round. I asked him about the residents in Dunham Village, explaining that I was concerned because I was selling apartments to elderly people. "Are they generally in good health?"

"Many have existing medical conditions and they need repeated treatment to keep those conditions under control, but on the whole, most are settling down well."

I slipped the strap of my daffodil bag over my shoulder. "What happened to Mrs Whisby? I heard she died suddenly."

Meg Farrell had sent a chit round with the news. There was a momentary pause, quickly covered as Roberts slammed the metal drawer shut. "Whisby? Yes, yes, I remember. It wasn't so very unexpected. She was 86 and had a medical history of bronchitis."

Roberts held the door open. "I have several visits this morning." It was a dismissal, but apart from that slight pause, his words had held nothing sinister.

I went back to the sales office. A man and a woman were sitting on the sofa waiting for me. I greeted them with a smile, put the sign I had left on the table in the drawer and asked their name.

"Sylvia Henderson, and this is my husband, Kenny."

Kenny grunted something and wandered over to the window, distancing himself from the proceedings.

Sylvia sat opposite me. She tittered and threw her head back, her long fair hair flying over the shoulders of her expensive blue and white-flowered linen dress. "Kenny's shy, but business is business, isn't it! My mum's name is Brenda Moffat. She's seventy-three, she's got rheumatism, and the house is too big for her. So it's sensible for her to downsize. I've told her she's moving into one of these flats."

Some mutterings from the window were tersely interpreted by Sylvia. "Don't be silly, Kenny, of course she's got to move. Pops died ten years ago and Mum's become silly and started rambling."

She leaned over the table towards me. She had sapphire-blue eyes like a Persian cat. "It's really embarrassing. She can't remember even simple things and she's sitting on a fortune in that old house. Now Kenny's got a great idea and needs the capital to get started. Getting started is the most difficult part of a business, isn't it."

Isn't it. Always a statement, never a question.

Kenny came over. "Let the old girl stay in the house. She doesn't want to move. I've told you we can manage. Come on, Sylvie, let's get out of here!"

But Sylvia pushed his hand away. "She's *coming*, it's all arranged." Kenny was not going to change her mind. She told him to go and wait in the car. Kenny muttered something and walked out.

"*The Helpline* was just what I needed," Sylvia said briskly. "Their doctor certified Mum as incompetent and I moved everything over to the solicitor and now we have Power of Attorney. He got the house sold in next to no time and the house-clearing firm sent almost everything to auction."

"Have you got the advert?" I asked.

"I was told to destroy it," she snapped. "I've not met you before. How do I know you're part of the set-up?"

"Oh, I'm part of the team, I've taken Renée Tournai's place," I said smartly. "She was here before."

"I wasn't talking about her, I was talking about Rowene." She rapped her knuckles on the table. "But whoever you are, you can give me the forms to sign."

I looked at her, disliking her rudeness and undecided how to continue. It sounded like a scam. Doctor and solicitor working together to put Power of Attorney into place. I couldn't see where the house selling and clearing came in, but it looked like a neat package, hard to touch, hard to bring to court, everything done carefully and "legally". I opened the drawer to find the folder and she said she'd come to pay the final sum and get the keys. "Now!" She almost grabbed the papers out of my hands. "Where do I sign?"

She had bought one of the cheapest and smallest flats. I wondered if I should seek advice about the rights of elderly people.

"Do you want her to have cleaning and laundry help?" I asked.

"She can do that herself." She took the pen with her left hand, ticked the boxes and signed both forms.

As she handed them to me her fair hair flowed round her shoulders like angels' wings. Her mother would move into the flat on Saturday morning. "I kept back enough furniture so she doesn't have to sleep on the floor."

For the first time in fifteen years I was meeting something worse than the man with the gun in my nightmares. I hoped I would never see Sylvia Henderson again. I gave her the keys without the mandatory smile or handshake.

"It may be some time before you get your money back from reselling the flat," I observed.

"You mean when my mother dies?" She was brazen about it. "All things come to an end, isn't that what they say?" Then she went on calmly. "My mother's a sick old woman. She wouldn't help us when we needed help. Rowene put me in touch with the right people. They did everything quickly, but it cost me."

She got up, flicking her golden wings over her shoulders. "There's only one thing I care about and that's Kenny. He needs the money and she wouldn't help him. In a few days the whole thing will be over and done with, and I hope to God I never see any of you lot again."

Touché! As I watched her leave I wondered why speed was so important. Brenda Moffat might live for years and Sylvia's money would be tied up in the flat. Once again I wondered who Rowene was. MS were the initials on the little flag on the map.

I read through the forms Sylvia had signed. Brenda Moffat lived in Richmond. I knew Richmond in Surrey, but this was Richmond, North Yorkshire. I sat back and thought for a moment, then I took the notebook out of my shoulder-bag and made a list of the names and places of the clients I had met:

Thomas Cameron—Aylesbury

Edward Dermott—Glasgow

Julia Whisby—Norwich

Gillian Conrad—Norwich

Hal Goodison—London

Sylvia Henderson—Richmond, North Yorkshire

And there had been others, like Margaret Avery, the Reddings and John Murray and his wife, people with no connection to *The Helpline,* to Rowene, or the strangely worded advertisement. Heals had only advertised locally, so how, and why, had contact been made with Cameron in Aylesbury, Dermott in Glasgow and Henderson in North Yorkshire?

Sylvia had said, "In a few days the whole thing will be over and done with." At the time I thought she was referring to her mother moving into the flat, but suppose she had meant something darker?

Years spent exposed to criminal activity at Inner Temple had sharpened my wits, but I reminded myself I was *not* a detective, I was a saleswoman trying to earn a living, and not very well according to the Tylers. The Moffat mother would probably live for another fifteen years just to spite her objectionable daughter!

I walked over to the map on the wall. The houses were moving slowly. Too slowly. Trish Porter had said there had been violence shown against the scheme. No-one else had mentioned that.

At eleven Tim Harvey breezed into the sales office. "I've got your tablets!" He threw a chemist's green-coloured bag on to the table.

I was impressed. "I wasn't expecting them until Monday."

"Pleasure, anything for you, Paula." He lingered over my name. "Just let me know what you need and when I go into Swaffham I'll get it for you."

"Thanks, I'll remember."

There was something attractive in the warm way Tim embraced me into his world. He perched himself on the edge of the table, all chummy and nice. "There's a good film showing in Swaffham tonight, would you like to come?"

I was cautious. "Maybe, when I've got a bit more time."

His lips went down. "D'you like it here? The other woman only lasted a month."

"Why was that?"

"Pat said she wasn't a good team member. She said Audrey snooped. That was her name, Audrey Simpson."

"Where was she snooping?"

"Here, in the office, and questioning people. And she was crotchety. Always picky and interfering. Not like you, Paula, you're different. People really like you. They've told me." He spoke in short phrases, like a gangster in an American B movie. "I'll make us a coffee." He slid off the table.

Still lives with his mother, I thought. I decided to be coy and learn all I could about Audrey. I didn't tell Tim, but I'd already spoken to Corrie Smiley. She had plenty to say about Audrey Simpson. "She was fifty-eight, efficient enough, but abrupt. Trouble was, she didn't know how to turn the charm on, too down to earth, like, an' always asking questions. She tell me she think something's goin' on in the Village. Thing is, she don't know what. Soon after, Pat sack her."

I turned as a furious Pat Heals erupted into the room, tip-tapping over the wooden floor. She was dressed in a well-fitting dark-grey suit with an off-white stripe. On the left lapel of her jacket was an emerald brooch which exactly matched the colour of her eyes. She was one of those slightly built, attractive women. She reached the table just as Tim came back with two steaming mugs of coffee.

"What are *you* doing here?" Her eyebrows twisted up.

Tim, sulking, pointed a mug at the chemist's bag on the table. "I brought Mrs James's tablets."

"All right, but you're not paid to deliver *coffee*, are you."

Anger popping out of his eyes, Tim banged the mugs down on the table, hating Heals for treating him like a juvenile. His aggrieved shoulders hunched up as his bustling bottom propelled him out of the room. I quickly mopped up the coffee Tim had spilt. Abruptly Pat dumped her bag on a chair and faced me.

"Mr Sellick showed me the letter and articles you wrote." I found myself sketching the sharp lines tightening round her eyes and mouth. "You should've passed them through me. You had no right, *no right,* to go direct to Sellick." I was taken aback at the ferocity of her manner. "I lead this team, everything should come through *me.*" My silence irritated her. "My money's in this undertaking." Her voice rose shrilly. "Another thing, you should have informed me personally about the Gazette's interest in the RH project. You're the newcomer here. You know nothing about the place, all the work, all the dreams, that have gone into making this project work."

I frowned. She shouldn't be blaming me for doing her job, she could have arranged for the editor to visit Dunham Village herself.

"And *I* shall accompany Ms Porter and Mr Sellick round the Village on Monday," Pat continued crisply. "I know *everything* about this project, so I can explain its history and what we hope to achieve."

"Miss Porter mentioned that Mr Sellick had some bad luck with an earlier project."

"You mean the Lincoln housing plan? That was a disaster because the builder cut corners, and that was proved in court. They had to pay substantial damages.

This project is quite different. Of course there are always people who enjoy making trouble, but this time Doug Sellick has given us a real vision."

"I agree with you," I said calmly. "That's why I wrote the adverts."

"I see." She turned the table diary round closing the subject. I watched her slender red-manicured fingernail move down the list of names and dates. "You're entering everyone who enquires about the properties, as well as those who come?"

I was short. "Everyone."

"I understand you're asking for the letters and advertisements that were sent out from the main office."

"*They* give me the letters," I responded mildly. I hurried on. "There was an advertisement, but it was different from the one you sent out to the local press. It mentioned a representative and an organisation called *The Helpline*. What does that mean?"

She pulled herself up sharply. "Again, it's none of your business, but I'll answer you anyway. I don't know who the representative and *The Helpline* are, and I don't know who's sending out these corrupted adverts. Probably someone with a grudge against Mr Sellick. When the project was first mooted there were many objections, and some people were incredibly unpleasant and antagonistic." She turned to me, her manner cold. "If you have any adverts or letters I want to see them."

"There was only the one and I threw it in the bin," I lied. "Some of the clients have mention someone called Rowene. Mrs Henderson, a client, was expecting her to be here. Is she the representative?"

Heals looked at me sharply. "You're very persistent. I thought the representative was Audrey Simpson. She was here before you. She was forever probing into things, just like you, Mrs James. When I questioned her about the representative she became rude and offensive and I had to sack her. I hope Mr Sellick hasn't made another error in appointing *you*."

I ignored her rudeness. "What about Renée Tournai?"

"She was hopeless at the job. I wish I *knew* who was interfering and why they're trying to discredit the Village. And I don't know anything about Rowene. If you meet her you must tell me at once and you must give me everything that's passed on to you. Now, is there anything else you want to say?"

"Yes, could you tell me why some flags on the map have more than one name?"

I pointed to the flags within the red line and her face darkened. "Those properties have *nothing* to do with you." With an effort she pulled herself together. "The explanation is quite simple. In the beginning the nature of the Retirement Homes was not properly understood and people bought bungalows or flats for elderly relatives who were too old or too sick to manage on their own. When Miss Farrell realised what was happening it was decided to inform the relatives that the clients should be in a more suitable environment. Then the properties were resold. The wellbeing of our clients," she added tartly, "is very important to us. Why did you ask?"

"Curious, that's all."

She picked up her bag and briefcase. "Curiosity lost Simpson and Tournai their jobs. If you're not happy working here I suggest you start looking for another place. Oh, and don't write any more advertisements for the Village. We already have plenty. Just sell the properties, Mrs James, and do the job you're being paid to do. And in future if you receive negative comments or papers about Dunham Village let me know at once. Oh, and you may be asked to work some afternoons. Martin Spencer's in hospital and will be away for at least a fortnight. I'm going over to see Miss Farrell before she leaves for Norwich. Mary will take over this afternoon. And you may have to explain to any clients that Miss Farrell will be consulting with Mr Sellick all afternoon."

"When will she be back?"

Pat grimaced. "Later this evening." She turned suddenly, her voice high and shrill. "Why did you come to Norwich? There's nothing here for you, Mrs James. In fact, if I were you I'd go back to London before something unfortunate happens."

I stared at her. Did she know what she was saying? Pat swept out, her head high, my finger sketching the defiance in the tension of her shoulders and short angry steps.

Three more people came and looked round the site. Dr Njella, a biologist working at the University of East Anglia, said he had chosen an upstairs flat on behalf of his parents. It had a good view over the golf course. There was no mortgage involved. His solicitors were Parr, Parr and Bretherton.

"Good, they're next door to our main office in Norwich." I gave him the standard form with my name and details of the flat and asked him to give it to Mr Bretherton.

When he left, I reached for the phone. Miss Farrell answered, sounding edgy. "Yes, yes, Audrey Simpson showed me a curious letter about a representative and something called *The Helpline*. I told Pat Heals and she's dealing with it. Rowene? No, she's never worked here. When will I be back? Later this evening. *Look* at the time! I should have left half-an-hour ago. The story of my life!"

I was ready to lock up when Hal Goodison popped into the office and loped up to my table. I hid my dislike and asked how the golf was going.

"It's a great course, but I've come about the front door. It's sticking. You need to send the carpenter round to look at it."

I made a note in the diary and said I would pass it on. "I'm sorry, Mr Goodison, but I'm locking up now, is there anything else you want?"

"D'you play golf?"

I lied and shook my head.

He leaned over and tapped my arm. "Whenever you want a game, let me know. We'd make a great team."

Goodison was one of those men who never listen.

At five o'clock Mr Jolley and his wife came to tea. Mr Jolley had a leather Gladstone bag filled with tools, and I showed him where I wanted the *Daisy* picture hung in the sitting room. He said he would first do the measurements and come back after tea to hang it.

While we were waiting for him I showed Enid my garden. I was apologetic. "It's not really a garden. I call it my courtyard."

"But it's lovely!" Her response was unexpected. "It catches the afternoon sun, almost anything will flourish here." We walked round the pots and hanging plants and she suggested I should get a small willow. "It will bring you good luck."

I would welcome some luck. Then we went back inside and I showed her the original *Wild Marjoram* in my bedroom. The colours glowed in the afternoon light.

Enid had a habit of bobbing her head and shoulders to one side when she was speaking. "It's quite beautiful. Tell me, did your mother work with anyone when she was composing her garden themes?"

Inexplicably, I said brightly, "Oh yes, Mr Siskin was always there, ready to help."

"*Siskin!*" The name rebounded jarringly. Head and shoulders bobbed again and she raised her left hand in acknowledgement. "Of course, the Lavender

149

Series! Such a beautifully created work." We went back into the kitchen and I made the tea and put out the sandwiches, the Victoria sponge and cups and saucers.

Mr Jolley came into the kitchen. "Great! Tea and sandwiches!" So I poured out the tea, passed the salmon and cucumber round and got to know Mr Jolley's wife.

Enid Jolley was a tall, bony, down-to-earth woman in tweeds with a round face and wide-spaced brown eyes under strongly marked brows and wavy grey hair piled high over her forehead in the style of Queen Mary.

She was saying how lucky she had been. "I had a wonderful childhood. My father landscaped gardens for the rich and famous, so I grew up learning about plants, trees and grasses."

It wasn't just luck, I thought, as I refilled their cups and cut the Victoria sponge. Enid Jolley was bright and intelligent and curious about life. She had won a scholarship to the Studley Castle Horticultural College in Warwickshire when she was eighteen. "And now I lecture two days a week there, and two days at UEA, and the rest of the time I'm at our garden centre near Brundall." She seemed comfortable with her life and appreciative of the good things that crossed her path. "When William retires that's where we shall live."

I wondered what had drawn them together.

Jolley smiled. "I've just rebuilt the garden centre and finished the house. I've kept it simple, but Enid insisted on a conservatory for her plants." He smiled. "I think the room is as much for her as for the flowers!"

I laughed. "We all need a room to escape into."

A strange expression crossed his face. "Why do you say that?"

Feeling foolish, I stumbled into my explanation. "Well, I've been running away from people, things, the world, for most of my life, and it would be nice to have somewhere to feel safe."

My voice faded as I saw the man with the gun step out of the shadows near the kitchen door. I waited petrified for the shot, but he disappeared back into the darkness. It was the second time he had stepped outside the bedroom shadows.

With an effort I pulled myself together, fearful I was becoming mad or madder. I gave a short harsh laugh. "My mother loved her conservatory. She found it soothing to sit there and paint, especially as she got older. It was really hard for her when she kept dropping her brushes and pencils."

"That must have been very upsetting," Enid said. "Was it a neurological disorder?"

"I don't know. The doctor said she had flu."

While we were having more tea I invisibly sketched Enid's distinctive Edwardian face with its generous mouth and prominent cheek-bones under long, low brows.

"How did you know MJ Jeffries was my mother?" I asked abruptly.

"*Wild Marjoram!* As soon as William said you owned it, I knew who you were. I read an article about it years ago in a gardening magazine. I have a print of *Wild Marjoram* and all Jeffries' books and two of the original canvases illustrating alpine plants." Enid smiled disarmingly. *"Wild Marjoram* illustrates Marjorie Jeffries' life particularly well, don't you think? I mean she was rather wild when she was a young woman, involved in murder but, like marjoram itself, she relished the beauty and taste of life."

I was taken aback at the comparison. Enid asked me if I painted.

I told her I preferred sketching. "I used to write stories and illustrate them, but my life has taken a different path since then."

"And do you like the path you're travelling?"

I stared at her. "Actually, I find it quite daunting."

She put her hand on my arm. "You're a strong woman, you'll find a way to navigate the problems."

Mr Jolley got up. "I'll see to the picture now while you two have a chat." I sighed with relief as he passed the door and safely left the room.

I poured out another cup of tea for Enid. "You know, I had the impression earlier, when you were speaking about *Wild Marjoram,* that you knew my mother."

"Yes, we met in 1937 in Berlin." The words hung back as if she were reluctant to continue.

I waited patiently, and Enid went on slowly. "I was seventeen and already set on a career in horticulture. My father had arranged for me and my mother to travel round Germany and Austria to see the great gardens. While we were in Berlin in '37, my cousin, Sally, invited us to meet the painter MJ Ackert at the British Embassy in Wilhelmstraße. Sally's husband, David Delaney, was a legal attaché at the Embassy. We all met again the following year at the Exhibition of Fine Arts, a few months before Marjorie J Ackert changed her name to Jeffries and left Germany."

Her shoulders bobbed impulsively. "Marjorie was exhibiting two portraits and a painting of the Brandenburg Gate. I was immensely impressed with her interpretation of the *Friedenstor*. Such a big, heavy, Germanic sculpture with its four horses and Greek goddess. Marjorie had seen it shrouded in the hazy mist of a hot summer day and had softened the outline. Very impressionist! And then there were the two portraits."

"Who were the sitters?"

"One was a portrait of the British Ambassador in his naval uniform, looking very bull-doggy beside the furled Union flag, but the second was a sketch of her cousins. It was full of love and understanding."

Her words defined the painting so well I felt the tears prick at my eyes.

"Your mother and my mother became friendly and we invited Marjorie to stay with us in Rhyll in North Wales. She sketched my mother and David Delaney. I still have David's sketch, but Mother loaned her painting to a museum in Virginia."

I was amazed. Madge had shown me a photo of a woman standing beside a Welsh dresser. It seemed incredible that people I had met so recently were mixed up in the strange Norfolk nightmare I was living in.

"Such a pity Marjorie stopped painting portraits," Enid went on, "but Dieter Ackert must have been a big obstacle in her life. Perhaps she could no longer bear to look into the faces she was painting and see the truth. War, the act of violence, sullies everyone it touches." Her voice dropped suddenly. "Nothing is ever the same again."

I couldn't see my mother ever flinching from the truth, but the remark was disturbing. "Were you involved in the war?"

"I never talk about it." She looked up as her husband came into the room. Jolley was frowning. Enid started carrying the tea things over to the sink. I told her to leave everything. It would all go in the dishwasher later.

"My mother once told me the past was never far away," I said, "but more and more, I feel I hardly know her. Until very recently, I didn't even know she painted portraits."

"Then I'm right, she *was* hiding from the past." Enid had recovered from her dark thoughts. She had her back to me as she placed the tea things in the sink and I continued sketching her, noting how her short dark jacket accentuated her long back.

"We've met before," I said suddenly. "I remember sketching you!"

She turned round, looking astonished.

My pencil traced the gold band round the bottom of her jacket and a picture began forming in my mind. "A room was full of paintings. You were talking to a young man across the room. I was standing with my mother near a painting of a boat on the Thames." The long evening dress in dark blue silk had emphasised her heavy build. The memory-spike was growing stronger. "You were wearing a short, light-blue jacket and long blue evening gown." I hesitated as the picture blurred and then came back into focus. "My mother was talking to a man who didn't look well. And standing next to Mum was another man in evening dress with his wife." A stronger picture was forming in my mind. "It was the Summer Exhibition at the Royal Academy in Piccadilly."

It was 1963. I was twelve years old. I was wearing green sandals, short frilly white socks and a green and brown tunic with a stripey brown and red patchwork pocket. I could see it all so vividly.

I am standing next to my mum on a hot summer's evening in a room with a high ceiling with windows. There are all kinds of paintings, all kinds of sizes. The large room is filled with people in evening dress, people talking, endlessly talking, about paintings, about people.

It's a glittering occasion full of glamour pulsating to an incessant hum of conversation. I love the beautiful clothes and the string quartet playing Schubert. I want to skip and dance round the magnificent room, but I know Mum will send me home if I do, so I stand quietly beside her and pretend I'm dancing.

The man who looks ill greets Mum. "Good to see you, Marjorie. Last time we met was in '49, remember?"

"My first exhibition after the war," Mum says.

"You captured your father so well. History will acknowledge him." He nods soberly. "It was a privilege to have known him."

Mum is quiet, her lips tucked in at the corners. She always does that when she's upset. But why should she be upset with the big grey-haired man with the long upper lip and the sham smile that never reaches the cold brown eyes?

"We had our time in history, Sheldon, and it wasn't kind to Section 23. We lost too many agents and the traitor in our midst was never found."

Cold Eyes is Sheldon. He draws a thin smile with his lips and shifts his walking-stick to his left hand. "You were always clinical in your analysis, Marjorie. You forget there are people who are alive today because of us."

The skin on his face is drawn tightly round the sunken cheeks. He has a tremor in his right hand. I'm sketching him on my invisible pad. Mum says she's sorry he hasn't been well. Sheldon dismisses her regrets.

"But you're right about our time in history, Marjorie." His voice is quiet. "We were tested beyond human constraints and now we pay the price with our health."

With a curt nod he moves away and talks to a man in uniform. Waiters are circulating round the hall with glasses of wine on trays. Mum takes some red wine and the waiter hands me a tall glass of orange juice with ice, soda water, a slice of cucumber and a straw. The bubbles go up my nose and I sneeze. It's the first time I've had cucumber and soda water in orange juice. It tastes...different!

Two young men approach Mum. The one with wavy red hair is Callum Strachan. He points to the painting of two men in a skiff. "I've rowed a lot on that stretch of the Thames and you've captured the light beautifully."

They talk for a moment about the men in the skiff who will represent England in the Olympics.

Then his companion steps forward. "I got your note. I'm Arno Müller's nephew, James Mitchell."

James looks just like Heathcliff, dark, smouldering and dangerous.

Mum smiles. "I'm so glad to meet you at last." She feels inside her bag. "Arno wanted you to have this."

She gives him a small box. James opens it with an exclamation. I peer forward and James holds up a chain with gold links. "When did he give it to you?"

"Before Emden," Mum replies quietly.

James puts the chain round his neck. "I wanted to ask you about Arno. He and his wife brought me up when my parents died. I've recently been told he was a double-agent. I don't believe it, Mrs Denby. All I want is the truth. I would trust what you say."

Mum's face has closed in. "This is not the place, or the time, Mr Mitchell, but I'll say this: I never believed Arno was the traitor in Section 23. He was shot and captured on our last mission at Emden."

"But there are no records of what happened to him."

Mum looks up at him. "I still don't know the truth behind my father's death. In war not all deaths are signed off neatly by a coroner. Many simply 'disappeared'."

He nods. "The 'Vernebelt', I know, but—"

"What are you doing here, James?" Sheldon has come back, an angry scowl darkening his face.

Mum hesitates. "Mr Mitchell wants to know the truth about his uncle, Arno Müller."

"The truth?" Sheldon laughs harshly. "In war truth is grey and not always welcome." He frowns at James. "All we know for certain is that Arno was captured at Emden with Elèna. The writers they were escorting died on the pavement. Only Marjorie and her chemists survived the ambush. Within a few weeks we began receiving transmissions from Arno and on his advice we sent over forty agents into Holland. Later we learned that they had all been captured and murdered."

James steps forward, his hands clenched. "Do you believe he was turned?"

Sheldon shrugs. "All we know is that he disappeared. But Arno's not alone in suffering recriminations. Stefan Radevsky was convinced Jürgen Bergmann had betrayed him, and others thought you were the mole, Marjorie, and I know, yes, I know I was suspected as well."

"We all were," Mum responds quickly. "The loss of so many agents was a terrible blemish on Section 23. The past is always with us, Sheldon, that is the burden we bear."

Sheldon turns to James. "I'm told you're off to Rome tomorrow." His eyes narrow. "How did you get that gold chain?"

"I gave it to him, Sheldon. Arno wanted his nephew to have it."

Sheldon nods, his face sour, and walks away. Mum touches James's arm. "People will always have their doubts. I know, because many still have their suspicions about me."

James looks surly. He thanks Mum for the gold chain and walks away with Callum and they join a group of young people. Callum kisses a girl wearing a long slinky silver-green gown that shows all her curves. I wonder if they're lovers. I long to wear a dress like that. I sip my drink and sneeze again.

Sheldon comes back. "You think I was harsh with James, Marjorie, but he's young, he hasn't struggled in war." He bends closer to her. "Colonel North has arrived. Something's afoot. Did you hear he's head of WATID now? North tells me your husband was involved in an attack in Pforzheim near the end of the war."

Mum steps back. Her face is strained and her eyes have turned black. A man in a dark suit hurries up and gives Sheldon an envelope. Sheldon tears it open, his eyes skimming down the paper. He looks up. His voice is abrupt. "No message!" The courier turns like a soldier and marches quickly away.

"What is it, Sheldon?"

"This *is* why North is here." Sheldon taps the message. "It's unbelievable! Someone from the past has just turned up in West Berlin." He gives Mum the telegram. "They kept his name pretty quiet."

My eyes move between them. Their shoulders and necks are full of tension. My hand is busy sketching the tightened muscles as I hear her whisper, "Jürgen! Gott sei dank! Now, at last, we may learn what really happened."

Sheldon grunts. "Don't set your sights too high, Marjorie, the Soviets wouldn't have returned him if he had anything left to tell us. You can be sure they bled him dry."

Mum says the Russians only exchange the sick and the dying. "And we give them back working spies!"

"I hope Bergmann's not too sick," Sheldon said. "We'll want to interrogate him."

"Interrogate?" Mum is angry. "You should be laying down the red carpet for him!"

"Nonsense, Marjorie, we don't know what he's told them. A lot of people will want to kill him for fear of what he's said." He touches her arm lightly. "I can hardly believe the old bastard's bounced back over the Glienicke Bridge."

Mum is firm. "I hope he has the answers to some of our questions."

Sheldon shrugs. "We'll see. Enjoy the exhibition, my dear, that's why you're here."

Sheldon pats my shoulder and smiles as he moves away. I pull Mum's arm. "Can I have some more orange?"

She corrects me sharply. "May! May you have more orange!" She signals to a waiter who gives me another glass of the curious tasting orange-cucumber drink. Then we start walking round the room and Mum points out some of the paintings and tells me about them.

I ask her if she really painted portraits. "You only paint plants and things now."

"Questions, always questions, Kindchen?" Her voice is affectionate. She looks at me. I'm nearly as tall as Mum now. "The war, the past, changed everything. I changed. I wanted to learn more about plants, their colours and shapes and their importance in our world. And people began buying my canvases. That's what happened. Yes, Paula, that's how it happened."

A man and woman stop us. They congratulate Mum on her work. She is relaxed with them. Then Mum stops at a painting called Cityscape. She tries to explain what Richard Diebenkorn has done to create the picture. A couple join us and leave quickly. "That's Marjorie Ackert," I hear the man saying to his companion. "Her father was a Nazi."

His companion, an elderly woman with a long, cross face, says it's a disgrace Ackert is exhibiting. She's wearing a beautiful silk-patterned ivory-coloured shawl draped over her back and shoulders. I would do anything to own a shawl like that. I sketch it quickly. My friend Josie never fusses about clothes, but something deep inside me knows she's wrong. Clothes and colour define us, they influence what we do and how we think.

But when I try to explain this to Josie she says, "Balderdash! You don't have to get all dressed-up for slopping round the house." She's interested only in training for the Olympics.

Mum pulls me along quickly. "Don't stand there vacillating, child, it's getting late." She glances at her watch.

"What did they mean about the Nazis and why did they call you Ackert?"

She doesn't reply.

"Why isn't Daddy here?" I ask her.

"He didn't want to come."

Another waiter comes up with more drinks. At the same time two people stop and talk to us.

"I don't know if you remember, but we met at the Embassy in Wilhelmstraße before the war."

They shake hands. "Of course, I remember. You're David Delaney and you were very kind when we first came to London."

Mum is being gracious.

David brings his wife forward. She says, "I'm Rosa, David's second wife, and as you see we're expecting an addition to the family."

Mum congratulates her and quickly sketches Rosa on the back of an envelope she finds in her bag. It's a line drawing, almost a cartoon, but drawn with affection.

She signs it MJJ, London, RA 1963. David and Rosa are delighted. I've been sketching David on my invisible pad and now I draw Rosa. When I get home I'll draw them properly on paper.

David smiles. "My father and I had the privilege of meeting Dieter Ackert in 1930. Dad thought he'd changed a lot. Everyone was hoping Ackert would become president after Hindenburg and the '32 election. It was devastating when he was shot."

Sheldon re-joins us with Colonel North. North has thin peppery-brown hair combed sideways over his head. He is shorter than David Delaney and Sheldon, but when he speaks everyone turns and listens.

The Colonel shakes hands with Mum. "It's been a long time, Marjorie, but I had to come and see your work. Sheldon tells me you've heard the news about Bergmann."

Delaney looks surprised. "Jürgen Bergmann?"

Sheldon answers him. "You've not heard? Bergmann's in West Berlin. The details will be on your desk when you get back to the Foreign Office."

A curious expression comes over David's face. I can't read what he's thinking. He turns and introduces Peppery-Hair to his wife. "The Colonel was in overall control of our agents in North Europe during the war."

Rosa clasps her hands. "Oh, a master spy!"

I like Rosa, she says what she means, but everyone else looks embarrassed.

"It's good to meet you again, Delaney," the Colonel says. "I knew your father when he was at the Embassy in Wilhelmstraße. I heard you talking about Ackert just now, and you're right, Germany needed a strong man with vision. Many hoped Ackert would be that man, but by January 1931 there was a hint, nothing more at the time, that Ackert had a secret plan. He never confided it to me."

Mum says sharply, "I never knew about a secret plan!"

We have to move back to allow a group of people to stand in front of The Rowers on the Thames. After a while they move on and another group takes their place. It's a moment or two before I pick up the conversation.

"You were too young, Marjorie," Colonel North is saying. "He would never have involved you but, in my opinion, Ackert was too insular a man to fit into

Nazi idealism. I gained the impression he was building his own party. Of course he would have kept that carefully under wraps before going public. Then there were rumours that the Nazis themselves didn't trust him."

Sheldon agrees. "From that moment, Ackert was targeted. I don't know what he was doing on the march, but it was foolish to be so prominent. Whoever had it in for him had the perfect opportunity to get rid of him. And the police, who were very jittery, opened fire at one point. Later that day Rik van der Vendt was arrested, but neither he nor the police had anything to do with it. The Nazis shot Ackert, there's no doubt about it."

Colonel North seems less sure. "I knew the police chief, Hans Falk. He was well placed to know the facts. His men had orders not to shoot Ackert under any circumstances, and there were witnesses who swore they heard shots coming from a different direction. Falk always believed the communists executed Ackert and Adler Schiffer." He pauses and glances at Mum. "But I think there was a conspiracy. The country was in crisis. Dieter Ackert upset a lot of people, Marjorie. Behind the charm he could be abrasive and difficult. You must face the truth, he made a lot of enemies. It could have been anyone who fired the shot, but the outcome brought dividends for the Nazis.

"They immediately claimed Ackert and Schiffer as martyrs to the cause of National Socialism and they hoped the conspiracy, and Ackert's secret plan, would die with him. Of course, when Van der Vendt threatened to reveal the truth, the nightmare started up again.

Sheldon breaks in. "We still don't know who murdered Van der Vendt."

"We shall never know."

Mum is bitter. "Conspiracies were everywhere, it was only the truth that was absent. In the beginning I thought the mole in Section 23 was someone in the Foreign Office. Later I thought there was another explanation. When I became part of a new unit, I told the Colonel of my suspicions."

North nods. He has sharp features like an eagle and he has kept his figure. Dad is always talking about keeping his figure.

Sheldon frowns. "What unit was that?"

The Colonel says it was a small group set up in late 1942. "We were chasing shadows in Belfast. Irish loyalties were complex and diverse."

"You mean Hannagan and the bombings?"

"Hannagan's still alive. He's a very dangerous man, and very good at killing." North turns to Mum. "Now that Bergmann's in West Berlin we should learn more. In fact I'm leaving for Bonn tomorrow."

Mum looks up. "You'll be speaking with Jürgen?"

He nods and shakes hands, including mine, and hurries away. Mum is frowning.

David Delaney looks troubled. "He's a difficult man to read."

Sheldon moves closer to Mum and I hear him whisper, "North was on a fishing trip. Did he find the fish he was baiting?"

Mum is concerned. "I don't know."

A waiter comes up and says something to David. He turns to his wife. "Forgive me, darling, something's come up."

We all turn. David is making his way over to a middle-aged woman who appears to be arguing with James Mitchell. She has her back to me, but I start sketching her figure in the blue evening dress with its box jacket. Mitchell is pulling away, shaking his head. David's wife looks ill. "Baby's coming!" she gasps. "I'm going to be sick!"

Mum says the room is too hot and sends me to find a chair while one of the waiters hurries across the room to bring David back to Rosa. I'm excited at the thought of seeing a baby born. Will it just drop out? Will it start crying? Sheldon and North shuffle away muttering, "Take care! Good luck!"

Rosa and her husband leave before I can find a free chair and I never see the baby. Everyone begins to leave and I'm bundled into a taxi. Before Mum gets in, she hears her name being called across the pavement.

She waves. "I'm coming!"

She tells me to wait in the taxi. I watch her run across the road and disappear into the mêlée of beautiful gowns and dinner jackets moving like dancers round each other. I get out of the taxi to get a clearer view. Mum is talking with the darkly handsome James. I turn and see Callum Strachan. He's near a street lamp. It gives an aura over his red hair. His companion is the pretty girl in the clinging gown. Callum is waving for a taxi. Mum and James run over to them. There is a flash of light near my shoulder and Callum collapses onto the pavement.

A man wearing a black jacket, with a black hood over his head, is leaning against the back of my taxi. He hasn't seen me. He raises his left hand and I *glimpse a rifle. He's preparing to fire again. There are shouts. People are running towards us. I press myself against the taxi, too frightened to cry out.*

The man with the gun is walking away. He mixes with the crowd coming from the other direction. I see Mum running towards me. She's frightened and angry because I'm on the pavement. She pushes me quickly into the taxi and shouts at the driver to take me home. I look out of the back window as the driver accelerates. The gunman is flagging down a taxi. I'm sure he's coming after me. He thinks I can identify him, but all I saw was a man with a gun and a black hood over his head.

I'm so relieved to see Dad when I get home. I try to tell him what happened. He wants to give me my bedtime chocolate milk drink, but I'm still frightened and I revert to the familiar baby names. "Mama went to see a friend, Dadda, and there was a man with a hood." I'm giving little gasps as I speak. "He was standing behind my taxi. Mama and James were running towards Callum. I saw the flash from the gun as Callum moved in front of James. Then Callum fell onto the pavement." I look up. "Who was the man shooting at? Mama or James or Callum?"

Dad takes my mug and holds me close. "Well, what do you think?"

I explain the angle of the gun. I've learned a lot at the shooting club. "I think Callum got in the way. The hooded man was trying to shoot either James or Mama. Then the man with the gun got into a taxi and, Dadda, I thought he was going to chase me and shoot me as well."

"Did he see you?"

I shake my head vigorously, rubbing my forehead against his jacket. "No, Dadda, he had a hood over his head, a black hood. He couldn't see me and I didn't see his face."

Dad gives me my chocolate drink again and I tell him about a man called Ackert who was killed by the Nazis. Dad frowns. "I know all about Ackert and he's not important. You being in bed and asleep when your mother gets back, now that's important. No more talking, honey, it's lights out."

And the room falls into the warm safe blanket of darkness that wraps itself round a sleeping child.

The memory-spike was dying and I was surfacing back into the present. My mind stirred uneasily. I didn't want to leave yet…something Mum had said. It was important. It was gone. Someone was shaking my arm.

"Are you all right, Paula? You've seemed so distant the last few minutes." Enid's uncertain smile met my unfocussed eyes. Enid's jacket and James Mitchell had been the triggers into a hall filled with paintings.

I reached out to Enid, talking quickly. "There was a man, tall with greying hair and cold eyes. Sheldon Asquith. And David Delaney and his wife. She was pregnant. And you were there, at the Exhibition, arguing with James Mitchell. Later, his friend, Callum, was shot dead."

She stepped back. "My goodness, you're as direct as your mother! How do you remember all that?"

I asked her what she had been talking about with Mitchell. She was guarded. "Mitchell? I don't remember the name, but yes, I was at the exhibition. It was a great social event. I remember speaking with the president of the Academy and some of his guests. I don't remember seeing you at all, but David and Rosa were there." She laughed ruefully. "I love art exhibitions. I was at one in Berlin when I fell in love."

She was leading me away from Mitchell. I wondered why she had lied. I knew I wasn't mistaken, that head-bobbing was very memorable, and so was the straight line of her shoulders and the wide flat back. I smiled. "Did anything come of it?"

"There's nothing like your first love. I was very young, and the path I was on was full of sunshine in a world full of shadows. It was bewildering and magical."

I felt a lingering regret that I hadn't experienced anything of the magic of love with Richard, but it was not an answer to my question.

"What happened to him?" I probed.

"The war happened. The war changed everything. After all, you shouldn't fall in love with the enemy." Enid stopped suddenly. "Goodness, I'm rambling! I've never spoken about that time to anyone before." She looked searchingly at me. "There's something of the unnatural about you." She smiled uncertainly. "But returning to Marjorie, I met her again when I was in Ireland."

"In *Ireland*?" I echoed.

"In 1944. I was there collecting seeds and plants for my master's degree. I'd already decided on building a bank of seeds for the future. Marjorie said she was lecturing in Dublin at the university. I thought she was running away from the war."

I struggled for a moment to express the words I didn't want to say. "Was my mother a Nazi?"

Enid looked at me quizzically. "Well, she *was* the daughter of Dieter Ackert, but if you want my opinion, I always saw her as an honest person, perhaps too uncompromisingly honest at times."

"Uncompromising" pointed to a difficult person, one who might make enemies. Enid smiled. "You have an unusual memory! How do you recall things after all these years?"

"It's just a quirky thing. And I can't remember anything until something triggers the process of recall. But what interests me is my mother. I'm trying to find out more about her. She died just before I was sixteen. It's really helpful meeting people who knew her."

But instead of understanding Mum better, I was getting more and more confused. Nor did I find Enid Jolley easy to read. She was a self-contained woman, wrapped up in her work with the steely resolve that goes with making that work successful. Not a person to get close to, despite all the head waggling. Then Mr Jolley came into the kitchen and told us the picture was up and we went into the sitting room.

"What an intimate portrait!" Enid exclaimed. "It's the same as light and shade in a flower border, the scent is intensified and grows muskier through the brushwork."

She stepped nearer. "Who painted her?" She looked at the bottom of the portrait. Her voice trailed away. I could almost hear her thinking, *Wasn't that the man she ran off with?*

"Van der Vendt, now wasn't he murdered? And Marjorie was involved." She lowered her hand. "Yes, yes, a tragedy that he died. He was very good. Look at the detail on the daisies in her hair. *Bellis perennis* is the formal name. Such an interesting flower for the artist to choose. Chaucer called it 'the eye of the day'. It represents purity and innocence." She turned to me. "Was Marjorie happy?"

I raised my eyebrows. "She wasn't happy at the end of her life. There were problems, arguments and she wasn't well. I told you she kept dropping things. It made her sad. It's hard for a child to understand what's going on." I hesitated. "And the passage of time hasn't made it easier."

Enid frowned. "Marjorie wouldn't have liked feeling vulnerable."

Mr Jolley picked up his bag of tools. "I'll just take these out to the car. Be back in a minute."

I thanked Enid for coming and talking about my mother.

"You've made me remember," she said slowly. "It's true, the past is always there, in the shadows of a room, in the dark corners of the mind." She looked at me, frowning. "I suspect Marjorie recognised those shadows. There's a lot of Marjorie in you, Paula. It will be interesting to see where the paths in your life take you."

And where the shadows destroy you. Had she whispered those words? Or had I plucked them from my heart?

Jolley came back and helped his wife into her coat. "I told you my wife knew a lot about plants. Did I tell you she's a professor of plant ecology at the university?"

I was reproachful. "No, you did not. I wouldn't have dreamt of asking her to come round to see my little yard."

"But you're wrong!" Enid's interruption was swift and passionate. "It's the *little* gardens that count. All the people who love their own small plot of lawn and plants and shrubs, *they* are the people who really matter. They keep the love of gardening alive, and incidentally, keep *us* alive and breathing. Did you know that Voltaire said we must cultivate our gardens? You have only to think of the Chelsea Flower Show and all the interest in the small gardens they create."

Inspired by her words, I invited them to my birthday lunch on the sixth of June. Secretly, I hoped I would learn more about my mother.

"Sorry, Mrs James, I'll be busy, but Enid can come." Jolley turned to his wife and after a short hesitation, she nodded.

"Twelve-thirty all right?"

She nodded again, and I noticed how the tension in her shoulders had increased. I wished now I hadn't suggested it. Mr Jolley put his coat on and I offered to write him a cheque for putting the picture up, but he refused and thanked me for the tea. At the front door, Enid bent down and picked up a postcard lying on the mat.

"That's Ranworth Broad near Wroxham. We went there recently to visit the wildfowl centre. It's well worth a trip."

I took the postcard quickly. After waving them goodbye, I turned the card over. I was glad Enid hadn't read the message on the back: *Stan's dead, murdered. If you want to live, Mrs James, give us the Pforzheim miniatures. We know you and your father have them.*

164

In my head, I heard my mother shouting Stan's name at my father. But who was Stan? There was no signature, no way of getting in touch, no way to stop the persecution. I didn't have the miniatures. I knew my father wasn't alive.

In the kitchen, I took the other postcards out of my bag:

Why did you come to Norwich?

We know you came to Norwich to meet Denby.

The postcard from the Norwich Art Gallery.

And now the *Stan* card.

The postcards were alarming, the anonymity disturbing and threatening. I wondered who was behind them. And there was another question: why had Enid lied about speaking to James Mitchell?

Saturday, 30th May 1981

I had a phone call at eight in the morning from the Norwich office. "Mary's sick, could you take over at Swaffham?"

I drove down under a drizzly grey sky with a migraine throbbing on the left side of my head. On arrival at the sales office, I was pleased to find I was on my own. I made some weak tea, took some more migraine tablets and waited for customers. Three people turned up and looked round. They came back to the sales house saying very little and went away again. Four people telephoned and I made appointments for Tuesday afternoon. I wandered over to the map on the wall. There were more initials on the little flags. MA, that was Mary Andrews. She had sold three flats.

I walked back to the table feeling the usual sickness and giddiness that comes with migraine. Unlike some sufferers who go to bed and close the curtains, I have always kept working, determined not let the migraine master me; but today I couldn't wait to get home.

A little later Corrie came breezily into the room, her cheerfulness grating on me. "They sent me down to help out, it's always busier at weekends. That's great news Trish Porter comin' here on Monday! She hasn't always backed Sellick, he mess up on some things." Her voice reached me from the kitchen where she was hanging up her coat and bag. "But it's deeper'n that, it's personal with her. If she give us a good write-up, that'll be great for Dunham Village." She poked her head round the door. "I'll make some coffee and you can tell me all about Monday."

165

I told her I'd prefer tea to coffee. I gave her the news as I sipped the tea. "Trish said she might add the Village to her 'Around East Anglia' series. What did you mean by 'personal' just now?"

"Trish Porter's Jewish and there were stories about Sellick and the South African Nazi Party in the war. Lawrie Heals tell us Doug like all the banners and uniforms and that, but I never hear him say anythin' against the Jews, and I've known him all my life. He's a good bloke, Doug is, but people lost a packet on the Lincoln project. That's why Dunham Village is movin' slowly." Corrie peered up at me. "You don't look so good, Paula."

"Migraine," I said tersely.

"Go home, I'll look after everything."

"Are you sure?"

"'Course I am!"

I had just picked up my bag when Doug Sellick walked through the door and came up to my table.

"I knew from the moment I saw you that you had drive and ambition, and by God, I was right!" Sellick gave me another welcome cheque and explained it was for the articles and arranging for the editor of the Gazette to go round the Village.

"I'll be here Monday. The Gazette's carried a few adverts of the Retirement Homes, but this is the first time Porter's stepped out of her office for us. I'm here today because we've run into a bit of a problem." He turned to Corrie. "I'll pop in later and we'll talk then." He bent down and muttered something.

Corrie looked pleased. "Ted'll be ever so glad."

Sellick turned to me. "OK, get your things, we're going down to the old church."

I went into the kitchen to get my coat from the back of the door. As I was reaching to get the coat, a wave of nausea swept over me. I waited a moment until it passed, found some tablets in my bag and swallowed a couple with some water. I heard Sellick calling me impatiently. Sellick wouldn't pander to illness.

I got in the buggy and he drove down to a corner of the Village where the last large clearance of land was taking place. En route I could see that the builders had redoubled their efforts. Sellick pointed out that many of the properties on the east and west side of the golf course were in the process of being finished.

I saw Goodison practising his putting in his garden. He waved as we passed by. Turning sharply right, Sellick followed a lane down to a derelict church and an old graveyard. He waved his arm. "There's the reason for the hold-up."

An excavator was working on the site removing earth and putting it to one side. The place seemed to be filled with people. To the right was an angry group waving placards and chanting: "Save our old church!" and "Stop the desecration!" A policeman was standing nearby. Opposite were two caravans, and in front of them were people working at the graves.

We got out of the buggy, my head throbbing from the bumpy ride. Sellick seized my arm. "Look round, Mrs James, the graveyard hasn't been used since the 1850s, and the church is in a poor state, but there are still people who protest against development on what they describe as 'sacred' ground. Protesting is an English disease. I've told them no houses will be built here. We have to keep the church because it's a protected building, but we need the old cemetery for roads leading to Peterborough and Norwich. Any land left over will be grassed or planted with flowering shrubs. And I've ordered a memorial to be placed here. It'll record the history of the church and any names we find on the coffins."

I asked if anyone knew the history. His response was immediate. "The curator at the local museum knows all about it. The church was built in 1426 for a thriving mediæval town with an agricultural community. They did well until Old Ironsides, worst disaster this country's ever known in my opinion, sent in his troops in the Civil War. They broke up the church altar and reduced the town to a hamlet with a few farms, and over the years the church crumbled away until now it's just an empty shell."

He tapped my arm. "Ah, here's the man who can explain it better. We met during the war and he's really made something of his life since then."

A big, good-looking man in his early sixties greeted us with a wave. Bob Stevens was wearing jeans and a blue open-neck shirt. Half-moon glasses were sticking out of the top pocket of his dark blue jacket.

I asked him why he hadn't simply bypassed the churchyard.

"Two reasons. We didn't want a cemetery on the edge of a village for elderly folk, and we need space for the main A47 road. I don't know what all the fuss is about, there's been no Christian service here for over a hundred years." His voice had a rough edge, but was not unpleasant. "Of course, we'll keep what's left of the church and bend the road round it. English Heritage have agreed to that."

Stevens waved towards the caravans. "Over there are church officials and council officers. We always work closely together and everything is done with dignity and respect. This isn't the first time old burial places have been moved. When Thomas Hardy was an architect in 1867 he designed a road through a graveyard. The Church have already designated a place where the bones will be re-interred with a full Christian ceremony."

I looked at the protesters who were waving their placards. "Why do they worry about people who were buried so long ago?"

"They want the dead to sleep quietly, or maybe they're reminded of their own mortality. It's easier when nobody remembers who were buried in these old sites, but these are local people and their past history touches their lives." Stevens smiled. "But let me take you round the site and you can see for yourself how we're dealing with the problems." He looked at me. "You're not squeamish, are you?"

I was paler than usual because of the throbbing migraine. I said I had a cold and sore throat. Stevens grunted. "You shouldn't be wearing high heels on a building site." I pointed out that I hadn't expected to be on a building site. He shrugged.

We walked over to a half-dug grave where some archaeology students from Cambridge University were carefully moving back the soil. Their tutor explained they would be taking some of the bones back to Cambridge for the study of diseases from the fifteenth century.

Stevens pointed to a pile of boxes lying on plastic sheets. "We use these boxes for bones in case we have to replace any coffins. The council and the local Church insist we keep exact records. Not all the graves have headstones, because the poor, and those who died in plagues, were just thrown into a pit. When they're buried again we'll erect a pillar and inscribe on it all the names and dates we can find, and that will be part of our social history."

As we walked over the site, I saw a priest talking to the group of local men and women. Stevens nodded. "Digging up old graveyards is happening all over the country. A railway line, a road or airport is needed, so they've got to dig to build, and there's less and less space for the living and the dead. Mind you, re-siting old graves isn't as grim now as it used to be. The bones don't get dumped in an ossuary or charnel house. They're either re-interred or the scientists want 'em."

"And you build your rail track, your new arterial road or retirement homes," I responded drily.

Stevens shrugged. We walked over to where a student was gently removing top soil with a small hoe. Two more students were waiting with brushes and trowels. Their task was to clean the coffins and make a note of the names and dates of birth and death.

Sellick was telling Stevens I had only recently joined the firm, but Stevens frowned and held up his hand. "Wait!"

One of the students kneeling by a grave had shouted something. The hoe swept across the soil again.

Again, the student shouted urgently. He began to move the soil quickly aside with both hands revealing the body of a small child in the scooped out cradle of earth, his legs bent awkwardly, the side of his face stained with dried blood, the fair curly hair darkened by the soil. A light-blue tee-shirt and blue cotton shorts were his shroud. Socks and shoes were missing. No coffin, not even a box, no quiet sleep for him. I felt the shock of his open eyes. This body had not long been in the ground.

Sellick was visibly shaken. He pulled me down as he bent over the small corpse. "Look, the poor bugger's had his head bashed in." He stood up. "D'you know what this means?" He shook my shoulder impatiently. "It means murder. That means the police."

"And that means the digging has to stop," Stevens added dourly.

Sellick scowled at me. "D'you know how much it costs to build a road? A fortune! And stoppages cost a double bloody fortune."

But all I heard was *murder!* The word screamed inside my head and the memory spikes shot up: Amy dying. Callum falling. The stranger bleeding on the yellow flagstones. The knife glinting in the sun. My head throbbed. I was suddenly cold. And then I was sick. Stevens looked at me dispassionately. "I knew you'd be squeamish."

He called the policeman and a priest over and told them to stay by the dead child. Sellick pulled me away, his voice harsh. "Go home, and don't broadcast what's happened. I'll stay with Stevens and wait for the police. The child was probably local. They'll soon find out who did it."

I drove the buggy back to the office. I told Corrie what had happened. "That's shockin'," she said. "*Shockin'*! And you look *awful*, Paula."

She wanted to make me a coffee, but I told her I'd be sick again. I was quietly desperate. "I just want to get home."

I lay down on my beautiful blue leather sofa with a bottle of mineral water, a supply of migraine tablets and a packet of plain biscuits. I wanted to close my eyes and sleep and let the tablets do their job, but I could not rid my mind of the image of the dead child, his open, lifeless eyes, the congealed blood on his head wound. A local child, Sellick had said.

I knew from my time with Selwyn Freeman that the investigation would begin with painstaking house to house enquiries to find the child's identity and his parents. There would be a compilation of statements, meetings with the Social Services, the arrest of the perpetrator of the crime and finally, trial, conviction and imprisonment. I thought I'd left it all behind. I leaned back, feverish, my head throbbing. And suddenly, painfully, the suppressed memory of the death of my child surfaced.

Just over a year ago, I had been over two months pregnant. I hadn't told Richard. I couldn't understand at the time why I held back, but I had felt nervous, uncertain how he would take the news.

It was a bright Sunday morning in April 1980. I was alone in our London flat while Richard was having another "catching up on work at the office" day. It was about ten when I felt piercing pains and cramp, then shock, vomiting and a rush of blood and placenta from the vagina. Somehow, I got myself to my feet and cleaned up the debris of what should have been my baby. I consoled myself by thinking that the uterus had evicted the foetus because it was damaged, but the rest of me wept for the baby I had wanted. The bleeding lasted all day and the pain would not stop. I phoned Richard and asked him to bring a Chinese take-away home. I couldn't face cooking or eating a meal. Later that evening, I told Richard what had happened.

"Is it…all over?" His voice was thin. His features had tightened into a blank withdrawal. I felt no warmth from him, no reaching out to hold me close. He never referred to the loss of our child again. That night I slept in the spare room, saying I was feeling sore, which was true; sore and drained and sad, and the bleeding wouldn't stop.

I continued to feel unwell and the next day, I had a high fever, a horrible smelling discharge and an infection. The doctor sent me to hospital where I had a dilation and curettage. They kept me in overnight. In the morning, I waited for Richard to come and drive me home. In the end, I took a taxi.

As I opened the door of our flat, I knew at once it was empty. There is something cold and echoing about an empty place. Everything belonging to Richard had gone. Propped up on the kitchen table was a note. He had sold the flat. The new owners were taking possession the following week. Neatly attached to the note with a pin was a cheque. In the note, Richard explained that the cheque represented my half of the value of the flat, of my home. The letter was signed 'R'. No goodbye, no thanks for the good times, regrets for the bad, a short, cold, chilling statement signed with an initial. There was a postscript: *Leave the keys on the kitchen table.*

I had had no idea he was selling the flat. It had all been done behind my back over several weeks. The deception was like a savage blow. I wondered if I had any legal recourse to stop the sale, but what would that have achieved? Richard no longer wanted to share his life with me, and there was a child, a child he wanted. My marriage was over. The next day I packed my things, leaving instructions with the caretaker to send the removal crates on when I could give him an address. Then I took the train to Norwich.

There had been no time to mourn the loss of my child. Until now. I sat on my sofa and let the tears fall unchecked. I had kidded myself that I had dealt with my miscarriage, with Richard's infidelity, the divorce and the loneliness. There had been no emotional breakdown, no self-pity, only lethargy and an inner despair. I had hoped that by moving away from London and changing my job, changing my life, the pain and deceit would be put behind me.

I remembered the sense of relief when I was on the train to Norwich. But now I wanted to escape again, away from my dead baby and the chilling note on the kitchen table, away from the moment the grave had opened and revealed a child's broken body, away from the face in the shadows and the threat of a bullet through my head. But where would I run? Even in my dreams, there was nowhere to hide.

That night, the faceless man stepped out of the shadows. His voice echoed eerily round the bedroom. *I know she's dying*, he said. I whispered back to the darkness. "But *how* do you know she's dying?"

The question was important. I *knew* it was important, but my mind was like a cryptogram, and though memory kept trying to decode the message, the pathways were so ragged and the brain so incoherent, the clues to the code were obscured. I pulled myself up and packed the pillows behind my back.

I had thought Amy was the woman who was dying, but now I questioned that assumption. Amy had died brutally, her blood staining her blouse and the rug. Somewhere in my mind, I began to search for another woman who was dying, but the shutter snapped down and the shadows merged with the night.

I put the bedside light on to disperse the pricking, taunting phantoms and dozed fitfully until the early morning sun glimmered through the window.

171

I had a shower and a cup of tea and some tablets. The migraine was better, but as usual there was still a dark shadow aching behind my forehead. I phoned Trish Porter at her home and told her what I knew about the child in the scooped-out grave. The facts were already on the television and radio. The two-year old boy had been battered to death by the latest boyfriend of a young, inadequate mother. His explanation when questioned? "The kid wouldn't stop crying, so I shut him up."

The mother had carried her child's dead body over to the abandoned graveyard and had scraped out a space on top of a grave with her hands and covered the little body with earth. Did she leave the brute who had murdered her child? Or did fear hold her back, or a perverted loyalty restrain her? The due processes of law were set in motion, but the depressing fact remained—the boyfriend would be out of prison in a few years and would probably be "shutting up" the child of another partner.

Heals had rung me late on Saturday asking me to stand in for Mary on Sunday morning. I was about to leave for Swaffham when the doorbell rang and a man in blue dungarees told me he'd come about the boiler.

I looked at him blankly.

He explained impatiently that he serviced the boiler every year at the end of May for Captain Dalton.

I frowned. "I understand he's in Australia."

"That's right, Mrs James. That's why I've got a chit from his solicitor, Careless-Adams. Here it is."

"Carless-Adams," I corrected. "Yes, but—"

"I come every year," he began again.

I was firm. "But it's Sunday."

"I always come on a Sunday. I work for Eastern Boilers, see, but I do the boilers special for the captain on the last Sunday in May for a special rate."

"Oh! Well, I can't afford to have the boiler serviced, I've only recently moved in."

"Yeah, that's right." He was very determined. "That's what the captain said, that's why he wants me to put in new safe boilers. Read the chit, you'll see it's pukka."

The piece of folded paper confirmed what he was saying. Both boilers had to be changed and as the property was still legally in Captain Dalton's name, the work had to be done. It added that the heating engineer, Dwayne Raynier, had already been paid for the work.

Dwayne nodded. "If I can come in and just see the boiler before I go upstairs?"

Resigned, I stood aside, and he went straight to the kitchen. He was in his fifties, brisk and cheerful. There was a lively beat to his step. He told me he came from the Caribbean.

"I joined the army."

I asked him if he'd been back home.

"Nah, don't think I'd like the heat now."

He looked into the sitting room as he passed the door. "You've changed things, much more homey-looking." He saw my surprise. "Like I said, I used to look after the boilers when the captain lived here."

He opened the door that housed the boiler. "Look, this is an early type. Things have improved since I put this in. The captain said you gotta have a safe boiler, an' he's right. And the new ones are more efficient, so you can save up to a hundred pounds a year. Now that's worth considering, isn't it, specially if money's tight, like you say. An' I tell you what, I'll put a couple of shelves up in the cupboard when I've finished and you can keep your ironing there."

"That's very kind, but how much will *that* cost?"

"No worries there, Mrs James. The captain's paid for the work already. He lived in this flat for years. He said he felt responsible."

I was hesitant. "Well, it's very generous, but—"

Dwayne swept on. "He can afford it, he's well off. No worries there."

Perhaps I worry more than Dwayne and Captain Dalton. "Phone Careless-Adams," Dwayne said finally. "He'll tell you it's OK. His home number's on the chit."

Carless-Adams sounded only vaguely annoyed at being disturbed at home early on a Sunday morning. He said Captain Dalton had been in touch with him. "Both boilers have to be changed and Captain Dalton has paid in advance for the work to be done. You'll find the engineer very helpful."

I thanked him and put the phone down. I asked Dwayne if he had to do the work today.

"That's right, today. My mate's bringing the new boilers so we'll start upstairs and then come down and put the new boiler in for you. I'll have to put the water off at the mains for a bit, so you'd better fill the kettle if you want to make coffee."

"How are you going to get into the upstairs flat?"

"No worries there, I got a key. If all goes well, I'll be down after lunch."

"Look, I have to be out this morning. I may not be back when you've finished upstairs."

"That's OK! I got a key for this flat too." He felt in his pocket and showed me both keys. "The captain gave me the keys so I could always get in if there was an emergency, like."

I was concerned. I didn't like all these keys belonging to someone I didn't know.

I tried to explain and Dwayne said, "Look, Mrs James, the captain'll have my balls if I don't do the job properly!"

He was earnest, but Dwayne was a stranger and I phoned the solicitor again. This time Carless-Adams was quite acerbic. "Mrs James, everything has been arranged by Captain Dalton. I must remind you that the house is still legally in his name. He has told me that Dwayne is thoroughly reliable. *You are in good hands.*"

The words were heavily stressed. I mentioned the keys. The crisp tone was reinforced with a distinctly frosty edge. "Many workmen have keys to homes where they do work on a contractual basis. Again, I assure you, you have nothing to worry about. *It has all been arranged, Mrs James.*" He sounded really annoyed.

I should have stuck to my guns and told Dwayne and Carless-Adams I'd have the work done another day, but my cautious inner voice held me back. The house was not yet mine. Suppose the boiler blew up on Monday? Where would I stand then? I worry too much, but I would worry even more if the work were left undone. So I thanked Carless-Adams, nodded tersely to Dwayne and drove to Dunham Village.

I was hoping Sunday would be busier than the weekdays. I arrived at the sales office at a quarter to nine and sorted through the newspapers. Head office phoned and told me Corrie Smiley would be coming down early and would take over the afternoon shift.

I went into the kitchen and made some tea. In the next half-hour, twelve people came in. Four were interested in purchasing bungalows, two wanted apartments and the others wanted to look round. It took a couple of hours to sort everything out, but in the end, I sold two bungalows.

Corrie came at two and I left and drove home, taking the cash and paying-in books with me. I'd go to the bank tomorrow. I got home and found a message on my kitchen table. *I need some parts and will be back on Monday about ten.*

I had a sandwich and a cup of tea, but I felt restless. Yesterday, another leaflet had come about properties in Damgate Lane. I decided I should face the demons from the past and go down the lane to the cottage. I reminded myself I had been a child when the man came to tea and died in our garden. Perhaps I would understand better what had happened if I went to Yorkstone Cottage and tried to see it through adult eyes. Picking up my jacket, I got in the car and drove to Acle.

I drew up outside Yorkstone Cottage in Damgate Lane. It was such a strange feeling to see it again. Childhood! What a mixed blessing it is! I walked slowly over to the low wooden gate. The cottage looked just the same, sitting comfortably within the green lawn and flowered garden. The regal lilac-blue lavender hedge, Loddon Blue, looked splendid and well cared for. Jeffries had used *Lavender Angustifolia* and its aromatic blue foliage for the cover of her book on lavenders. I looked over the gate. I wondered who was living in the cottage now. In my mind I saw the two deep comfortable armchairs, the sofa and the Welsh side-board, the love-spoons with our names, and the large chestnut dining table and chairs by the windows.

Over the hedge at the bottom of the garden was Brownleas, the house where Bobby, the lively black and white springer spaniel, had lived with his owner, Mrs Lacey. I hadn't seen Bobby since that last visit to Yorkstone Cottage when I was fifteen and Bobby was two. It all seemed such a long time ago.

I was standing by the gate when a man came towards me walking past the bushy lavender hedge. I stepped back.

"Why, it's Gerry Scott!" He was wearing a black bomber jacket and jeans and looked very different from the man in the white milkman's coat, but he was easily recognisable by the way he walked. "I was told you'd gone back to Cambridge."

He opened the gate and I heard the familiar squeak as it swung to. "Surprised to see you here, Mrs James."

"I used to stay in this cottage during school holidays."

"That must 'a been nice." He walked over to a white van parked nearby and drove off.

I had been as surprised to see Scott as he had been to see me. In our short conversation, he had said absolutely nothing. I leaned on the gate peering up the path and in that moment, I decided to face my fears. The last time I had seen the flagstones by the front door they had been covered with blood. I had glimpsed them recently in one of my freak memory storms.

Slowly, because fear can only be slowly overcome, I pushed the gate open and walked up the winding path bordered with lavender. Before I turned the corner I paused, catching my breath as the heady fragrance of lavender settled on my chest. I moved forward, my legs heavy, my breathing laboured. I was fearful that time had not washed the blood away, but the yellow flagstones held only the inert form of a black and white springer spaniel stretched out in sleep in the sun.

Tentatively, I whispered his name. "Bobby?" My heels rang on the paving stones as I stepped closer. He opened his eyes and raised his head, the white spot above his nose catching the sunshine.

I was delighted. "It *is* Bobby!" Bobby was an old dog now, his muzzle grey, his eyes a little sunken, his eyebrows standing out white against the black fur on his face. He struggled to get up, his back legs weak, but his tail was weaving a loving greeting.

I knelt down, putting my shoulder-bag on the stones. "Hello, old friend, what are *you* doing here?"

He put his nose in my hand and snuggled closer. I stroked him, gently pulling his ears in answer to his soft grunts. "And do you know, Bobby, meeting *you* is the best thing that's happened to me for a very long time."

I was startled by a voice behind me. "And it's the best thing that's happened to Bobby!"

I stood up quickly and met the serene gaze of Mrs Anna Lacey from Brownleas. She was still slim, dressed in a simple but expensive frock, plain jacket and brogues, a double string of pearls round her neck.

"How lovely to see you and Bobby!" I bent and stroked him. "I feel fifteen again. Bobby was a puppy when we first met and he must have been nearly two when my mother died."

And my world fell apart.

Fifteen, playing with Bobby and the two Siskin sisters near the lavender bushes, while a man was murdered and the flagstones turned from yellow to red. The lavender was so strong I gasped as the scent filled my lungs.

Mrs Lacey let her eyes run over me. "You haven't changed much over the years, Paula. A little older, just as self-contained." Her voice was sharp. "And a little battle-tested, perhaps."

I was surprised she hadn't said "battle-scarred". She pointed to my bag. "The daffodil on your bag is most beautifully stitched."

"I bought it for the hope and renewal of life the daffodil might bring."

"A lovely thought." The scarcely noticeable Irish accent struck me anew. Bobby's voice was English, of course, with a light English spaniel bark.

"I always thought you were a clever girl, Paula, perhaps hugging yourself too much inwardly. Of course, things were difficult."

There was the unspoken 'after all that happened'. And I disliked her remark, *hugging yourself inwardly.* As a child, I had always been afraid of Anna Lacey.

I forced a smile. "You must be wondering what I'm doing here. I just wanted to see the cottage once more. I'm afraid I'm trespassing." I tried to steady my breathing; lavender always affects me badly. "I was told that my mother left the cottage to a friend. Was it the man who just left?"

"Good heavens, no! I thought you knew. Marjorie left the cottage to a fellow gardener. There's a story behind the bequest. Marjorie had saved the family's lives during the war. Henry died in 1952. That's why I'm here. His son, Werner Siskin, inherited the property from his father. He's decided to move in and I've been airing the place for him."

I stepped back. I was thoroughly confused. "Siskin, you said?"

"That's right."

Bobby stood up and stretched his front paws and yawned. I had read that yawning was a sign of happiness in dogs. I was glad Bobby was happy for I was baffled. While I was trying to retrieve my wits, I bent down and stroked his soft fur. "Bobby and I were such good friends. I remember we once explored the windmill in Acle, and Bobby climbed up the steep steps with me."

Anna nodded. "And we were grateful to have an active young thing to take him for walks. Marjorie sketched Bobby. I must show it to you. She captured that depth in his eyes that all dogs have, as if they're communing with you. Afterwards she told me how well he'd behaved. Dogs, you see, have a natural sense of their own importance and behave much better than children!"

I picked up my bag and Bobby wagged his tail. "It's been lovely meeting you and Bobby, Mrs Lacey. I'm glad I came, but I must go now."

I went back to the car, conscious that she was watching as I drove away. I wondered how she knew so much about me. Mum had never said Anna Lacey was a friend.

When I arrived home, I poured out a glass of wine and sat in my courtyard. I needed to think things over. I received a small income from the sale of Mum's books on plants and shrubs, but that had almost dried up. Younger, more exuberant gardeners, with vast audiences on television and radio, had captured that market.

I went back over the conversation. I couldn't understand why Mrs Lacey had said Mum had left the cottage to Henry Siskin. It was incomprehensible. Bizarre. No, it was bloody impossible.

I had wanted a family for my big dolls house. Dad had found some wood and had created the Siskin family. They were about a foot high with movable limbs. Mum had dressed them, crocheting and sewing their clothes, and she had painted the Horticultural Society's Certificate, framed it, and hung it on the wall in the dolls house sitting room with portraits of the Siskin family: Henry, Maria and Werner. Unfortunately, Maria and Werner had sustained fractures and were thrown away. I had begged Dad to make Suzy and Jenni for me.

Mum had brought the wooden toys to life by telling me stories about them. Mr Siskin was a landscape gardener. He had lived in Germany before the war, but had been forced to leave the country just before hostilities began. Siskin, his wife and baby son were smuggled out of the country into England. She had even commemorated Mr Siskin in her *Siskin Series of Lavender* books. But she had never told me her stories were about real people. So when Mum said, "Mr Siskin is the keeper of my memories," I had laughed, thinking she was joking. Maybe the joke was on me.

Mr Siskin's tools, his wheelbarrow, spade and garden fork, his trowel and clippers were made by Dad. The Siskin family had lived in the dolls house and I had played with them since I was four years old. Rosebuds were entwined round the house name, Lintwhite Villa.

I had no friends in Acle, because we lived in London during the term, and Suzy and Jenni, Mr Siskin's wooden daughters, became my dearest companions. They were completely real to me. They joined in all my games and loved Bobby as much as I did. Jenni was the daring sister and sometimes quite naughty, while Suzy was demure and infuriatingly virtuous. "She's such a goody-goody," Jenni would whisper. They'd been as frightened as I when the fox looked over the hedge. I had been fourteen. I could still smell the lavender, still smell the fear as the stranger fell, his blood staining the flagstones.

Mum had said, several times, that I was to have a special gift on my thirtieth birthday. Something to do with Siskin. For some reason, it had amused her. My mother was so strange about some things. About a lot of things.

I found another postcard on the mat before I went to bed. There was no stamp. It had been delivered by hand. It said: *Time's running out for you and Denby.*

I hadn't seen my father since I was fifteen. I felt increasingly alarmed by the cards. I wondered if I should take them to the police, but I didn't want anyone asking about the past.

Monday, 1st June 1981

No migraine today, only a faint shadow behind my eyes. I left before Dwayne arrived with the spare parts. The roads were busy and I was fifteen minutes late. Behind the sales office the small car park was filling up. I parked between a dark blue Morgan and a green Ford Fiesta and hurried into the sales room. This was Trish Porter's Walk-Around-the-Village day. I saw Corrie and a tall thin saturnine man coming out of the kitchen with Meg. Trish and two colleagues were talking animatedly with Tim and Goodison near the sofa. Pat Heals, looking annoyed, was escorting two clients over to Corrie's empty table. Corrie limped over quickly and shook hands with the two women.

I slipped into the kitchen to make a cup of tea and took two capsules, hoping it would keep the migraine as a background shadow. When I walked over to my table Pat Heals greeted me coolly, eyeing the cup I was carrying. "You could have got that later." I flushed at the reprimand. "While we're going round Dunham Village you'll have to stay and man the phones with Corrie. I hope you'll be busy today. Trish Porter thinks your articles will make a difference. We'll see!"

Meg Farrell greeted me with a smile and Pat went over and joined Tim who was looking bored. I glanced round and was amazed to see Mitchell standing near the kitchen door. As I got up to go over and talk with him, Trish came up to my table. "I'll keep your articles in mind as I go round," she said, "but we may see things very differently, you know."

"Not too differently, I hope," I said, but Trish had already moved away.

When I looked back at the kitchen, Mitchell had gone. A moment later, Doug Sellick strode through the doorway with three people in tow. He greeted Pat with a nod, but saluted Trish with a kiss on both cheeks. "I see you're still running that old Morgan," he said.

"It's the only car I'll ever drive," she replied tartly. "Why haven't you invited me round before this?"

"Because the Village isn't finished yet. There'll be a proper function when it is, and I'll let you cut the ribbon and bash a bottle of the champers against a wall." He looked round. "Well, are we going, or just standing here talking?"

Bob Stevens arrived in a rush. He nodded coolly at me and then joined Sellick. "It's a better day than yesterday," he smiled, shaking hands all round. "I'd have been here earlier, but I got held up. I hope you're going to like what you see, Miss Porter, we've put a lot of thought into the Village."

"I'll report on what I see, Mr Stevens. Hopefully, you've included a lot of new ideas."

I stood up as a middle-aged, dark-haired man in a long leather overcoat walked up to my table.

"Nice of you to get in touch again, Paula. What's going on here?"

Before I could say anything, Trish Porter stepped forward. "Nils Hanson! What's brought *you* here?"

Hanson smiled. "Good to see you again, Trish. Well, I couldn't resist my old friend's invitation. Paula and I knew each other in London."

I introduced him to Sellick. "Nils works on the *Manchester Guardian*."

"I hear you had a problem over the weekend," Hanson said.

Sellick hunched his shoulders up. "Local affair. Police already have the moron who killed the child."

"So I've heard. Paula told me about your ideas and sent me the brochure. I'd say you've done a good job by incorporating the local features. It's marrying imagination with economics."

Sellick liked that, but Pat tossed her head, annoyed at being left out. I introduced her to Hanson. "We're just going round the Village," she said, her voice high and sweet. "I think you'll be interested, particularly in the golf course. Did you know Erik Maroc designed it?"

"He must have liked your ideas. Maroc doesn't often leave Frejus these days."

"Well, it wasn't the money," Sellick retorted. "He's a rich man and he still charged the earth, but he liked the idea of a retirement village with the emphasis on activity, plus turning an ugly tarmacked aerodrome back into a beautiful part of the countryside."

As they moved out, I heard Hanson say to Pat that he wanted to see everything.

Meg came over. "I've done my bit by turning up, now I'm going back to my office." She looked tired.

When Corrie had sent her clients out in a buggy and the room was clear at last, we sat down quietly together.

"She's a real bitch, that Pat," Corrie said viciously. "You set this up with Trish, but Pat'll take all the credit. She can't help it. She's always been bossy, but that were a real coup bringing Nils Hanson down here. D'you know him well?"

I nodded. "He's a good reporter. Who was the man with you earlier, tall, dark-haired?"

"That's Ted, my old man. He's Doug's driver now. We're real happy about that."

We were busy all afternoon. None of Trish Porter's party came back to the sales flat. I imagined they'd gone on to the restaurant in the club house. I was about to pack up when DCI Quinn and DS Penry came into the office.

"I thought you didn't work here in the afternoons," Quinn said abruptly.

"I don't usually. This is a special day. Trish Porter's here, she's going to write some articles about the Village. I'm leaving in a minute, but you can talk to Mary or Mrs Heals. One of them will take over the evening shift. Oh, here's Corrie, she may be able to help you."

Corrie had been taking more clients round the Village. "There're police everywhere," she said. "Wha's goin' on?"

A uniformed officer followed her and spoke softly to Quinn. He nodded, picked up his coat, signalled to Penry and they all left the room.

Corrie and I waited for Mary. She was over an hour late, but just before she arrived, Penry returned on his own. "It's bad news," he said at once. "A man has been shot in the carpark. I'm sorry, Mrs James, it's Major Denby, your father."

I told Penry he was mistaken. I explained that my father had died eleven years ago. In a train crash. In Paris. "Funnily enough, Mrs Conrad was saying my father was alive, but she was so confused I just dismissed it." I fumbled for the words. "I don't understand what you're saying."

Penry sat down heavily. "I don't wonder you're confused. I've been reading the file. It's an incredible story. In a way, your father *did* die in that crash in 1970, because from that time, he became an undercover agent and he had to 'disappear'. I wasn't working with DCI Quinn then. I joined the Force in 1973. I don't know how much you know, but Major Denby was involved in the theft of paintings from a museum in Pforzheim, in Germany, during the war.

"Quinn told me that Denby and a fellow soldier, Scott, turned Queen's Evidence in 1970, and Denby handed Colonel North a notebook in which he'd written down all the transactions he'd made—dates, names, photos—of the sales of the Pforzheim pictures, and he helped North get a whole lot of them back. Then North asked him to join his team hunting Hannagan, an Irishman who had worked with the Germans in the war. Denby knew a lot about Hannagan. Unfortunately, he couldn't get in touch with you without blowing his cover."

"But Mrs Conrad said he was living in her house. I didn't believe her, of course, but was it true?"

Penry was reluctant. "Well, yes. Cedric Conrad left his wife a fortune in diamonds, the 'Pretoria Diamonds' they're called. He'd mined them in South Africa. They made him a very rich man. Then we heard that Hannagan knew about the diamonds. He's running short of money for his Cause. I think Denby got in the way and that's why he was shot."

"Because of your stupid rules, I was stopped from seeing my father again."

"If Denby had talked with you, he would have put you in danger. Trouble was, your father was a bit of a wild card and he didn't always tell North or Quinn what he was doing. Quinn didn't like that, and that's why we don't know why he was waiting in the carpark. Perhaps he'd had a tip-off about Hannagan; or perhaps he was waiting to get in touch with you."

It would be nice to think my father had been waiting to talk with me, waiting to take me away to a safe place where there were no guns and no violence.

Penry said my father's car had been taken away for examination. "And I'm sorry to have to ask this, but will you come into Swaffham and identify the body?"

Corrie looked upset. "Does she have to? I mean, she's just had a terrible shock."

Perhaps Corrie's response made me stronger. I told Penry I would go with him.

As we left, Corrie called out, "Don' worry, Paula, I'll look after everything here."

Penry drove me into Swaffham and I saw my father after all. Penry told me the murderer had been hiding in the back of the car. A silencer had been used. It had happened quickly.

In my mind, I saw the faceless figure rise up from the back seat and shoot my father in the back of the head. And I saw the swirling circles of purple and mauve move round him, his eyes glazing with death as he lost consciousness and died from his wound. I wished I could have spoken to him. I wished I could have held him close once more, but when the light of life is gone there is nothing left, except to mourn. And I had been mourning the death of my father for fifteen years.

Penry offered to drive me home, but my car was in the carpark at Dunham Village. So Penry took me back to the sales house. And then I drove home.

I had the strangest feeling that my life was being "arranged". Ever since I came to Norwich, things had fallen into place as if they had been pre-contrived. Like finding the flat. An estate agent's pamphlet had been left on the hall table in the bed-and-breakfast place where I had first stayed. The agents were helpful, the rent was reasonable and I had moved into the flat two days later. Then came the offer to purchase the whole house. I was convinced *Wild Marjoram* had been placed in the window of the art shop to catch my eye. And there was the job I'd gotten so quickly at Sellick's, then later, Porter's offer of a job, all so easy. Much too easy.

When I got home, Dwayne had gone. The kitchen looked immaculate. On the table were two keys and a note: *Both keys returned.* Beside them was a booklet containing information about the new boiler. I couldn't help remembering another time when a key and a heartless note had changed my life. I looked in the boiler cupboard and saw the two shelves Dwayne had put up. I put the keys on my key-ring. Keys open doors, but grief closes them.

Tuesday, 2nd June 1981

The police had reopened the carpark to the public. I was Dr Roberts' first patient. After examining me, he sat down and wrote up his notes. "Has the treatment helped you?"

"Yes, you were right, the capsules are much better than tablets."

"Good. But as I said before, you need to rest. I'll write out a repeat prescription and Tim will bring the medicine to your office."

Corrie was answering the phone when I walked in.

"Thursday then, at three o'clock, Mr Davis. See you then." She put the phone down. "You feelin' better, Paula? You shouldn't have come. I'd have managed. You don't look too good. P'raps you'd better see the doc?"

"I've just seen Dr Roberts, he's given me a repeat prescription."

I went over to the map on the wall and had a shock. The bungalows Cameron and Dermott had bought were for sale and so was Mrs Moffat's flat. I told Corrie I had to go over to see Meg Farrell.

Meg was sympathetic. "Are you feeling better? Corrie told me what happened."

I said I was fine, but that I'd just seen the map. "I can't believe three people I've seen recently have died. What on earth happened?"

"They were probably more ill than perhaps you or their relatives realised." Her Scottish brogue sang with regret. "And perhaps you should have persuaded them to consider a nursing home."

"They all seemed positive that Dunham Village was what they wanted. But what happened to Mrs Moffat?" The unfortunate mother of Sylvia Henderson.

Farrell shook her head. "She got up in the night and fell down the stairs. Did you know she was suffering from Parkinson's and shouldn't have been left on her own?"

My voice was harsh. "I never saw Mrs Moffat. Everything was arranged by her daughter. She told me her mother had rheumatism. She never mentioned Parkinson's." I was really angry now. "You know, Meg, they're not honest. They hide things, and now I feel terrible."

She patted my arm. "As I said before, some of these people should never have been brought here, but you can't argue with relatives. I know, I've tried. Of course, there'll be an investigation. Three of your clients have died within a week of purchasing a property."

"What kind of investigation?"

"Well, the coroner's been informed and there'll be an inquest. You'll be called as a witness."

I didn't like what I was hearing. I knew all the blame would be heaped on me. I tried to offload some of the guilt. "You must also be worried about these deaths, you're in charge here. Did *you* see Mr Cameron? He was over eighty.

And I did query about him being left here on his own. How did he die? And Mr Dermott? He wasn't ill, he'd had a stroke, but he was managing well."

Meg looked annoyed. "No, I didn't see Mr Cameron or the others, although I'd made a note to visit them in a couple of days. Mr Dermott? He was found dead in the bath. He'd taken an overdose. And Mr Cameron fell and hit his head. He was unconscious when the cleaner found him. He died later in hospital. No, Paula, you were the first to see them, and as I said, perhaps you should have asked more questions and made sure the older people were *compos mentis* and physically able before they bought a bungalow."

Farrell's reassuring Scottish brogue had become a sharp attack. "I can't *believe* Mr Dermott took an overdose." I shrugged helplessly. "And you're wrong, I did ask questions, but no-one has told me to refuse a transaction because the client is elderly. And besides, Pat Heals objects when I ask questions."

Meg frowned. "What kind of questions?"

"I ask the clients how they heard of the Retirement Homes and why they decided to come to Swaffham. Mr Dermott came from Glasgow. How did he know about Dunham Village in Norfolk? Dermott, Cameron, Moffat all came from outside Norfolk. Moffat lived in Yorkshire and Cameron came from Aylesbury in Bucks, but Pat told me she'd only advertised Dunham Village in Norfolk. So how did they hear of the Retirement Homes in Swaffham?"

Meg looked at me. "I've no idea."

I hesitated. "Why does Pat Heals dislike me?"

Farrell wavered a little. "Well, you're young, exciting, attractive. And Sellick's never rushed down to the Village before to see any of his salespeople. Pat's jealous of you, Paula, and if I'm honest, I think she'll try to get rid of you."

"Perhaps Sellick will have other ideas."

"Not with these deaths," Meg countered promptly. "You'd better get a good lawyer!"

Feeling thoroughly dispirited, I went back to the show house and asked Corrie what she would do if there were a coroner's enquiry. She sat on the fence. "Dunno. Looks bad."

Three clients came into the room asking if they could look round the Village and Corrie took them.

A few minutes later, Tim Harvey sauntered into the sales office. He put the familiar green chemist's bag on the table. His large figure and bustling cheerfulness filled the room and lifted me out of my despondency.

"I'll make some coffee," he said. "It'll cheer you up." He was back in a few moments. "I've fluffed up the milk so it looks like a cappuccino!" As I sipped the hot coffee, I told him what Farrell had said.

"I'm not a medic," I objected. "The clients deliberately chose Dunham Village for their relatives. They didn't want a nursing home. Meg Farrell's going to tell the coroner that I'm at fault for selling the properties to people who are sick."

Looking serious, Tim sat opposite me. I liked the way his fair hair curled riotously over his well-shaped Saxon head and as he talked, his wide dark eyes ignited into life. "You're in trouble, Paula, they're out to get you. Like they did Audrey. You've been asking questions. Pat Heals doesn't like it."

I leaned back wearily. "Why doesn't she like it?"

"You've got to be careful of Pat," Tim warned. "She can be nasty. Sellick relies on her completely." His eyes darkened. "I wish you weren't working here. Pat got rid of Audrey because she was snooping round, asking questions. Like you do. Just sell the properties, Paula, that's why you're here."

"Tim, I have to ask questions to learn my job, and I want to earn those bonuses Sellick promised me. My articles are appearing in the Gazette this week. And I want to write more to push the Retirement Homes. Anyway, how does Pat *know* I'm asking questions?"

"One of the relatives said something." Tim was dismissive. "Look, you've already written the articles. Why get mixed up in all the problems?"

I heard Gillian's voice. *All the nasty goings-on.*

Tim's voice rose. "After all, you're not involved, are you?"

I wished I knew. A scam isn't difficult to operate: keep it simple, plan it carefully, seduce the clients with the promise of big rewards, execute the plan smoothly and rake in the money. It happens all the time, and when the clients learn the truth they seldom complain, no-one likes to look a fool. But I was puzzled about the part *The Helpline* played. I wanted to dig further.

"One of my clients, Sylvia Henderson, talked about a helpline, and a representative called Rowene. Do you know anything about them?"

Tim was annoyed. "Audrey asked me the same thing. I didn't know anything then and I don't know anything now."

I wondered how far Audrey had got in her investigation. I needed to unlock Tim's knowledge. "We can't talk here, Tim, let's go out for a meal tonight and get to know each other better."

He lapped it up. "That'd be great!"

"I'll meet you at the Red Club. Eight o'clock OK?"

He nodded, his eyes bright with expectation. He came quickly round the table and stood in front of me. Before I could stop him, he pulled me up, held me in his arms and kissed me. "You're the best thing that's ever happened to me," he said thickly, and kissed me again. It was surprisingly nice, soft and lingering, his aftershave attractive.

The best thing that ever happened to me. Someone else had said that. A long time ago.

Stiletto heels pecked furiously across the parquet flooring. "What the *hell's* going on here?"

Tim sprang back, tripped over the chair and banged his head against the table as he fell. Pat Heals thumped her black handbag on the table as I bent over Tim. Blood was trickling down his face.

"Leave him, he's shamming. He doesn't want to look me in the eye."

I didn't blame him. Pat looked demonic.

"You've come early," I said weakly.

"If all these shenanigans are going on, it's a bloody good thing I did!"

I was surprised at the force of her anger. Tim groaned and I reached down and pulled him to his feet, giving him my hanky to hold against his forehead.

"Haven't you got anything to do?" Heals screamed at him. He scowled and stumbled out of the door.

"Shouldn't he see a doctor?" I began.

"Why? He's *walking*, isn't he?" Heals almost choked. "How long have you two been at it?"

"A kiss—is just a kiss!" I quoted flippantly.

"I don't believe you!"

"Does it matter?" But it *did* matter. Perhaps Tim's yielding lips were the attraction.

"I shall tell Ray Bradley, the chemist, that I don't want Tim in the Village anymore."

I was shocked. "Look, there's nothing between us—"

Pat burst out furiously, "You may think the articles you wrote have given you a status, but I've worked hard to lay the foundations for Dunham Village and I won't let you or Harvey or anyone else mess it up."

She turned abruptly to the table diary. Her slim finger moved down the columns. "You're entering everyone who comes or phones?"

I nodded.

"And you know you mustn't keep any cash or cheques on the premises?"

"I go to the bank every day."

She looked round. "Where's Corrie?"

I pointed to the door. "Here she is."

Pat's face grew dark. "So, she's been taking clients round the Village while you and Tim skulk in here?"

She was being ridiculous. "Corrie's very good with the clients," I said crisply. "When we're busy, we take it in turns to drive them round the Village."

"I'll report this to Mr Sellick," she said furiously.

"Good!" Now I was angry. "I don't know what you've got against it."

Pat picked up her bag and tip-tapped her way out of the room past Corrie. Pat wasn't comfortable. Her shoulders were high and tense as she stumbled, uncharacteristically, over the door-sill. I wished now I'd mentioned *The Helpline* and seen her reaction.

Corrie had loved every minute. "She hates me because I limp. She once said I make the place look untidy. Sly old bitch. She thinks Sellick's got the hots for you, Paula."

"Rubbish, of course, he hasn't."

"*I* know that, but the old bat thinks he has."

Despite her lack of support, I liked Corrie. She was good-natured with a ready smile and large dark-blue eyes in a plain, square face framed with short light-brown hair and a thick fringe. She had broken her leg as a child and it hadn't healed properly. It didn't bother her or her husband, but she hated Pat Heals for calling attention to it.

My key-ring was lying on the table. Corrie ran her finger up and down the flowered shafts of the little keys Amy had given me.

"They're so pretty. What do you use them for? And what do the numbers mean?"

"A friend gave them to me. I think they're good-luck charms." I wondered, as I always wondered when I saw the little keys, what Amy had wanted to tell me.

I found the EDP and the East Anglia Recorder on the doormat when I got home. No postcards, thank God. After a light lunch, I settled down to read the

Recorder. I wanted to keep up with what was happening over the whole area so that I could direct articles for the Retirement Homes to the best market. I was still hoping the project would survive the publicity from the coming coroner's inquest.

At the bottom of the first page, I noticed a paragraph:

Estate agent found dead: Coroner's report

Mrs Audrey Simpson, aged fifty-nine, was found dead at her home in Cambridge two weeks ago. She had recently been working in Norwich and Swaffham as an estate agent. She had been prescribed Benzodiazepine tablets for a sleep disorder. The post-mortem established she had taken a large overdose of the tablets with a considerable amount of alcohol. Mrs Simpson was recently divorced and had been depressed for some time. However, an airline ticket to San Francisco was found in her handbag and a neighbour said she was excited at going to California to visit her daughter. The coroner commented that depression often leads to mental instability, but as there were anomalies which had not been resolved, he must record an Open Verdict.

Further down the page was another article. A woman walking her dog had found the body of a woman on a beach in Great Yarmouth. The police were asking for information. A short description of the dead woman and her clothes followed.

The phone rang. It was Corrie, nervous and apprehensive. "The p'lice have been. They're askin' questions about a body found in Yarmouth. A woman. One of our business cards was in her pocket. Then they show me a photo. Oh Paula, it was Renée Tournai! D'you remember I told you about her, how she was sacked an' everything?"

I told her about Audrey Simpson.

"You mean, they're *both* dead?" I could hear her breathing heavily. "Why would anyone want to kill them?"

"We don't know they were killed. Perhaps Renée committed suicide like they say Audrey did."

"I don't believe it." The words rushed out. "Audrey was always so full of herself. She was going to America to see her daughter, and Renée tell me she was glad she was going back to Paris. She hate that Pat. They argue all the time.

189

Tha's why she was sacked. But she tell me she didn't care, 'cos she didn't like Norwich."

"Well, it's certainly a coincidence that two women from the same firm have died."

Too much of a coincidence.

Corrie was hysterical. "Someone's pickin' us off, one by one, someone who don't want the Village built! In the early days, when Doug Sellick was negotiating for land, the Acle office was bombed and there was a fire here at the head office. An' last year the coffee machine was spiked with drugs an' we were all sick. There's been a lot of opposition to the Village. That's some nutter out to get us. Which of us'll be next?"

The phone went dead. No-one had mentioned bombs or fires or drugs.

Then Sellick phoned. His voice was hard and unpleasant.

"DCI Quinn has been to see me. He gave me the most extraordinary story about your father being murdered in the carpark behind the sales house. Then he said two other women who once worked in the office have been found dead. And of course, he knows about the dead child at the church. Things are suddenly going badly, and I'm not happy about it." And the phone was slammed down.

My heart was thumping unsteadily. There were no commiserations for the loss of my father. It was all about Sellick's Village.

The foyer in the Red Club was decorated with heavy crimson and gold drapes between tall Doric columns. There were gaming rooms and a bar upstairs, and two restaurants and a bar on the ground floor. The place was full when I arrived at eight o'clock. Tim was waiting for me in the foyer, elegant in evening dress, his young, attractive face alight with mischief. I had put my hair up, and the sapphire necklace, earrings and bracelet were a perfect accompaniment to my close-fitting red gown with its thin, silver shoulder straps.

As we followed the waiter to our table, Tim whispered: "You look like Aphrodite!"

We sat down and I asked him how he felt. Tim frowned. "I slipped, it was nothing." He pointed to the top pocket in his jacket. "I've washed your hanky. It's got your initials on it, so I'll keep it to protect me, in case Pat pushes me over again!"

Tim's self-deprecating humour was attractive. And unexpected. The waiter brought our orders: grilled trout and salad for me; fillet of beef, chips and whisky for Tim.

"Your husband was a fool to let you go," he said, tucking into the beef. "I didn't know that falling in love could change everything so quickly. And now all I want is to live my life with you."

I couldn't believe he was serious, but his offer of love, reaching out to me in my loneliness and hurt, was appealing.

Richard had accused me of being prosaic. "There's no romance in you!" he once said. Well, romance or not, you have to have enough money to live on. I pointed this out to Tim, but he dismissed the finances of love with a flourish of his fork, finished his steak and ordered a third whisky, which I was paying for.

"We'll find a way. All *I* know is that I'm hopelessly, wonderfully, madly in love with you. We've only just met, Paula, but you've magicked me!"

With a pang I thought how young he was.

"There's an enchantment about you, darling." He leaned forward. "I love your hands, your face, the way you move, the way you talk. I want to hold you in my arms, kiss your lips, your eyes. I want to dance round the world with you. I never knew love could be so full of pain and desire."

Despite myself, I was swept up into his emotions. Richard had never wanted to dance round the world with me. There was something engaging in such abandonment. And Tim made me feel young again.

"Darling, *darling* Paula, let's leave this bloody awful place, let's leave the whole dirty wretched business behind us."

The dramatic moment was lost as he leaned back in his chair and laughed. "D'you know, Heals thinks you're a spy!" He tipped the whisky down his throat. "Maybe you are, but I don't care."

I sat back, angry at myself for being beguiled, but interested in Pat's remark. "Who am I spying for and what is there to spy on?"

"Nothing! It's just Pat being fixated. I told her you were learning on the job, and she said you only got it because Sellick had known your mother. Is that right?"

I said I didn't think he really knew her.

"OK, but you won't be in his good books if your clients keep falling dead all over the place! Pat said Sellick's thinking of letting you manage the Dunham project while she goes to Wales to set up more Retirement Homes. But Sellick won't leave you in Swaffham if things go wrong."

How much more wrong could they go? I told Tim I wondered if *The Helpline* was running some sort of a scam.

"What kind of a scam?"

"I don't know, but I think a lot of money may be involved. I'd go to the police but I don't have any facts. You go round the Village, Tim, you know what's going on."

He leaned back in his chair. "So you've only come here to find out what I know, eh?"

"Not really, Tim. I do think the Retirement Homes is a really good idea, but now there's going to be this inquest and I'm worried. What I want is your help. The death of that poor child was a shock, and now Corrie's told me about attacks on the agency. What's going on? D'you know, I think Sellick's only keeping me on because I've had some good ideas, like advertising more widely."

Tim grinned, the smirk lingering on his lips. "Pat told me all about it, how you got in on her act. She's mad as hell. She said Sellick was all over you." He frowned. "He hasn't tried anything, has he?"

I thought of Sellick, sixty-plus, pug-faced, smelling of cigar smoke. "Don't be silly, Tim. I just want to know what's going on."

What I really wanted was to vindicate myself before things got to the Coroner.

"Yeah, well, I move round the Village and I hear a lot. People are distressed. The family home's been sold. It affects people, and sometimes they say silly things to disguise how they're feeling. You're saying all the things that Audrey said. She got sick when the coffee machine in head office was spiked. But honestly, I don't think there's anything dodgy going on in Dunham Village. It's just coincidence that the three clients died."

I sat back. I was not convinced. "Most people who come are local. Did anyone die when Audrey Simpson was in the sales office? You see, I've been thinking that Moffat, Cameron and Dermott may have been drugged—"

"And then murdered?" Tim was highly sceptical.

Despite his scorn, I rushed headlong into committing myself. "D'you think Dr Roberts was involved?"

Tim was disdainful. "That's a big leap, isn't it, from no facts to accusing a respected physician of murder! Roberts wouldn't risk his name in anything dubious. And what evidence do you have for drugs? None. The post-mortems will give the facts, but I doubt they'll find anything. The people who come here are old and often more sick than they let on. I know, I give them their medicine. You're playing the detective when there's nothing to detect. Just like Audrey

192

Simpson. She was always asking questions about *The Helpline* and a 'representative'. That's why Pat sacked her." He took my hand. "Paula, darling, why don't you just find another job?"

And then it hit me. Tim didn't know Audrey Simpson was dead. He was shocked when I told him. "It was suicide. The coroner said she was depressed about her divorce."

Tim snorted. "Rubbish. Audrey *wanted* the divorce. She hated her old man, he was always playing round. She was saving up to go to America to visit her daughter. I can tell you she was *mad* when she was fired. I was there when she threatened Pat."

"*Threatened* her?"

"Audrey was stupid. She said she knew secrets about the Village."

"Corrie told me there'd been a fire at the Norwich Agency, and something about a bomb."

Tim nodded. "Yeah, that's right. Norfolk people are set in their ways, they don't like change, and Sellick let a lot of people down on the Lincoln build. He lost a lot of trust. That's why the money side's going slowly." He frowned. "And now the police are all over the place, because of the dead man in the car park." He looked up. "I don't like the police."

"Why's that?"

"Because of what happened at Bath."

"Go on."

"There was a girl. She died. Overdose. That's why I didn't finish my degree. Now all I do is deliver medicine to old people." Tim was on his fourth whisky.

A waiter came and cleared the table and offered Tim the sweet menu. He pushed it aside. "Damn the puddings, get me another whisky!"

The whole ambiance had turned sour. I was sharp. "You've had enough, Tim, we ought to be going."

"Enough is never *enough*," he shouted roughly. "Where's that damn whisky?" He stopped suddenly. "See that man over there, two tables to the right?"

It was Goodison with Lionel and Edna Redding. I shrugged. "OK, it's Hal Goodison and two people interested in buying a bungalow."

He nearly choked. "Hal nothing! It's Henry, plain old Henry Goodison. He's here to keep an eye on us."

"He couldn't possibly have known we would be here tonight," I objected. "And talking about the police, why are they asking questions about Lawrence Heals?" Tim looked startled. "They asked me where he works. I said he was at the Acle branch."

Tim shook his head. "He's gone back to South Africa."

I watched him throw his head back, his mood suddenly expansive, almost genial. I didn't want to think it, but Meg Farrell had mentioned drugs. "Tim, if you're smoking cannabis, you shouldn't mix it with alcohol."

"It's recreational. Anyway, it's nothing to do with you."

"It is, if you want to spend your life with me!"

Tim stretched his hand out to me in mute appeal. "No more questions about the Retirement Homes, please Paula. Forget Audrey and everyone. Just listen to me. I want to leave this awful place. I want to chuck it. I tell you, I want out. I've been feeling like this for a long time. Come away with me, Paula." There were beads of sweat on his forehead. "It's funny, we spend all our lives in a box we call our home and end our lives in a box in a churchyard."

People were looking round and whispering, but Tim was oblivious to them. He held both my hands. "Don't you understand, my darling, I'm frightened. I don't want to be consumed by flames or buried in the dark, dank earth. Hold me close, keep me alive."

Then he turned and grabbed a waiter's arm. "Where's my drink? Get me another whisky!" Tim's fork was banging a little ditty on the empty glass on the table. "Where's my drink? Where's my whisky?"

And I was forgotten.

"Hello, 'ello, old man, what's going on here?" A shadow fell over the table. Hal Goodison clapped his hand on Tim's shoulder and sat down beside him.

Tim's response was extraordinary. He jumped up, his chair clattering to the floor as he shouted and lashed out at Goodison. "Leave me *alone!* You're as bad as the others, but I know what you've done. I know who you are!"

Voices were surging round us. A waiter picked up the chair and Goodison dragged Tim down hard and I heard him gasp. Another man came over and suggested we should leave. Goodison nodded. "Leave him with me, Franklin. After a couple of coffees, I'll drive him home."

"Very well, Mr Goodison."

A waiter poured out coffees for all of us.

"Coffee makes me sad," Tim said thickly. "I wan' another whisky. I wanna be happy."

Laughing, Goodison put his arm round Tim's shoulder and held him down firmly. "And have one you will, Tim, after the coffee. Then we'll have a party and we'll all be happy together."

Tim struggled to get up. "Paula, why are you letting this *scum* treat me like this? He's a liar and a murderer. Lawrie told me."

"Lawrie's as big a fool as you are, Tim." Goodison tightened his arm round Tim. "Now drink the coffee and then we can go."

I stood up, desperate to get away from Goodison, hating his smarmy, pseudo-smiling mouth. "I'll take you home, Tim."

Goodison waved his hand at me. "He's too drunk even to walk to the door. Let's get him calmed down first. Come on, Tim, drink the coffee, and then we can *all* go home."

I sat down reluctantly. Tim swallowed the coffee with a grimace and Goodison took the cup from his hand as Tim's head sank slowly down onto the table.

"Poor old Tim." Goodison looked at me, the ugly sandy-coloured patches on his bald scalp glinting under the lights on the table. "It's all getting to him. He was a brilliant student, chemistry, you know, bright but unstable. Cannabis. A girl died. Nothing proved, but he was sent down from Bath."

Chemistry! Not Roberts, but Tim! Perhaps he was being blackmailed because of his drug habit.

"Why are *you* here, Mr Goodison?"

"I like to gamble in the evenings. I could see you were having trouble with young Tim, so I came over to help. And you're just as bad, Mrs James, encouraging him in this nonsense, snooping round asking foolish questions." His deep-set light brown eyes swept coldly over me. "Why are you playing this ridiculous detective game? You may have once worked in the criminal courts, not as the big-time barrister you pretend to be, but as an insignificant secretary."

"Now, look here," I began angrily.

Goodison stood up and leant over the table. "Get off your high horse, Mrs James. You're just a very ordinary woman doing an ordinary job badly." Spittle flew out of his mouth onto my dress. "You're intent on creating mischief with your endless snooping. I will personally see that you and Tim are sent packing from Dunham Village." He looked down at Tim. "The idiot's been selling drugs again. His future's in jail, and you'll end up there, as well."

I didn't believe him. I didn't want to believe him. Tim raised his head. He pushed himself up and looked straight at me. I held my breath. His eyes were iridescent, his lips parted. In that moment, I was spellbound.

He turned to Goodison, his fists clenched, his mouth suddenly enormous as the cry tore out of his throat. "You poisonous sod, you will not have her! She is not for killing!"

Goodison stumbled to his feet, fear shrill in his eyes. Tim's fist smashed into his face and Goodison fell back, sprawling across his chair.

I'm standing on the edge of the room
I am a part, and not a part,
of what is going on.
Noise is filling the room,
I see everything and
register nothing.
Goodison is pulling himself up.
He's reaching inside his pocket.
I see the gun.
I hear the shot.
But the shot is not meant for me.
Tim sways and falls on top of Goodison,
And Goodison screams as the gun
Is pushed into his ribs.
The men are locked together,
And purple and mauve are
Seeping in and out of
Their life's pulses.
Lionel Redding is rushing over.
The room is full of shouts and cries,
The sharp abrasive scrape of chairs,
The surge of movement, forward then back.
Tim lies huddled on the floor
Blood is soaking through his shirt.
A young doctor in evening dress,

pushes his way through the crowd.
He bends over Tim, his sleeve red
from the blood on Tim's shirt.
My eyes see everything,
my brain records nothing.
I am back in a world far removed
from the screams and mayhem.
I am a sixteen-year-old girl,
looking through a half-open door
watching Amy die as the bullets spit round her.
My mother is facing the old man's gun
and the colour is running from the rose
on her shoulder.
And the streetlight shines on Callum
as he falls dead at her feet.

Brandy is being forced down my throat.
I choke and push Penry away.
Chief Inspector Quinn's voice,
disembodied, crackling and hissing, tells
Penry to take me home.
"I'll see her in the morning."
Penry takes my arm.
I move with feet of lead.
I'm in the car and Penry is driving me home.
Penry takes the key from my evening bag
and opens the door.
I sit at my new kitchen table
in the beautiful gown
and silver slippers red with Tim's blood,
and, slowly, slowly,
I become conscious of where I am.

"Feeling better?" Penry pressed a mug of hot, sweetened tea into my hand, his voice coming through a fog-horn. "Can you tell me what happened?"

My hands trembled round the mug. The tea was sweet and sickly.

"Tell me what happened," Penry said again, but my mind was all over the place searching for an earlier murder.

"Goodison had the gun," I heard Penry say. "He shot Harvey and it looks like he accidentally shot himself as Harvey fell on him."

I tried to understand, but the words were not Penry's words.

Tim was shouting, "She's not for killing!"

How extraordinary that Tim should say those words. My life has been one long wait for the bullet that will kill me.

He must have loved me to give his life for me.

I looked up, my eyes searching Penry's face. "Tim said Goodison was a murderer. Lawrie told him."

"You're sure about that?" Penry's voice sounded almost normal. He took out his notebook.

"It was confusing," I said slowly.

Penry asked me if there was someone who could stay with me.

I told him I wanted to be alone.

He said a WPC could stay the night. I repeated, "I want to be on my own."

On my own. *On my own.*

Penry's Welsh voice, soft and soothing, "Well, get some rest. You'll feel better in the morning."

I agreed, my voice toneless. "In the morning. Goodbye, kind Mr Penry."

At last I was on my own, but I could not stop the tears. Tim had drunk too much, had taken drugs and said he loved me. I was seeing in him the double of myself, pathetic in our shared weakness, hapless in our dealings with people. When I saw the gun, I thought the faceless man had found me, but Nemesis had hung over Tim and taken his life.

I slept in a fever of bloodletting. The old man's blood on the flagstones. Carnation petals falling on Tim's face. Droplets of blood on daisies in a field. A dead child in an open grave. A dead baby in my womb. And in my dream, I heard the shot.

Playing the detective, Goodison mocks.
The Auctioneers will kill us, my father says.
I love you hopelessly, wonderfully, madly.
Hold me close and save my life.

In my dream I wept for Tim, for the man whose life I couldn't save, but I have known, from the age of fifteen, that the dead are taken from us and we are alone.

I woke from a haunted night, my cheeks wet with dreams' tears, and I lay apathetically watching the early dawn colouring the window. Unable to sleep, I dragged myself up and stood under the hot, clear-running shower.

Wednesday, 3rd June 1981

Penry was right, I felt better in the morning. Everything was always better in the daylight. DCI Quinn came round at ten. As always, he was carrying his grey raincoat. He hung it up on the hook in the hall. I saw him glance in the mirror, his eyes watching me. He followed me into the kitchen. I had already made some coffee, and we sat together at the wooden table.

"I'm sorry about your father," Quinn said. "We didn't always see eye to eye, but he was determined to bring Hannagan to justice." It was a muted commiseration. "Penry was worried about you."

"Oh, I'm all right," I countered quickly. "Where is he?"

"Taking statements. So I've come to see what you remember. In your own words, tell me what happened at the Red Club."

"I've written it all down." I passed him my statement.

"I still need to hear you tell me what happened."

So I told him what I could remember. And as I talked I sketched Quinn's greying hair which had receded into a widow's peak. I had sketched him many times with my invisible pencil, capturing the strain in his thin face and grey eyes, but never catching what was in his mind.

"But what were you *really* doing at the club, Mrs. James?"

I couldn't understand his question. *Really doing?*

"Having a meal with a friend."

"Yes, Tim Harvey, the young man working for the chemist in Swaffham. And the other man, Henry Goodison?"

I shook my head. "He joined us later."

"What were the two men arguing about?" Quinn took out his notebook.

"Tim didn't like Goodison." Then I mentioned Audrey Simpson. "Tim didn't believe she committed suicide."

And I reminded him he had asked me about Lawrence Heals. "Tim said Lawrie's gone back to South Africa."

Quinn grunted. "But why did you go to the club with Harvey?"

I moistened my lips. "I wanted to learn more about *The Helpline* and a 'representative' called Rowene."

"You mean you went there to pump Harvey?"

"Tim wasn't co-operative, but one of my clients, Mrs Sylvia Henderson, mentioned *The Helpline* and Rowene. The point is this, three people who recently bought properties at the Retirement Homes came from Glasgow, Richmond in Yorkshire and Aylesbury in Bucks. I was told that Pat Heals had only advertised the Retirement Homes locally, so how did the relatives of my elderly clients know about Dunham Village? And why did my clients die so quickly after being left here? Lots of local people have bought properties and nothing's happened to them. And Sylvia Henderson said some worrying things."

"Such as?"

"Sylvia hated her mother. She said, 'In a few days the whole thing will be over and done with.' Four days after moving into her upstairs flat, Brenda Moffat was dead. Mr Dermott also died just after moving into his bungalow. He came here, he said, to play golf. I know people don't always let on about how ill they are, but, despite a stroke, Dermott wasn't a sick man. And another thing, Tim was frightened." I heard the tremor in my voice. "I've kept notes about everyone who bought properties through me. You may find my notebook useful."

I passed it over to him and he slipped my statement into it. "Good, I'll hang on to your notebook for the moment. Has anyone else mentioned this helpline?" I shook my head. "All right. Now then, what was your relationship with Henry Goodison?"

"There was no relationship." I was annoyed. "If this is a formal interrogation I want a lawyer."

"This is informal, but events are moving fast and I need to know what you know."

"Patricia Heals is friendly with Goodison. He bought his bungalow through her. I thought he was a creep. Pat is Sellick's right hand and she's put money, a lot of money, into the Retirement Homes."

I got up and switched the kettle on. " I didn't know Goodison would be at the Red Club last night. It's all down in my statement."

If you'd only bother to read it.

"So you're saying these men were not your lovers?"

I nearly threw the kettle at him. Quinn raised his hand. "All right, all right! but Mrs Heals told us she saw you and Harvey kissing in the sales office."

"And I told her a kiss is just a kiss. There was *nothing* between Tim and me."

"How long had Harvey and Goodison known each other?"

"No idea. I only met them last week when I started working at the sales office. You'd better ask Goodison's friend, Lionel Redding. He rushed over to help Goodison when he was shot. He was *very* concerned."

"And you know Redding from where?" The question hung in the air.

"They were interested in looking at bungalows. It's all down in my notes." A hint of exasperation had crept into my voice. "I didn't know they knew Goodison. I'll tell you this, though. Goodison was trying hard to shut Tim up at the Red Club. Tim was drunk and silly. And that's really all I know."

The doorbell rang with its annoyingly high-pitched trill. "I'll get it," I said. "The kettle's boiled so you can make the coffee this time."

Penry was on the doorstep shaking the rain off his anorak.

I glanced up at the leaden sky. "I thought it was going to be a nice day."

"It's been changeable all week." Penry was in a good humour. "You're looking better."

I thanked him for his kindness of the night before and led the way to the kitchen. There were three welcoming mugs of hot coffee on the table.

"Got anything for me?" Quinn asked.

Penry handed him a piece of paper. "This backs up what Tim Harvey told me about Goodison," he said. "Interpol are interested in him. They believe he was involved in the death of a young woman in Spain. You should have got Harvey to repeat his suspicions to the police, Mrs James."

But I knew Tim would never go to the police.

Penry sat down and passed Quinn a file. "I spoke with Commissar Agüero in Madrid early this morning. It's all down in the file. As you can see, they didn't have enough on Goodison to push for an extradition."

Quinn looked surprised. "Your commissar spoke very good English."

"Well, no sir, I speak rather good Spanish!"

Quinn grunted. Then he asked me again why I had come to Norwich.

"Why do you keep asking me the same stupid question?"

Penry opened his notebook. "Things happen round you, Mrs James. Setna was murdered the night he questioned you. He thought you knew more than you were saying." He looked up. "And now two men die at your table in the Red Club."

Quinn nodded. "We need to talk, to understand, what is going on since you came to Norwich. Now, this flat. Do you rent it or own it?"

I replied cautiously. "I'm in the process of buying the house, but I'm still waiting for completion. It was owned by a Captain Dalton and he gave me the option to buy as long as he could stay on as a sitting tenant in the upstairs flat."

"And you have the money to buy it." It was a statement, not a question. Quinn knew everything about me, my finances, my parents, my jobs. "Tell me about Captain Dalton."

I looked at Quinn blankly. Penry said, "You must have spoken to him, invited him in for a drink?"

"No and no. Captain Dalton's in Australia and the solicitor, Mr Carless-Adams, is acting for him."

Quinn said, "I've spoken with Sir Selwyn Freeman. According to him, you're a hard-working, honest, loyal and intelligent young woman." He sounded as if he didn't believe a word. "Then I spoke with your ex-husband, Richard James. Now he wasn't quite so complimentary." He looked at his notebook, "He agreed you work hard but, in *his* words, you were too close to Sir Selwyn. And your nature is dark. When I pressed him on that, he said you're obsessed by unknown fears." The rubber band snapped the notebook shut. "What did he mean by that, Mrs James?"

I thought of Richard, unfaithful, uncaring. "Obsessed by fears? Perhaps, and what else? Oh yes, a 'dark' side."

Richard would have enjoyed telling Quinn about my dark side. A sudden memory-spike took me unawares. I saw a flash. And the fox blinked. I felt the colour drain from my face and my heart raced uncomfortably.

Penry leaned forward, concerned. "Are you all right? D'you want a drink of water?"

I nodded, grateful for his concern. I sipped the water and waited until my heartbeat slowed down. "Let me tell you what Richard means by my 'dark' side. I sometimes get brief glimpses of something that happened a long time ago when I was young. And then the memory stops, leaving me, well, quite frightened."

"Is that what happened just now?"

I nodded. Penry glanced at Quinn. "That's what I told you, sir."

Quinn was watching me narrowly as he asked me to explain. "I get these memory-flashes when someone says or does something that triggers a series of pictures. Then I see the whole scene, hear the voices, watch the action, just as if it's on a film. The funny thing is, I'm always standing outside and looking inwards like a spectator reporting on what's going on. My mother said a memory like mine is a gift. I think it's a curse." I was bitter. "It's called eidetic, or flash-bulb memory. Usually, people lose the gift as they grow older, but a few retain it."

I paused, trying to collect myself. "Richard told you I'm obsessed by fears. It's true. I can be thrown into a panic when a curtain billows in the wind, when a car backfires, when a cup falls and breaks or a painting at an auction reminds me of a frightening time."

When I had tried to explain it to Richard, he had accused me of being emotional and hysterical. *If you're not careful, you'll become a danger to yourself and to others.*

Was he thinking I would attack the insipid woman he had taken into his life? I had been overcome by humiliation and shame when Jane Donovan told me the affair had been going on for over two years. And I never knew! Why had he made love to me during that time? I dragged myself back to Quinn and Penry.

Quinn was saying, "Is that how you felt when you saw the tin can photo?"

Only a moron would call it a tin can photo.

"I have a recurring memory of the time a stranger, an old man, died in our garden." I went on unsteadily, "One of the truly frightening things I remember is the fox. He had small bright eyes. I remembered the fox just now."

Quinn's voice was sharp. "Tell me about the fox."

"I was standing behind the lavender hedge near the garden gate. It was a bright summery afternoon and Suzy and Jenni were playing with me."

"And they are?"

"Mr Siskin's children. They were large wooden toys with articulated limbs, but to me they were completely real, as human as you are, not toys at all. I played with them all through the holiday, but one day two old friends came to visit my parents. Mum said it was a special day. They were talking about a secret society called *der Ritterorden, the Knights' Order,* part of *The Brotherhood.*"

I surrendered myself to the memory. "It was a lovely hot day in late July. It wasn't long after my fourteenth birthday and I remember there were lots of bees and insects that summer, and the scent of lavender …" I faltered. "The scent of lavender was everywhere."

The camera in my mind began to flicker. The heat-haze of the morning had turned into bright afternoon sunshine, the heat intensifying the scent from the lavender bushes. Mum was talking about her friend, Jürgen. He was nearly seventy. He had been ill. She hoped the journey would not be too much for him. My mind explored a little further. *Knicks!* Yes! she had wanted me to curtsey to the old man, and I had objected.

The camera turned again and in the misty shadows I saw the table outside the front door of Yorkstone Cottage and the large yellow flagstones that formed the patio. On the table was a big tray filled with cups and saucers, plates and forks, a cake knife, a coffee jug and a large walnut cake; to the side was a bottle of brandy and glasses. The memory became stronger. Yes, it was a *celebratory* party. I was fourteen years old.

July 1965

I am behind the hedge with Jenni and Suzy Siskin. It is late afternoon and it's a special day because Jürgen has come to Acle.

Jürgen Bergmann, Mum and Dad, are sitting round the eucalyptus table on the patio with Bruno Roth, who has driven Jürgen from West Berlin to the cottage in Damgate Lane. Earlier today Mum showed me a pencil sketch of a confidant young man with pleasant features. I scarcely recognise Bergmann in this tired, shrunken figure with heavy, folded fatigue lines pressing down to his chin.

I curtsey to the tired old man as he sits at the table on the patio's flagstones. I'm wearing sandals, a blue tee-shirt, shorts, and a loose jacket with deep pockets. Jürgen frowns. My clothes are too 'modern'. He shakes my hand limply and asks how my schooling is progressing. I reply politely and Jürgen tells me he's waiting for another car to arrive.

"An old friend is coming to join us to commemorate a day we celebrated seven and twenty years ago." He smiled. "That was the day we joined the Ritterorden. In those days," he lowers his voice playfully, "it was a secret society!"

He looks too old for cloak and dagger assignations. I bob another dutiful curtsey, and Mum tells me to go down to the end of the garden to play until she calls me for tea. I pretend to run off but turn back to join Suzy and Jenni behind the lavender bushes. The Loddon Blue lavender is growing in long wide planter boxes faced with Cotswold stone. It forms a thick hedge all the way from the patio to the wooden gate opening onto the pavement.

There's been an air of excitement from Mum all morning, but Dad is grumbly and cross. I position myself behind the lavender bush overlooking the patio, kneeling down on the low wall supporting the bush. I part the thick spiky stems and secretly watch the group round the table.

The old man fascinates me. He is a desiccated figure, his clothes hanging loosely on him. A greyish-white feathery crown adorns the dome of his head. His skin is like parchment, brittle and lined. Only the dark blue eyes bring colour to his face. My fingers sketch the weary, folded facial lines and sunken cheeks, and I add Mum and Dad sitting at the table.

Mum looks happy as they talk quietly together. Dad has opened the bottle of brandy and is passing the bulbous glasses and box of cigars round, but Dad is not happy. His face is closed up. Everyone is speaking in English, because of Dad.

Mum smiles at her visitor. "Surely it would have been more pleasant to travel together?"

"It was thought better to travel separately. Remember, Marjorie, they have permitted him to come so that he may answer our questions."

"I know, I know! The best thing is that you're here among your friends. It's been a long time, Jürgen."

She leans across the table and lovingly strokes his arm. Jürgen kisses her hand. He says he was taken prisoner in 1945 by the Communists. "When they had done with me, I was sent to work in the mines. Now that my heart is weak they use me as a pawn to be exchanged for Soviet spies."

His voice is toneless, it has no lilt, no rise and fall. Dad salutes him with his glass. "You survived, Jürgen, that's what matters. Amongst all the evil, the camps and the deaths, you were one of the good Germans. Prost!"

Jürgen raises his glass in return. They wait patiently while he lights and puffs at his cigar. "It's good we can meet today, this very day, when we sealed our vow to the Ritterorden."

"The day that changed the lives of so many." Mum's voice is husky with emotion. She raises her glass. "Arminius!"

Jürgen acknowledges the tribute. "Arminius! We all prayed the Austrian Kapo, like Varus, would fall on his sword, but it took longer before he succumbed to poison. Many owe their lives to the courage of people like you and Elèna."

Jürgen leans back against the comfortable fat green and red cushion tied to his garden chair. The short burst of energy has weakened him. "I'll share something with you." He is speaking slowly. "The vow we took that day kept me alive in the horrors of the camp in Siberia." He stretches out his left hand. "See, in that first year I lost two fingers and two toes to frost-bite. But you're right, Erich, I learned how to survive."

Dad is watching Jürgen, his eyes alert. "You're quite sure you want this meeting to go ahead, Jürgen?"

The old man nods like a puppet, up and down, up and down. "Ich bin mir sicher!" He accepts a hot cup of coffee with a smile that stretches the pale parchment skin. "We will see what happens!"

Jürgen turns as the garden gate opens and closes with its familiar loud squeak. Mum frowns and tells Dad he should have oiled the hinges. Dad looks cross. "Later. I'll do it later."

"The professor has arrived." Jürgen sits up straighter. "Now we will learn something of the truth."

Holding Suzy and Jenni close, I creep along the bushes that line the path to the squeaky gate. The air is shimmering with heat, and the scent of lavender lies heavily over the garden. A car-door slams. There are steps on the path. The gate squeaks again. Two people have arrived. Footsteps sound behind short, tappy, clickety steps. Then a small sharp head appears over the hedge and small glittering brown eyes are flickering over us. The fox smiles and his mouth opens and closes.

The fox frightens me. Clutching Jenni and Suzy I crouch down behind the lavender bush and scuttle down the path towards the house. Again I kneel on the low wall and gently part the bush and watch the adults sitting round the table on the flagstone patio.

A big man, wearing a long brown trench coat, is walking up to the table. A stocky man marches behind him. He tells Dad his name is Hans Meyer and he's Professor Baumgartner's driver. The professor is the man in the trench coat.

Dad shakes Meyer's hand and tells him to go to the Riverside Inn for lunch with Jürgen's driver, Bruno. He throws his keys to Bruno. "Take my car. Your Trabant will attract too much attention. Give us a couple of hours, then come back and pick your passengers up."

They leave their car keys on the table and Dad hands Bruno some money for their meal.

Meyer turns to the man in the long coat. "Enjoy your lunch, Herr Professor."

The professor is old, like Jürgen, but he has more vitality. He is well over six feet tall, with a smooth plump face, a thin, straight, grey moustache, keen dark eyes and a scar shaped like an arrow over his left eye. He possesses authority. He sits down next to the fox who is leaning against his chair, his pointy nose and sharp beady eyes fixed on the lavender bush. I hiss softly. The fox is watching me.

Jürgen sits back, twiddling his cigar between the thumb and third finger of his right hand. Mum looks up with a smile and offers the professor a slice of walnut cake. "Ich freue mich, Sie wieder zu sehen, mein alter Freund! We were all such good friends in '37 when we joined the Bruderbund."

Jürgen leans back, his head against the plump cushion. "1937? We were knights in shining armour then, tilting our lances at the evil in our world."

Dad grunts. "Time has moved on."

Jürgen puffs at his cigar. "And there is no place for us today." He raises his glass. "Well, Herr Professor, I hope the journey was comfortable." There is no warmth for the newcomer.

"Comfortable enough." Baumgartner stands up and walks over to the lavender hedge. "There was a child." He peers over the bushes. "I do not like children." His voice is waspish. "They annoy me with their probing eyes."

I'm sure he's going to tell Mum he saw me and Jenni and Suzy, but he says nothing.

Mum is soothing. "Paula's playing at the bottom of the garden. She won't come up to the house until I call her."

The professor grunts and returns to his seat. He takes his cigar and his glass of brandy as Jürgen's tired voice remarks, "You've worn better than I, Baumgartner, but then you were on the right side when the barriers came down in 1945."

"But I was thoroughly interrogated. I told them I did not commit atrocities, but Neumann and Harte, our superior officers, were callous. They smeared us with their brutish acts. They were hanged for their crimes."

His speech is curious. It is phrased in short emphatic bursts. There is a grating gasp in his voice. "Andreas and I were saved from the gallows, not by a Bruderbunder, for not one of you came forward in our defence, but by three men and three women from the Resistance who cleared us of wrong-doing. Now, Jürgen!" He waves his cigar towards the listless man and laughs harshly.

"Jürgen's called the 'good German who came in from the Cold'. Am I so different? Like many of my generation, I remained a practising Catholic throughout the war, and I swore by Our Lady, and by Arminius, that I would fight the plague called Nazismus. And I swear before you that I fulfilled my vow."

The professor clenches his hand and the fox blinks. "I was never a Nazi. I was always a Bruderbunder. I was, I am a psychologist, not a soldier. I always kept within the law."

Mum nods. "You were a brave man to make the journey, Felix. The doctors at the hospital told us you had suffered a Lungenentzündung." She turned to Dad. "Pneumonia, Erich. We're all so glad you're better now. It was good of you to come."

"It was important to me. There are things that have not yet been settled."

The professor turns to Bergmann. "We worked together to get twenty good men and women out of Nazi Germany. That should not be forgotten."

Jürgen nods. "We played our part."

"But the part is not yet played out." Baumgartner drains his glass. "I know you had me brought here." He pauses again. "Yes, brought here. To probe into the past. To learn the truth."

Mum pours him a coffee. He nods his thanks and leans back against the fat purple cushion.

Jürgen responds. "I was held in Moscow for two years while they squeezed everything out of me. They wanted information." A grey look passes over his lined face.

"Yes, yes, I read about the exchange. At least you can spend what is left of your life in western luxury."

"But the damage has been done. My heart is worn out. Now that you're here, professor, we have questions, and we need answers."

The professor nods. "It's good to be out of the house." He accepts another piece of cake. "It's been a long time since we took the oath of Arminius, yet the past is still with us. That is why you asked me to come, to look back into the past so that we can live again in the present."

I don't know what he means, for everything he says has a hidden meaning.

Mum nods solemnly. "That is well put, Felix. We will never recover until we learn the whole truth."

Jürgen clears his throat. "But the position needs to be clarified." His voice is suddenly stronger. "There are three objectives to be discussed. These objectives have been agreed by the authorities. Let us call them: The Berlin Agenda."

He holds up the three fingers of his left hand. "One: Who betrayed Radevsky? Two: Who betrayed Elèna and Arno Müller, and what became of them? Three: What were the circumstances surrounding the deaths of Marcus and Curt Ackert?" He leans forward. "Is that understood?"

The professor glowers and says nothing.

Jürgen insists, "Remember, Felix, you have come of your own free will to tell us what happened."

Baumgartner explodes, repeatedly banging the head of his cane on the table so that all the plates and cups and glasses jiggle up and down. In protest, the fox opens and closes his mouth. "Now I tell you also, the truth cannot be confined to your three questions. As I said earlier, there are still things to be settled. I, too, have an agenda." He hesitates and turns to Mum. "The name of this village?"

Mum is apprehensive. "Acle. The name is Acle."

The professor nods. "So, my timetable will be called The Acle Agenda. As you all know, our world is still a dangerous place, but I have not come here in any sense of contrition. I want my side of the story to be heard." He pauses. "You mentioned the boys, Marcus and Curt, Marjorie's cousins."

Baumgartner's voice is harsh. "Peter Schiffer knows the truth. He should be here, supporting me, but you chose not to invite him. Very well, if I must stand alone, so be it." He turns to Mum. "You were told the brothers died in a Russian Kriegsgefangenenlager, a POW camp, is that correct?"

She nods. The professor is terse. "Nein, nein, the boys never saw active service. They were never in Russia. They never left Bremen. In December 1939, they were indicted for treason against the state. The truth is they were too close to Dieter Ackert. The Nazi Party feared the boys knew Ackert's secret. And they no longer trusted you, Marjorie, because of the Radevsky affair, and the boys paid the penalty." He laughs abruptly. "You could say that Curt and Marcus were guilty of sedition through familial links. I tried to talk to them, but I was turned away, and they were summarily beheaded by the guillotine that very day in 1939."

Mum is standing and shouting, her hands raised to her head, pulling at her hair, tears flowing down her face. "Why did he lie to me? Why did Peter lie to me?"

"Why did he fabricate the story of a Russian camp?" Baumgartner shrugs. "Perhaps the truth was too terrible."

Mum is beside herself, moaning uncontrollably. She falls back in her chair, rocking to and fro in Dad's arms. Jürgen leans over and pours out a brandy and tells Dad sharply to quieten her. She drinks the brandy and is calmer.

"Sehr gut, that is one truth out of the way. And now I'm thinking of the summer of '37, Rik van der Vendt and Groningen."

I think Groningen is such a lovely, grumbly name.

Dad frowns. "But Rik is not on our agenda."

Jürgen quickly adds, "That is so, Baumgartner. The terms for this meeting are that you stay with the Berlin Agenda."

The professor interrupts him savagely, "No, I will not. You see, I know all your dirty secrets." He smiles as Jürgen raises his voice in protestation. "Yes, yes, I agreed to the agenda in West Berlin. I needed to get away from doctors and out of the country. I wanted to meet Jürgen and Marjorie again." He turns and faces Dad. "And, of course, the murderous Englishman."

"What's that?" Dad gets up and strides round the table. His face is full of anger, but the professor laughs up at him.

"All stridency and contention as usual! I will answer your three questions, but on my terms, Denby. Sit down, otherwise I shall call this meeting to an end." He bangs the cane on the flagstones. "And that is final."

Jürgen is plucking nervously at the red patches breaking out on the dry skin on his face. He signals angrily to Dad to sit down. The professor is smiling. He knows he has won the exchange. "Now then, Marjorie, let us go back to that day in March 1937, when you and Peter Schiffer were lovers, but you chose to run away with the Dutchman."

Jürgen's thin tone rises above the rich bass voice. "The Dutchman has nothing to do with the three questions on our agenda." The dry skin on his face is flaring up again. Baumgartner watches him, his eyes narrowing.

Mum is now in control of herself. She passes the professor some more cake. "I hope, Felix, we can have a proper dialogue. We want the truth about our friends who died."

"Very well, but let us approach these agenda in a different way. I want to take you along a path."

Jürgen interrupts harshly. "The only path we have to follow is the one agreed to in Berlin."

The professor is calm. "Marjorie is right. The reason you had me brought here is to learn the truth. My path will lead us to the whole and not the half-truth of the Berlin Agenda. Which truth do you want, Marjorie?"

Mum forces a smile. "Just the truth, Felix. So let us start at the beginning. The Nazis had infiltrated the Bruderbund in 1937 and six of our friends were executed. It was then that we formed our own secret inner circle, the Ritterorden, the Knights Order, to continue our fight against Nazism. Our password was 'Arminius'. That night we celebrated and went to the Ball. You were there, Felix, with the Conrads and poor Ralf, such a handsome young man."

The professor pooh-poohs Ralf's handsomeness. He says it was foolish to get involved with the woman. "But if you want to talk about Ralf Linburg, I will help you. Now tell me what you remember."

Jürgen leans forward. "He's not interested in our agenda, Marjorie, this is all about Baumgartner's verdammte path."

Mum reaches over. She holds Jürgen's arm. There is desperation in her voice. "We are the lost generation, Jürgen. How long must we live under a life sentence? We need a conclusion, a line drawn under those days. Felix knows the truth, that is why we agreed to meet."

Dad grunts. "I said this meeting was a mistake. I can see now it's going to be a bloody disaster."

"Nonsense, Erich! It's eighteen years since the war ended and we need to know what happened to Elèna and Arno. And I want to know who betrayed Radevsky. These are the reasons that Felix is here."

Felix Baumgartner sips his coffee and eats his cake. He's enjoying the discord.

Mum puts the cake-knife down. "Very well, Felix, I'll do as you say." She leans back against the dark red cushion tied onto the chair.

"I saw two people in love. They danced, their bodies close together, but I never believed they were sexually intimate. Gillian Conrad was married. She would not have enjoyed a full-blown love affair. The titillation of love was thrilling enough." She shudders. "It was a terrible ending to a sweet romance."

The professor snorts. "I interested myself in the case because Linburg was a Bruderbunder. But it was to no avail. Conrad had learned that Linburg was distributing leaflets against the Third Reich. Normally that would not have worried Conrad, for he was no lover of the Führer, but when he discovered that Linburg was planning to run away with his wife, that was another matter and he denounced Linburg to the authorities. Linburg and his friends were dragged before the Sondergericht and found guilty, the inevitable verdict from the Special Court. And that is why Linburg and his foolish friends lost their heads under the axe."

"Why are you so cruel?"

"The ones who are cruel, Marjorie, are those we love who betray us. And I have no reason to lie."

Dad looks up. "Just tell them about Elèna and Arno, damn you. That is, if you know."

Baumgartner parts his lips, but he is not smiling. "Ah, yes, Number Two on your Berlin agenda. I know their fate, but first let me tell you about Cedric Conrad. You were with Conrad when he played a trick on us in Pretoria. I was part of the German Mission negotiating for the same industrial diamonds as Conrad and the British Government. Conrad won that contract unfairly and our mission went home with nothing. I was lucky to keep my head. Meissen, the mission chief, was hanged. Failure was always heavily punished." The professor draws on his cigar. "Conrad was as big a rogue as you, Denby!"

Dad shrugs. "A rogue in peace is often a hero in war, but I realise now this is a personal issue. You failed in South Africa and now you want revenge. A bit late for that, surely?"

Baumgartner's hand clenches on his stick and the fox blinks nervously. "Yes, we lost the diamonds, but time will catch up with you, Denby. The authorities still want to know what happened to the four dead Canadians at the Pforzheim museum. I'm sure you will you'll be found guilty and will hang for their murder."

Dad leaps to his feet. "I've had enough of this. I want you out of my house. Get out, Baumgartner, get out!"

His features are puckered, his eyes protruding with fury as he lunges across the table. But Mum and Jürgen are restraining him. "We must hear what Felix has to say. Or we'll never know what happened to Elèna."

Mum is desperate. Slowly, Dad sits down, but he is simmering with fury.

Baumgartner has not reacted at all. He sits back composedly, a cigar in one hand, a brandy in the other.

Mum says war is not only about soldiers. "We're all victims in war, Felix. Pretoria is not why you're here."

Jürgen raps the table sharply with the handle of his knife. "It is of Radevsky and Elèna I wish to speak. Perhaps the great psychologist could tell us who betrayed them?" His mouth primps up sarcastically.

The professor leans forward and grips the fox's head with his big hand and the fox snaps his mouth shut. "Well, you should know, Jürgen. Radevsky himself was sure you had denounced him. He even wrote to tell me so! The truth is, a Dutch Nazi betrayed Radevsky. His name was Arno Müller." Mum tries to interrupt, but the professor raises his voice. "I know Müller was with you, Marjorie when Radevsky was killed in Groningen, but Müller was a double agent, working for Dutch Intelligence and MI5. He was our mole in your Section 23. Now that makes the fourth murder, and I'm warning you, there's a fifth."

Mum's lips are drawn back. "But Arno saved my life in Groningen. I never believed Jürgen betrayed Stefan."

Jürgen says nothing and Dad swears under his breath. He pours more brandy into his glass and drinks it quickly.

Baumgartner smiles. "No-one knew whom to trust, but in this case Müller was only partly responsible for Radevsky's death. I know the truth, because I was there, in Gestapo Headquarters."

Dad is pouring coffee for Mum and Jürgen. "I've a nasty feeling more dirty linen is going to be washed. The trouble is, I'm beginning to believe the bastard. As he says, he has no reason to lie."

Baumgartner smiles frostily. "First I want to return to Van der Vendt, for the truth begins and ends with his murder."

Jürgen hits the table with his fist, taking everyone by surprise. "Van der Vendt has nothing, nothing, to do with the Berlin agenda. I repeat, we do not have to sit here and listen to this buffoon."

Baumgartner draws his thick eyebrows down. His voice is sour. "Very well, Denby, get my driver. I wish to return to West Berlin."

Mum jumps up. Tears are running down her face. "No, Felix, I won't let you leave. Only you know what happened to Elèna. If you think Rik is important, then I, we, must cooperate."

A smile creeps along the professor's lips under his moustache. "Sehr gut. The truth then. Rik van der Vendt: painter, womaniser, political activist, fool. You first met him in 1931, Marjorie, when Rik was painting your father's portrait. Now Ackert and Van der Vendt found they were two of a kind, and

Ackert told Van der Vendt his secret. Later in 1937 Van der Vendt learned about another secret: Hitler's plans for Holland in the coming war.

"Despite the promises, Hitler had decided not to treat Holland as an equal with Germany. The Netherlands would have no sovereignty, it would be a puppet state, subservient to Germany. No wonder Van der Vendt was murdered! Then over the radio in 1937 we discovered that Dieter Ackert's daughter had been arrested; but I can confirm Marjorie had nothing to do with Van der Vendt's death. All old history, you will say."

Baumgartner stretches his hand across the table and his fingers dig into Mum's arm. "You wanted the truth, Marjorie, but more often than not the truth is a curse." He releases her and leans back. "Van der Vendt brought the curse down on himself."

Mum's eyes are huge as she stares across the table. Jürgen is agitated and the red spots on his flaky skin are flaring up again. "Stick to the Berlin Agenda, Baumgartner."

The professor shouts, "My path will lead us to the truth."

Mum rounds on him robustly. "All Jürgen wants, all I want, Felix, is for you to answer the three questions."

The professor grunts. "Then I will ask you this, do you want the grey half-truth or the whole spectrum of truth?"

She draws back. "The colours of truth!"

"At last we're speaking the same language. As you know, politics in the early thirties were volatile and—"

Jürgen thumps the table with his hand, "We don't need a lesson in history from you!" he shouts.

"Van der Vendt's murder—"

Jürgen stands up unsteadily. He is a sick man who has reached breaking-point. He leans on the table breathing heavily. "You have no remit to bring Van der Vendt and God knows who else into this discussion." He clutches his chest and groans, falling heavily back into his chair. "Elèna, my god-child!" he whispers.

His eyes are closed, and the chalky skin is filled with pitted lines, pinching his mouth and chin. Dad runs round the table and coaxes Jürgen to drink some brandy.

Then Dad turns to Mum, and I hear the bitterness in his voice. "Baumgartner's playing with us. You can either listen to him or take my advice and pack him off to Germany before things get worse."

Baumgartner titters. Mum looks drained. She turns to the professor. "Time is running out and soon your driver will be back and you'll have to leave."

Dad snaps, "If you've something to say, Baumgartner, get on with it, or I'll bloody drive you back to West Berlin myself."

"Ever the pragmatist, eh Denby! Very well then." The professor placidly places the tips of his fingers together. "Rik van der Vendt's body is fished out of the Reitdiep Canal, near the university, and Marjorie is arrested. But the Nazis do not want the daughter of the great Dieter Ackert to be charged with murder. It's not good for their image. According to the story," he turns to Jürgen and raises his glass, "they send Jürgen to Groningen to get Marjorie out of the mess. Of course, it's nonsense, because Jürgen is already in Groningen, in the very same police station as the one Marjorie and I are in."

Mum is bewildered. "But, Jürgen, I was told you were in Bremen!"

Jürgen is silent. He fiddles with his napkin.

Baumgartner nods. "Once it's established that Marjorie has no knowledge of her father's secret or Hitler's Dutch plans, she's released into Bergmann's custody and transported quickly over the border back to Berlin where she can do no harm. Rik van der Vendt was murdered by Arno Müller acting under the orders of Jürgen Bergmann, his handler in Bremen. In England, Selwyn Freeman handled Arno for MI5. And that is another truth."

Mum is whispering to Dad, holding his arm for support.

Jürgen pulls himself up. He is brusque. "In order to survive, yes, survive, *Marjorie, it was necessary to work with the enemy. You cannot always choose your partners. Nothing was black and white, the colours were neutral, hard to define, and shadows constantly threatened our lives. Before I left West Berlin I warned the authorities that Baumgartner would get up to his old tricks, but I never believed that you, Marjorie, would be so easily beguiled by his lies. Baumgartner may be a Bruderbunder, but he was also a member of the Gestapo."*

Dad is lighting a cigarette. "But Radevsky accused you of the same thing, Jürgen. He said you were working with the Gestapo. Maybe you're lying, not Baumgartner."

The professor nods heavily. "The colours are beginning to reveal themselves. Now let us proceed down my path to the final truth."

But Jürgen shouts, "Gott verdammt! This path is leading nowhere. Why do you believe him?"

"Because it smells right." Dad is firm.

Baumgartner looks round the table his face grim. "Good, then I continue. Jürgen had his finger in many pies. Bremen is near the Dutch border and the Dutch and German police have co-operated closely over the years. That is how he came to know Müller. Jürgen helped Arno Müller become an MI5 agent. Is that right, Jürgen?"

Jürgen nods calmly. "Yes, Müller was one of my moles." He looks straight at Mum. "History records the battles, but war is underscored by personal conflicts. My war was about one man. Dieter Ackert." His voice trails away into a murmur.

Baumgartner nods. "And therein lies the truth. In late 1939, Jürgen instructed Müller to get himself attached to the newly-formed Section 23, in the hope that he would partner you, Marjorie, on your missions into Europe."

He pauses to savour his wine. "Now it becomes difficult, because people will let emotions confound the facts. I was at a meeting in November '39 when Bergmann told me he was hoping to turn Marjorie into a double agent. I gave him some tips on how to handle you, and after all, early in the war, no-one knew whether your allegiance lay in London or in Berlin. But of course it was all flummery and nonsense. Jürgen had had his own agenda from early 1931.

"In '31, we learned that Ackert was arranging a march to take place through the streets of Bremen. It was to end at the Town Hall. On the steps of the Town Hall Ackert would give a speech and reveal his secret. At first his friends were sure the secret involved the setting up of a new Partei. It seemed such an obvious step."

The professor reaches out to Mum, who clasps his hand. "It's not difficult to understand that Ackert, and all those of the Great War generation, were suffering from fatigue. Ackert had been wounded at Ypres and again at Verdun, and old wounds fester, they wear the body down as the years pass."

Baumgartner drops Mum's hand abruptly. "Ackert was weary. There was to be no crowning of a king to lead his people to prosperity. Instead, Ackert told Adler Schiffer, Jürgen Bergmann and myself that he'd decided to emigrate to America and he wanted his supporters to follow him."

Mum is distraught. "I don't believe you, Felix. My father…" She chokes on the words. "My father would never have left his homeland. It would have been a denial of everything he'd campaigned for."

Baumgartner nods. "But the war had taken its toll. Ackert was still carrying bullets in his body from that war, as I and many others still do. Were you too young, Marjorie, to see the lines entrenched in his face, the stiffness as he moved, the dark moods caused by the infections from those bullets?"

Mum sits down, her face puckering, her hands clasped round her head. "I don't know, I don't know! I only ever saw him as Vati, the man everyone adored." She turns to Dad. "Was it like that, Erich? You were wounded, did it change you so much?"

Dad answers her slowly. "War changes everyone. Soldiers return from the front, but life at home is different. They are different. The pace of life has changed, but the pain and the dark memories are always there. Many commit suicide." He looks at Baumgartner. "Is that how it was with Ackert?"

The professor nods. "A defeated nation began clutching at men like Ackert. He wanted Germany to regain tolerance, respect and honour, but it was hard to create utopia in a post-war Germany of gross inflation and bitter conflict between the far right and the far left.

"When Ackert told us he was emigrating, we were aghast. We were his closest friends, comrades who had fought shoulder to shoulder in war. Ackert had saved Adler Schiffer's life in the trenches, and Schiffer's commitment to Ackert was total, as was mine. After the war Schiffer and Ackert taught at the university, Bergmann became a policeman, and I finished my medical studies and was affiliated to the police. We all believed that Ackert was the one sane voice in a murderous world. Emigrate? Unmöglich! Impossible!"

Jürgen's eyes are closed. His lips are moving silently as his fingers tear the fine linen napkin apart.

Baumgartner nods. "And, Jürgen, you were determined he would not leave."

Mum gets up unsteadily. "Unsinn, Felix! My father would never have emigrated." She reaches out to her friend. "Jürgen, you were my father's oldest friend, tell me this is all nonsense!"

Jürgen's voice is muted. "It is not nonsense. Dieter Ackert was a hero, the only man that could push the Nazis out of power. He had the charisma, the background, the gift of oratory, but his path was coming to an end. Dieter was tired and sick. The battle had become too strong and too long."

"It's a shock for you, Marjorie," Felix breaks in, "but, as I said, we are deceived most by those we love. Now I can reveal what happened on the day of that infamous march in '31 when Dieter Ackert, Adler Schiffer and Jürgen Bergmann were approaching the Town Hall."

Jürgen is suddenly on his feet, shouting. "I've heard enough. It's time to put a stop to this rubbish."

But Mum is urging the professor to continue.

"Yes, you've waited long enough to learn the truth, Marjorie. Sit down, Jürgen, we're at the end of the path."

But Jürgen is refusing to sit down. He's getting noisier and noisier, objecting to everything the professor is saying. Dad pulls him down. "Let the man have his say."

Dad gives Jürgen some brandy and the old man tosses it down, his face working. He continues to shout, trying to drown Baumgartner while his hand keeps banging noisily on the table like a drum beat.

Baumgartner shouts above the noise. "I was there, on the steps of the Town Hall, as the head of the march approached with Ackert and Adler Schiffer in the lead. There were thousands marching behind them, thousands more were lining the streets and cheering them on. But there were rumours that the Nazis, the communists, even the police, were out to stop Ackert talking to the people.

"Usually, Ackert, Schiffer and Bergmann marched three abreast, as they had done in battle, but this time, Jürgen Bergmann was walking behind Ackert and Schiffer. At first I thought he was trying to slow the march down, but as they reached the Town Hall, a shot rang out and Ackert fell dying across the steps. Adler Schiffer, turning to help his friend, was hit in the head and chest and died immediately. From my vantage point on the steps above, I saw what happened. Then the police, the Nazis and the communists opened fire. Many died and many were arrested."

The drumming has stopped. It is eerily quiet. Baumgartner nods. "Jürgen revered Ackert, but he could not stand by and see him betray Germany. Jürgen Bergmann shot Ackert in the back at close range. The protection you enjoyed in the war, Marjorie, has been Jürgen's penance for the crime he committed in the name of the Fatherland."

Mum is staring wide-eyed at Jürgen, her mouth open, her shoulders limp. The old man slumps down in his chair. His skin is grey with defeat. He is quiescent.

218

Dad frowns. "You're sure about this, Baumgartner?"

"I swear by the Holy Mother that Bergmann murdered Ackert."

Mum is bewildered. "But he was your friend, Jürgen, he loved you."

Jürgen whimpers, "I followed Dieter through war and peace, then out of the blue the old fool says he's throwing it all away. If I hadn't shot him, someone else would have killed him."

He looks up, his voice steadying. "You're the best of the family, Marjorie. You never compromised your beliefs, you never lied. Even during the war, you knew exactly what you were fighting for. Yes, I shot Ackert and Adler, and yes, the guilt lies heavy on my heart, but by protecting you I was seeking absolution for the sin of killing Dieter."

Dad is incredulous. "Let me get this straight. You're saying you worked with the Nazis to keep Marjorie safe, because you killed her father?"

Baumgartner nods. "That's exactly what he's confessing. In life, the colours get blurred, nothing is as it seems. And now the lying has to stop. For that was not the end of the matter. When Marjorie was sent on undercover missions into Holland and Germany, Jürgen gave orders to the police not to fire on her. In return for their compliance, Jürgen broke the main Dutch Resistance and forty-two brave Dutch men and women were tortured and executed. I didn't know then that Marjorie would be teamed with Elèna, my wife. The imponderables of war defeat the best of intentions.

"In 1939, while Holland was still neutral, Arno told Jürgen that Marjorie was meeting Radevsky in Groningen. Jürgen informed the Dutch police and the officer in charge made sure Marjorie and Arno escaped from the ambush.

"Much later, I discovered that Arno and Jürgen had made a pact. A large sum of money was deposited in a bank in Berne in Arno Müller's name, and the commitment was made that Marjorie Ackert would survive the war."

Jürgen looks up. "You are Ackert's daughter and part of the magic that lies in Ackert's name. We had to keep you alive. Of course everyone was suspect in Section 23, Müller, yourself, Elèna, even Sheldon Asquith, head of the section. Arno used his time well by shifting the blame from one to the other."

Slowly Mum cuts the last piece of cake and Dad passes the slices round. He asks the professor what became of Arno.

Baumgartner smiles. "Arno is a survivor. He was captured in '42 with Elèna at Emden. I'd begun to suspect Arno might be working for the British, so I had to reappraise my ideas about Jürgen. Within a day of Arno being captured at

219

Emden he had escaped from his prison cell. I saw Jürgen's hand in that. And money, lots of money. Money used as bribery. Is that not so, Jürgen?"

The professor calls Jürgen's name twice before Jürgen slips out of the grey silence he has wrapped round himself.

"Bribery saved a good man from the gallows. I made sure he reached Switzerland safely. The last I heard was that Arno married a Swiss girl and has two children."

Baumgartner turns to Mum. "The truth is even more complex than you allow." He turns to Jürgen. "Radevsky was sure you were the traitor, Jürgen."

"Enough of the lies!" The words wing towards me over the lavender hedge as Jürgen pulls himself up. "You will not pin this death on me, you coward. I have proof that you *betrayed Radevsky!"*

The cry bursts out of Baumgartner's mouth. He stands up and faces Jürgen across the table. "All right, I admit it. Radevsky had turned Elèna, my wife, against me. When they became lovers I lost everything, my honour, my family, my home, my career. All because of that slut."

"Stop it!" Mum is on her feet. There is uproar as she screams and throws cups and plates onto the patio. "Stop it, I say! Elèna was a beautiful young woman." Her voice rises menacingly. "What happened to her, Felix?"

Felix's breath is rasping painfully. "Yes, yes, it was terrible. Terrible! She died in Gestapo Headquarters in Bremen."

"But there are no records." Jürgen strikes the table with his hand. "I searched the records. Her name was not there."

"Correct! No records." Baumgartner's voice is clipped. "It was difficult when it became known that Elèna, my wife, was working with the Dutch Resistance. Only my superb record saved me from the gallows. But I'm not a traitor. I stood by our vow to the Bruderbund. No-one suspected a Gestapo agent of helping dissident Germans to escape. And Jürgen, you could not have done it on your own. Is this worth nothing?" Baumgartner turns to Mum. He seems to be pleading. "The death of Van der Vendt—" he begins.

But Jürgen breaks in, "Van der Vendt's death is a red herring. We no longer need Baumgartner. Erich! Telephone his driver at the restaurant and tell them to return here. It's time they went back to Germany."

"No!" Mum is on her feet. She has recovered from her frenzy of tears and plate-smashing. "Felix is right. He saved many lives, just as we all did. And yes, like all of us, the trauma from those times have left him damaged and disturbed,

as his doctors will testify. What separates him from us? By the end of the war the Ritterorden and what was left of the Bruderbunder had rescued over six hundred talented souls from the Gestapo. Those were Germans helping Germans, like Felix, like Jürgen, Elèna, Arno and me." She looks defiantly round the table. "It's a story that needs to be told."

Baumgartner sits down and I can see he is tired and old. "Yes. I played my part against our enemy. Elèna and Radevsky were a personal issue."

Dad nods. "Right then, tell us what happened to Elèna."

Suddenly a bundle of black and white fur bounces up against me. I am delighted to leave the passion and the drama and take Bobby down to the bottom of the garden where I throw twigs for him to collect and bring back; but after a few moments Mrs Lacey calls him, her fluting tones reaching into our garden. Bobby puts his head on one side, and then runs across the grass and squeezes through the hole he has made in the hedge.

I hear Anna Lacey's voice: "Where have you been, you naughty boy?" And Bobby's happy springer bark tells her he was playing with Paula, his friend. I run back to my position at the lavender bush. All I can hear is glass breaking and angry voices. Something has happened. I kneel on the wall and carefully part the lavender stems to get a clear view.

Mum, Dad, Felix and Jürgen are standing angrily round the table. Jürgen's cup and saucer are broken on the flagstones. Mum's chair is lying on its side, her red cushion stained with coffee and wine.

"Tell them the truth, damn you!" Dad's voice is raised.

The professor draws himself up. Everything about him is strained. "Elèna died! I watched her die. Why can't you be satisfied with that?"

But they clamour for the truth and the professor steps back, his chair clattering onto the flagstones. Anger fills his face and voice. With a sharp cry, he raises his cane and stabs the fox's mouth sharply into Jürgen's hand. The old man screams, his cries piercing the air as he pulls the fox from his hand. Dad runs round the table, but the professor's pistol is pointing straight at his heart. Dad stops, his hands raised. His voice is soft. "This doesn't have to go any further, Baumgartner. No-one has to die. We can talk this through."

"Stay where you are, Denby. I despise everything you stand for, and it would give me great pleasure to put a bullet through your heart, but as Marjorie said, this is a German matter."

The pistol moves and points at Jürgen. "The doctors at the hospital allowed me to come here. As you know, I have been ill and my life is drawing to an end. I have nothing to lose."

Again the pistol moves. "Keep your hands up, Denby, and step back!"

The professor is breathing heavily, his neck sunken into his shoulders. The gun is steady in his hand.

His voice is a grating whisper. "It was your testimony, your lies, Jürgen, that told against me. It's time to settle old scores."

But Mum entreats him. "No, Felix, wait! I must know what happened to Elèna."

Felix shakes his head. "It is foolish to trawl over her death."

"Just tell me what happened!" she cries.

"Very well. Elèna was interrogated and then stripped of her clothes. Now turn with me and see the flames devouring the living, naked, breathing woman as her body twists in the burning coals of the furnace."

Pain is everywhere, distress in every raised voice. Jürgen's hand is pressed against his heart. "You will die for this."

"No, you will die. This is the moment to confront your past."

Dad moves forward, and Baumgartner fires his pistol at his feet. Dad stands still. With his left hand, Baumgartner picks up the car keys on the table. "Keep back. Zurück!"

There is an enormous crash as the table is thrown onto its side and Jürgen drops back into his chair. Cake, glasses, brandy, hit the flagstones. A shot. A cry. The professor is shouting in German, his weapon pointing at Mum. Dad is inching forward. The colour from the rose pinned to Mum's dress is running down her shoulder. She is leaning on the upturned table. Such a curious expression is fixed on her face. It's as if she has turned to ice.

Another shot. Jürgen slumps forward in his chair, his eyes closed. Dad runs round the table, the broken glass crunching under his shoes.

Another shot, and Baumgartner staggers forward.

The cake knife glistens in the sunlight. In an instant Mum's hand is as red as cadmium paint and the paint is dripping over the yellow flagstones.

Baumgartner groans, his hand round the knife in his chest. Then he crumples forward over the upturned table, the groan dying in his throat.

Mum steps back. Her mouth is open in a silent scream as Baumgartner slips to the ground. The scent of lavender is overpowering. The sun has turned black, and purple and mauve are staining the paving stones.

I fall onto the ground, retching, and my vomit is full of lavender leaves and flowers. I wipe my mouth and watch as Dad bends down and pulls the knife out of the professor's chest and drops it behind the table.

Steps are hurrying along the path and the drivers, Bruno and Hans, rush into view. "Mein Gott, was ist hier geschehen?" Bruno is flabbergasted. "We heard shots. What happened? Is he dead?"

I watch Dad stoop and pick up the professor's gun. "Look, man, Baumgartner shot at us. How the hell did he get a bloody gun? Wasn't he searched?"

Hans raises his hands. He's shaking. "I don't know how he got it. I'll have to account for this, you know." He's panic-stricken. "We'll have to give statements. Und mein Gott, die Polizei! What will they make of this?"

Dad interrupts quickly, "No police! Keine Polizei! Ruhe sie sich, Hans!"

But Hans is visibly distressed and Dad grips his arm. "Now listen to me, Meyer! Baumgartner came here willingly. He was a sick old man. How did he die? He slipped and fell on the knife as the table collapsed."

I watch them, my legs trembling, my heart thudding. Lavender is in my mouth, my nose, my lungs. There is blood running down the sleeve of Dad's jacket.

Mum is leaning over Jürgen. She's hysterical. "Jürgen's dead!"

Bruno runs over to her. "Was he shot as well?"

Dad's answer is short. "Heart attack. He shouldn't have been here at all. He was an old man with a weak heart, facing a pistol and threats. He knew Baumgartner was a conniving bastard, but no-one thought he was carrying a firearm."

But I know Jürgen had to come. He was a man with a terrible secret. His heart had died within him long ago.

Dad tells Bruno to take Mum into the cottage. "Give her a brandy, then come back here."

Bruno puts his arm round Mum's shoulder. Her steps falter and Bruno carries her into the house.

Hans looks at Dad. "What am I going to tell them in Berlin?"

Dad nods grimly. "Car crash. Look, we'll do it this way. You've delivered him here, and you and Bruno go to the nearest pub and have a beer. You're letting us talk together privately. That's what they wanted. Stick to the truth. Now, let's see. We'll say...we'll say you left the keys in the car. There's been a disagreement. Baumgartner gets annoyed and rushes down the path and drives off. He's in the devil of a mood and crashes the car. It bursts into flames.

"You might get your knuckles rapped for leaving the keys, but that's about all. I'm amazed they let him come over. Perhaps they hoped he'd unlock some secrets, but they should have anticipated the consequences. As long as they get a body back I don't think they'll worry too much. If they've any sense they'll cremate what's left of him."

Hans looks unconvinced. Dad picks up Baumgartner's coat and together, they carry the professor's body to the car in the lane. Dad tells Hans to follow him in his car. "I'll crash the car with Baumgartner in it."

Before they leave, Dad comes back and helps Bruno carry Jürgen into the house and I hear him phone for an ambulance. Mum is talking, her voice high and unsure. A little later, Dad comes out alone onto the patio. He calls my name. "I know you're there. I know you've been there all the time."

I stand up, my legs shaking, the sickness on my breath. Dad is standing very straight. For the first time I see him as a soldier, strong, in command. His voice is curt. "Where did you get the gun?"

I fidget.

His voice whips round me. "The gun! Who gave you the gun?"

"Josie gave it to me. It's her brother's gun. He's in America. She said I could have it for a week, to practise. It was in my pocket." And then all my fear floods out. "I was so afraid the professor was going to kill Mama and you. I had to stop him." I'm frantic. "The bullets are blanks, I didn't know they'd kill him!"

"Give me the gun."

I go round the lavender bushes and give him the gun. He nods, examines it and puts it in his pocket with the professor's gun.

I listen to his hard soldier voice. "You didn't kill him. The blank coming over the hedge unbalanced him and that helped me get at him and save your mother. Now there's work to be done here." He looks me up and down. "First get rid of those disgusting clothes and clean yourself. Then look after your mother. A bullet nicked her shoulder. I've cleaned the wound and dressed it. Your job is to make her some hot, sweet tea and clean up the mess out here. I shall be back soon.

Now, you are to forget everything, do you understand? Everything you've seen and heard today. You're never to talk about it. Is that understood?"

I nod. I understand what he is saying and what I have to do. He bends down and picks up the cake knife and the professor's stick and takes them into the house. When he comes out, he passes me without a word and I hear the cars drive away. I say nothing about the wet blood on Dad's sleeve.

I change my smelly clothes and wash my mouth out. Then I sweep up the mess on the patio flagstones and put all the broken bits of glass and crockery in the kitchen bin. I go back and pull the table upright and wipe it down. I wash the red-stained stones clean with the outside hose, and then I push the chairs close into the table.

I'm remembering Dad's expression when he was angry with the professor, the moment when anger changed his face and turned him into a stranger. I'm surprised when Mr Chase, our neighbour, comes hurrying down the path to the front door. "Is everything all right? We thought we heard shots and someone shouting."

I look at him, nonplussed. Mum joins us in the garden. She has changed into a brown top and jeans. She is calm.

"Shots? No, of course not, Michael, it was fireworks!" Her smile is brittle. "We were celebrating with friends from the old days when two of the fireworks exploded prematurely. I stumbled and upset the table and everything fell to the ground and broke. Erich thought I was burned. I'm afraid we were all shouting."

She turns to me. "You've done well, Liebling. Now take the covers off the chairs, they all need a good wash, and after that put the kettle on."

She takes our neighbour's arm and I watch her walk with him to the garden gate. "I'm sorry we disturbed you, Michael, but one of my guests has been taken ill. The excitement was too much for him. We're expecting the ambulance any minute."

"Of course, of course! Is there anything I can do to help?"

A siren blares and an ambulance pulls up. "Forgive me, Michael, but I must go back to my friend."

"Of course! My wife will pop over tomorrow."

"That will be lovely. Ah! here are the men."

She pecks Michael on the cheek. I follow the ambulance men into the sitting room and they take Jürgen away on a stretcher, his head is covered by the blanket. Hans follows and climbs into the ambulance. When they've gone, Mum *collapses onto the sofa and I hear her begin to cry. In the Bible they talk about women weeping, and for the first time I feel the depth of their grief in the total submission of her tears. With a jolt I remember what Dad said about making hot, sweet tea and I go into the kitchen.*

My mind was in chaos and the smell of lavender kept sweeping over me in waves of sickness. A cup of coffee was pushed into my hand, and as I began sipping the hot, comforting liquid I became calmer. The sickness passed and the memory-spike faded.

I've sometimes wondered if other people experience the same retrieval of the past through sound and colour as I do. How much had I revealed to Quinn? I watched him flipping through my notebook. "Tell me, Mrs James, how many children would remember everything like that? And what was the fox about?"

Penry broke in. "What she was saying made sense, sir. Rik van der Vendt and Dieter Ackert were both alive in the thirties. My father taught history at Westminster School and he admired Ackert. He was sure Ackert was shot in Bremen by the Nazis. He wrote a book about it." He looked at me accusingly. "It didn't have anything to do with Bergmann."

Penry's father knew nothing. Quietly, I replied, "It was a long time ago, but I do remember the smell of lavender. It made me ill."

"How could you remember so much detail?" Quinn was sceptic.

I tried to explain. "I have no control over the memory-spikes. That's the name I use for the moments of recall. They transport me into another time. Sometimes I'm a spectator looking in from the outside; occasionally, I'm part of the scene itself. Sometimes everything's just black and white, sometimes there's colour. But the memories need a trigger, a sound, a word, which activates the hidden film-reel in my head." I looked at Quinn, my voice strained. "The reel starts turning and I hear a shot or a woman groaning. Or I may see a rose dripping blood and everywhere carnation petals are falling. Just as suddenly, it all disappears and I'm left feeling completely disorientated and very, very scared. Time makes no difference. I can recall twenty years ago, a year ago, but I couldn't tell you what you said when you questioned me about Setna a few days ago, not unless there was a trigger to start the process."

Quinn turned to Penry. "Perhaps you and your psychology are right. We just have to dig deeper to find the truth about the missing miniatures. Now, Mrs James, who were the people round the table?"

Had he heard nothing I'd said?

"My father and mother, their old friend, Jürgen Bergmann, and Professor Felix Baumgartner."

"And where was the fox?"

"It was confusing." I could not talk about the fox.

I looked up, meeting Quinn's cold eyes. "I was peeping through the lavender bush. It was a limited view. The next day we drove down to London and I went back to school and into a new form. I forgot all about it. Until now."

Not really true, there were always those teasing flashes of memory and the unanswered questions about the big man who came to tea.

"I wonder where they crashed the car," I said suddenly.

"You're sure there *was* a body?" Penry asked.

"Quite sure. He didn't move, there was blood everywhere."

"The local police should have a record." Quinn looked at Penry who made a note and Quinn went on, "What happened to the fox?"

"No idea."

Quinn grunted. "Can you sketch these people?"

I could sketch the men. I took my sketching book out of my shoulder bag, found some pencils and sat and waited for the features to become clear. When the first sketch was finished, I handed it to Quinn. It showed a tall, heavily-built man, dark suit and tie, dark eyes, heavy brows, thick white hair and a scar over his left eye.

"But you talked about him as if he'd been a Nazi criminal. He wouldn't have been allowed out of the country if he'd been in prison."

"Mum said he was a very disturbed man. He'd been treated badly after the war, and it took time to clear his name. He blamed Jürgen for that. He came to Acle and there was some kind of accident and he died. He said, *In life, the colours get blurred.*"

I handed Penry the second sketch, showing Jürgen Bergmann.

"He looks very frail," Penry said.

"He'd been a prisoner of war in Russia. I once saw a sketch my mother had drawn of him much earlier. I would never have recognised him as the same man."

"You're very good," Penry said, and added unexpectedly, "I was good at art at school, but I decided to read psychology at Durham instead. And then I joined the Force, but I've always been interested in art."

So that's how he knew about Van der Vendt and MJ Jeffries. He held up my sketches. "You've made these men come alive. I wish I could do that."

My mother, I thought, would have liked Penry. Quinn wasn't interested in Penry's brief encounter with art. He took the sketchbook and turned some pages. "We could do with you on our team. You see a lot when you look at people." He read the names out. "Sellick, Gillian Conrad, Corrie Smiley, Stevens. Peter Schiffer." He looked up. "How well do you know Schiffer?"

I shrugged. "I've met him a few times recently. He told me he'd known my mother and, for some reason, he thought I had some of her paintings."

Quinn showed the next sketch to Penry. "She's caught you there, Penry." He paused very slightly over the sketch of himself and looked up. "You're very good. You should do this for a living."

I mumbled something, and Quinn closed the book. "Now then, how old were you when Baumgartner died? Thirteen, fourteen?" Quinn was trying to work it out. "You could have imagined his death. I mean, children don't know what death is. Perhaps he didn't die but was hurt in the accident. You react strongly to things. Like those metal boxes! Were you *more* than a secretary, Mrs James? I mean, did you work for any of the Secret Intelligence Services?"

I laughed. "You mean MI5, CI2 and so on? That's nonsense. I'm a secretary, a very ordinary woman doing a very ordinary job." The loathsome Goodison had said I was doing an ordinary job badly. "I'm what I am," I added quietly.

"Scarcely ordinary with such a background! You *know* things and I need to know what you know. At the moment I want to know why you chose to come to Norwich at this particular time."

I suppressed my frustration and answered him. "My husband had left me. I suppose you could say I was running away from the past."

But Quinn's eyes darkened. "That's it? You just wanted to get away from your ex?"

And suddenly, I snapped. All the fears, the nightmares, the deceit and heartbreak, the miscarriage, gushed out of me. "You talk as if divorce is easy to deal with! It isn't. You go hammering on and on at me, searching in the wrong places."

Quinn was unaffected by my emotional distress. "Tell me more about Yorkstone Cottage. We've seen Scott going in and out. What would he be doing there?"

"No idea."

Penry referred to his notes. "Setna had a photo of James Mitchell who works for CI2. There's a connection between Mitchell, Sir Selwyn Freeman, a miniature painting, and you. The painting was found on the body of a dead man in Yarmouth. That man was Stan Parry. He fought with your father in 1944 at Pforzheim. You see, Mrs James? There's always a link leading back to you."

I was crisp. "You're trying to create a mystery where there is none, but I do remember something about the miniature. Sir Selwyn was very excited when it was found. It was a portrait of Princess Victoria. Did you know Selwyn's an authority on English miniaturists?" Now I was coming to the sticky bit. "I saw Mitchell briefly when he was leaving Sir Selwyn's rooms at Inner Temple. I never spoke to him. The photo Setna showed me was of a much younger man, and I didn't recognise him as Mitchell. I did see him at the Riverside Inn recently, but again we didn't speak, and I saw him at the sales house. But it's odd you mentioned Parry." Quinn looked up expectantly. "I've been receiving some strange postcards since I've moved here. They're in my bag and Parry's name is on one of them."

Penry passed me my bag. I burrowed inside for the envelope with the postcards, taking care to bury my revolver under a silk scarf.

"It's puzzling," I said. "I don't understand them at all." I hoped I wasn't going to regret showing Quinn the cards. I put them on the table, picture-side up.

Penry turned the first card over. "I see what you mean: *Why have you come to Norwich?*"

Quinn held the second one up. "What exactly does 'Pforzheim' mean to you?"

"It's a word I heard years ago. I know now there was a robbery; paintings were stolen."

A memory-spike, my mother's voice. *Bremen is part of my past and Pforzheim is part of yours.* Why was I remembering that?

"And why does this postcard mention you and Denby and miniatures?"

He passed it over to me. *If you want to live, Mrs James, give us the miniatures. We know you and your father have them.*

Quinn leaned forward suddenly. "You may see your father as a war-hero, but murder was done at Pforzheim and your father was involved. Details have recently come to light, and now there's going to be an official report on what happened at Pforzheim."

"How do they know he was involved?"

"There was an eye-witness. He's only just come forward. Colonel North wants to speak to you about it."

"An eye-witness after all these years?" It seemed incredible. "But I don't know anything about Pforzheim. I wasn't even born then." I felt an overpowering sense of injustice.

"Let's go back to the card about the art gallery."

"Schiffer seems to think I have my mother's paintings, but I'm sure she sold everything."

"Do you know Schiffer well?"

"No, are you interested in him?"

"We've been keeping an eye on his art gallery." He picked up one of the postcards. "What can you tell me about this: *Stan's dead, murdered. If you want to live, Mrs James, give us the miniatures. We know you and your father have them.*"

Again memory was pricking at my mind. "When Amy died, I was in shock. Almost everything about those years just disappeared somewhere in my brain, but when I saw the Chirico painting, snippets of memory kept coming back. I remember I was standing behind a door. I heard my mother say, 'Stan has the medallions', and Dad was really angry."

Quinn frowned. "What medallions?"

"I don't know."

"And you're sure Parry never tried to get in touch with you?"

"Quite sure."

Penry said, "Tell me about the Chirico painting."

"There was a man standing in the street beside a building with tall arches. He was holding his arm out as if he had a gun. It brought Amy's murder into my mind."

Quinn leaned forward. "You said there were four postcards, but there are only three here."

I had pushed one into the hall table drawer. Penry went and found the card. He passed it over to Quinn. *Time's running out for you and Denby.*

"These cards are threatening," Quinn frowned. "Why didn't you tell me about them earlier?"

How could I possibly tell Quinn about my complicated life?

Penry took the card. "There's no sender's name, no phone number, how do they expect you to get in touch?"

Quinn said, "They're waiting."

"Waiting for what?"

He ignored my question and said it was time they looked round Captain Dalton's flat. He asked me if I had a key.

"Yes, Dwayne gave it to me."

"Dwayne?"

I was on the defensive. "He services the boilers for Captain Dalton on the last weekend in May."

"Go on."

"If you'd read my notes, you'd see that Dwayne saw to the boiler upstairs on Sunday, but had to return on the Monday to put in a new boiler for me."

Quinn couldn't hide his astonishment. "You mean you let this stranger into your flat while you were out?"

"The solicitor said he was all right."

"And that satisfied you?"

"Look, I'm only the tenant. The house belongs to Captain Dalton. I don't want to be responsible for the boiler blowing up. And the solicitor vouched for Dwayne."

"Hmm. And the keys?"

"I asked him to leave the keys with me. I didn't like him having keys to my flat."

"So this man, this stranger, has spent time alone in your flat and has been upstairs on his own." His grey eyes glinted with disbelief.

I was guarded. "I had to go to Swaffham. It was all arranged. It's all in my notes."

"And you've never met Captain Dalton?"

"No."

Quinn got up again. "OK then, if it's all right with you, we'll go upstairs and make sure your heating engineer left things properly. After all, you don't know anything about him, and he's been poking round a lot in the house."

I gave him the key, alarmed at the way he had described Dwayne's movements. An hour later, Quinn rang the doorbell. "Nothing upstairs to worry about. The new boiler's in and the place is clean and tidy." He handed me the key and joined Penry waiting at the gate. I watched them drive away.

Wednesday, 3ʳᵈ June 1981

After everything that had happened, I felt the time had come to protect myself from the men who were after the Pforzheim treasure.

I always kept my mother's Walther PK in my shoulder bag. It was only a matter of time before Quinn searched my flat. I needed to find a good hiding-place. I went into the guest room and opened the wardrobe door.

The wardrobe was full of memories. My old shoulder-bag was still there and the shoe-box with my little bear with the scorched ear. I lifted him out of the box and put him on the pillow on the bed. He looked almost happy. Then I knelt down and opened my mother's canvas bag. Lying on the top, carefully folded, was the silk rose-patterned scarf my father had given Mum before she died. I rocked back on my heels, the memory-spike bringing her vividly into my mind. This time, it was at the inn near the bridge over the River Bure.

July 1960

I'm nine years old. Mum is wearing a pretty blue smock and her short fair hair is waving back from her face in the breeze. This time she's painting an elderly man and his granddaughter on one of the Broads cruisers. It's lunch time and cruisers are coming and going all the time. I rush round being a generally helpful nuisance, catching the ropes from the boats as they ease in and out from the staithe. When I'm tired, I come and sit near Mum and watch her paint. People stop by the easel and Mum does her best to answer their questions.

After a while, I clamber up onto the bank and sit behind a yellow flowering shrub. To my delight, I find a carpet of daisies and begin making a daisy chain, half-singing to myself as I fit the tiny stems together. Without really noticing, I glimpse a man sauntering down to the staithe. He stops by the easel. Their voices carry clearly up to me. They're speaking in a mixture of German and English.

"You're not returning my calls."

"It's finished. I can't go on like this."

"Come away with me, Hanna."

"No, it's finished, Franz. Go away." I peep round the flowering shrub. "Don't make a scene, Erich's in the inn."

The man is a stranger. He's handsome with long fair hair, like the picture of the knight, Lancelot, in my book of King Arthur. And his voice is like music. Why is Mum angry with the handsome knight?

"Erich this and Erich that! What do you want with a stolid, stupid Englishman?" The handsome knight is softly mocking. "We could be happy again in Germany and you could paint all day."

"And the child?"

"No child, just you and me."

"I won't leave Paula. There's your answer, Franz. It's over, I want you to go away."

"You've said that before."

"Go away and leave me alone. Why are you making it so hard?"

"I risked my life for you, Hanna. Have you forgotten Holland and the Gestapo on our heels?"

"Perhaps we should have died together then."

"You're bitter, but what happened was not my fault. Look, I have a gift for you from Hugo Fricke, our professor at art college. He died last week. I was with him at the end. He wanted you to have the box with his pencils. And the sketches."

I put the daisy-chain on my wrist and creep further round the shrub. "You weren't such a prissy miss in those days, Hanna. Amazing how well the old man caught that glow in you, but he was well versed in love. I was jealous you were so intimate with him."

Her voice is strained. "A portrait, it was just a portrait, Franz. It was good of you to bring them. And the pencils, but now you must leave."

He stands looking down at her. "Is this to be our final farewell, here by an English river, beneath a hot, blue summer sky? Surely you can give me one last kiss for all the memories we share."

I see his face change as he pulls her roughly up into his arms. I creep further round the bush. They're standing very close and very still. Mum trembles as he lets her go.

"And now my gift. Zur Erinnerung! A rose, the single rose for memory and romance." I watch him press both his hands round Mum's hand as she holds the rose. "Only remember me!" He turns and walks quickly away. But I have seen his face. He is angry.

Mum sinks onto her painting stool. She's crying. I scramble down the bank and run up to her.

"He loves you, Mama, he didn't mean to hurt you."

"You saw?"

"He brought you a present. And a rose."

She has dropped the rose. It has thorns. Her hand is bleeding.

"Yes, yes, Liebling, a present from my old professor at college."

"And a rose," I insist. "A rose with thorns. He was angry, that's why he pressed your hand into the thorns."

"It was an accident." But I know Franz did it deliberately. He was punishing her for not going away with him. Mum washes the blood away with water from a bottle and wraps a cloth round her hand.

"The rose was for remembrance, for Erinnerung," I say.

She nods. "My professor, Hugo Fricke, has given me his crayons." She smiles. "He sometimes painted people with clothes on and sometimes without."

I gasp. "Mama, did he paint you without any clothes on?"

"Once or twice." Her lips dimple at the corners.

"Can I see the painting?"

"It was a sketch, not a painting, and no, you may not see it."

"Why did the man call you Hanna? That's not your name."

"Ein Spitzname, Kindchen."

"And was Franz his nickname, Mama?"

"Yes, yes, his nickname."

"What did Franz want you to remember?"

"Goodness, were you watching all the time? We were sharing memories of our time at college with Professor Fricke. Show me your daisy chain. It's very pretty, Liebling. Now, help me pack and we'll go and find your father and you can have something to eat."

Looking back, I could see it was clever of her to mention naked sitters in a sketch, knowing it would excite and scandalise a small child. Earlier in the day, she had painted a frog in the reeds. The frog had told her all his secrets. His name was Herr Willi Frosch. He was tired of eating flies for supper. He wanted some wurst. So Willi climbed on board one of the cruisers.

"The cruiser over there, Paula, the one I'm painting. Willi told the little girl, she's the same age as you, *Liebchen*, that he was really a prince, and if she gave him some wurst for lunch, he would turn her into a princess. Well, of course, the little girl…"

The story lasted through lunch and all the way home. I had never seen Mum so animated, and Dad was drawn into the story. "Oh, yes," he said. "I think Willi Frosch will soon find the key to the secret cupboard."

The next day, Mum knitted a frog with bright black eyes, a green waistcoat and a brown scarf hanging jauntily over his left shoulder. Willi Frosch was plump and huggable.

It had all been such fun and by bedtime, I had completely forgotten the stranger who loved Mum. Until now. My mother had had an enchantment about her at that time, an enchantment she had captured in her painting of the bistro in Berlin. Something had happened to her between those early years and the last two years of her life when her skin thickened and she grew more and more irritable as the brushes dropped from her hands.

Willi Frosch was lost when our house was sold after Mum died.

I had not wanted to remember the past after Amy's death, but the tentacles of those dark days were dragging the past into the present.

Remembering.

Driving down the lane to Acle and Yorkstone Cottage in the summer holiday, passing a windmill and a church standing in a field.

"We went there when we were living in Acle in the war." Mum's voice was echoing down the years. "It's called Hemblington Church and the wonderful fresco on the wall was only recently discovered. It had been painted over to protect it from evil men who wanted to deny the truth. And nothing has changed, Paula, evil people are still trying to destroy what we hold dear." She had turned to me with a smile. "We must go to the church on Sunday and rejoice that truth has triumphed."

Remembering.

Dad pointing out the pink-footed geese on the sugar-beet fields and the red kite floating lazily through the air.

I was fifteen.

The summer of 1966

Mum has set up her box easel and canvas stool in the garden. As I walk past I stumble and my mug of coffee spills over the painting-bag. I'm struggling to clean it when I find the rings, an Odala ring that Mum takes off when she's painting, and a ring with two straight gold lines with crooked ends and a curious inscription.

"What's this?" I ask, holding it up.

She snatches both rings from me, slipping them into the pocket of her smock. "Not everything is for you to see or understand."

Mum is becoming increasingly impatient, her moods changing rapidly. Tonight she sits on my bed next to Willi Frosch. I notice how lines of fatigue have formed round her mouth and jaw. I reach over and touch her. "I'm sorry I upset you!"

Mum tells me her headaches have made her tetchy; her brushes and pencils keep falling from her hand. She smiles ruefully. "And that makes me bad-tempered. I've been given a different medicine now, so hopefully, I'll soon be better. And I do so want to be better."

She holds up her right hand. "And to make amends, I want to explain about the rings. You know this one, the Odala ring. It's gold and very special. I wear it above my wedding ring. My father gave it to me the night before he died. It signifies kinship, family, not just your own family, but with all those who have the same ideals. The other ring you found is called an Eif ring, the ring of self-sacrifice. My mother was given the ring after my father died. Why? Because he died heroically. When she died, the rings were given to me, and they will pass on to you."

She gives me the Eif ring. I say the lines look like SS signs. She shakes her head. "The SS may have used them, but they're part of an old German Runic script, ancient symbols that represent belief and structure in our lives."

She leans back against the bed's footboard, the lines on her face relaxing. "It's time we talked. Tell me, Liebling, where do you think your future lies? I knew, from the earliest age, that painting would be my passion and would make my life beautiful. Now, what passion makes your life beautiful?"

I think about it for a moment, frowning as I hold the Eif ring. I like hockey, but I wouldn't call it a passion.

Mum is watching me, a smile lingering on her lips. "You haven't realised it yet, Paula, but you have a very unusual talent. I don't know where it will lead you, but you'll need to be careful."

I'm sure she's going to say I have a talent for languages, because I'm good at German, Latin and English, but I don't see why I should be careful.

"It's the way you see things," she says. "You observe changes in speech and movements, like an artist or an actor, and instead of accepting the obvious scenario, something in your brain works out what's being hidden, what people

are afraid to say openly. It's a funny kind of mental crossword, and you're quite unaware of it. I think it's called cryptesthesia. It's made up from Greek words. Lots of medical terms come from Greek. Now, if I'm right, cryptesthesia is a kind of extra awareness to what is going on round you. It's a very special gift."

I'm unimpressed. "How will I earn a living with this 'mental crossword' thing?"

"You'll have to be careful. It's never wise to disclose all you know and, if someone is hiding something, it's more important to find the reason than to reveal the knowledge." She pauses. "You might become a writer. I like the way you interpret your characters and illustrate your stories. Or perhaps a translator, you're good at languages. Or maybe a detective, a barrister or a politician."

I enjoy writing essays, but writing books takes so much longer—all those words! Translating sounds dull, and detectives get killed and, as I point out, the politician who came to talk at the Town Hall left covered in egg! But the barrister sounds interesting.

"You'll have to work hard," Mum says.

My lips go down. "Why does everything have to be so hard?"

"Well, perhaps you'll fall in love with a wonderful man and have ten children!"

That sounded even more like hard work.

"You play the violin. Perhaps you'll go to music college and play beautiful music every day."

I frown. "You have to practise a lot. Mr Modigliano keeps quoting Schumann: 'Übung, Übung, Übung. Practice, practice, practice', and in time, he says, you might get a rare and wonderful moment of joy. It seems an awful lot of work for one little moment of joy."

"Well, not a violinist, then."

"Do painters have this, what was it, crypto-thing?"

"Some have it; others, like actors, use it without realising it. I expect spies, who have to hide their own identities and discover other people's secrets, have it. We all have things to hide, Paula, that's part of our human nature." She laughs quietly. "A good painter is careful what he keeps in and what he leaves out of a portrait, that is, if he wants to earn money."

"But you said I can't paint."

"I said there are still things to improve, but I like your last story. It's the best you've done, and you've sketched your characters beautifully. Show it to me when it's finished." She looks at me reflectively. "And there's something else. You have a remarkable memory for recalling events and conversations. It's just as if you're seeing things on film."

I shrug. I'm not interested in that. "There is something I would really, really like to be. I want to be good at clay pigeon shooting like Josie Kent. Josie wants to be in the next Olympics. She's very good. I want to be in the Olympics."

Mum leans back and I know at once she's going to be a damp squib. "You shouldn't want to be like another person. We're all unique and you should be developing your own qualities. Having a crush on Josie's brother will not make you a great shot."

"How did you know?" I gasp.

"Teenagers are not good at hiding their emotions. Clifton Kent is not the man for you." I think rebelliously that parents are dried up prunes. "Josie Kent is doing what she wants. Set your sights high, Liebchen. As I said earlier, you have a remarkable memory and you're good at languages and writing stories. Maybe you could become a journalist."

She looks at me, smiling, trying to make amends for snubbing me. "Yes, a journalist. You'd travel a lot, you'd like that."

I rush headlong into danger. "Maybe I could write a biography of my family, if you would only tell me about them." It's an old gripe. "I don't know anything about your early life, or what your father did. All I know is his name, Dieter Ackert. Everyone at school has grandparents. Please, please tell me about your mother and father."

She gets up abruptly, leaning for support on the bed. Her mood has changed, her voice is harsh and slow. "There are things too difficult to speak about."

"Please tell me" never works with Mum. The career conversation is over.

On reflection, I don't think my mother understood me very well. The special gift of awareness she credited me with hadn't helped me in my marriage. I hadn't noticed Richard moving further away, growing to hate me.

The Chirico painting had unlocked a flood of memories. The trauma induced by Amy's death had turned me into an emotional and unpredictable teenager and a cautious and insecure adult. Whenever a door slammed, or light and shade deceived my eyes, erratic surges of pulse would turn my heartbeat into a racing engine, and I would struggle to forge a way through the day.

From time to time, I would go back over my stories, my pencil eager to develop the idea behind *Bobby and the Apricot Lady*, but then the lavender would choke me and I would try desperately to clear my mouth of the suffocating leaves. And the story would be abandoned once again.

In the guest room, I pulled the canvas painting bag right out of the wardrobe and began foraging in it. I found the box with Hugo Fricke's expensive pencils among the acrylic paints, the two small glass bowls, the tub of Gesso, linseed oil and turpentine and the old plate Mum had used to mix her colours on. Near the bottom of the bag, I found her flowered smock wrapped round a long-stemmed rose with thorns. *Only remember me.* The parting had been painful.

There was half a torn roll of kitchen paper used for drying the brushes, some old newspapers and a painting of Willi Frosch, the clever frog. I took it out. I would have it framed and put on the wall.

An English broadsheet, dated May 1966, was folded open at an article on the death, in July 1944, of Admiral Canaris who had been head of German Intelligence. Rory Temsley, the journalist, was convinced that a handful of German agents had remained at liberty in Britain throughout the war. He wrote that he had been given access to secret information by an agent whom he called 'Miguel'.

Beneath was a short biography of a titled woman, Lady Brigid O'Hara, who moved freely between Eire and the UK carrying information to German agents, like Miguel.

Miguel told Temsley another German agent lived in East Anglia. He said she was known by the name "Hanna". Unlike other agents who were caught using codes which had been broken at Bletchley Park, Hanna had invented her own means of sending information to Berlin. She had used an Odala ring. Temsley had asked Miguel if "Hanna" was German. He replied that he thought she was an Englishwoman who taught art to wounded men and women. He went on to say she worked with a German who had given her the Odala ring.

According to Miguel, Hanna had used a German Zapp spy camera to photograph documents. The papers were then "shrunk" to the size of a microdot, which Hanna hid in a tiny cavity beneath the Odala symbol on the ring. A young Spaniard, Felipe, a friend of Miguel, would secretly meet Hanna and place the dot into his own carefully constructed Odala ring. Felipe's ring would be passed on to Lady Brigid, and this ring would be carried by her and different agents across Europe until it was delivered to the headquarters of Section III of German Counter-Intelligence at 76, Tirpitzufer, Berlin.

Temsley had become more and more intrigued about the identity of "Hanna". He had immersed himself in the stories he heard from the spies who had worked with her. Miguel told him that Hanna taught art and textiles at a school in Norfolk. Felipe, who had known Hanna well, had been killed in a road accident in Berlin in late 1944 on his way to his German masters. He had left a notebook behind in his London flat and Temsley, trawling through the coded pages after the war, became convinced that Hanna had used Felipe to send Canaris information about manoeuvres being carried out by Allied Forces in the south of England in preparation for D-Day. Miguel told him that Hanna moved in the highest circles, meeting important men who held high ranks, men who might let slip a hint of vital news to an attractive woman.

Temsley thought he had found the answer to how nine E-boats had been able to position themselves off Lyme Bay in Devon without being seen by Allied patrols. It was the time when a major US and UK exercise, Operation Tiger, was taking place. Allied ships, filled with US soldiers, were sailing through Lyme Bay en route to Slapton Sands on the morning of the 28th April 1944, preparing to exercise landing on Utah Beach in Normandy on D-Day.

When Kapitän Bernd Klug discovered that only one Royal Naval vessel was protecting the T-4 convoy of 8 large tank landing ships he immediately ordered his E-boats to attack with torpedoes and gunfire. In the ensuing conflict more than 700 Allied soldiers were killed or drowned, and many others were injured. Leaving many boats on fire and bodies floating lifelessly in the cold waters of Lyme Bay, Klug's E-boats slipped silently away with all their crews unharmed.

On board were American prisoners who would be interrogated when the boats reached France. Until all the floating bodies were identified, Allied Intelligence had feared that BIGOT officers might be among the captives, men who knew all the details of the D-Day invasion plans. To their relief, all the BIGOT officers on board the landing ships were found among the dead.

Temsley was convinced he had solved the mystery of the traitor who had informed German Intelligence of Operation Tiger, but he did not think the traitor was Miguel's "Hanna". Reading the article again, I thought he was pointing the finger squarely at my mother.

I lowered the paper for a moment, remembering the memory-spike that had opened up the Art Exhibition to me. Sheldon Asquith had been there talking to Mum about her father, Dieter Ackert. He had asked Mum which country she was fighting for in the war. Mum had been upset.

Further down the article Temsley had written a passage on the significance of the *Bruderbund*. "They were Anti-Nazi," Temsley wrote, but he believed they were following a secret agenda of their own.

Sitting on the floor in the guest room I read the articles again. Franz had called my mother "Hanna". He had given her a rose with thorns for remembrance. Mum's father had preferred "Hanna" to "Johanna". Baumgartner had said he knew secrets about Mum. *Dirty secrets*, he had called them. People are complicated. They do strange and unexpected things.

Before her last birthday Mum had talked to me about the Odala ring. She had been unwell and was in bed lying against some pillows. She had passed a ring over to me.

26th February 1967

Engraved on the inside of the band is the name Dieter Ackert with dates of his birth and death. Gently, I slip the gold ring on to my finger.

Mum's voice, her whole demeanour, is so serious I feel intimidated. "You're the new generation, Paula, untouched by the poison in our lives. But the links we have to the past influence not only my time, but yours as well. My father loved his country for the literature, the music, art and science. Years later I had to make a decision, to follow his path or the wider virtues of decency, respect and honour. Some friends and I formed our own secret club within the outlawed Bruderbund. We called it Das Ritterorden, from the old Chivalric Order of Knighthood. We wore our fathers' Odala rings to remind us of our duty to family and country in that dreadful war."

I have never seen her so serious. "Earth is a killing field, never forget that. Somewhere in the world there is a war: a little war or a bigger war. The killing can be on the battlefield, in the jungle, in the home, or on the street. Life is a desperate struggle for many people, and sometimes that desperation puts a flame to our world and consumes it. We bear the burden of their hate and mad ideals."

She takes the ring gently from me and puts it on her finger. "I have tried, through my work, to lead a life of truth and worth."

She hesitates. "Things are said, and the lie, the calumny, sticks." It's as if she's speaking to herself. "But if duty is done, then honour is maintained. One day, Paula, you may have to remember that courage and duty come at a price." She begins to pick at the duvet, breathless and agitated. "Sometimes compromise is necessary."

"But how will I know?" Panic is in my voice. It all sounds so difficult, so serious, so grown-up. "How will I know?"

"Common sense will guide you."

"Would an Odala ring help me?" I ask.

She smooths the duvet and her voice is stronger. "It isn't the ring, child, it's what lies deep within you that tells you what is morally right. The ring is only the outward symbol of what is decent and honourable, and the crucifix is the inward spiritual symbol for love and good in…in…" She fumbles for the English word, but only finds the German. "Menschlichkeit."

"Humanity," I tell her proudly. The word has been on our vocabulary list for this week.

"Of course. Humanity. Parents should leave their children a legacy. 'Truth and Humanity' are my legacy to you, Paula, you must carry them with you throughout your life. Later, let us read Lessing's play together. It's about Nathan, a wise man who lived in desperate times, desperate like our own. Lessing understood the colours of truth. It's a pity, Paula, that children today learn only about the terrible wars of this century. There is so much more to learn about the goodness in people."

My mother's words were often difficult to understand, and now I found them impossible to live up to.

I was folding another paint-smeared rag when I felt something hard and knobbly. I spread the rag out and found another ring. It was my father's wedding ring. The date of their marriage was engraved on the inside. I was disappointed. I hoped I'd found the microdot ring. I put it in my pocket.

I continued looking through the bag. That's when I found the sketches tucked inside one of the broadsheets. The girl in the sketch was young. She was naked and beautiful, her limbs stretched out inviting her lover into her embrace. In the second sketch, she was an innocent child running naked through water rippling across a sandy beach. The third showed the shadowy form of her nude lover above her. They took my breath away.

No wonder Franz had been jealous. Fricke had held nothing back. I recognised her instantly from the *Daisy* painting: wide-eyes, generous mouth, slim nose and rounded chin, her short, fair hair swept back. Where is the line between art and pornography? There was a magic in her, a power of attraction that Schiffer had felt. I didn't want Schiffer to know I had the sketches. His hands must never roam over her.

I was putting them to one side when a piece of paper fluttered out. It was a short letter from Rommel. It was dated 1937. It was about a portrait he wanted Mum to paint of his wife, discussing her dress, shoes and jewellery, and his wish that she be painted in their garden near a hibiscus. There was nothing political in the letter, and nothing about a fee. I folded it carefully and put it in my pocket. I did not want the police to find it. I would hide it somewhere safely. I replaced the newspaper exactly as I had found it, except for the sketches, Dad's ring and Rommel's letter.

Then I gave the painting bag a final shake to rumple it up. I wasn't so surprised about the Rommel letter, because I now knew Mum was painting important people at that time, but I still didn't know what to think about "Hanna". Temsley had almost convinced me that the spy was Mum.

I put the bag back in the wardrobe and went over to the dolls house and lifted off the grey fitted cover. The blinds were down, making it look funereal. I tried to open the doors but they were firmly locked. Strange, they had never been locked before. Even when I was fifteen, I was still making up stories about the family who lived there. The name, Lintwhite Villa, was entwined with tiny rose-buds and leaves.

Perhaps Amy had shut out the light and locked the doors as a gesture of disapproval.

I replaced the cover, pulling the edges straight so that they fitted snugly over the roof. Then I went back into the kitchen and put the Odala ring and Dad's wedding ring in my shoulder-bag with the revolver, the sketches and the Rommel letter. I hoped they would be safe under the watchful daffodil.

Trish Porter phoned in the afternoon. "I've been told you were at the centre of the drama last night at the Red Club. Why didn't you give me the story?" Her voice was charged with deep disappointment.

My response was flat. "Well, it's been rather difficult. Police and everything."

"Yes, of course." Sympathetic drop of voice, but swiftly moving on. "Anything to give me now?"

"When Chief Inspector Quinn says it's OK, I'll write it down for you."

"You seem to be at the middle of several things, Paula. The trouble at the Retirement Homes, and now lovers fighting and dying over you."

Oh God, this was crass. A wave of irritation swept over me. "No lovers! I was there for a meal and a talk. As I said, I'll give you the story when I can." I hurried on. "Have you decided to promote Dunham Village in your paper?"

"Now is not the time to advertise a place where there's been a murder. I'll wait till it all settles down and then go round again with a photographer, but if you're interested, I've got a job for you. There's been a break-in at an art gallery. Some pictures have been stolen, police baffled, that sort of thing. I've made an appointment for you at four o'clock today, OK? This is the address and the name of the man you'll be speaking to."

I wrote the address down as she spoke: The Norwich Art Gallery. Peter Schiffer.

"I can't do this." I was breathless with anxiety. "I've met Schiffer and I didn't like him. I found him confrontational and unpleasant."

"Tell me more!"

I could feel her excitement.

"It's a personal matter." Talking was making it worse. "I'm sorry, Trish, I'll go anywhere, but not there."

Trish was surprisingly compliant. "No worries. You're leading an interesting life, Paula. If there's a story in all this, you'll let me have it?"

"I promise. And there *is* a story, a huge one, and if I survive the next few days, you'll be the first to know."

Why did I say that?

Slowly, I lowered the phone, Trish's insistent voice echoing down the line until the final click. *If I survive the next few days.* Saying the words made the threat of an impending disaster seem uncomfortably close. Quinn knew something. He had said that my coming to Norwich had prompted an interest in the Pforzheim miniatures. I began to believe Quinn was right and the recent deaths were related to me and the past.

Thursday, 4th June 1981

I got up early and had a refreshing shower. I pulled on a dark red skirt, white shirt, a black loose-fitting jacket with two red slanting pockets, and black open-toed sandals with high red and black wedge heels. All women have "signal colours" that express their moods, and red and black are the colours I wear when I feel my back is against the wall. I swung my daffodil bag over my shoulder. And the telephone rang.

It was Sellick. His voice was cold. "I hear you were involved in a fracas at a night club?"

Rather more than a fracas, I thought. I hoped he didn't have any details. "I was not directly involved," I lied, "but it was very distressing."

"I'm sure it was. More to the point, it wasn't a good advertisement for Dunham Village. I don't expect my staff to be a part of murder in nightclubs, especially in some sort of love-triangle with guns."

I was an embarrassment to him.

"I've discussed the concerns you raised in your letter with Mrs Heals. She agrees that some people who bought properties should have gone to a nursing home and, because of everything's that happened, you had better count this your last day at Swaffham. Come to my office Monday morning at ten. I may have a job for you later in Yorkshire."

The phone went dead. I had lost my job. Panic began to set in. Thirty on Saturday, unable to keep my marriage, unable to hold down a job, nothing substantial achieved. Goodison's words rang in my head, "You're just a very *ordinary* woman doing an *ordinary* job and doing it *badly.*" It was true. It must be true. My life was running off the rails. Judd's twelfth step had become unattainable.

I was glad Corrie wasn't in the office when I arrived at the sales house.

"Oh, there you are, dear!" I turned. Gillian Conrad was standing in the doorway.

Adjusting my face into a smile, I greeted her. Gillian, with her endless chatter, was the last person I wanted to see. Better just get on with the job. No-one had to know this was my last day. Gillian was clutching a brown envelope and her big paisley bag.

"I really *don't* like those metal boxes!" She pointed at *Stack*. "There's something *daunting* about them."

At that moment, Corrie came in. "You talkin' about the *Stack?* Can't see why anyone'd want to put together some old tin cans hangin' in space like that." She made a face. "Just plain borin'."

Gillian said, "*That* is because you do not understand, dear. You haven't been *educated* to understand."

Corrie gave me a hard look.

"How can I help you, Mrs Conrad?" I said quickly.

"Well, dear, I would rather talk to you alone. I've something very personal to say."

I looked at the table diary. "A Mr and Mrs Hill should be here. Ah, here they are! You take them round, Corrie."

Her shoulders huffed up, Corrie nodded. "Suits me, don' want to be where I'm not wanted."

A young voice came from the doorway. "I'm Kate Thompson. I know I'm early, but can I join you?" She had come to look over the Village on behalf of her parents.

Corrie cheered up immediately. "The more the merrier!" And they all left, chattering together.

Gillian sat down. "I can't speak with that girl with her big eyes looking on." With an exclamation, she leaned forward, pointing to the silver frame on my table. "I have a print of *Wild Marjoram* at home."

I told her I had the original painting. "Then your mother knew you needed protection. It's an oregano, sometimes called sweet marjoram. Your mother must have foreseen danger in your life, so she painted the herb to act as a shield for you. It's strange, isn't it, that her name is mirrored in the word marjoram? She was as wild and beautiful as the plant."

I stared at her. Enid Jolley had said something similar.

"But I'm here today because of my will. Have you met Isla McGovern?"

"No, I haven't."

"Of course, you haven't, dear, she's the marketing manager in my business and I've been talking a lot with her ever since I met you. Isla is as capable as any man in the finance department, so I've written a new will and left my shares and assets to her. I want you to look after my will and send it to my solicitor when I die. And I don't want Peter to get a penny."

She gave me the brown envelope addressed to Mr Elliot Smithson, Cornhill Chambers, Norwich. "Elliot" and "Smithson" fell smoothly into place as Gillian's solicitor.

I put the envelope on the table. "The will has been witnessed and signed?"

"Everything is correct." She folded her hands on her lap.

I leaned back. "Why do you dislike your son-in-law so much?"

"He turned Stella against me." She pushed her neck forward like an enquiring tortoise. "Have you ever met him? No, but if you were to, you would find him charming and irresistible." Her hazel eyes darkened. "Last night I stood by the pool watching the fish swimming round the stones. I talk to them often, because Cedric's soul is in one of them. A beautiful thought, don't you agree? I enjoyed seeing the light rising from the pool and reflecting back from the stars.

"However, early this morning, I glimpsed Peter from my bedroom window. He was standing near Elliot's car in the driveway, but when I got downstairs and opened the front door, the car had gone and there was no sign of my son-in-law. And now Chief Inspector Quinn has told me Major Denby is dead. Eric was waiting for Hannagan. Hannagan wants the diamonds. You remember, dear, I told you about the Pretoria Diamonds, but Hannagan's as stupid as the young man who's been harassing me."

She rearranged the silk scarf round her neck. "And then Quinn asks me about the stolen miniatures! He's convinced I'm the friend your mother talked about. Denby thought so too. I told both of them they'd been left with a higher authority." She laughed. "They thought I meant God!" She was suddenly serious. "But it was all so long ago, and the mind wearies over time."

Pat Heals came into the office and Gillian waved her hand towards the paintings on the walls. "Such pleasant landscapes, but Judd's *Stack*'s another matter. Paula's mother was a famous painter."

Gillian leaned back. She looked troubled. "I said it was all so long ago, but the night I danced with Ralph Linburg in Berlin is like yesterday. We danced through the night, but then he lost his head." She tittered suddenly in a scary way. And then her voice broke. "They used an axe, because he was my lover." She nodded, her eyes fixed on *Stack*. "It was Cedric who gave the order. When Cedric was dying, I took away his tablets, but I let him keep his head."

Could I believe what she was saying?

"War and love are such strange bedfellows," Gillian continued, a smile sweetening her face. "There was Baumgartner and his frumpy wife. They

247

divorced and he lost his reputation as well as the financial support from his wife's family. And he was stripped of his place at the university because he had married Elèna, his student. Elèna was Cedric's niece. Such a beautiful young girl. Then Elèna left Baumgartner. Baumgartner was a Bruderbunder. He worked as a psychologist for the army and made a name for himself. Such a curious world!"

Pat hesitated. "My father fought in the Burma campaign. It was a terrible conflict. He came home a damaged man, sullen and difficult. My mother died in the 1947 flu epidemic and I tried to carry on. Doug Sellick had known my mother in Norwich and he invited my father and me to join his business. I'm very grateful to Doug."

My pencil had been busy recording her on my invisible pad, sketching in the drooping lips and the shell-shaped beauty of her ears.

Gillian was firm. "My husband gave Sellick a lot of money, but I refuse to throw the firm's money away. Are you sure you want to throw yours away, Mrs Heals?"

There were voices outside. Pat turned. "More clients, more business, hopefully more money!" She sounded quite upbeat. "I trust Doug, Mrs Conrad. I'm sure he'll turn it round. Now, about Corrie?"

I explained Corrie was showing prospective clients round the Village.

There was a nod, no tirade. This was a new Pat, or perhaps Gillian's story had softened her.

"She should be back soon," I was saying, when I was interrupted by Stella running into the room.

"I've been looking *everywhere* for you, Mother." Stella waved her hand as Meg Farrell followed her. "It's all right, Meg, she's here!"

Meg nodded and went out.

Stella picked up the brown envelope on the table. "Smithson? Is this the will you've been talking about?"

Gillian was defiant. "Yes, and because I don't trust you or Peter, I'm leaving it with Mrs James."

Stella stared down at me. "My solicitor will hear about this. Influencing a senile old lady to make a will is a criminal offence."

"I haven't influenced anyone," I began, but Stella had already taken her mother's arm and marched her out of the room, Gillian twittering inanely. Corrie passed them as she came back into the office with her clients.

"What's going on?" she asked.

"Just Mrs Conrad," I explained, and while Corrie was writing out the details for her customers, I told Pat quietly that Sellick had said this was my last day. "Although," I went on, "I'm seeing him on Monday about a possible job in Yorkshire." But that seemed doubtful.

"It's a big county," Pat said. "He's probably hoping to lose you in it. Take a word of advice, concentrate on making a success of selling the properties and he might let you come south again. After all, if you get involved with lovers and gun duels, what else can you expect?"

Was she joking? At two o'clock, I packed up my things and said goodbye to Corrie. I'd been at the Swaffham sales office for just two weeks. I could truthfully say it had been a remarkable experience. I looked at Judd's *Stack* for the last time as I carried my things out to the car. I still hadn't reached the twelfth step. Perhaps the metal cans would crash down and that would be the end.

With a limp wave at the guard, who smirked knowingly, I drove through the gates of Dunham Village for the last time. I didn't hold out much hope for the Yorkshire job. Sellick would want to get rid of me as quickly as possible.

I got home, made a pot of tea and put the radio on. The news was all about the Royal wedding. I let the commentator's words circle over my head as I beamed into my own thoughts. Had Gillian really murdered her husband? My thoughts squirrelled round. Quinn was right, criminals were waiting for my mother's old friend to step forward with the miniatures.

A little later I switched the radio off and went to bed. I looked at *Wild Marjoram.* "My mother was right," I said aloud. "I need protecting. I wish you would do your job!"

Friday, 5th June 1981

I had tea and toast in the morning. No work to go to, I could take it easy. The phone rang and I went into the hall, but whoever was at the other end put it down smartly. Someone checking I was in. I found my revolver and loaded it before I put it back in my bag. The doorbell rang with its sharp trill. Quinn was waiting outside, his thin face unapologetic.

"What is it now?" I was abrasive.

"You want to speak on the doorstep?"

Resignedly, I stepped aside. "I've made some tea." Maybe he would go after a cup.

He put his raincoat on a chair and sat down while I poured out the tea. I asked him where Mr Penry was.

"He'll be round later."

Quinn took the tea with a nod and sweetened it, as always, with three lumps of sugar. "Mrs Conrad's solicitor is missing, but his Rolls Royce has been found in Mrs Conrad's garage."

I was taken aback. "She talked about him only yesterday at the sales office. She'd seen his car and her son-in-law near the front door, but when she went down, they'd gone. Are you investigating Mr Smithson's disappearance?"

"We are. Mr Smithson contacted me yesterday. He'd phoned Mrs Conrad and explained that her son-in-law, Peter Linsey, was involved in fraud. He's been swindling the company for years."

I thought of Gillian, frail, determined, rambling. Quinn went on, "Mrs Conrad must have spoken with Linsey and he went mad, threatening her and her daughter with a pistol. They ran into the nearest room, locked themselves in and phoned 999. Fortunately, a patrol car was nearby. They arrived just as Linsey shot the lock off the door, and arrested him. They found the women huddled in a corner of the room behind an upturned table. It's a good thing we got there before Linsey did some real damage. Now then, what exactly did she say?"

"She talked about her will, her son-in-law and a young man who was threatening her about some diamonds. And she talked about my father. You could have told me my father was in Norwich, Mr Quinn. I wouldn't have betrayed him."

Quinn ignored my accusing eyes. "It was out of my hands. Your father told me that he and his wife were friendly with the Conrads. We all thought Mrs Conrad had the Pforzheim miniatures and we were hoping she'd hand them over to Denby. She denies having them. We also need to know what she's done with the Pretoria Diamonds. Hannagan and a group of neo-Nazis are nosing round for them. Unfortunately, your father had a personal vendetta against Hannagan, something to do with your mother. Denby was a loose cannon. If he'd told us what he was doing, we might have saved his life."

I told Quinn that Mrs Conrad thought her dead husband's body was in one of her fish in the outside pool. "I don't know if he's a Lion-head, or a Shubunkins, but she speaks to him every night by the side of the pool."

"You're not serious?" Quinn said.

I hurried on, "Have you thought of this possibility? Mrs Conrad may have given the diamonds to Miss Isla McGovern who's on the board of her firm. In fact, I think McGovern will take over the firm."

Quinn hunched forward, frowning. "That's *exactly* what I mean. How is it you always know more than I do? We've only just learned that Isla McGovern assaulted Linsey yesterday with her umbrella. That was after Smithson told her about the swindle, and now I've been told Mrs Conrad's made her managing director."

The doorbell again. Penry was on the step, his collar turned up against the drizzling rain. "Our lovely summer!" he said.

I asked him if Mrs Conrad was all right.

He nodded. "Linsey was out of his mind, but he's in custody now. Mrs Conrad and Mrs Linsey are shaken but OK."

"Have you found Mr Smithson yet?"

"We're still looking."

Penry shook his jacket vigorously before hanging it up. A police car drove off and I saw Quinn's Ford Escort parked outside.

"Got anything for me?" Quinn asked as Penry came into the kitchen.

"Yes, sir." Penry's eyes flickered over me as I made coffee. "It's Stella Linsey's diary. She'd engaged a private investigator to follow her mother."

Quinn nodded. "Sounds good." Penry opened the diary and passed the small brown leather book with gold insignia and gold clasp over to Quinn. He read the page quickly. "Who's DK?"

"David Knight, the PI."

"OK, let's see now. Knight reports that Mrs Conrad met Paula James in the restaurant at Jarrolds. They talked for a long time."

Quinn turned some more pages. "Mrs Linsey didn't like you. She calls you an impertinent jumped-up interfering spying bitch who's trying to, what's this word? Oh yes, influence a senile old woman."

He put the book down on the table, my beautiful new kitchen table, sullied now by the brown, gold-tooled diary and its disgusting entries.

The sniping continued. "Why did you arrange to meet Mrs Conrad in Jarrolds restaurant?"

It is so easy to make one's life look a lie. "It wasn't arranged. I went there for lunch. Gillian joined me and we sat and talked."

It didn't sound convincing, even to me. "I was sorry for her. She was old and unhappy."

"It's Gillian Conrad's birthday tomorrow," Quinn said unexpectedly.

I stared at him. "It's mine as well. My mother's friend is supposed to give me the Pretoria miniatures tomorrow."

Quinn nodded. "That's right. Everyone's waiting for these miniatures to surface and for you to make the next move."

Now I was really frightened.

When Quinn and Penry left I scrubbed the kitchen table, but I knew that however hard I scrubbed, the ugly words in Stella's diary would always be there, staining the wood.

About ten o'clock I started locking up for the night. It was dark and wet outside. It had been a miserable early June day, and the night was closing bleakly.

I went into the kitchen to make a coffee. I never closed the kitchen blind, I liked seeing the street lamp shining through the window. Tonight it was illuminating slanting shafts of driving rain. As I poured hot water onto the coffee powder, I thought of my mother. Coffee making had been a ritual for her. She would not have approved of instant coffee.

I put the jar away and remembered the rubbish had yet to be put out for the morning collection. I pulled the black bag out of its bin under the sink and went out into the yard, holding a towel over my head against the streaming rain. I left the bag in the dustbin near the gate.

As I was turning to go back indoors, Gerry Scott loomed out of the street-light. He crossed the yard quickly. "I gotta talk to you about Major Denby."

"My father's dead." I felt my voice rising. "Look, I'm sorry, but I've had a terrible day. I can't talk with you now."

I felt thoroughly ill-used. It had been a bloody awful day.

I stepped inside the kitchen, Scott following me closely, the rain bouncing off his short black jacket like sprigs of heather. "I know he's dead. That's what I gotta talk to you about." He looked over my shoulder. "That coffee smells good."

I sighed and gestured to him to come inside. He hung his wet coat on the hook on the door and sat down at the table. I hoped to God he would go away soon. I was always hoping my uninvited guests would leave quickly, but Scott looked very solid at the table.

I dried my hair with another towel and offered it to Gerry who ran it over his short bristly crop. Scott was of medium height, fit, slim, with hollow cheeks, dark brown eyes, and thin regular features. He spoke with a cockney rhythm and I had never felt any antagonism from him.

I gave him the coffee I'd heated up earlier and made another for myself. Standing with my back against the sink, I looked at him over the rim of the mug. "I was surprised to see you at the cottage. Now I'm surprised to see you here. I suppose you're not really a milkman, so who are you?"

"Yeah, well, I was a milkman once. A long time ago. I'm Sergeant Gerald Scott, Scotty to my friends. I served with your father in Special Operations."

I nodded. "You were with him at Pforzheim."

"That's right, and that's where all this begins, see, at Pforzheim. That's why I'm here. The major told me I had to come an' see you if anything happened to him." He looked at me, his eyes steady. "What d'you know about Pforzheim?"

"Some paintings were stolen from a museum."

"That's right. It was like this. They was all down in the basement, big beautiful paintings by the greatest. I read their names: Picasso, Van Gogh, Rembrandt, people like them. Charlie Havilland knew all about art an' he showed us how to cut the paintings free without harmin' 'em. Charlie chose the pictures and showed us how to pack fifty-five into each of our rucksacks. They was carefully rolled up and they filled the bergens. Then the major took one of the Canadians' backpacks and filled it with a lot of miniatures and medallions.

"Well, we must 'ave got over four hundred of them paintings packed away. Then there was the other things we took, just for ourselves. Me? I found some Russian knives, all gold decoration. I still got 'em, and the others found stuff to fill their pockets.

"When we got back to England the major took control and became our accountant. He hid all the large paintings in a disused windmill in Acle. He called it the Pforzheim pot, an' when he thought the time was right he sold a paintin' here, an' a paintin' there, an' we got paid. He got a lotta money for them paintings an' we felt safe with the major in charge. We called ourselves *The Auctioneers* 'cos we sold a lotta stuff through auctions in Europe, America and Hongkong, as well as to private buyers."

"When I was young, I heard my father say *The Auctioneers* would shoot my mother and me if they didn't get the miniatures."

"Yeah, that was when your ma found the major's collection an' she gave 'em to a friend to look after. This friend's supposed to give you them little paintings when you're thirty. Tomorrow. I'm not kiddin' you, them miniatures are worth thousands and *The Auctioneers*'ll kill anyone who gets in their way."

"Who are *The Auctioneers?*"

"All them in our unit at Pforzheim. That's the major and Stevens, Redding, me and Parry, Arthur Lake and Charlie Havilland. Then Ly got jealous of the major and accused him of keeping some of the paintings back for himself, and he turned the others against us. The major said he didn't trust Ly. He accused him of stealing some of the paintings and keeping the money for himself. Well, it was open war, see, between them and us. I stuck with the major. Stevens would have none of it. He left *The Auctioneers* and Ly and Charlie took over. I'm pretty sure Art Lake killed Parry and Setna. Setna was working for Colonel North like the major and me. They nearly caught up with Mitchell, an' almost got the major an' me a couple of times."

"Who are Ly and Redding?"

Scott's answer was brief. "Same man, Lionel Redding."

The softly spoken Redding I had met at the sales office in Swaffham hadn't looked like a murderer.

"OK, now tell me what happened to my father."

"Like I said, it's all about Pforzheim. Redding and the others are after the miniatures. They're worth a fortune. Anyways, they found out we was holed up in Conrad's house. Then there was whispers that Hannagan was hangin' round Dunham Village where you work. That really scared the major. We was told the IRA leaked it out. See, the IRA don' trust Hannagan, and the major hated him. There was bad blood between 'em, somethin' to do with your ma. The major wanted to get you out of the country, out of danger. It's not just *The Auctioneers* watching you, there's some ugly Nazi-types in Norwich They heard Conrad left his diamond fortune to his wife. Anyways, the major had a plan for gettin' you out. Colonel North and Quinn don't know nothin' about it. I was there, in the background, near the sales house, watchin' to see who was comin' an' goin', ready to help the major.

"While the major waited in his car, I stayed on the road in the car keepin' watch, and Mitchell hung around the sales room waiting for Hannagan to act. Then I saw a geezer in a black coat slip round the side of the sales house. He had someone workin' with him, a short fair-haired bloke with gunman written all over him. The next moment Black Coat's running round to the back of the house. The major gets out of his car lookin' interested. He walks around a bit, talks to Mitchell and then gets back in his car. An' that's the last I seen of him.'"

"Did you recognise Black Coat?" I asked.

"Nah! But if it was Hannagan he could look like a street Arab one minute and a bishop the next. Then Mitchell told me the major was dead."

"I didn't know my father still cared," I said quietly.

"He's always been worried about you," Scott said. "Always known where you was, what you was doin', everythin' about you. You didn't see him, but the major was at your wedding, outside the church. Trouble was, we was always marked men and couldn't get near you. But now the major expects me to see you're all right. That's why I come tonight."

I was moved by his words. I wished I'd known. I wished I could have told my father how sorry I was for doubting him.

I felt a surge of anger. "None of this would have happened if you hadn't stolen the Pforzheim paintings in the first place."

Scott shrugged. "The Yanks and the Russians, they was worse than us. An' it was easy. So easy. An' then it went wrong when your ma found the major's miniatures. The major figured it like this. Your ma coulda given the miniatures to Conrad's wife to look after. The old friend your ma told you about. She says she hasn't got them, but somebody's givin' 'em to you tomorrow. An' that's why everyone's closin' in on you."

I didn't like the sound of "closing in on you". I'd been observing Scott. He fitted the profile of the intruder in my flat: strong and quick on his feet. "Did you break into my flat, assault me and then run off?"

He shrugged.

"Not very brave for an ex-soldier!"

My contempt did not disturb him. "I was looking for the miniatures and you caught me by surprise. I could've killed yer if I'd been yer average tea-leaf. You was right to change the locks."

I had an unpleasant thought. "My parents gave me a sapphire necklace and matching earrings for my fifteenth birthday. I hope they weren't stolen from Pforzheim!"

"Nah, they weren't stolen."

I looked at him, my eyebrows raised as I caught his canny sidelong glance.

"You shouldna left 'em lyin' round. A burglar woulda lifted 'em. They're very nice, not top drawer, but *very* nice."

I was never going to get the better of Sergeant Scott. His voice was rough.

"You're playin' a fool's game if you think you can ignore Redding and Havilland. They're killers. They won't have no trouble in making you speak."

I began to feel desperate. "If you know so much about these men, why doesn't Colonel North arrest them?"

"The colonel won't do that until he knows who the top man is. The major thought it was Redding, but Redding's not a leader. Then he thought it was Peter Schiffer, but the colonel was dead against that. Art's good at killing, but he's not a thinker. An' there's Charlie, see. I think it's him, but the major had this idea. Your boss, Selwyn Freeman, could be pulling the strings from the inside. Freeman knows a lot about paintings and he's a born leader."

"Or it could be Sergeant Scott," I said softly.

He nodded. "Could be, but it ain't. But the colonel'll find him. The trouble is what's happening now. *The Auctioneers* want the miniatures *and* the Pretoria Diamonds. The colonel was hoping Mrs Conrad would bring you the miniatures. Then the Nazis and *The Auctioneers* would attack. Then we'd get 'em all, see."

"Now look, I don't want to be used as bait," I objected.

"Well then, tell us what your ma did with them miniatures!"

"I don't *know* what she did with them. Why don't you hang round, Sergeant Scott, and maybe you'll see the 'old friend' handing them over to me tomorrow!"

"That's what I'm plannin' to do." Scott gulped down the hot coffee I had made for him.

"Tell me where Stan Parry fits into all of this," I said.

"Stan was pally with the major after the war. I knew he was living on a boat in Martham Pits hidin' away from his old woman. The major had unloaded the medallions onto Parry to look after. Then the major found a buyer for the medals an' he asked me to go and get 'em. So I went down to Martham Pits, but Parry was dead in his boat. I spoke to Liz, the girl Parry was livin' with. She'd seen a fair-haired man, tall, big build, go on board, an' she'd run away. Sounded like Arthur Lake. Good soldier, poor civilian. Art likes trouble.

"Anyway, when Liz come back, Parry was dead. I asked her about the medallions, but she didn't know nothin'. The medallions weren't on the boat, but I know what Parry done with 'em. He hinted it to me. He'd sold 'em on, not knowin' the major had found a buyer. The major let me have one when we was in Pforzheim, but I'd 'ave liked the lot."

I told Scott that Parry had sewn a miniature into his jacket. "Sir Selwyn Freeman's an expert on miniatures and he confirmed it was part of the stolen Pforzheim treasure."

"That's right. The major gave Parry his own miniature for lookin' after them medallions. I know you worked for Freeman. Like I said we've been keepin' an eye on you all these years."

Hidden eyes will be watching you. So my father's *Auctioneers* were linked to me. Quinn was right, I knew things. But what things?

I leaned forward. "Mr Scott, I didn't know my father was in Norwich. I was told he'd died in a train crash in Paris years ago."

"Yeah. A man died near him on the train, and the major swapped passports, wallets, identities, but *The Auctioneers* saw right through it. Anyway, he bought this house and a small flat in Norwich and I've a place in Yarmouth, so we was able to move between the three of 'em."

I had to stop him there. "You're telling me Captain Dalton was my father and this is his house!"

"That's right." And he went on, his voice rough. "It was a bad day when your ma found them miniatures and hid 'em. It's brought us a lotta grief. Your ma put you in danger. The major tried to protect you. Now he's dead, an' there's only me left to see yer right."

I was distressed at his words. Mum couldn't have foreseen what would happen.

"Do *you* know where the diamonds are?"

"They're not in the house. The major thought Conrad sold 'em." He paused. "Did you know the old lady had a PI tailin' her? Mrs Conrad talked a lot with you, didn't she?"

"She liked telling me what life was like before the war." I felt my way carefully through the words.

Scott leaned forward. "Somethin' I wanted to ask, what happened to Denby's left arm? It was stiff."

I heard myself saying, "There was blood on his sleeve, running down his wrist."

"I knew he'd been shot." Scott lit another cigarette. "Did you get any more postcards like that Norwich Cathedral one?" I nodded. "Redding sent 'em. He was trying to frighten you."

"He succeeded. I'm very frightened."

Scott laughed mirthlessly. "So would I be if Redding an' Havilland was after me."

I decided to bend the conversation away from art. "Tell me, Mr Scott, what's so special about the medallions?"

He frowned. "Well, see, they're history, like." He spread out his strong, capable fingers. "You wouldn't think I was interested in history, an' me a lad from a boys' home in Kentish Town, but it was the only thing at school I liked. I could see it all happenin' in pictures in my mind. Well, I saw the medals in Pforzheim, and I couldn't take my eyes off 'em. It wasn't just the jewels, it was the story they told of the war, *my* war. I wanted to feel 'em, to read what they said. They're dedicated to the German top brass, all gold with rubies and diamonds. They was for their widows to wear, proud like for what their men done. I see it like this, them medallions are a part of my war. We was promised a fair share, but the major took them as well as the miniatures. The major didn't play fair. He took what he wanted. I woulda liked some of them medallions."

Scott was a curious mixture. A killer with a conscience, a covert historian, an intruder with probing fingers, a man who lived by his own rules.

"I know who's got 'em now," Scott went on. "An' no-one's gettin' in my way, including no stupid Nazi gang, neither."

"What Nazi gang?"

"Somethin' Parry got 'imself mixed up in. I warned him he'd be in the middle of a war if he wasn't careful, an' now he's dead."

Scott stood up. "You don' look so good. I'll go now, but I'll be back. Maybe you'll have remembered somethin' about them miniatures by then."

I was puzzled. "You seem so sure I know where they are."

"You know all right!" He put his head to one side. "Kids know things without them knowin' they know, see what I mean? That's why I went to look round the cottage."

I was quick. "Oh, there's nothing there. There was hardly any storage space."

He looked at me, and I moved back at the accusation in his eyes. "I'm right, you *do* know somethin'. That's why everyone's closin' in on you."

What had I said that meant so much to Scott? "All *I* know is that I'm very frightened."

Scott slipped his coat on, a sardonic smile creasing his face. "So you should be, Mrs James. The major said you know where them little paintings are, and that's good enough for me. I'll be back soon, but if you want to live longer you should take them little paintings quick to Quinn."

Scott's car was parked in the front near the street lamp. I walked with him to the front door and watched him hurry down the darkened path in the rain to the wooden gate that led on to the pavement. As the gate opened, Scott turned and waved.

The bullet came out of the night and Scott fell backward against the street lamp. Stunned, I watched dark figures rush along the pavement and bend over him. In the swirling rain, a man straightened up. He swung the gate open and began running up the path. I stood motionless in the doorway, silhouetted under the porch light, too numb to move. I saw him raise his arm. I saw the gun. Then pandemonium broke out. Shots hit the brick wall above my head. Shouts filled the night air. Police sprang out of the darkness, running across the lawn and along the wet pavement. Screaming police cars skidded to a halt in the middle of the road.

Out of the night came Quinn's voice. "Lay down your weapons, Redding, and you, Lake! Get your hands up. *Now!*"

A shot rang out. A dark mass of men struggled in the rain near the gate. Another shot. The mass parted and three struggling figures were pushed into a police van that had drawn up beside an ambulance. The van drove off at speed.

I ran down the path. A police doctor was bending over an officer lying on the pavement besides Scott's inert body. I heard the doctor speak to Quinn. "'He's been lucky, but he'll have a sore head and back for a bit."

The injured policeman was carried to the waiting ambulance. The doctor moved over to Scott. Another examination, pictures, and then Scott's body was driven away in a black mortuary car.

Quinn saw me standing at the gate and shouted, "Get her out of here. This is a crime scene."

Penry ran over to me. "You shouldn't be here, let's get back in the house."

"It was the man with the gun again." I shuddered. "He tried to kill me."

Penry took my arm. "No-one's going to kill you." He hurried me up the path and into the house. "We'll have an officer standing at the gate all night and the whole place will be cordoned off. Everything will have to be examined, including your flat and the front garden."

I had collapsed onto my dark-blue sofa. Penry found the brandy and poured some into a glass. "Drink this and you'll feel better."

The brandy warmed me, but my hands had slipped down to the bottom of Judd's metal ladder. All hope had gone. I was sure I, and not Scott, had been the intended victim. I huddled down on the sofa. I was marked for death until the "old friend" came forward with the stolen miniatures.

"Scott?" I whimpered.

"He never knew what hit him."

Quinn came in and sat down in an armchair. He looked even more tired than usual.

"Who was the man with the gun?" I asked.

"Arthur Lake, and the other two were Lionel Redding and Charlie Havilland. They all served with your father. They were at Pforzheim. Now then, Mrs James, where are these miniatures your father had?"

"I don't *know*!" I cried. "If I knew where they were, I'd give them to you. I don't want anything to do with them. I don't want to go to the British Museum. I don't want anyone else dying for them." Desperately, I cried, "I can't go *on* like this."

I kept seeing Scott fall and the man with the gun running towards me. I was hysterical. "I can't go through that again. You've got to stop them coming after me!"

"What's this about the British Museum?"

"My mother told me to take the miniatures there."

"So you had them at some point?"

"I *never* had them. Mum told me she'd left them with a friend, and when I was older, I was to take them to the British Museum."

Penry. "Who's the friend?"

"I don't know! I keep telling you. I. Don't. Know!"

It was true. I couldn't go through such a terrifying experience again. I rocked forward, my arms wrapped tightly across my chest. "My mother said she wanted to save the miniatures for posterity. But she never told me where they were."

Exhausted, I leaned back against the cushions. "*Why* does everyone think I've come to Norwich to get them?"

Quinn frowned. "Because your mother arranged it." He thought for a moment. "Do you know if it's a woman or a man?"

"No!"

"Perhaps it's just a question of making the right connection," Penry suggested.

I interrupted him wildly, "What if this 'old friend' is no longer alive? Have you thought of that? The miniatures may never be found and I'll be hounded for the rest of my life!"

The thought was so terrible I said death would be preferable than living like this.

Quinn interrupted quickly, "We're going to get to the bottom of it. Denby's cache of miniatures is round all right, or there wouldn't be all this activity. Someone knows something."

"But I don't!" I stared at Penry. "Who will hold the gun next time?"

Quinn got up heavily. "What you need is a good night's sleep. Besides the officer at the gate, I'm leaving another officer outside the back door. Scott's car will be collected by our people soon, and two scenes of crime officers are waiting to look round your flat now." He nodded at Penry who turned and went out of the room. "You're not to leave here until the miniatures are found. Remember what I said, *you* are the key to their recovery." His voice rose. "Good, here they are." He went over to the two men and the woman with the camera, all wearing white overalls with face masks.

I told them Scott came in through the back. "We talked in the kitchen and then we walked through the hall to the front door and Scott went down the path to the gate."

The officers nodded. "When we've finished, we'll move you if we have to." They moved out to the kitchen.

"I'll be back tomorrow," Quinn said.

I trembled. Scott had said he'd be back. And then I was struck by another thought.

"Tomorrow's my birthday. Jane Donovan's coming with a friend." I struggled to stand, gripped by a terrible possibility. "Suppose it's Mum's friend?"

"What time are they coming?"

"Half-past twelve." I fell heavily back onto the sofa. "I don't want Jane to come. I don't want a party. I want to be left alone. And there's another thing." I looked at him wide-eyed. "I haven't bought anything for lunch!"

"A party, eh!" Quinn looked thoughtful.

"I'm going to cancel it."

But Quinn was firm. "No, let it go ahead. Nothing's going to happen to you, because I'll be here." He looked down at me, his eyes brooding. "Do you know I'm beginning to believe you genuinely don't know where the Pforzheim miniatures are. But you know *something*. Penry's psychology could be right. Remember now, there are two policemen to keep you safe tonight and tomorrow. Keep thinking about the miniatures, Mrs James, we don't want any more violence."

After Quinn, Penry, and the forensic officers had gone, I went into the kitchen and made a pot of tea. There was a rap on the door.

"Everything all right, Mrs James?"

It was reassuring to see PC Jenkins in the courtyard. I told him I was making tea.

I closed the door and glanced up at the clock with its spring flowers painted round the wooden frame. The hands stood at midnight, the haunting hour of familiars, ghosts and fairy folk. I thought they had all visited me in one form or another that day. It was as if a hundred years had pressed down upon me. I made the tea and gave a mug to PC Jenkins and another to PC Burton who was standing near the front-door.

Then I took a mug of tea into my bedroom and got into bed. I needed to think. My mother had wanted to save the paintings for posterity. Sitting up in bed and holding my hot drink, I thought, *Posterity be damned!* The greed emanating from the robbery at the Pforzheim museum had led to Amy's murder, my father's death and years of fear for me.

Gillian Conrad had said death and love were impossible to understand, but my mother had understood them. I wondered why I was such a pale reflection of Marjorie J Jeffries. Where she had been brave, I was supine and inadequate; where she had lived and loved, I had failed and was alone; by the time she was thirty Marjorie J Ackert was famous in Europe, and I was nothing, an ex-secretary, a failed estate agent, nothing to show for my life. What would my mother think of me? But then, the other side of my brain riposted, she should never have put me in this impossible situation.

I lowered the bedside light to dim. I couldn't sleep in the dark. Someone might be waiting beyond the shadows to attack me. As I lay down, I stroked the running horses on my fleece and wished I could run beside them to the land of fantasy and dreams.

Saturday, 6th June 1981

I woke with a blank mind. Sometimes sleep forms mental patterns, and problems are solved, but this time there were no patterns, no connections to offer Penry. I went into the kitchen and put the kettle on. Such a comforting thing to do.

PCs Jenkins and Burton had been replaced earlier, but both had returned for a morning shift. I made hot mugs of tea for them and a pot for myself that I carried into the sitting room. Leaning back on the sofa, I remembered the D-Day landings. I always thought about them on my birthday. So many strangers who became a part of my life, because they had been *there*, on the Normandy beaches. And because of them, I was alive and I was *here*.

What part had my mother played that day? Whenever I had spoken about the war, she had always praised Britain's courage. "Only the cowards ran away to America. Everyone else stayed and defied the enemy." But the newspaper articles had confused me.

I sighed. Thirty years old today and no-one to wish me Happy Birthday. Amy had always greeted Mum with a joyous *Alles Gute zum Geburtstag.* They had embraced, their friendship forged from childhood until their passing only a week apart. I showered and dressed, bright colours for a birthday lunch.

Corrie phoned, her Norfolk voice sharper than usual. "You're seein' Sellick on Monday. He's offerin' you a job in Yorkshire. I was wonderin'... If you go, will you take me and Ted as well?"

I couldn't hide my astonishment. "Well, Corrie, it's not up to me, and I probably won't accept the job anyway." I hurried on and asked if she had made a sale with the Hills and Kate Thompson.

"Yeah, they're coming back this mornin' to sign on the dotted line."

Pat would be pleased.

A few moments later, Jane Donovan phoned. "Just to let you know my guest and I are bringing the food for today, so you'll have nothing to do except enjoy your birthday. And," she added, "let's make it a party!"

"I'm not sure about a *party*."

Or about lunch.

"Nonsense, it's a special date, your thirtieth, and we're going to celebrate it."

I lied and told Jane it would be lovely to see her. I put the phone down quickly.

Jane belonged to the unhappy past. And Jane was so much older. She'd been more of an acquaintance than a friend. I had been unhappy at being on my own, no birthday wishes, no friends. I should be leaping up and down that someone was prepared to lay on a birthday treat for me. How contrary can you be?

I looked through the post. A birthday card from Jane Donovan. *With love and best wishes.* I thumbed through the bills; more advertising stuff and a large brown envelope. On the back, the name and address of the solicitor, Parr, Parr & Bretherton. It contained the deeds to the house and the relevant paperwork. I now, officially, owned No. 3, Eversley Road. In a way, it was like a birthday gift from my father. I told myself I would celebrate later, after the day was over.

Today was looming as an obstacle. I had slipped down Judd's ladder yesterday, but I felt I was back on the second step today. Each step had conveyed more knowledge about my mother and myself. My mother had reached the tenth step behind Radevsky until Arno Müller pulled her down to safety. But the steps had lied. She had never been in danger.

Coming out of the hospital and painfully climbing the steps to our flat in London, I had not expected to find so cruel a note from Richard. I had fled down the stairs and out into the street in dark despair. Almost without knowing what I was doing, I had found myself on the train to Norwich. And ever since, the need to escape had filled my mind. I had an uneasy premonition that today could be the end, or the beginning, of my life.

With a grimace, I thumbed through the rest of the post. There was a circular from the bank with a new plastic card; a letter from Sellick outlining the terms of the job in Yorkshire. Then I saw the postcard. The front had a photo of a Kafka pompom dahlia. Above the photo were the words *Birthday Party* in purple, the colour of death. I turned the card over. It had the wheelbarrow sketch Mum had painted with HS imprinted on its side. In the barrow were a pair of gardening gloves and a trowel. Mum's dahlia paintings were always called *The Siskin Paintings.* A message on the left read: *Saturday, 6ᵗʰ June, I shall be joining Paula Denby to celebrate her thirtieth birthday.*

Denby, my maiden name. Was this the unknown who was bringing the miniatures to the party? I was alarmed. The writing was large, generous and quite unlike the other postcards. I burrowed into my shoulder-bag for the safety and security of my revolver, but instead my fingers closed on Mum's rosary. I opened the velour pouch and let the heavy chain fall through my fingers. The beads and the words that accompanied them had soothed my mother.

I wanted to pray for help, for guidance, but faith and patience are needed when carrying one's Cross to Calvary, and both were in short supply on my part. My mother had talked of *Wahrheit und Menschlichkeit*, Truth and Humanity. I wished I could share her belief. Sadly, I put the beads back in my bag.

I found all the postcards and read them again. Then I went into the hall and made a phone call.

Jane rang the bell at exactly 12.30. As usual, she was dressed in sober colours: brown trousers, white blouse, dark-red jacket with gilt buttons and brown shoes with flat heels. Her straight, grey-flecked brown hair framed her thin face and was drawn up at the back with a silver comb. She had two carrier bags filled with Indian take-aways in foil containers and packets of salad things which she dumped on the kitchen top before turning and embracing me warmly with a "Happy Birthday, darling!"

I responded impatiently. "Who did you say was coming with you?"

"Mother, of course, she's following with the wine. Oh, and we've invited a few friends to join us as well."

I panicked. "I thought it would just be you and me!"

"That wouldn't be much of a party, darling, so we invited some people your mother knew."

This was all about my mother, not me.

Jane put an envelope into my hand. "I'm giving you this before anyone comes. Your mother wanted you to have it on your thirtieth birthday."

The envelope contained a passbook for the Artists' Building Society in Ipswich. My mother had been paying into it up to her death. After that a G. Long had continued giving the same sum every year. The passbook held long lists of numbers, starting from the date of my birth in 1951 to 1st June 1981. A considerable sum of money had accrued. I looked quickly through the pages and asked Jane why there was a large sum in early June 1967.

"Marjorie instructed me to sell the house in Ealing after her death and asked that I and the firm should be trustees for the account until your thirtieth birthday. I'm glad you've got the passbook now, Paula. The money's probably come at a good time."

I wondered if Jane had the miniatures as well, but Mum had never spoken of her as a friend. Still, the money was very welcome. Jane's mother, Anna Lacey, came into the kitchen and greeted me with a cool nod. She had brought some wine, a bottle of malt whisky and a sad tale to the party.

"I had to take Bobby to the vet yesterday." She reached out and touched my arm lightly. "He was an old dog, and there were problems. I'm glad you saw him again before he died."

I turned away. Dear Bobby. I had loved him so much when I was a child. Why do those I love die? And why are tears and lavender leaves filling my throat?

Jane tapped me on the shoulder. I moved away from the annoying finger and opened the door leading into the courtyard. PC Jenkins gave me his empty mug with a smile.

Mrs Lacey laughed. "*Two* policemen, front *and* back! Isn't that a *trifle* extravagant?"

I faced her, hating her pomposity. "Not when a man died outside my house yesterday. He was shot in the head. Perhaps you would rather go home?"

Anna Lacey was robust. "Of course not, dear, not with two policemen on the premises. But why was the man killed?"

I closed the door, filled the kettle and switched it on. "People think I have paintings worth a great deal of money. Do either of you know anything about the Pforzheim treasure?"

For a moment there was an uncomfortable silence, then the doorbell rang. I saw Anna turn, expectation on her face, but Jane was already hurrying out of the room. She returned a moment later with Enid.

"We have an unexpected visitor," she said tartly to her mother.

Anna turned, a prick of annoyance in her eyes. "You should have told us, Paula. How can Jane plan the day without knowing how many are coming?"

I explained quickly that I had invited Professor Jolley because she had helped me with my garden. I couldn't understand the fuss.

Jane stepped forward, her hand outstretched. "Professor Jolley and the Bank of Seeds? This is such a pleasure. Please tell me if I've got this right: the Bank is to safeguard the seeds from, now what is it? Pestilence, disease, and war, for future generations! The world will owe you a great deal, professor, in the years ahead."

Enid thanked her. "But I'm not staying long. I've just popped in to wish Paula a happy birthday." She turned to me. "I've got two presents. An Agave Americana cactus. The leaves arrange themselves at the base in these pretty rosettes." She put the flower-pot on the table. "And here's the sketch of my cousin, David Delaney. He wants you to have it."

The drawing was executed in pen and charcoal by my mother. The date was 1944. I recognised the man immediately. "I stood beside him at an art exhibition in London years ago." I turned to Enid. "I told you about it. Were his wife and baby all right?"

"Absolutely fine. They called the baby Frances."

A birth and a death. Poor Callum.

Anna joined in, the acidity quite gone from her voice. "Please stay, I'd be grateful for some extra help preparing the food. The buffet is our birthday gift to Paula, and Jane is too busy organising everything to help me."

Enid seemed to respond to the warmth in Anna's voice. "I'd love to help." They walked amicably over to the kitchen unit where Anna had been preparing a green salad. She gave Enid some lemons to cut into quarters to go on the salad dish. They kept their voices low as they talked quietly together.

I looked round as Jane called out. She was foraging in one of the cupboards. "What do you have for coffee?"

"I'm sorry, only powdered coffee in a jar."

"My dear, I live on it, so easy to use. I wouldn't get through the day without it."

"Why did you and my mother keep so much from me?" It was a question I had to ask. Quinn thought I knew a lot, but he was wrong.

"We were advised by the police not to get in touch with you when your mother died. You were so young and the police wanted everything to settle down after Amy's murder. We thought it would be safer if there was no connection with the past."

My mother had refused to go on a Rhine cruise until it was "safer". Perhaps "safer" had been more important than I had appreciated.

Jane found an inlaid marquetry tray. She wiped it down and started to fill it with cups and mugs. "And at the time we thought it better to keep a distance because of the charges laid against Marjorie."

"Charges?"

Anna interrupted us. "I need two or three flat oven trays for the foil cartons."

I found the trays and Anna put the food into the oven, saying, "Marjorie's father, Dieter Ackert, was too close to the Nazis, and Marjorie herself came under suspicion. And there were threats, of course."

The kettle boiled and Jane found a large jug in the cupboard. "Clarice Cliff!" she exclaimed. "Now which one is this?"

Enid broke in, "It's the Ravel pattern. I've got a whole set of Crocus at home. What a genius the woman was!"

"Bizarre! I love the Bizarre patterns." Anna Lacey smiled. "Such wonderful shapes and colours. Now where's that coffee?"

Jane frowned. "Shouldn't we wait?"

"He may have been delayed," Anna sounded cross. "He said he particularly wanted to meet Paula."

Jane nodded. "I'm hoping to know more about Lisa. Now where are the sugar bowl and the cream jug?"

I found them, but Anna was tense as she took them and put them on the tray, the lines accentuated near her eyes. "He's been talking about Lisa?"

"Yes, he mentioned her when we had lunch together in London."

"You had lunch with him and you didn't tell me?"

Jane looked embarrassed. "He wanted to tell you his news himself."

Anna interrupted her, "Did you know he's had a job here, in Norwich, for the last two months? But he only 'dropped in' yesterday to tell me his plans and to say he must meet Paula for some unfathomable reason. That's why I said he could come today."

I was intrigued why this stranger should want to meet me, and piqued at Anna's open disdain for me. Who on earth were they talking about anyway?

"I gave him the bag and contents as you suggested," Anna went on. "He said he wanted something that would serve as an introduction to Paula. He hasn't met her for over twenty years, but he's more interested in her than in his old friends!"

Enid and I looked at each other bemused. Hurriedly, I asked Anna when the food would be ready to serve.

"Give it half an hour, time for everyone to arrive." She turned away busying herself with the food.

Enid touched my arm. "You're so like your mother, though fairer and taller. I thought Selwyn was in love with Marjorie when he came to Berlin, but he was a difficult man to read. I served with Marjorie in Section 23 and Jane joined us a little later."

"And my mother kept open house for all of us when we were off duty," Jane finished triumphantly.

I faced them. "You all knew my mother, *that's* why you're here today."

Which one of them, I wondered, was Mum's 'old friend'?

The fretful-sounding doorbell trilled and Jane ran out, returning with Selwyn Freeman and Madge Conway, the American I had met at the Art Gallery. Selwyn embraced Jane. "Sorry I was so long, I've been talking with Mrs Conway."

He turned to me with a smile, but I confronted him, my sentences short and angry. "You knew my mother all those years ago. Yet you never *once* spoke about her. Why have you come?"

The smile was wiped from his face. "Colonel North and Jane invited me."

"Are you Mum's old friend and have you brought the miniatures?"

Selwyn's fastidious features froze. "I don't have the miniatures, but I've been told you've got yourself mixed up with some unsavoury characters since you came to Norwich."

He handed me a bottle of malt whisky and two bottles of red wine.

"They're very welcome," I said distantly. Red wine gives me migraine. I put the bottles on the kitchen table.

Anna stepped forward. "A man was shot here last night, Selwyn."

Madge said. "That sounds just terrible. I hope I'm not in the way, Mrs James." She looked round. "I'm Madge Conway. I met Paula in an art gallery in Norwich recently."

Anna broke in. "Will there be any more of your friends coming, Paula?"

"Madge isn't a friend and I didn't *know* she was coming," I said frostily.

Madge turned cheerfully to Anna. "No need to worry about your arrangements. I won't be staying for lunch."

Selwyn frowned. "Do we *have* to stand round in the kitchen?"

"Of course not!" Anna seemed to cheer up. "Let's all go into the lounge and have something to drink."

We followed her into the sitting room. "What a useful gate-legged table," Jane remarked. "Do you have a tablecloth or mats to protect it?"

"Mats are in the drawer in the bookcase near the table." I had bought the mats one rainy evening in Norwich Market because they showed pictures of the beautiful old buildings in the city.

"They'll do fine. Mother, you sort out the drinks and I'll get the coffee."

I showed Anna where I kept a few bottles and wine glasses in the cupboard at the bottom of the bookcase. Selwyn nodded. "Brandy, that's good."

I went into the kitchen and gathered up all the bottles and took them into the sitting room. Madge was talking to Anna. She was pressing her about a visit to Ireland.

"I'm sure we met in Dublin in 1939."

Jane came in with the tray. "You were in Dublin then, mother!" she said cheerfully, filling the cups with coffee and handing them round.

"Yes, of course, but I'm sure I would have remembered meeting Mrs …?"

"Conway, but Madge'll do fine. I'm a voice from long ago a bit like Professor Jolley here who has one foot in the past and one in the future."

Everyone looked confused, and Madge said, "I'm referring to the Bank of Seeds you've created. Such a brilliant idea for safeguarding the future." She looked round. "Are all the guests here?"

Jane shook her head. "Not yet."

Their voices merged into the background as Enid explained cactus care to me. It appeared that succulents need loving treatment. There were 'pups' and propagating parts, drainage, rotation, fertilisation, re-potting and lava rock pebbles to be mastered.

Selwyn had been listening. "Just water it," he said grumpily. "You don't have to nurse it!"

I turned, startled, as Quinn came into the room. He acknowledged Selwyn with a nod and came up to me. Jane joined us and Quinn accepted a Beaujolais and wished me Happy Birthday.

"Well, Mr Quinn, are your policemen doing whatever it is you want them to do?" Jane raised her glass with a smile.

I wasn't surprised they knew each other.

"They know exactly what to do, Miss Donovan."

The front door trilled again and a few minutes later the sitting room door was thrown open and Anna came in with Trish Porter. Anna looked annoyed. A surge of relief flooded through me as Trish came over.

She accepted a glass of wine and turned to me. "Are you all right, Paula?"

"I'm glad you're here," I replied quietly.

Trish was wearing a plain black jacket and flared trousers with a blue V-shaped blouse gathered into a flowing dark-blue tie. Her hair was brushed back behind her ears, and she had a black and white washed leather bag over her shoulder.

"You didn't say it was a party. And isn't that Sir Selwyn Freeman, the barrister? And there's Professor Jolley. I wrote an article on her work only last week." Enid turned on hearing her name and joined us.

Trish smiled. "Lovely to meet you again, Professor Jolley! Bio-diversity is one of the 'in' words, and your Seed Bank at the university has made Norwich famous."

Enid nodded. "It's becoming an international work. South Africa has now joined us in collecting their immense diversity of seeds and I've heard the Chinese are showing an interest as well."

Jane came over. "My mother would love to talk with you again." She tucked her hand into Enid's arm and they walked over to the sofa where Anna and Selwyn were sitting.

Trish raised her eyebrows. "Any particular reason for inviting me?"

I didn't answer her at once. Quinn came over and joined us.

"Miss Porter! What's the press doing here?"

"I'm here as Paula's friend."

Quinn said he didn't think journalists had friends. Trish smiled disarmingly. "You must be thinking of policemen, Chief Inspector."

Selwyn walked over with a brandy in his hand. He nodded at Quinn and smiled at Trish. "Who's this?"

"Trish Porter," Trish replied crisply.

"And what do you do?"

"Editor of the Swaffham Gazette."

His face lit up. "Oh, then you must come over and meet Anna Lacey. She's forever writing letters to the editor of this or that paper, complaining about something or other. You've probably already had letters from her."

His voice faded as he took Trish's arm and steered her over to the sofa. After a few moments, Quinn left me and joined them.

Enid sauntered up. "I've brought you a coffee." She pointed to the *Daisy* picture. "Marjorie seems to be everywhere."

"I feel that," I said. "Tell me, why do I think everyone in this room is tense? Or perhaps it isn't everyone, but just one person."

Everything felt false. The sour smell of fear was reeking through the room.

"Who do you think is tense?" Enid asked quietly.

"Well, I would say you are, and perhaps Anna Lacey."

Enid smiled slightly. "Marjorie was very perceptive and you seem to have inherited that quality, but Selwyn Freeman is the most anxious here. Or perhaps it's you?"

"It's no wonder," I said. "I witnessed a violent murder last night."

"Life hasn't been easy for you." Enid looked round the room, her eyes brooding. "There's an interesting collection of people here. I expect they all have something to hide. You shouldn't be so trusting when meeting people. They're not always what they seem, Paula, and some may be dangerous." There was a threat in her words.

I stared at her. "What are you saying? Who may be dangerous?"

She turned abruptly and joined Jane near the table.

Quinn came up. "Do you know why Mrs Conway's here?"

"She came with Selwyn Freeman. Or perhaps she's my mother's 'old friend'."

"Now that *would* be interesting," he said.

We went over to the sofa where Madge was sitting with Selwyn. Madge was cheerful. "Hello, Chief Inspector, have you come to join the party or are you on duty?"

Quinn smiled. "And what are *you* doing here, Mrs Conway?"

Jane and Enid joined us. Madge put her glass of wine down. "I had a phone call from Colonel North asking me to come with my old friend Sir Selwyn. We were talking about Marjorie Jeffries in the car on the way here. I first met her in Berlin before the war at the American Embassy. The British Attaché and his wife were there with a young girl and her mother. They were accompanied by a handsome young man in German uniform. That girl was you, Enid."

Enid Jolley stared at her. "I don't remember you. Yes, I was there, but I forgot all about him when I returned home and took up my scholarship at Studley Castle."

"Perhaps, but it's a connection with the enemy which Marjorie may have kept in mind."

I was sketching Enid. Her jaw was tense, her shoulders high and tight. "I wouldn't know," she said shortly.

Madge turned to me. "I have a surprise for you, Paula. A gift from your mother. I was told to give it to you on your thirtieth birthday."

"The Pforzheim miniatures?" I cried.

"I've no idea, but perhaps this is the key that will answer all your questions."

She gave me a box and a key and wished me Happy Birthday.

I heard myself gasp as I raised the lid. The box was full of pen drawings with old German Gothic writing.

Selwyn reached over and picked one up. "The Radevsky cartoons!"

Everyone crowded round as I spread the drawings out on the table. Some were more like sketches than cartoons, but the wicked humour Radevsky had used to lambast the Nazi leaders was present in every one. They were clever and damning, cruel and brilliant, an astonishing insight into the Nazi character and the social scene of the time.

I had never seen Selwyn so confounded. "Oh, my God! Well, if the Dutch police hadn't killed him, the Gestapo would have done. There was no hiding place for Radevsky after he drew these."

Clearly, as if I had been transported to Groningen, I saw the staircase and the splash of blood on the twelfth step. And I heard the windmill's sails rasping in the misty night. Fear and desperation had urged Radevsky forward up the steps. There was the same fear, the same smell of death in this room.

But who was holding the gun?

Enid asked me what I would do with the cartoons. I didn't hesitate. I put them back in the box and gave them to Quinn. "You and Selwyn represent the law here. I don't know why Mum wanted me to have the cartoons, but I'm leaving them with you. Do what you judge to be right."

Anna got to her feet. "The food should be ready to serve now."

"But your friend hasn't come," I pointed out.

"There's no need for him to come," she replied shortly.

Enid said she would help her with the food and they left the room. Quinn went over and pulled the gate-legged table out with Jane and placed the mats ready. A few minutes later, the table was covered with bowls of rice and curry, poppadoms and onion bhajis and a large salad bowl. And at the side were dishes, forks and spoons. Everything smelt delicious and I thanked Jane and Anna for their birthday gift.

Enid joined me on the sofa with a plate of curry and a glass of wine. She pointed to the *Daisy* painting on the wall. "Children are often surprised by the separate lives of their parents."

It was such a perceptive remark that I stared at her. "That's very well put. I never understood my mother. She was brilliant, talented, and sometimes over-forthright in her manner, but she lived an amazing and varied life."

I looked round the room, at the groups of people talking and eating together. It looked peaceful, but I felt increasingly uneasy.

"Do *you* know anything about the stolen miniatures?" I asked abruptly.

Enid looked surprised. "I've never heard of them."

Madge looked up. "They're part of the Pforzheim treasure stolen during the war."

I was astonished. "What do *you* know about them?"

"The FBI have been working with British Intelligence for years trying to trace the treasure. That's why we were in the gallery the day you came, Paula. DCI Quinn is part of Sir Selwyn and Colonel North's team. I thought Schiffer had the van Goghs and Monets, until I met him and changed my mind."

Selwyn leaned forward. "Mrs Conway is here to throw more light on the Pforzheim heist. As Quinn will attest I'm still part of MI5, and because of my connection with Marjorie and Denby, Colonel North has co-opted me into this investigation."

"My mother told me that when I was thirty, an old friend would give me the Pforzheim miniatures. If my mother's friend is here, please come forward, and let's get this over with."

No-one moved and the moment passed.

I stood back. It was imperative I should know where everyone was, and what they were doing so that I could anticipate the next attack. Anna, Selwyn and Enid were together on the sofa, and Jane was pouring out a coffee for Madge at the table. Selwyn had sequestered himself on the end of the sofa with a small table full of curry dishes and my bottle of brandy.

Trish had joined me again. She repeated her question. "That was a dramatic moment! Is this old friend the reason you invited me round?"

Trish was no fool. I lowered my voice. "You're here because you've nothing to do with these people. I want you to keep your eyes open and tell me what you think of them."

Trish's voice in my ear again. "Why is there a policeman outside the front door? And why was the woman who met me at the door so disappointed when she saw me?"

I could feel her journalist fingers aching to write, but I was firm. "No notes! You're here as my friend, not as a journalist. Like I said, I want you to talk with these people and learn all you can. The policeman? A man was murdered here yesterday. I'll tell you about it later."

"Tell me now."

"Later! I want you to keep your eyes open."

She put her hand on my arm. Her voice was urgent. "Paula, why was Anna Lacey so disappointed when she saw me?"

"She was expecting a friend, and you weren't the friend."

When I was a child, I had sketched Anna and discovered a tall self-assured woman with beautiful eyes, slim face and high cheekbones flattering the delicate shadows of her cheeks. Now, as I sketched her on my invisible pad, I saw a woman who had been hurt, my pencil etching in the pain-pinched lines.

Jane came by with a tray of glasses filled with red and white wine and Trish chose red.

"I have a proposition for Paula. Perhaps you can help her consider it."

Jane put the tray down. "I'd love to help."

"My friend, Dr Mark Fisher, the curator at the Old Catton Museum, needs some help. There have been thefts at the museum."

I broke in swiftly. "I don't want anything to do with art."

"Fisher wants a different perspective, not another artist. At least go and see him."

I frowned. Jane said, "It sounds interesting, Paula, right up your street."

More like up my mother's street, I thought dourly. I dropped the card in my bag and told Trish I'd think about it.

Picking up the tray, Jane walked over to the table and Anna passed us holding two jugs filled with coffee. Lowering her voice, she reprimanded me, "Paula, mingle dear, get into a birthday mood."

Birthday mood be damned. At any moment a maniac might leap through the door or crash through the window, waving a machine-gun and demanding the wretched miniatures.

"Why did you phone me today?" Trish said. "What's going *on* here?"

"You wanted a story, Trish. Well, you'll have it by the end of the day."

Trish looked mischievously round the room. "Let's see now. You have a famous botanist, a leading barrister, a darkly intense woman waiting for a friend, a Chief Inspector, lost treasure, a journalist and the daughter of a famous artist.

It's an Agatha Christie setting." She smiled. "So which one of us committed the murder?"

"This isn't a game, Trish. Last night three people were arrested. They'd just killed a man who'd been talking to me about the stolen paintings."

She stepped back. "The Pforzheim paintings?"

"They're worth a lot of money and the people looking for them are pretty desperate."

"How much money?"

"Thousands."

"Do you know where these paintings are?"

"No, but my mother found them and left them with an old friend who is to give me the miniatures today on my birthday. He, or she, may be here now or may come later. And there are at least two armed gangs ready to fight for them. That's why I wanted you here, a friend, supporting me."

I looked around, my senses unusually alert, everything standing out in sharp detail, my finger curled round the grip of the revolver in my jacket pocket. "I keep checking where everyone is, so I'll be ready when one of them leaps up and starts shooting."

I didn't tell her about the tension in the room, or the smell of fear, or the revolver in my pocket.

Trish looked shocked. "But surely you know a little more about this friend? Your mother must have said *something*." She gestured round the room. "Any idea who it could be?"

"Any one of them," I said promptly.

"Oh no!" She pursed her lips. "I'd put my money on Anna. She's so controlled and alert."

But Mum had never treated Anna Lacey as a close friend. "Go and talk to her," I suggested. "See what you make of her." Trish joined Anna at the table where she was putting the used cups to one side. Anna looked up with a smile and Trish offered to help carry the cups into the kitchen and wash them.

I walked over to the armchair where Jane was eating her curry. I asked her how well she had known my mother.

"Well, it's odd really." A frown darkened her neat features. "Although we lived just over the hedge, I was away at university when she first bought the cottage. I only met her in 1941 when I joined Section 23 after I'd graduated in law. Then in 1946 I was asked to join the War Crimes Commission. As a lawyer and Dutch speaker, I was useful, amongst many others of course, and the judges at Nuremberg needed all the help they could get. I met Marjorie several times when she gave evidence to the commission."

"She never mentioned the commission to me," I said slowly.

"None of us ever spoke about the terrible things we heard."

I saw my mum so clearly in that moment. The 'judges at Nuremberg' had sparked a memory. Mum, lying in bed towards the end of her life, a bitter smile on her lips.

May 1967

"How will your generation judge my world, Liebling? After the war, Churchill wanted to shoot all the Nazi and Communist villains, but the Americans wanted a judicial process that not only offered to punish the Nazis for their crimes, but also condoned the violent acts perpetrated by Stalin and his cohorts."

I ask, "Did Churchill shoot all the villains?"

"No! But he should have done. Stalin is dead, but the world is still held to ransom in his shadow. And now Stalin's heirs will go on committing terrible crimes, and perhaps your generation will have to go to war to stop them."

I caught up with Jane as Anna was going round, refilling cups with coffee.

"When I left the commission, I got a job as a solicitor in a firm in London," Jane was saying. "After Nuremberg, it was wonderful to talk with ordinary people about their everyday worries. Towards the end of May 1967, Marjorie asked me to visit her. I was shocked at her appearance. She told me she was dying of cancer and her husband had disappeared. I gathered there was a scandal involved and she was concerned for you, Paula. She asked me to draw up papers making Amy and me your official guardians, but Marjorie insisted that I was not to approach you if everything was going well. Then Amy was murdered and I sent you the literature about Inner Temple. Once you were in Chambers, it was easy for me to keep an eye on you, and of course, I was also one of your trustees." She raised her glass, a smile filling her eyes. "Happy Birthday, Paula!"

"I didn't realise how close you were to Marjorie," Anna said sharply.

Jane tried to appease her. "You know it wasn't possible to stay in touch when I joined the commission, but we made up for lost time by taking our holidays in Dublin."

Madge interrupted her. "When did you say you visited Dublin, Mrs Lacey?"

"I didn't say."

"Your daughter mentioned you were in Dublin in '39."

Anna nodded impatiently. "Yes, I was there. My elderly aunt was ill and I stayed with her until she died." She turned to Jane. "You remember Aunt Niamh?"

Jane's eyes lit up. "Of course, I first met her when I was about eight." She turned to us. "It was really difficult because Auntie spoke such a strange mixture of English and a language I'd never heard before."

"Niamh spoke Irish," Anna explained briefly. I sketched the defiance glinting in her eyes.

Jane nodded. "She told me stories about the Red Knights of Laoìs, a mediaeval kingdom in Leinster with beautiful queens and brave chiefs. She took me to see Lea Castle when I was small. It was a beautiful ruin. I was really upset when you didn't take me with you in 1939, mother. Auntie Niamh died while you were there."

"Why didn't you go?" Madge asked.

"I don't know why you're so interested," Anna said belligerently, "but Jane was at Durham University and I didn't want her studies interrupted."

Madge nodded. "Perhaps you met Marjorie while you were in Dublin visiting your aunt?"

Anna frowned. "I didn't meet her, but the Irish liked her work and Marjorie sold many canvases over there. There were rumours going round that she was a Nazi. Did you meet her in Dublin?"

"Several times," Madge said cheerfully. "She was actually there to lecture at the university. She couldn't get a visa to the USA. The FBI always viewed her politics with suspicion."

Selwyn leaned forward. "I was in Dublin in 1939. Some German paratroopers had landed in the south, and we were working with the Gardaì to track them down. Despite Irish neutrality we shared a lot of intelligence. We didn't want Ireland invaded by the Germans, and the Irish didn't want the Germans, *or* the English, on their soil."

Anna was sarcastic. "I wonder who they feared the most!"

"I was in Dublin in 1939 collecting plants and seeds as research for my degree," Enid broke in. "And both the north and Eire agreed to contribute samples."

Trish turned to Madge. "What were *you* doing over there?"

"I was a cub reporter. Irish-Americans wanted to know what was happening to their relatives in Ireland. The paper sent me out to get the bigger picture."

Anna looked at Madge and Selwyn on the sofa. "You both look very cosy."

"It's a lovely sofa." Madge patted the cushion. "I like it when the seats are soft and large."

"Well, it's got to fit all sizes," Anna re-joined spitefully.

Both Madge and Selwyn were well covered. Selwyn grunted and drank his brandy. Anna walked away and I saw Madge's eyes following her.

"I don't ever remember my mother saying she'd been in Dublin," I said.

Selwyn frowned. "Marjorie wouldn't have talked about that time."

I passed Enid and Anna as I helped myself to more curry. They were arguing. I was surprised. Strangers don't argue. Anna glanced at me, frowning.

"I'm mingling!" I assured her.

I joined Madge and Selwyn on the sofa.

Jane was going round offering more wine.

Selwyn poured himself some more brandy. "Now Paula, Chief Inspector Quinn has discussed the matter with me, and he's right, *you* are the key to finding the lost artwork. When you joined us at Inner Temple, we wanted to protect you. Amy's death was a shock. No-one could have anticipated you would be witness to her murder."

Enid was offering more curry to everyone. Quinn accepted some with a smile. "Unfortunately," he said to me, "the neo-Nazis are using Ackert's name to give legitimacy to their cause. We know there's a Nazi cell here, in Norwich. Perhaps they've been in touch with you?"

I was short. "No, they haven't."

Jane handed me a hot coffee. "We're not accusing you of anything, Paula dear, we're trying to find answers to the awful things happening in your life."

Selwyn leaned forward. "You should tell the Inspector the whole truth, Paula, otherwise he, and others, will continue to doubt you."

My eyes blazed. "*You* doubt me?"

"The problem is," Quinn broke in mildly, "you attract trouble, Mrs James. Tell me, why did you apply for the job at the Retirement Homes in Swaffham?"

"I saw it advertised in the local paper."

"I can see it was a good idea to choose a sales house where all the comings and goings wouldn't be remarked on."

"What comings and goings?" I asked furiously.

Trish turned to Quinn. "Why don't you leave the poor girl alone?"

"I'd like to," Quinn replied, "but I have to tell you that Denby was positive you knew who had the miniatures. He convinced both me and Colonel North."

I was as cold as ice and very fearful.

Madge broke in. "The FBI sent us over to make contact with Paula and Schiffer. He was Marjorie Jeffries' lover and he knew all about the Pforzheim paintings. Jeffries was smeared with being a Nazi in the war. It's not unreasonable to think you know where the miniatures are. The FBI think you're working with the Nazi cadre in Norwich."

I tried to break out of the net they were pulling round me. "Of course I'm not. I told Mr Quinn about a possible scam going on at the Retirement Homes. Why would I do that if I were part of a conspiracy with the Nazis?"

Quinn nodded. "To throw suspicion elsewhere. You insist you don't know where the stolen paintings are, but everyone else is certain you have them."

"Is that why you've come today, Selwyn, to represent me when Quinn arrests me?"

"If you need me, Paula, of course I'll represent you. Well now, are you about to tell us where the miniatures are?"

And I had thought he was a friend. "I've already told you," I said thickly, "I don't know who has them or where the damn things are."

Trish stood up, her voice more trenchant than normal. "You have no proof that Paula's involved. If you had proof you'd have arrested her before now. Your argument is all circumstantial: she knew him, he knew her. That's misfortune, not proof of wrongdoing. I believe her when she says she doesn't have the miniatures."

Selwyn frowned. "But Quinn is right, Paula is linked in there somewhere."

Quinn turned to me. "We're dealing with violent people. You had proof of that yesterday." He was looking at me, his manner quiet. "If you're not involved with them, why don't you help us?"

"I'm trying to, but there's nothing more I can tell you, except that I'm frightened."

Selwyn's beautiful voice was rougher than normal. "Of *course* you're frightened." He paused. "The trouble is a lot of your problems are due to your mother. Marjorie was a remarkable woman, but some people believed she had close ties with the Nazi movement and that's why the neo-Nazis are homing in on you for the Pforzheim treasure and, of course, the letters."

What letters? Now I was sure there was a conspiracy: *They* knew everything, and I knew nothing.

Madge picked up her bag. "I'm sorry my box of cartoons didn't solve the mystery. Well, I've done what Marjorie asked of me and I'll be on my way. We've been called back home, and Ailie and Bette are waiting for me at Heathrow Airport."

She shook hands warmly with everyone. Jane said her mother had gone into the kitchen. "Ah, here she is! Mother, Madge is leaving now."

Anna smiled frostily, keeping her hands to her side. "Have a good journey, Mrs Conway."

Madge nodded. "Goodbye, Hanna."

"Anna, it's Anna!" She turned brusquely and went back into the kitchen.

I accompanied Madge to the front door. "You need to take care, Paula, there are dark forces in that room." Madge felt in her pocket. "Here's my card. Ring me when you know the truth."

I watched Madge get in the car. She had deliberately called Anna Lacey "Hanna". I walked slowly back to the house. PC Burton smiled. "Happy Birthday, Mrs James, hope it's all going well!"

"Not really."

"You've got DCI Quinn to help you."

But Quinn was part of the problem. I closed the front door and went into the sitting room.

Everything had been tidied away. Selwyn was sitting moodily on the sofa by himself, drinking brandy.

Trish came back into the sitting room. "Everything's washed up and put away. Now Paula, I hope you'll think over what I said about the museum job."

"I'll let you know."

When today is over.

Jane came out of the kitchen. "I'm making more coffee. Enid has offered to help. We'll bring it into the lounge in a few minutes."

She went back into the kitchen and Anna joined us as the doorbell trilled.

"I'll get it!" I said.

But Anna was quicker. The words shot out. "I know who it is."

Trish looked up. "The party's nearly over, do *you* know who it is?"

"No idea," I said, "but Jane and Anna were arguing earlier about someone called Lisa. But I may have got that wrong."

I had got it wrong. The newcomer was slim, mid-forties, dark eyes beneath thick tufted eyebrows, light-brown hair waving back from a square face, a narrow arched nose and what my mother liked to call an 'obstinate chin'. He was holding two carrier bags.

I was standing by the door and he didn't notice me as he passed, turning aggressively to Anna. "Lisa phoned me, she was in tears. You should never have gone round there."

Anna drew herself up, her colour heightened, but something deeper was etched in the taut lines round her mouth. "You could have visited the girl later, but this is neither the time nor the place to discuss the matter."

"Quite right," Quinn said. "Well, don't hang round the door. Come in and have a drink."

Jane and Enid carried in trays with coffee, mugs, cream and sugar. Anna and Selwyn opened more bottles and poured out the wine. I accepted a mug of coffee, but I couldn't take my eyes off the newcomer. He was so oddly familiar. I tried to cling to my senses, to think the unthinkable. I stepped back while everyone else moved down the room to the table where drinks were being offered. I kept trying to put the stranger into some sort of context.

When I was a child, my father had created a family of large wooden toys with articulated limbs. They lived in Lintwhite Villa, my dolls house. Mum had dressed them and made up stories about the family: the father was a renowned landscape gardener and very brave; the family had escaped from Nazi Germany and had settled in Norfolk.

I saw in the newcomer the same characteristics as the father doll—dark hair waving back from a low forehead, the same tufty eyebrows and square chin.

I had been slowly edging my way down the room towards the gate-legged table. The stranger turned. "You're Paula Denby!" he exclaimed.

"How do you know?" I asked breathlessly.

"Your hair!" he replied promptly. "I saw you when I was fifteen. You were two years old with a mop of honey-coloured hair. You haven't changed much."

I was unsure if it were a compliment, or an insult, to be compared with my two-year-old self.

He hurried on. "You won't remember me, Paula, but I'm Werner, Henry Siskin's son. I used to live at Brownleas. I've changed my name back to my father's old name, Zeisig, because I've been working in Germany."

He raised his glass. "This is a special day, your birthday, and I have paintings, a surprise gift and a diary to give you." He looked round. Everyone was watching him. "Last night, I found my father's old diary. It's full of secrets from the war." He turned back to me, his eyes dark. "Full of secrets about your mother, Paula. Full of ugly secrets about the people in this room."

Spite was in the words and in the thinning lips. There was a tightening of tension in the room. No-one had moved.

Siskin.

My mother's voice. *Mr Siskin is the keeper of my memories.*

Abruptly, I asked him if he were my mother's old friend. "You said you have some paintings for me?"

He nodded, his tufted eyebrows lifting. "Indeed Marjorie was my friend, and yes," he held up one of the carrier bags. "I have two pictures to give you."

Only two? But hundreds of miniatures had been stolen.

"Well, *I* haven't any secrets from you, darling." Jane was cheerful, her arm round Werner's shoulder. "Paula! Friends! Let me introduce Dr Werner Zeisig, a brilliant young scientist working on a cure for cancer. His father was a well-known landscape gardener in Europe. The family came over in 1939 and settled with us and Werner's been my baby brother ever since. Now Werner, you already know Paula, Anna and Selwyn, of course. So that leaves Miss Porter and Chief Inspector Quinn."

Zeisig nodded at Trish. "But we've already met. Your advice was very helpful, Miss Porter, but I may yet take matters into my own hands."

"What was that about?" I whispered.

"He came to the Gazette yesterday," Trish said. "I didn't know what to make of him. He said his father was a spy in the war."

Quinn joined us, his voice low. "What else did he say?"

"He had enough information to turn today into one hell of a party. And he didn't say it in a nice way. He mentioned Selwyn Freeman and Paula Denby by name."

Werner came over and shook hands with Quinn. "We've also met." Quinn looked surprised. "In my father's diary. He wrote about a young police officer, Carter Quinn. That was you, Chief Inspector."

"Perhaps I should have a look at this diary," Quinn said grimly.

Werner laughed. "Can you read Gothic script? No, I didn't think so."

I stepped forward. "Why did you send me the postcard?"

"That's simple, I didn't want to miss your thirtieth birthday."

"Why? What's it got to do with you?"

He frowned. "You'll understand well enough when I read you the diary." He felt in his jacket pocket and pulled out a green leather notebook. "I read this last night for the first time. It's all about secret and shameful things that were done in the war."

I didn't like what he was saying. And I didn't like Werner Siskin.

Compulsively, I checked again where everyone was sitting. Anna and Selwyn were on the sofa with Enid, while Trish and Quinn were now in the two armchairs. Werner came over and sat down between Jane and me on the hard-backed chairs round the table.

"First, let me tell you a little about myself. I gained my doctorate at Oxford and now I'm a chemist and research fellow for a German pharmaceutical firm, and I've just been appointed managing director in our branch in Norwich. So I decided to come to Acle early to look over Yorkstone Cottage and, of course, to meet my old friend, Anna Lacey, and tell her that Lisa and I are planning to marry. Because of my work, decisions had to be made quickly, and Lisa and I are moving into the cottage at the end of August."

Before Anna could reply, he turned to me. "I'm so grateful to Marjorie for leaving Yorkstone Cottage to my father in her will. He's left it to me and soon Lisa and I will be enjoying living in Acle."

"But *why* did she leave the cottage to your father?"

Werner was taken aback. "Did she never speak of it?"

"Never."

Perplexed, he appealed to Anna, and Anna responded immediately.

"Marjorie always admired Henry Siskin. In 1938, when she first heard that the Siskins were to be sent to a concentration camp, she began organising their escape. Unfortunately, Henry died in 1952."

"Do you have sisters?" I blurted out.

"Werner's an only child," Anna answered sharply. "Why do you ask?"

I shook my head.

Werner was explaining to Jane that when he was sixteen, he had an accident riding his friend's motor-bike. "Unfortunately, I broke my leg and now I walk a little stiffly."

Just like the toy in the dolls house, I thought. On an impulse, I asked him if he were happy.

Werner looked surprised. "Well, I'm getting married. I own a property in Hamburg, a cottage in Norfolk and my work is valued and worth doing." He paused for a moment. "When I was a child, I used to watch you over the hedge at the bottom of the garden. You seemed so confident, so precious and loved by your parents. I was envious because I was a poor immigrant boy with no future."

"Well, you're the lucky one now." I gave a self-deprecating laugh. "I'm divorced. I'm not doing anything worthwhile, in fact I've just lost my job. So however confident I may have appeared as a child, you've succeeded in your life and I've accomplished absolutely nothing."

Werner laughed, amused. "Time sorts us all out. I'm glad we've met again, Paula, it puts the past into perspective."

He picked up one of the carrier bags. "I only found it this morning, pushed down hard behind the cushions on the sofa. It may have belonged to your father, Paula."

I gasped. Fifteen years behind the cushions and he was as malevolent as the day I first saw him looking over the bushes. The fox was staring up at me, his bright eyes blinking, his mouth opening and closing. The smell of lavender was everywhere, dripping into my eyes, choking me and blood was pouring over my hand onto the yellow stones.

With an exclamation, Quinn stepped forward and pulled the cane from Werner's grasp. "What d'you think you're doing?"

Werner laughed. "It's a joke, that's all! Ein Scherz!"

Trish asked me if she could keep the cane. I nodded and turned away as she took it.

"What a fuss you're making about a walking stick," Anna snapped. "But Werner's right, time *has* sorted you out, Paula. Where have all your haughty ways got you as you traded on your mother's fame? Marjorie could do nothing with you. We know she would never have left the Pforzheim paintings with Eric. Your father was a wastrel. He didn't even go to his wife's funeral. Marjorie would only have left the paintings in your care, Paula, so why are continuing to deny all knowledge of them?"

I was nearly crying with rage. "I've explained a million times that my mother gave the miniatures to a friend. She *never* gave them to me. And she never told me who the friend was."

There was a cough and Werner stood up. "I know about the paintings." He looked round the room with a self-satisfied smirk. In that moment, I hated him as much as I hated Anna.

"You mean the Pforzheim miniatures?" Quinn urged.

"The miniatures, yes. I visited Marjorie towards the end of May in 1967 to celebrate my doctorate. Where? At the house in Ealing. The front door was open. I heard Marjorie arguing with Erich about paintings from Pforzheim. Miniatures, he called them. He accused her of hiding them and he threatened her."

The memories came flooding back. It must have been about the time I first heard Mum and Dad arguing.

"Major Denby left the house in a rage, and I went through the hall and into the conservatory where I found Marjorie. She wasn't looking well, but she was pleased to see me. I'd brought her chocolates and flowers and I told her about the firm in Hamburg I was about to join. We had some Schnapps to celebrate my doctorate. It was very pleasant. Marjorie was proud of what I'd achieved. I told her I'd heard the argument about some miniature paintings, and Marjorie said Paula knew all about them."

I stood up, my chair falling over in my agitation. "I know *nothing* about them!"

Werner picked the chair up. "Why are you so upset? I'm telling the truth. Marjorie said the miniatures were with an old friend, and this friend was known to you by name. She was quite definite. Marjorie said this friend would come forward on your thirtieth birthday." He looked meaningfully round the room. "Perhaps he or she is in the room now, and you've already arranged for the transfer to take place."

It sounded reasonable, even plausible. I turned to Werner, my manner short and unpleasant. "I see you've come here to make trouble for me."

But Quinn was emollient. "You're sure of this, Zeisig?"

Werner was undisturbed by my outburst. "Quite sure. I was twenty-nine in 1967 and it was my birthday. I've never forgotten that moment. It was all so mysterious. Erich left the house and then the phone rang. Marjorie went out into the hall and I went over to look at the dolls house. I'd forgotten how big it was. It was called Lintwhite Villa. Such a clever pun on names. I knelt down and opened the doors and some large wooden figures tumbled out. I was filled with disgust and threw them straight back into the dolls house. Then Major Denby came back. Marjorie was refusing to tell him where the miniatures were. She said her friend would give them to Paula on her thirtieth birthday. So it makes sense that Paula knows all about them."

Anna interrupted him brusquely, "I don't remember you coming round to celebrate your doctorate with *me*." She sounded bitter.

Werner turned on her savagely. "You were always ready to reprimand me for this or that or for nothing. Marjorie was *always* pleased to see me."

Quinn stood up. "That's enough, Zeisig. Now, Mrs James, is this friend in the room?"

"How would I know? No-one's approached me. I keep telling you, my mother never gave me a name. But if you *are* here," I looked round, "why don't you come forward?"

But again, no-one moved.

"There's a lot of money and lives at stake here," Quinn said. But everyone remained where they were sitting, their faces puzzled. "Right then, let's see the paintings Siskins' giving you." He looked at me. "There must be a reason why your mother held them back. Could they hold the key to the Pforzheim robbery?"

"*You* seem to hold the key to a lot of things, *Carter Quinn*!" I said coldly. "Why didn't you tell me you knew my mother?"

"I'd hazard everyone in this room knew her," he replied quietly. "And I bet they all know how much the stolen miniatures are worth as well."

An undercurrent of expectation rose in the room as Werner handed Quinn a watercolour in a plain light-oak frame. Mum had painted it in the nineteen-fifties. It was a two-storey building with a large rose garden and blue shutters. It had hung on the wall of our lounge in Ealing.

"It's The Rosary," I blurted out. "Mum said an old friend lived there."

"*The* old friend?" Enid cried.

Jane echoed her. "The friend with the Pforzheim miniatures?"

Selwyn frowned. "Why did Marjorie give *you* these paintings, Jane?"

"They were listed in Marjorie's will. I collected them myself and left them in my mother's care. Marjorie insisted that Paula must have them on her thirtieth birthday. If, however, Paula were dead, the paintings were to be handed over to Colonel North in MI5."

Selwyn shook his head. "Why should Marjorie hold the paintings back until now? There must be something in them if North is involved." He turned to Werner. "Show us the other painting."

Werner held it up and Enid frowned. "What a curious choice of subject."

"It's the first time I've seen it," Selwyn said.

The subject was a small bird in a cage.

Selwyn asked me to tell him about the picture.

"Mum painted it when I was thirteen. We'd found the bird lying motionless near the bird-bath in the garden. It was in shock. Mum put it in a box and covered it with a warm piece of cloth. The next day she bought the cage and we nursed the little bird back to health."

I felt myself relaxing as the memories returned. "I used to rush home from school to feed him and clean the cage. Dad called it a spinus spinescens, so the little bird became Spinny. Dad said it must have escaped from a bird sanctuary because it came from the Andes. We advertised, but no-one came forward, so when Spinny was better we released him into the garden. I put out a bowl of water and a coconut shell filled with his favourite suet pellets and madeira cake crumbs and for a few days he came back, but then the visits stopped and I never saw Spinny again."

Quinn shook his head. "I don't get it. Why should your mother save a rose garden and a bird in a cage for your thirtieth birthday?"

Standing to one side, I let my eyes enter the cage with the little Andean siskin, and in that instant, I began to read the message my mother had painted into the picture for me. My mind went from one step to the next, just as if I were climbing Judd's ladder. What had Werner said? *Lintwhite Villa, such a clever pun on names.* I glanced at him, trying not to make my dislike influence my judgement, but Werner knew the name was important. My mother had said, *Mr Siskin is the keeper of my memories.* I had laughed thinking she'd been referring to my wooden toy, but suppose she had meant Siskin's son?

It was Trish who alarmed me next. "Spinny's talking to you, Paula! Tell us what he's saying."

Quinn leaned forward, his forefinger jabbing at the picture. "It's called a barley bird. I've seen them eating flax and barley."

The last step up the ladder. I was now certain I knew where the paintings were, but there must be no sudden movement, no sign of recognition, or I would alarm the man or woman with the gun.

288

Selwyn laughed. "You're right, Quinn, it's a passerine, a finch. It belongs to the Fringillidae family." Trust Selwyn to be an authority on garden birds.

"I thought it was a goldfinch," Werner said.

"Similar, but this bird is smaller." Selwyn looked up, his eyes narrowing. "It's a linetwige, a flax-eating warrior bird. In English…" he turned, his eyes suspicious. "In English, that's a siskin." My fingers curled round the butt of the gun in my pocket. "Siskin is your name, Werner."

"My name's Zeisig."

"But Zeisig is Siskin in English. You said something earlier." Selwyn's voice softened. "Yes, you said it was 'a pun on names'." He looked at Werner accusingly. "You know something." He looked round. "No-one is to leave this room. See to it, Quinn."

Quinn went to the door and called Constable Jenkins who was told to stay outside the sitting room door. "No-one is to leave or enter this room."

I watched Selwyn turning the picture over and over, his silvery head bending over the frame. Selwyn was intelligent, he might work out the answer. If only I could find a way to leave the room and get to the miniatures first.

Selwyn came over to me. "Finch? Passerine? Is it some kind of clue to the Pforzheim theft? Marjorie was a devious woman. I wouldn't put it past her to leave a clue to the paintings *in* a painting."

"You talk as if you didn't like my mother."

He looked at me, frowning. "Your mother was a great painter, but she lied when it suited her and she used people. And sometimes, her idealism was questionable." He shrugged. "The passage of time, and her death, doesn't change the truth, Paula."

The truth as *you* see it, I thought savagely.

Enid came closer, squinting into the picture. "If you recognise something, you must speak up, Paula."

Anna joined her. "Everything Selwyn says about your mother is true, and if there is a clue in the picture, you must tell us, Paula."

"How can a bird tell you anything?" Jane wondered.

On an impulse, I picked up *The Rosary* picture.

"I *do* remember something. There was this woman who worked with Mum in the war."

Don't sound too sure, hesitate a little.

289

"Mum used to take me to visit her at The Rosary. I remember the rose garden, full of scent and colour. Lots of people lived in the house. They wore funny hats and we had tea with…" I hesitated, confusion in my eyes. "I think it was, yes, it was a Sister Vlinder." My eyes sparkled. "I'd forgotten all about it."

Trish frowned. "What kind of 'funny hats'?"

"I'll draw it for you."

I found a sketchbook in the bookcase. "They all wore them." As I drew Sister Vlinder in her large stiff Dutch hat with wings turning upwards, I went on talking, giving convincing details about the big room and the women hurrying to and fro. "There were sick people in the room. I remember the rustling of the long skirts as the sisters moved round." I had to lead them away from examining the bird in the cage.

"Sisters?" Selwyn asked.

Jane leaned over my shoulder. "Goodness! That's the habit of the Sisters of Saint Clare in West London!"

"That's *right!*" I was really excited now. "Mum called them the Poor Clares and Sister Vlinder worked there."

Anna shook her head. "But the Poor Clares concentrate on prayer, they're not a working order."

Werner interrupted her rudely, "You had to go to London one weekend and Marjorie took me to The Rosary when I was a young boy. The nuns who came to Ealing were a working branch of the Sisters. They cared for the sick and the poor. Marjorie was much loved by the Sisters. There were a lot of German women there."

I was alarmed. Werner knew as much as I did.

Quinn took my sketch. "We'll find Vlinder," he snapped.

We all turned as PC Burton came into the room. "She's come back, sir!"

He stood aside as Madge breezed in. "I was driving away when I saw a man turning into the garden. I've been waiting round the corner, interested to see the guest Anna's been waiting for. As he hasn't come out, I've come back. I want to know what's going on."

Anna was sharp. "What's it to do with you?"

"I'm interested in everything going on here. You could introduce us!"

Selwyn got up. "Madge Conway, FBI. Dr Werner Zeisig!"

"FBI?" Werner's eyes glinted. "Any particular reason you're here?"

"Yes, the Pforzheim miniatures." She pointed to the two pictures lying on the sofa. "Are these part of the stolen art?"

"No." Werner looked round. "But Paula knows where the Pforzheim treasure is. And so do I. And you're right, Freeman, the secret's hidden in the name, but if you want the whole truth, the *greater* truth, I have it here." He waved the diary above his head. "My father writes about the Poor Clares in Ealing, about Marjorie's friend, about the Pforzheim theft, the miniatures and the secret lives of everyone in this room." He paused. "And I know about Hannagan."

Quinn was visibly shaken. He turned immediately and told Jenkins to stand outside the front door. "Now, Zeisig," he turned towards the German, "tell us about this diary."

Werner spoke calmly, "We came to England in 1939. My father writes in the diary that he worked for the British in the war, but there are different kinds of war. From 1943, my father, Marjorie Ackert, Colonel North and a young policeman, Carter Quinn, were searching for two Irish dissidents, Hannagan and Hanna. This diary tells their story."

There was not a sound in the room.

Werner turned to me. "There are things that we, as children, never knew about our parents. How could we know about events that happened long before we were born or when we were small?"

I nodded at Enid. "You said something similar, about the separate lives of parents."

Werner nodded. "My father would have understood that. When you stand at the forefront of great moments in history, as he did, you stand alone. My father admired Marjorie. He once told me they'd worked together on important projects. I thought he meant garden projects, but I was wrong." He looked round the room, a strange smile on his face. "In these pages, my father mentions The Rosary. He writes that it's not as innocent as it looks with its blue shutters on the windows and the sweet-smelling rose garden. One of the German nuns told him that a woman had brought an Irishman to The Rosary. He'd been shot in the shoulder. She thought his name was Loon. She never spoke to the woman."

I heard the sound of an indrawn breath and felt something like an electric shock run through the room. I looked round, tense and alert. Trish had taken a notebook out of her bag. Well, I couldn't stop her now.

Werner's voice dropped. "The war ended nearly forty years ago and though I'm German by birth, I spent all my early life in England, and I love this country.

I despise the Nazi period, but even so, I wouldn't have disclosed the existence of the diary if Lisa had not been upset."

Werner put the diary on the table and began speaking without reference to it. "The story begins in Munich, in May 1939."

The night sky is darkening when Henryk Zeisig receives an unexpected, and unwelcome, visitor. Herr Doktor Czerny greets Zeisig heartily with a firm handshake. Czerny, a leading figure in the Abwehr, German Intelligence, is a ruthless and scheming adversary, his reputation built on his success at implementing plots and intrigues. Czerny is in no hurry. Reluctantly Zeisig pushes aside the photographs of Graf von Schöning's extensive grounds and his notes for re-designing the gardens. He eyes his imposing visitor cautiously as he offers him a Schnapps. Czerny stays for over two hours and speaks at length to the renowned garden designer.

Three weeks later, Czerny's plans for Zeisig are reaching completion. Rumours have been filtered through to the Resistance movement that the Zeisig family are about to be arrested and sent to Dachau Konzentrationslager. From that moment the family disappear from sight. As Czerny has surmised, the Resistance has asked the British for help and a team has already been sent out to take Zeisig, his wife and baby son down the Dutch route to England.

The Zeisig family reach England and Czerny now has an agent who will be able to travel freely around the UK, ostensibly to design gardens and give advice about food production in wartime. This is an area in which Zeisig is an authority due to the work he did between 1918 and 1930 in post-war Germany. In reality Zeisig is in the UK as Czerny's eyes and ears to note troop movements, arms factories and new airfields.

After a short time, the Zeisig family is placed with Anna Lacey at Brownleas in Acle, near Norwich, and Henryk Zeisig's name is changed to Henry Siskin. Anna Lacey works for a charity that helps to home displaced families from Europe. Two years later, the Siskin family move into a small cottage near a windmill in Acle.

Back in Berlin, Czerny smiles under his heavy moustache as the letters and reports begin arriving on his table. Siskin's handler in England is a woman called Hanna. Siskin is not allowed to meet her, but is ordered to send his reports to certain 'drops' in London, shops from where Hanna collects the reports and sends them on to Czerny who is Siskin's control in Berlin. But everything is not as it seems. Within days of landing in England, Henry Siskin is closeted with Colonel North of MI5. Henry tells North about his meeting with Doktor Czerny. From that moment Henry becomes a double agent and North edits all the information Siskin passes on to Hanna.

It is during a later meeting with North that Siskin casually mentions Plan Grün. North knows the Plan involves the landing of German troops in Southern Ireland in preparation for an invasion of England. What he doesn't know, until Zeisig tells him, is that Czerny has already landed in Bantry Bay in Eire, his visit shrouded in secrecy. Czerny has spoken with top Irish officials, but his reception is mixed. In 1941 German High Command delivers an unwelcome message to Czerny. He is told that Plan Grün is dead. Kaput. The decision has been made at the highest level: Operation Barbarossa, the invasion of Russia, is to go ahead instead. Czerny is livid.

In his view, war with Russia is suicidal. He iterates and reiterates this viewpoint to his superiors. He writes that an invasion of England from the shores of Ireland would shorten the war and, as he vehemently points out, there are many Irish who would support the Germans. German High Command does not agree, so Czerny has secretly devised his own scheme: Plan Czerny. Over weeks and months, he has been building up a team of agents in England and Eire. It is Plan Czerny that Siskin discusses with Colonel North.

In late 1942, Czerny orders Siskin to make contact with an Irishman called Hannagan. This is the first time Siskin and North have heard of Hannagan. The Irishman, who has a pathological hatred of the British, is a German agent and holds the rank of Kapitän in the German Army, but Czerny has kept him under the radar. Now Czerny orders Hannagan to put his team into the field. They plant bombs in factories, mailing offices, schools, buses, trains and airfields. The SIS, the British Secret Services, believe the IRA is responsible for the crimes and time is wasted chasing IRA shadows. It is not until Siskin reveals Czerny's Plan that North learns the truth.

Now Czerny tells Siskin to team up with Hannagan. The Irishman wants to target the great houses and mansions where Siskin designs gardens. Siskin is alarmed. He meets with North and tells him he is frightened. "Bomben! I want with bomben nothing to do. Verstehen? Nichts!"

North decides to send the frightened Siskin to Ireland with Marjorie Ackert. She is going to Dublin, outwardly to lecture at the university, while Siskin will meet the great landowners in Eire. In the meantime North has circulated a rumour that Marjorie Ackert is pro-IRA and a Nazi sympathiser. Rumours begin to permeate the air, and many believe them because of the Ackert family history. North is hoping that Irish and English dissidents sympathetic to the Nazi cause will contact Marjorie. He tells her that Hannagan is in Dublin and she is to make every effort to meet him.

Madge Conway is also in Dublin. She is friendly with Marjorie Ackert and Lady Helena Ridgeway. Lady Helena is a rich socialite and well-known in Irish-German circles. She has long been an intimate friend of Doktor Czerny. Less well known is her relationship with Sir Robert Dorney serving in Winston Churchill's coalition government. Dorney is friendly with Daniel Malan, a South African politician, who has espoused the cause of apartheid and is an admirer of Adolf Hitler.

Czerny has arranged for Lady Helena to meet Madge, Hanna and Marjorie at the Davey Byrne pub in Dublin. But the meeting never takes place. Lady Helena is shot dead on the steps of her hotel as she leaves for the meeting. In Kildare Street, Marjorie is delayed by a drunken student who is protesting against her (temporary) appointment as Professor of Art at the College. The third-year student and the temporary professor are taken away to a Garda Station to be questioned.

Madge arrives in Duke Street alone. She is admitted into the Davey Byrne pub and is taken to a room where a young girl is sitting in the shadows at the back with armed men. Hannagan remains in the background. Distrust and suspicion are everywhere as news of the shooting of Lady Helena is broadcast over the radio, and Madge is quickly removed and driven away.

Immediately, North withdraws Siskin, Marjorie and Madge from Ireland, and the police and government agents throw a net round the city and break up Czerny's espionage ring in Dublin and London. But Hannagan and Hanna break through the net and disappear.

Quinn interrupted Werner. "In 1943, I was assigned to *Brega*, an MI5 attack group. Our task was to find Hannagan. He was using IRA-like attacks against armed forces waiting to be sent abroad to fight. That was when I met Madge Conway, Marjorie Ackert, Colonel North and Henry Siskin. The IRA never accepted Marjorie."

Selwyn sat up abruptly. "Not only the IRA, but the FBI had their suspicions as well."

Quinn's voice was harsh. "They were wrong. Marjorie Ackert was loyal to Britain."

Werner nodded. "My father agreed. I remember the last day of my father's life. Early in 1952, my father saw two people near the cathedral in Norwich. He was sure he had once seen the woman leaving Marjorie Denby's house. She was supporting a stranger, a man of medium height, looking unwell. For some reason, he excited my father's interest. On an impulse, my father took some photos of the two before hurrying home to develop the film in his small darkroom.

"My mother and I were having tea and I saw him go into his study. He was there for only a few moments when the doorbell rang. I think he found time to write this last page in his diary during those moments. I got up to answer the door, but *Vati* rushed out of his room and sent me back to my mother. When he didn't join us my mother and I went out into the small hallway. *Vati* was lying on the floor, blood everywhere. I phoned for an ambulance and went back to my father. He whispered two words, 'Kamera' and 'Hanna'."

"Did you find the photographs?" Madge asked urgently.

"Neither the camera nor the photographs were ever recovered. My father died before the ambulance arrived and my mother died a few days later. Neighbours kindly took me into their home before Anna came and rescued me."

Quinn nodded. "And when did you say you read the diary?"

"Last night, and I promised you a shocking revelation. The last thing my father wrote was Hanna's real name." Werner looked round. He was filled with his own self-importance. "My father and Marjorie always thought Hanna was deadlier than Hannagan."

He waved the diary above his head. "I can tell you now that Hanna is here, in this room. Has she come to collude with Paula and pass on the stolen miniatures? Or has she come to silence one of us?" He pointed accusingly at Madge. "You met her in the Davey Byrne pub in Dublin."

Madge rose to her feet. "Yes, I was in the pub that night." Her voice was strong. "The light was poor but I glimpsed a young woman at the back. When I came here tonight, I thought I recognised that woman. However, as I wasn't sure, I deliberately steered the conversation towards Dublin. Jane revealed more than she realised when talking about her Aunt Niamh. In June 1939, Anna was not with her aunt but in a Dublin gaol where her husband, Michael Donovan of the IRA, was about to be hanged, and *that* is why Jane was left behind in Durham."

She reached across. "I'd just like to see the diary first, before I say anything more."

The shot came across the room and Madge crashed forward. More shots, loud and deafening, and Burton, running forward, fell across Madge. Werner, half-turning, was caught in the chest and toppled onto the table, falling to the floor with the wine bottles and coffee cups and jug.

Selwyn stumbled to his feet clutching his arm, blood dripping through his fingers. I glimpsed Enid, crouching, moving round the room. She turned. I saw her pistol. Heard Quinn fire his weapon. Stunned, I watched Enid collapse and slide down the wall under the *Daisy* picture.

Then Anna was on her feet, her arm raised, the revolver circling the room. I fired through my pocket as Quinn swore and dropped to his knee, clutching his leg.

But I was watching Anna. Her back was arching, her arms reaching out to Selwyn. He fell beside her, cradling her in his arms, tears pouring down his face. Jane knelt beside the dying woman. "Oh my God, oh my God!" she kept weeping.

Quinn limped forward and bent over Burton. He looked up at me and shook his head, his lips pulled down. But Madge was alive, injured in her knee. Enid, lying with her back against the wall, blood pumping from a chest wound, was still breathing. Anna died within minutes, cocooned in Selwyn's arms.

Quinn steadied himself against the back of the sofa, cursing as he wound a tourniquet round his left thigh with his tie. Trembling, I went over and held the tie with my finger as he pulled it tight.

The acrid reek of discharging weapons, the sickening smell of violent death lay everywhere in the room, and life's pulse hung over us, as if time had forgotten to place the minutes into their allotted slots.

It had all happened so quickly, the moment of revelation confusing and inadequate. I still had no idea why both Enid and Anna had responded with gunfire to Madge's accusation.

Werner was dead, the diary clasped in his hand. Poor Lisa, lonely châtelaine-to-be of Yorkstone Cottage. PC Burton had died protecting Madge. Quinn had been shot through the leg, while a bullet had grazed Selwyn's arm.

In the hall, PC Jenkins was radioing for ambulances and back up.

Anna, Werner and PC Burton were taken away in a mortuary car, while Madge left in an ambulance. A further ambulance remained outside the house.

Both Selwyn and Quinn had flesh wounds which the police doctor, Thornbury, was treating. Police tape was covering the front and back doors and forensic officers were examining the crime area and working round Quinn. Jenkins was waiting with Selwyn in the kitchen.

Enid Jolley had insisted on staying. Thornbury took Quinn to one side. "I've patched her up, but she's got serious injuries. She should be in hospital."

Quinn, icy cold. "She wants to talk. I want to listen. Make her comfortable, doctor, but she stays."

"But when I need to take action, you must move aside, understood?"

Quinn jerked his head. Enid was lying on the blue leather sofa, her head supported by two cushions. She had been wounded in the chest. Her voice was weak. "You're bitter, but I want you to understand how it happened. It all began in Berlin. In 1937."

Quinn signalled to Trish, and Trish perched on the back of an armchair with her notebook so that Enid could see her.

"On the first day of our visit to Berlin, my mother met Leutnant Hans Bruch. He'd been ordered to get to know us." Enid paused repeatedly to catch her breath. "He won over my mother and introduced me to a young Irishman, Liam Hannagan, a captain in the German Army. We became lovers. I was besotted with him. I had never been happier. I met Marjorie Ackert in Berlin at a Fine Art Exhibition. She once said, in that dry way she had, that Berlin was a dangerous place. I thought she was talking about politics, but she was warning me about Hannagan.

"Then in 1939, my mother and I returned home to Wales. Hannagan told me to settle back into normal life and be patient, but nothing was normal after Berlin. I was a seething mass of hormones and desire. I went to Studley Castle and Hannagan contacted me again in my third year and I joined the IRA.

"When I had my degree, Liam told me to apply to Section 23 and pass everything on to him. My mother was Welsh, but my father had been Irish. Hannagan fitted perfectly into the pattern of my life."

She fidgeted with her jacket. "*Hannagan* wasn't his real name. He once told me he was the last prince of Ireland, and I built up a picture of him with a castle, a crown and a fiery black steed. He gave me the name 'Hanna' to mirror *his* name and confuse the enemy. He was a master of disguise, which helped him so often to escape.

"I thought I was helping to change the world, to make it a better place. How many have been deluded into thinking that? By 1952, I'd had a change of heart. All I wanted was to return fully to my studies as a botanist. The past had belonged to someone else, someone I no longer knew. I wanted to leave it all behind me, all the guilt, all the shame. When I told Hannagan I wanted to leave the IRA, he laughed."

Her words reminded me of Tim's desperate plea. *I want to leave this awful place. I want to chuck it. I tell you, I want out.*

Enid looked at me, her eyes dark with pain. "Recently, he told me to get in touch with Marjorie Ackert's daughter. Hannagan said you had paintings worth thousands and the Cause needed money. I was alarmed at how much he knew about you, Paula. I came here tonight to warn you. I didn't want you to die. I liked your mother, but Marjorie detested everything Hannagan stood for, and Hannagan doesn't have a forgiving nature."

She gasped suddenly, her hand on her chest. "From the moment Madge saw Anna and me in the kitchen, she began 'fishing'. Madge was clever. She wasn't sure at first which of us was Hanna, so she put all the emphasis on Anna. Anna and I knew each other in the old days, but from the 50s, we'd kept well apart, that is, until today. I had no idea Anna would be at your birthday party, Paula. It was a shock for both of us. I almost turned to go back home, but Madge would have told Quinn. Madge, Quinn, Mitchell and North have been working together for years hunting us down." She tried to raise her head, her eyes drowning in fear.

"Why did Anna shoot at us?" Quinn asked.

"The old loyalties. We'd worked together in the forties. We were comrades."

Quinn leaned over. "Where's Hannagan now?"

"I don't know."

"Rubbish! Did you play a part in the murder of four young policemen last week in Northern Ireland? I stood at the grave-side and saw them buried. We know Hannagan placed the bomb. He's got bloodlust running through his veins. Make amends for the terrible things you did for him, Enid. Tell me where he is so we can stop the killing."

Enid's breathing was becoming distressed, her voice faint. "I haven't been involved for years. People harbour old hatreds, old wounds, Inspector. The path you take in life has consequences. Don't forget what I told you, Paula, people aren't always what they seem."

Thornbury pushed Quinn aside as Enid coughed and blood ran over the cushions. She tapped the syringe, but Quinn held her arm up firmly. "Wait!" He bent over Enid. "Which of you killed Siskin's father?"

With an effort, she raised her eyes. "Panic. And fear."

She looked at me and gasped, "Tell William I'm sorry." She grimaced, and I saw her bite down hard. Spasms seized her body and convulsions shook her. The smell of almonds was everywhere. Thornbury was screaming at Quinn to get the oxygen mask from the ambulance. There was a fevered space of action then Enid was stretchered out by the paramedics. She was barely alive, but Thornbury thought there was still a chance to save her.

I was stunned. I sat down beside Trish. "What happened?" I asked Quinn.

"She bit down on a pill and released the poison." He sank down, his head in his hands. Trish looked at me, her eyes huge, her notebook lying crumpled on the armchair.

I was struggling to come to terms with the End I had known: Enid, the botanist who loved small gardens. Enid, the killer. Enid, the scientist who had built up the Bank of Seeds to save the world. Enid, who had murdered Siskin. Yet Enid had risked coming to the birthday party to warn me. She had looked round the room. *I told you not to be so trusting when you meet people. They're not always what they seem.*

I thought none of my birthday guests were what they seemed.

While Trish was giving her statement to a sergeant, Quinn pointed to the scorched hole in my jacket. "I'd no idea you had a revolver."

"I have a licence. I thought I might need it."

"How did you know Enid and Anna were involved?"

"I didn't." I shivered. "Why did Anna reveal herself? She could have stayed quiet and got away with it."

"You heard. Loyalties never die, and she feared her past would be brought out, but I never suspected poison." The forensic team left and Quinn called Jenkins to bring Selwyn back into the sitting room. Selwyn sank down onto a chair at the table and my fingers sketched the grief in his eyes.

Quinn pulled up a chair and sat down beside him. "Now then, sir, what was that all about?"

Selwyn's voice was a murmur. "I loved her." He looked up. I scarcely recognised this wretched man with the white face stained with emotion. "Anna knew Hannagan *and* Hanna, but she never talked about them."

Quinn glanced at me. He looked shocked. Selwyn carried on, his eyes lowered.

"We met during the war in 1939 when I was sent over to Ireland. I fell in love with Anna the moment I saw her."

Selwyn looked directly at me. "Anna was the most exciting woman I'd ever met. One day, she told me her story. She was involved with the IRA through her aunt and uncle who raised her after the deaths of her parents. Even when she was a child, she smuggled weapons and ammunition for the Cause. She married Michael Donovan, an IRA leader, when she was eighteen, but Donovan was hanged in the spring of 1939 in Mountjoy Gaol. She was with him in the prison before he died. I was there as Donovan's Counsel. They clung together before they were dragged apart. Then the hood was placed over Donovan's head and Father Kelly mumbled the words for the eternal damned. The trapdoor was released and Donovan dropped.

"I brought Anna back to England. The years passed, but the pain never left her. She told me she would never marry again. Once she helped Hanna when Hannagan was wounded." He turned to Quinn. "You may despise me, but I loved Anna absolutely. I never understood the term 'prisoner of love', but I understand it now. I protected her, I won't deny it, but I never betrayed her, and I *never* betrayed my country."

Selwyn was taken down to the police station to write a statement. He had said he never betrayed his country, but I knew the courts and public opinion would be against him. While Quinn was talking with Trish, I slipped out of the sitting room. I was glad to get out of that room of death. And I had not forgotten the hidden message in the siskin picture. I knew exactly where the miniatures were and I knew who Mum's 'old friend' was. My mother had been so much cleverer than Quinn and Selwyn.

I opened the guest room door and stopped on the threshold staring into a room full of bright sunshine, the glare dividing the room into light and dark. I waited, turned to stone, while red petals dropped round me.

Then the vivid splash of late afternoon sun faded and the petals vanished. I closed the door softly and walked towards the window, but before I reached it Quinn and Jenkins rushed into the room.

"Stay where you are!" Quinn's tone was sharp. "What are you doing in here?"

I improvised quickly and turned to walk over to the wardrobe. "My mother's painting bag. It's in the wardrobe. I wanted to look through it."

"Keep her away from the wardrobe," Quinn shouted.

Jenkins pulled me roughly over to the window.

"Why are you *treating* me like this?" I shouted furiously, but in Quinn's eyes I was still the criminal. I watched him tipping everything out of the canvas bag onto the floor.

"There are no paintings in the bag," I said shortly.

"Why did you rush in here?"

Could I go on with the subterfuge? The violence in the sitting room had terrified me. I no longer felt in control of my life. And Quinn would never give up. He dragged a chair over and sat on it. I was pleased his leg was still hurting.

"The painting of the bird gave me an idea." I was sullen, hating him for treating me like a felon.

Quinn nodded. "I was right. Everything pointed to you. When you went into the art gallery, Denby told us you were making a deal with Schiffer, especially when you met him again at the Riverside Inn."

"He was wrong," I said quietly. "And you've always been wrong."

"Tell me about the bird in the cage," Quinn said curtly.

I shrugged. "A spinus is a type of finch called a siskin. My mother once said 'Mr Siskin is the keeper of my memories'. I remember I laughed. Mr Siskin was a wooden doll who lived with his two wooden daughters in a large dolls house called Lintwhite Villa. A lintwhite, you see, is also a type of finch. That's when I knew the miniatures must be hidden inside the dolls house." I paused. "I didn't know then that the Siskins were real people. Old Mr Siskin, the gardener, was the friend she entrusted with the miniatures. Werner Zeisig had worked that out as well."

"You got all that from the picture? Okay, where's this dolls house?"

The house was standing against the wall partly concealed by the bed. Closely followed by Jenkins, I went over and pulled the grey canvas-fitted cover over the roof.

"That's some dolls house!" Jenkins exclaimed.

The words "Lintwhite Villa" were painted above the doorway, intertwined with rose-leaves and rosebuds. It had three storeys and an attic. Amy had needed a wheelbarrow to get Lintwhite Villa into her car.

Quinn grunted. "All right, Jenkins, let's lift it onto the bed."

I watched them struggle to lift it. Quinn sat on the bed and tried to push open the double-sided doors, but the two red knobs over the keyholes would not move. "They're locked! D'you have the keys?"

I hadn't played with the house since Felix Baumgartner died reaching across the overturned table with his gun. The desperate anxiety of that day had killed my childhood, and when Jenni and Suzy told me they were too afraid to play in the garden, I had put them inside and closed the doors. So who had locked them?

Quinn frowned. "If you don't give me the keys, I'll have to break the doors open."

Keys! The little keys! *I'll tell you what they're for when you're older.*

"My bag," I exclaimed. "It's in the sitting room."

Jenkins ran out and was back in seconds. The keys with their rose-leaf decoration on the shafts were on the key-ring.

Quinn told Jenkins to wait outside the door. "No-one's to come in." He turned to me. "Now then, tell me about these keys."

"Amy gave them to me for my sixteenth birthday. A few days later, she was murdered." I ran my thumb along the shafts. "She said she would explain about them later, but later never came." I took the keys off the key-ring. "I always thought they were good-luck charms."

"They're well made," Quinn said. "Look, they're decorated with the same pattern as the house name." It was the same rosy motif inscribed above the bistro doorway. "It's your house, your keys, you should have the honour." He put them in my hand, his eyes sombre and inward-looking.

But which key would open which door? I knelt down. And then I saw them. A tiny 3 and 6 had been inscribed on the backs of the doorknobs. They had not been there before. I fitted the keys into the locks and the double doors opened wide, one to the left, the other to the right, while a catch was released that held the roof down. Mum must have had the keys made soon after she found the Pforzheim miniatures. The sides of the house swung back revealing the interior.

I was hugely disappointed. There was nothing inside except the dolls house furniture. I had been so sure the rooms would be bursting with the Pforzheim treasure. I began releasing the blinds.

Quinn sat quietly beside me. "Now then, let's see what the house has to tell us."

I explained that the kitchen and study were on the ground floor.

"It's a well-appointed kitchen." Quinn pointed to the little coffee machine on top of the kitchen cabinet.

I told him a little of the history of the Siskin doll family. "But I never realised Mr Siskin was a *real* garden designer. At some time, the dolls representing Frau Siskin and her son, Werner, were damaged and thrown away. Later, I asked Dad to give Mr Siskin two daughters. That's when I got Jenni and Suzy and I began making up my own stories. Mum painted the garden diploma and put it on the wall with the Siskin portraits. Jenni loved the study. She was an academic at heart." It had a table, a captain's chair, a floor lamp and bookshelves filled with tiny books.

Quinn leaned forward. "Now go carefully, we're looking for anything untoward."

On the first floor was the lounge with a little sofa, two armchairs, two small coffee tables and a beautiful Welsh dresser with shelves and two cupboards. I took down the five love spoons. "See, their names are inscribed on them: Henryk, Sophia, Werner, Jenni and Suzy."

On the lower shelves of the dresser was a whole set of tiny dinner plates. A baby grand piano stood in the middle of the room. "It has a mechanism that plays a Schubert Impromptu." I touched the key that started the music. "Suzy loved playing the piano and Jenni envied her so much."

"I don't get it," Quinn interrupted. "You talk about these Siskin toys as if they're real people."

I looked at him uncomprehendingly. "They *were* real. To me. I had no friends in Acle except for Bobby, Mrs Lacey's spaniel. Jenni and Suzy were like my human friends, the sisters I always wanted. We lived and laughed together. Of course, they were real."

Quinn shook his head. "Are all young girls like that?"

I frowned. "Don't boys make up adventures? Jenni and Suzy were a part of my life, that's not hard to understand."

While I was speaking, I had been pulling up the blinds in the two bedrooms. I recoiled when I found Mr Siskin sprawled across the bed, his head smashed in, his legs broken. He was quite dead. A hammer was lying beside him. "I don't understand." I leaned forward to pick up the hammer.

"Leave it!" Quinn was crisp. He put the hammer into one of his forensic bags. "I think we can call this 'untoward', don't you?"

But my eyes had moved onto the adjoining room. Jenni was lying half off her bed, her arms broken, her head dented in, and Suzy was on the floor, decapitated. It was grotesque and heartrending.

Quinn bent down. "A murder scene no less."

"Who would *do* such a thing?" I lamented. "They were my friends. I loved them." Unwittingly, I was echoing Selwyn's voice. *I loved her.*

I bent forward to pick up the mutilated bodies. Again, Quinn stopped me. "Leave them. Hopefully, forensics will give us some answers."

"Answers?"

"When, why, who."

When? "It must have been before the keys were made and the house was closed down."

"Go on."

"My mother found the miniatures, perhaps a week or so before she died. My parents argued. Later, she said the miniatures were with a friend, and when I was older the friend would give them to me."

I stared angrily at Quinn. "I know the Who and Why as well. It was Werner Siskin, a revengeful young man visiting my mother and making a personal statement of his hatred for my parents and me."

The surface of the table in the study was covered with leather, but round the edge was the same rose-leaf decoration, the rosebuds running round the border of the drawer. Eagerly, I leaned forward.

"What is it?" Quinn held me back.

I quietened him with a wave of my hand. The trailing leaves were also decorating the top of the Welsh dresser with the two lower doors.

"Look for the roses!" I urged. I pulled the table drawer out and heard Quinn hiss. Three miniatures were lying inside. I picked them up with a shaking hand. They were three small portraits, two eighteenth and one nineteenth century. I held one up. It showed a fine gentleman with wig and lacy cravate executed on ivory.

"I'm sure this was painted by John Smart, an English miniaturist. Look how beautifully he's drawn the hands."

Quinn took it from me. "How do you know it's John Smart?"

"Smart often used a brown background in his work."

"How do you know all this?"

"I learned a lot from Selwyn."

"Three can't be worth thousands," Quinn said.

"The rest must be somewhere else. Keep looking for the entwined rose-leaves."

In a drawer in the Welsh dresser, Quinn found two keys attached to a ring and a ticket. On the ticket: *Keys to safe deposit boxes Numbers 519 and 520 at the Artists Bank in Ipswich, Suffolk.* On the back of the ticket was a personal message: *The Deposit Boxes have been paid up to June 15th, 1981. Alles Gute zum Geburtstag, Paula, Liebling, you know what you must do.* It was signed MJ Denby and dated 29th May 1967.

The paintings had been in deposit boxes all the time.

"What does she mean, you know what you must do?"

"I have to take the miniatures to the British Museum."

"We'll see about that. Colonel North must be told about this development. He'll want to be at the bank when the vault is opened."

I looked up and screamed. Staring in at the window was James Mitchell.

Quinn and Jenkins ran out of the front door. I looked quickly in the attic of the dolls house. Quinn came back, eyeing me suspiciously. I faced him, my hand in my pocket as Jenkins walked in with Mitchell.

I was driven down to Ipswich in a police car with Selwyn. Mitchell and Quinn went in another car.

"I'll resign," Selwyn told me. "If I go quietly, there'll be very little fuss. The past is a long time ago." But I knew, even as a child, that the past never goes away.

When we reached Ipswich, the bank manager was speaking with Colonel North. North introduced me to the manager and confirmed my identity. Nervously, I stepped forward, fearful of any more ugly secrets being exposed. Mr Cranmore, the manager, presented his keys and I showed him mine. I could feel Selwyn breathing over my shoulder as the keys were turned in the lock of the first large deposit box.

It contained hundreds of miniatures by famous painters. The second box held bundles of letters and photographs and more miniatures. I drew back and let Selwyn, North, Quinn and Mitchell sort quickly through them.

"Who are the letters from?" I asked.

"Stresemann, Adenauer, Churchill, Ackert and others of the thirties and forties." Quinn said I could read them later.

I turned to the photographs. Some were of Mum's family. I recognised Dieter Ackert at once, and the woman standing beside him with the large hat and the lacy bosom could have been my grandmother. Baumgartner was standing beside a beautiful young woman. Mum was smiling, looking up at Schiffer, while a scowling Selwyn stood behind her. Jürgen Bergmann, young and serious, was glancing to his left at an attractive Gillian Conrad and her dumpy husband, Cedric. It was like stepping back in time, just as all the future generations will step back into our time and look at us in our strange clothes staring out of greying pictures.

While Mitchell and Selwyn drove back to Norwich with Colonel North, I went with Quinn, expecting to be driven home. Instead, we headed for Ealing.

"There's still some unfinished business," Quinn explained. "So I've booked you and your friend, Trish Porter, into a hotel in Ealing for the night. She's already driven down there."

I didn't like the sound of *unfinished business*. "Is it something to do with the miniatures? And why Ealing?"

"It's nothing to do with the miniatures. James Mitchell knows someone in Ealing who wants to speak to you about your mother. I took the liberty of asking Miss Porter to pack a bag for you before we left the flat, and she'll meet us at the hotel."

"Why did you suspect me?" My voice was low.

"Your father was so absolutely sure you had the miniatures and perhaps, I allowed his judgement to overly influence me. But it wasn't only that. When you came to Norwich, everything happened round you. It was difficult not to see you at the centre of events."

"Am I in the clear now?"

"Oh yes. Yes, I'd say so."

He wasn't very enthusiastic.

The first thing I did on reaching the hotel that evening was to telephone Mr Jolley. I phoned four times during the evening, but there was no answer. Unlike Quinn, I didn't think Enid was still involved with Hannagan. I thought she had preferred to leave the violent past behind and marry William Jolley.

Sunday, 7th June 1981

It was strange to be back in Ealing where my parents had led their "separate lives".

We were in the dining room of the hotel having breakfast. I was edgy, worried about this unfinished business with Mitchell.

Trish was sitting opposite me. "I'd no idea you led such a colourful life," she said.

"I don't!" I responded. "In fact, I'd say most of my adult life has been quite mundane."

"And your childhood?"

"That was different."

She leaned back in her chair. "OK, what can you tell me about James Mitchell?"

"A mystery man."

She looked at me quizzically. "Are you pleased with your life?"

"Not really. The past wasn't always a happy place."

I turned. The scent of lavender was everywhere. I had half-risen when James Mitchell came forward. He drew up a chair at our table and the aroma subsided.

Mitchell still had moody, brooding eyes, but I was no longer captivated by him. I sat down and addressed him savagely, "Do you agree with Quinn that my father was untrustworthy, a wild card?"

"Ah!" Mitchell was startled. "You don't pull your punches, do you?"

"Nor does Quinn," I replied. "Well?"

"I liked your father, but he preferred getting results his way, which upset the management."

"Why are you here?"

He felt inside his pocket. "I was told to give you this to establish my credentials."

A roundel of coloured matches fashioned into a wheel and held together in its centre with a piece of wire was placed on the table. I gave a cry of disbelief. "The Wheel of Truth! My father made me one when I was a child." I looked at Mitchell distrustfully. "How can you *possibly* have one?"

He held his hands up. "It's not mine! My aunt told me to give it to you."

"Your aunt?"

"Is this connected with Quinn's 'unfinished business'?" Trish interrupted.

He nodded. "My aunt will explain everything."

Trish put a firm hand on his arm. "Mr Mitchell, we've both been through a very scary time. Some terrible things happened yesterday. Explain who your aunt is and what this is all about."

"Of course, I'm sorry. We're going to see my aunt who lives at The Rosary in Ealing." He turned to me. "Aunt Gertrud knew your mother. She gave me her Wheel of Truth to identify me as her messenger."

I was puzzled. "But The Rosary's a convent."

"Are you saying a nun can't have a nephew?"

"No, of course not."

Mitchell ordered a fresh pot of coffee and settled back. "OK, here goes. About fifteen years ago, I met you at an art exhibition. You won't remember me, Mrs James, but I spoke with your mother that day."

"I remember you clearly. You wanted to know if there was any news of your uncle, Arno Müller."

He raised his eyebrows. "Absolutely right. Well, Arno was half English, half Dutch. His mother's brother, Brendan Mitchell, took me into his family when my mother was killed in a climbing accident. My father was in MI6 and seldom at home, so Uncle Brendan and his wife, Aunt Lotte, brought me up. When I was fourteen Aunt Lotte took me to The Rosary to meet Aunt Gertrud who is Aunt Lotte's sister and your mother's friend. But time is passing. I said we'd be at The Rosary by half-past nine. Aunt Gertrud's an old lady. She wants to talk to you about your mother."

On the way to The Rosary, Mitchell told us he was leaving MI5. "I want to be a writer."

I told him no-one leaves the Service. "But you'll have lots of material to draw on."

"I don't want to write a 007 novel. I'm going to photograph and write about aquatic life."

A moment later, we turned into a side-street. I recognised The Rosary immediately. It was a low two-storey red-bricked building with blue shutters hinged back from the windows. Two large meandering borders of flowering pink, red and orange roses filled the cool summery air with their musky scent. It was exactly like the painting Werner Siskin had given me yesterday. I shuddered. Mitchell told us the building held a community of Catholic nuns who worked among the poor in the parish. "Some Carmelite nuns moved up here from Kent after the war," he explained.

"I thought they were Poor Clares," Trish replied.

"When they moved to Norfolk, the nuns bought The Rosary with the help of your mother and her friends."

"And your Aunt Gertrud lives here?"

"That's right."

An elderly nun, leaning on a brown walking stick, her shoulders hunched up over her neck, was waiting outside the building. As Mitchell ran up the steps, she stretched out her arms to embrace him. I looked on as he introduced Trish.

"An editor of a newspaper!" Gertrud was delighted. "You must come and talk to our children about your work. Children have a curiosity about life, you understand."

"Your children?"

"Orphaned, abandoned children. We give them security, a sense of belonging and an education."

Trish smiled. "I'd love to encourage their curiosity."

I bent down as Gertrud kissed me on both cheeks. "It's been a long time, Paula, *Liebling*. I'm so glad you've come with my dear nephew."

I told her I remembered visiting The Rosary when I was five. "There was a nun here with a big headdress. She was very old. Her name was Sister Vlinder. I sketched her when I got home. I remember she gave me some lovely cookies, which she called *koekje*."

"I'm happy you remember us so fondly." With a nod, Gertrud turned and walked into the house, her hand tucked into Mitchell's arm.

We went through a small hall and turned left into a light, pleasant room with a large table and Dutch high-backed tapestry-covered chairs. On the floor near the window lay two large old brown trunks. They looked out of place in the fresh sun-lit room.

Gertrud waved to us to sit down. "James had arranged for me to see you at your home on your birthday, Paula, but the meeting was cancelled by a Chief Inspector Quinn, who said it would not be, now what did he say, James? Oh yes, it would not be 'appropriate'. I'm sure Marjorie would be just as happy if I give you her gifts today."

Quinn, the old devil, still interfering in my life. My heart missed a beat as the door opened, but it was only a nun carrying a large tray with cups, saucers, milk and a welcoming jug of hot coffee. Gertrud whispered to her and the nun nodded and left the room.

As we sat down, Mitchell gave Gertrud the Wheel of Truth. "Paula recognised it immediately."

I broke in impatiently. "When did my mother give it to you?"

Calmly, Gertrud finished pouring out the coffee. "After we came to England, I carried on with my research work. I was a chemist at the time, but I wanted something soothing to do when work was finished for the day, so I tried my hand at painting. Unfortunately, I found it difficult to differentiate between certain colours, and Marjorie kindly designed this wheel to help me. She said she had made one for her little daughter. Sadly it did not help enough and I studied the violin instead." She looked up smiling. " As I hear sounds and rhythms perfectly well, I painted pictures through the music!"

"Do you still play?"

"Oh yes, we have a string quartet and we enjoy ourselves enormously. I'm fortunate that arthritis has not yet attacked my fingers, only my neck and back." She paused. "I must tell you that over the last fifteen years I've been paying a yearly sum into an account in your name. It was for the upkeep of two deposit boxes in a bank in Ipswich. James tells me you've now found the paintings."

I smiled. "The deposit boxes were signed for by a Mrs G. Long. My mother helped a Dr Lang to escape out of Holland during the war. Dr Lang was a chemist. In gratitude, she gave my mother her Crux Gemmata. I have it now."

"I hope it has brought you peace of mind and heart. Your mother and I became great friends. When Johan and I reached England and began working here, we were advised to change our names. The Nazis had long arms and several German refugees were murdered on British soil. I've become accustomed to being known as Sister Gertrude Long. Perhaps you will understand better when you see this painting."

Gertrud signalled to us to walk over to the window where a painting was hanging on the wall. It was dated February 1942 and signed MJ Ackert, De Grote Markt, Groningen.

I studied the picture. A woman in her early thirties was sitting at a plain wooden table with two men, one younger, one older. The wall behind them was covered with a light blue-grey wash. A naked bulb swung from the ceiling. Four small brown suitcases huddled together on the floor. A narrow shaft of light streamed into the room through a small window high in the ceiling. A branch hung darkly over part of the cracked pane. The tapering light picked out the bleakness in the faces of the three people round the table, their coats buttoned up to their necks against the cold spring day.

The younger man was facing the door. Blond hair unkempt, his left arm round the woman's shoulder, he held a revolver in his right hand, his finger round the trigger.

The older man looked ill, his cheeks sunken, his eyes lifeless, his weapon pointing at the door. The woman seated between the two men had dark curly hair escaping from her knitted blue woollen cap. In her left hand she too held a revolver. Fear bound the three together.

The charcoal and pen drawing with the blue-grey washed-in background was the perfect tool for such a sombre cameo. I recognised my mother's hand in every line. Frowning, I leaned forward. Lying on the table was a fourth revolver and an Odala ring, visual evidence of my mother's presence.

Gertrud nodded. "They were desperate times. This was painted just before we moved on to Den Helder."

"What happened to the two men?"

"Tomas, the old man? His family had been liquidated by the Nazis." She pointed to the door in the painting. "We heard men running up the stairs. Tomas stood up, firing as the police kicked the door open. He took the first bullets in his chest and head. Johan was a chemist like myself, and he and Marjorie and I crouched down behind the overturned table firing our weapons. Then shots came from the stairs and four resistance fighters hurled themselves on the police, pushing them further into the room as we rushed past and hurtled down the steps.

"A man and a woman were nervously waiting for us on the opposite pavement. They led us to a 'safe' house. But in those dark days, no house was safe for long. Eyes were always watching, informers were everywhere. The next day we heard that the resistance men who had rescued us had been summarily executed.

"Marjorie kept moving us on, always alert, moving us every few hours. We reached Den Helder and more men and women put their lives in danger to smuggle us out to England. You see, we'd been involved in important chemical research and the Nazis were determined to stop us escaping. Later that year we heard that our beloved friend, Teresa Benedicta, you may know her as—"

"Edith Stein," Trish said quietly. "She died in Auschwitz."

Sister Gertrud walked back to the table. "So many dear courageous friends. In England, Johan and I continued with our research." She looked round at us.

"There are no words that can express the outpouring of emotion towards those who have risked or given their lives to save another life. When peace came, I decided that my deeds should reflect my gratitude and so I joined the Order. For many years I've shared that gratitude and my joy in God with others less fortunate. So many good people have joined us in our work.

"In 1946, Marjorie bought this building and gardens for us and we started the work of The Rosary. Marjorie, and the other survivors who joined us, helped to make our project a success in the community. And that is why I want you, Paula, to have this painting. I know you will take great care of it."

I was in tears as I thanked her. So many had seen my mother as a difficult woman, unconventional, formidable, but at The Rosary, she had helped create a retreat for those who had lacked comfort and understanding.

While Gertrud had been speaking, my fingers had been busily sketching. Now I eased the page out and pushed it over the table to her.

Gertrud observed the sketch for a moment. "You're a gifted woman, Paula. and I thank you for your sketch. Marjorie told me you had talent and humour for writing stories and illustrating them."

Gertrud came round the table and I stood facing her. She looked up, her head to one side, her dark eyes measuring me up and down. "You're very like your mother, *mein Liebling*, taller and fairer in colouring, but similar in voice and the way you move. She would be proud of you, Paula."

Gertrud had been so close to my mother, and during such desperate straits, and the familiar term, '*mein Liebling*', caught at my throat. "Can I hug a nun?" I asked tremulously.

She laughed. "Of course, you may, you silly child."

Did I envy Sister Gertrud the quietness of solitude and the peace of prayer in her retreat? Yes, but *I* need people, people to sketch, places to record on paper, people who might make sense of this mad, unregulated world; and I need the sound of life in the movement of passing cars, the clatter of workmen, the chitter-chatter of people in the shops. People! People make my fingers itch to hold a pencil, to record the moment, to show the frailties and strengths of humankind.

"James tells me you've been an estate agent, but why aren't you painting?"

I tried to tell her that I would be compared with my mother and would always be a poor second.

"Nonsense! You have a different style altogether and you're looking at your modern world. Show me some of your work."

Reluctantly, I pushed my sketch-book over to her. She looked up suddenly. "What's this?"

I leaned forward. Bobby's eager face stared out of the page. "It's about a woman and her dog. I began it years ago, but I keep coming back to it."

"It's very good. What's holding you back from finishing it and letting others enjoy your work? You should understand, Paula, the gift is given to you to use and share with others."

"I'll think about it," I said cautiously.

"Caution is not always a virtue," Gertrud said sternly. "Courage, allied to talent, has changed the direction of men's thinking."

"I'll encourage her." Trish stepped in quickly before I could argue the premise.

"Good, a little help and that touch of love solve many problems. And when the story is finished, Paula, I shall want a copy."

"I'll finish it…for you," I promised.

Gertrud was delighted. "Splendid. Now I have a confession to make. These trunks were delivered to me here in early June 1966. At the time I was ill with the flu and the suitcases were placed in the cellar by Sister Vlinder. Unfortunately, she died a few days later from the same illness and the cases have been in the cellar, completely forgotten, until I stumbled on them a few days ago."

She asked James to bring one of the cases over. "There was a letter in an envelope attached to the top case. It was from Amy Eggers who wrote that she feared for her life. I immediately informed James and he told me that Amy had died shortly after Marjorie in 1967. I am very sad that I knew nothing of their passing at the time."

I opened the top suitcase. It contained sketchbooks from my mother. I caught glimpses of drawings of myself as a baby and portraits of Ackert, Schiffer, Baumgartner and Jürgen Bergmann.

I wanted to examine them, but now was not the time. I opened Amy's letter and read it out aloud so that it embraced everyone in the room:

Liebe Paula,

'These suitcases are for you. They're filled with your mother's sketchbooks. She gave them into my safe-keeping, and I have sent them to an old and trusted

friend at The Rosary as I fear that all is not well here. Sister Gertrud will contact you and give them to you when everything is safe.

Your mother and I were great friends, and she gave into my care her most precious gift, her daughter. I will try to fulfil her expectations, but The Auctioneers believe I have something they want and they are threatening me. Because I fear for my life and because I may not be here much longer, I want to tell you about your mother. Too many times, others have lambasted her and distrusted her. She has been treated badly, and I want to redress this and show you how dedicated Marjorie was to truth in a time of false truths, to her art, which consumed her life, and to her friends, for whom she was willing to lay down her life.

Marjorie was treated very badly by the art world after the war. Her connection with her father, and the dark rumours that were spread about links with the IRA and 'Nazism', damaged her, but no-one could put Marjorie down for long and she bounced back with her stunning books on plants and gardens. She hoped Mr Siskin would look after the Pforzheim treasure for you.

Most of all, I want you to know what an extraordinary woman your mother was: brave and resourceful, clever and ruthless. But Marjorie had many secrets and there were people who wanted her dead. I've decided that you should know the truth of your mother's activities in the war.

She led a dangerous life from 1937 when the Gestapo hunted the Bruderbunder down, executing many of our friends. Her closest companion in danger was Franz Helmann. They had known each other from art college. Both were later involved in rescuing Germans from Nazi Germany. Franz chose to remain in Germany during the war. He was very brave. Several times Marjorie and Franz met in Munich and Hamburg on secret missions. It was a miracle they survived the war.

Marjorie always loved Franz, but something happened during that time and things soured between them. I never heard the whole story.

In 1940 your mother began working for British Intelligence. Until 1942 I was Major Sheldon Asquith's secretary and I knew everyone in the Netherland/German Department. When Section 23 was wound down I worked with Colonel North. He was part of the XXI Committee which dealt with counter-intelligence and deception. He also created a special operations unit to track down dissident Irish working in England and Northern Ireland. It was Franz who warned him that an Irishman, code-named Lune, was working with the

Nazis and conducting a campaign of violence on the English mainland and in Northern Ireland. According to Franz, Lune was not part of the IRA. He was running his own war against the British.

In early 1943, after the collapse of Section 23, North put Marjorie back in the field to find Lune. MI5 thought the bombings were part of an IRA operation, but they were mistaken. In 1944 Marjorie told North she was certain 'Lune' was Hannagan, a captain in the German Army and a former IRA leader from Belfast. His companion, Hanna, was even more dangerous and elusive. I was always expecting to hear Marjorie had been found shot dead in a dark alley.

I'm convinced your mother was poisoned to prevent her discovering Hannagan's real identity. Unfortunately, neither Colonel North nor Dr Petrie agreed with me.

Paula, I want you to be proud of your mother. She had her weaknesses but, above all, she had great integrity as an artist and a friend, and she loved you dearly.

I shall pray every day to Our Lady that you are safe and your life is set on a good path.

Deine liebe Freundin,
Amy.

I put the letter down on the table. I had misjudged Amy. As a child I had seen her as cold and unemotional, but through the words in the letter, I discovered a different woman, a caring, loving friend, united with Mum through their wartime loyalties. And there was confirmation of my mother being poisoned, although I had thought my father responsible. For the first time, I saw my mother as Amy saw her, fearless and dedicated to truth.

The name Lune intrigued me. Where did it come from? And did it imply Hannagan was dark and mysterious as the moon? Then I remembered the four young policemen he had murdered. You can't be romantic about a man who lived with death and hatred. I asked James what he thought.

James's moody eyes did not change. "Killers aren't romantic. Death by violence is shocking. People write crime thrillers to titillate their readers as they try to learn the name of the killer or fraudster or blackmailer, but violent death isn't neat and tidy. It's bloody and horrific, and the victim faces terror and suffering. I worked closely with your father. He was worried Hannagan would use you in some way. He told me Hannagan had poisoned Marjorie and he was determined to get him. Perhaps that's why he was murdered."

James picked up the cases as I got ready to leave, but first, I asked Sister Gertrud if I might return and paint all the Sisters of The Rosary. To my delight, she agreed and we fixed a date, a weekend in a month's time.

"You must come," I said to Mitchell. "I'll paint you in somewhere. I know, you can be the gardener, and Trish?" I turned to her.

"I'll be a visitor with a bouquet of carnations for Sister Gertrud!"

"That will be lovely," Sister Gertrud said placidly, "but I prefer roses."

Mitchell drove us back to Norwich. We dropped Trish off at The Gazette and he took me on to my flat. As he pulled up at Eversley Road, Mitchell told me that Quinn had investigated the "scam" I had talked about.

"You were right," he said. "Martin Spencer and his friend, Lawrie Heals, were operating a 'Murder on Demand' scheme, which they called *The Helpline.*"

It was a clever and simple idea. Spencer had thought it up. He'd been reading some local and community newspapers and was surprised how much information they gave about local people who were ill, had dementia, had money in property or were well off. Spencer thought some people would like to get rid of certain relatives to get their hands on the family money. All they needed was a kindly, discreet, middle-aged woman to approach the family. Rowene was perfect for the job.

"They formed *The Helpline* with a solicitor who helped sell the old family home and arrange Power of Attorney and finances. They added a firm who sold off the contents of the old house, and a doctor who administered the fatal dose and the death certificate. A considerable sum of money changed hands. It wasn't long before *The Helpline* was in operation and aged, sick or unwanted relatives were being sent to the Retirement Homes. Spencer and Heals had already worked the scam in seaside places like Bournemouth and Newquay, but it was always a quick in and out. The business was folded up before they could be identified.

"They were clever and very careful. Roberts was the doctor in Dunham Village. He provided the drugs and signed all the death certificates." Mitchell frowned. "Someone should have picked up on that. *The Helpline* quickly found they had a growing clientele, which isn't good news for the rest of us!"

"But what went wrong in Dunham Village?" I interrupted.

"The first thing that went wrong was Lawrie Heals' dismissal from the Retirement Homes. Martin Spencer had used him to harass Mrs Conrad, hoping she would break down and reveal where the diamonds were. But she complained to Sellick a few days ago and he sent Lawrie packing back to Pretoria. Sellick was anxious to mollify Mrs Conrad so that she would keep supporting his Retirement Homes project. Spencer was now on his own. He was clever. He kept *The Auctioneers* separate from *The Helpline*.

"But he was not prepared for Renée Tournai, who was provocative and nosey. So they got rid of her. Then Audrey Simpson started sniffing round. She found things out and began blackmailing Spencer. So she had to go."

"But why did Sellick choose such unsuitable people?" I asked.

"He was looking for strong characters who would build up his empire, but the oddest thing of all is that Spencer fell ill the day you took up your appointment in Dunham Village. He'd been nursing a pain in his right side for a couple of weeks. The day you arrived, Spencer was rushed into hospital with acute appendicitis and operated on. Rowene had no orders from the boss and stayed at home, so there was no-one from *The Helpline* to meet the relatives and sick patients, except you. Spencer's been arrested and will be going on trial when he's better."

"So have you found Rowene?" I asked breathlessly. "I'm sure my clients were expecting her in the sales office. I know they were surprised to see me."

"Martin's talked. Rowene's flown the coop, but we'll find her."

I thanked him for the news and he drove off. I went into the flat. Forensics had finished their work, and I had finished with the house. I had decided to find a B&B and search for another flat. I picked up the post, packed a few things and drove into Norwich.

I found a B&B without any trouble. It was in a pleasant yellow-bricked house in a wide terrace. I told the landlady I would be staying for at least two or three weeks, because I was looking for a flat. As I signed her register, I remembered my flight from the empty London flat. I found it hard to compare myself with that sulky, miserable, uncommunicative woman.

Mrs Busby, owner of Orchard House, looked askance at the old cases.

"I'm doing research on some old books," I said boldly. "I'll keep them neatly in a corner."

"You're at the university then?"

An academic life suddenly sounded very acceptable. "I'm consulting with them," I lied.

In the evening, I sat in the unfamiliar room and read the post I had brought with me. Among the advertising leaflets was an official letter from Colonel Edgar North requesting me to confirm that I would be attending the hearing of the Pforzheim Report on Wednesday 10th June. Apparently, I should have replied to the original letter. I scrabbled about in my bag and found the envelope. The meeting was to be held at a hotel just outside Norwich. The proceedings would be heard in private.

The meeting would be reporting on the theft of paintings and artefacts from the Pforzheim Museum in 1944. New information had come to light, and statements and evidence would be read out. I was requested to post my statement with any knowledge I might have about the Pforzheim robbery to the colonel at the hotel as soon as possible. Enclosed was a stamped addressed envelope and a name tag attached to a thin blue lanyard.

I was aghast. I wanted nothing do with the meeting. I wanted to be purged of Pforzheim. The stolen miniatures had been found, there was no need to keep going over the details. In the end, I decided on a compromise. I would put everything I knew down on paper and hand it in at the hotel. If they had all the information, they would not need me at the meeting. I spent most of the night going through the cases filled with Mum's sketchbooks. I soon realised they were wonderful teaching material. My mother had written on some of the sketches, commenting on her use of different colours, the designs she had chosen, importance of background, use of different materials to create effects, the dyes she had mixed, the textures, all the minutiae that make up a successful painting. An art school or university would be interested in them. I put the books away and dozed fitfully until morning.

Monday, 8th June 1981

I left the house just after seven for my Monday morning appointment with Doug Sellick. I didn't want to wait until ten. Corrie had told me Sellick arrived at the office before eight every morning. I would catch him then and tell him I wasn't going to Yorkshire. I had my resignation letter in my pocket.

I drove into the small carpark behind the office, but it was full. Perhaps local residents had permission to use the space during the night. I reversed out and managed to find a place nearby in a narrow side street. It was still only a quarter to eight.

The main door was locked. It was annoying, but I would have to slip my letter through the letterbox instead of giving it to Sellick with a shrug of indifference. I turned and made my way to the car and drove back to the B&B. At one o'clock, I turned the television on for the news and watched astonished as neo-Nazis were shown storming into Sellick's agency earlier in the morning firing their weapons. A news reporter, standing outside in the noisy street, informed us that the Nazis had been quickly rounded up by armed police. We were told that Sellick had a collection of Nazi memorabilia including jewelled crowns, medallions, artefacts, uniforms, guns and swords. All had been stolen from palaces and great houses in Poland and eastern Europe during the war.

Sellick, together with Pat Heals and Jim Inglis, had been in his office when the raid took place. They looked white and shaken on television when the police escorted them to safety out of the building. Sellick later confessed to being blackmailed and threatened for his collection. Shocked, I realised that if I had arrived fifteen minutes later at the agency, I might have been caught up in the gunfire and violence.

A little later, I phoned Carless-Adams to let him know I was selling the house.

The smooth vowels flowed over the line. "I'm sorry to hear that, Mrs James, your father hoped you would be happy there."

I avoided responding to what my father may have hoped. "The house is on the market with a local estate agent. I just wanted you to know."

His cool tone hoped he might act for me in the future. I muttered something and put the phone down.

The very next day, I found a flat. It was empty, newly decorated and had no history of violence. The owner, a young man, accepted my offer. He wanted a quick sale. He was using Robert Jansen's Agency, a small estate office on the other side of Norwich. I chose another solicitor and told him that I had the cash to buy the flat. He said he could see no problems.

I read Colonel North's letter again, put my thoughts in order and started to write down everything I knew about the Pforzheim paintings and the stolen miniatures. Finally, I added everything Gerry Scott had told me. I pictured Scott sitting in my kitchen, his cropped head wet from the rain.

I drove to the hotel and handed my observations to the young receptionist. She said Colonel North's secretary would like to speak to me and I was connected to her on the phone. To my annoyance, she stressed that I must attend the meeting, which was being convened by the MoD. I was forceful. "But I've left my statement at reception. Surely I don't need be at there as well?"

"Colonel North may need to question you, Mrs James. It's essential that you attend."

Tersely, I confirmed I'd be there.

That night the news on radio and television was all about the neo-Nazi attack on Sellick's Estate Agency in the middle of Norwich.

Tuesday, 9th June 1981

I arranged for a firm to clear the flat in Eversley Road and sell all the furniture. I also hired "Jack—Van with Driver". Jack had a large folding trolley and together, we wheeled the dolls house out to the van. We added the microwave, the Clarice Cliff mugs and jug, the bookcase, books and photos, two suitcases filled with clothes and black bags full of bed linen.

"What about the rest of the furniture?" he asked.

"Too many memories," I retorted. Violent memories. But in the end, we dismantled the bed and took that as well.

Jack offered to put everything in his garage for a small fee when I told him I had a flat lined up. "I'll be able to move within a few weeks."

Later that day, I went to Jarrolds and looked round the store. Once again, I ordered a sofa, a nest of tables, chairs. Afterwards, I had a coffee in the restaurant and heard Gillian Conrad's voice all round me. I stumbled out of the store, feeling as if I were living with ghosts.

At five o'clock I went to the Old Catton Museum. Dr Mark Fisher was waiting for me. He wanted me to act as a sounding board, to watch, observe and note anything unusual. We went round the museum. Some of the rooms had been furnished in the fourteenth, sixteenth and eighteenth centuries, and the art gallery held some good paintings. There was a small staff. Everyone seemed happy with plenty to do.

My parents had never underestimated the importance of work as a means of enjoying life. I now had enough money to keep the wolf from the door, but work gave me the opportunity to meet people and sketch their personalities. I told Fisher I would let him know my decision after the North report.

Surprise had pricked his amber eyes. "The Pforzheim Hearing?" I was too astonished to speak. "I'll be there," he said. "We can talk about the job afterwards."

Fisher was not much older than I, too young to have been in the war, or to have known my mother, but if he knew North he might be involved with WATID or MI5. I left the museum feeling alarmed that the circle of disquiet might be starting again. The suspicion that everyone knew more than I hung in the air.

I drove on to the hospital. Madge was in a wheelchair. "I'm ready to go home," she complained, "but they're keeping me here because of the new knee-cap." She was also contrite. "If I hadn't returned to the house, that nice young policeman would still be alive."

I gave her my father's philosophy for survival in war: "Why did I survive when the man standing beside me was shot? You either accept it or go mad."

At the hospital, I was told that Enid Jolley had died in the ambulance. I phoned Mr Jolley later. Again, there was no reply. Again, I left a message.

What did I feel for Enid? What should I feel? We all struggle with life, but I would not have liked Enid's path. I felt that at last I had climbed Judd's ladder. Only doubts left by Dr Fisher were worrying me.

Wednesday, 10th June 1981

I was sleeping poorly. The shocking violence had finally caught up with me, and in my dreams I kept seeing Werner Siskin collapsing over the table and Anna Lacey falling, blood running out of her mouth. Tired and fractious, I longed for the solicitors to get on with the paperwork so that I could move into the empty flat. The house my father had sold me had been bought within a week of being put on the market.

I woke late, sprawled across the bed. The Pforzheim Report was due to start at 3.30 and it was already past ten, but there was a reluctance in me to get up and face the day. Slowly, I stood up. A wave of nausea swept over me and I hung on to the bedside table as the aroma of lavender filled my throat. I had hoped I would be free of the sharp-toothed grey leaves now that the miniatures had been found.

I stumbled over to my shoulder-bag. Nothing had changed. Somewhere, beyond these walls, my world was still a dangerous place of guns and violence. I found my revolver and loaded it.

Lansbury Hall was an imposing Elizabethan-style redbrick building with turrets and tall chimneys surrounded by large grounds. The owners had moved with the times and kept part of the building as their home, setting aside the rest to be used for conferences and special occasions. In the foyer I joined a queue near the wide staircase. Two police officers were standing by a table that had a large notice bearing the words *The Pforzheim Report.*

My revolver was in my coat pocket. I took the coat off and folded it over my arm and put the nametag with its blue ribbon round my neck. The directions in the letter were that I must show my passport and hand the colonel's letter over when I arrived at Lansbury Hall.

On reaching the table, I gave my bag to the uniformed policeman on the left and passed the letter and passport to the plain-clothes officer near the stairs. He glanced down the letter, opened the passport, checked the photo inside, asked for my name and address and confirmed both were on his list. This looked like being a very official meeting indeed.

My bag and passport were returned to me with a nod. I was given a slip of paper with a number and told to go up the stairs where I would find Conference Room 2B. At the top of the stairs, I turned left. Another policeman was on duty outside Room 2B. He was also holding a list and was ticking off names as people followed each other into the room. I noticed his eyes as he looked at me, wide-set golden eyes above high angled cheek bones. A Slavonic face.

The conference room overlooked a wide green lawn at the back of the building. Beams of sunlight were coming through two large windows illuminating the room with summer warmth. There was no dais. A table and four conference chairs were facing four rows of about fifty chairs. A woman in a blue-flowered dress, a dark blue blazer and low-heeled black shoes, was setting up a stenographer's machine at a table on one side.

The room was filling rapidly and people were finding their chairs. Several were in uniform. A Royal Marine had positioned himself by the door, a Browning pistol in a holster strapped to his leg. I saw James Mitchell cross the room. A moment later, Sir Selwyn Freeman joined him by one of the windows. Before the revelation of his relationship with Anna Lacey, Freeman had been a confident servant of the courts. Now his shoulders had shrunk and he moved like an old man.

I put my long, light-weight, green woollen coat on. A short, elderly man with a square face, leaning heavily on a walking-stick, nodded as he walked past me. He moved along the second row and sat down on a chair marked with the number 11. I was looking for chair 48 when Jane Donovan saw me. She stopped, nodded coldly and sat down in the front row. I had no idea how to deal with the death of her mother, the lost causes and the sorrow of the past week. And, perhaps, like me, Jane was fearing what might yet be revealed at the meeting.

The marine acknowledged DCI Quinn and DS Penry as they entered the room. Quinn was still using a walking-stick. His eyes rested on Jane, then me, then moved on to Mitchell and Selwyn who were making their way over to the chairs. WATID and CI2 were well represented. I turned as Madge Conway rolled through the doorway in a wheelchair, her legs covered with a tartan rug.

"It's infuriating," she muttered irritably as she joined me. "They've limited how much time I walk. Apparently it takes time for knees to settle. Like a cake, you know. In the meantime I have to use this bloody awful chair."

A man came across and spoke to her. An American. Madge nodded, her eyes moving round the room. The American took his seat in the front row. Madge stayed on the end of the back row with me.

There were nearly twenty people in the room. The square-faced man was speaking earnestly in German with a well-dressed man with a short beard. They turned as a colonel in the Canadian armed forces went up to them and spoke in fluent German. I caught a few words: *Pforzheim. Kommissar. Bürgermeister.*

There was a sudden stir and everyone rose as a short, thin man came hurrying down the room. He was accompanied by a policeman carrying two heavy briefcases that were put on the table. The thin man turned and faced us.

"Ladies and gentlemen, please take your seats."

Quinn and Penry sat on either side of him, and the policeman took a seat beside Penry, who was unlocking both the cases.

There were voices at the door. Trish was remonstrating with the guard. Quinn leaned over and whispered to Penry who hurried down the room. Trish gave him some papers. Penry glanced at them and Trish came and joined me in the back row.

I had recognised the thin man at once. He had changed very little from the day I first saw him at the RA Exhibition in 1964. Colonel Edgar North held himself straight, his stomach flat, his features sharp; only the thin strands of white hair stretching precariously across his head were fewer. My father would have said the colonel was just about holding his own.

He stood up and addressed us. "I'm Colonel Edgar North and the MoD has appointed me to report new findings on events that took place at Pforzheim on the 2nd, 3rd and 4th of October 1944. This is to be known as *The Pforzheim Consultation, Evaluation and Assessment Report.*

"Evidence has been submitted by *Polizeihauptkommissar* Lambert Weber, Obergefreiter Matthau Schmidt, a former German soldier, acting as night guard at the Pforzheim Museum in 1944, and by Mrs Paula James, the daughter of Marjorie and Eric Denby, Miss Jane Donovan a former agent in Section 23, Mrs Madge Conway FBI, and by DCI Carter Quinn, DS Owen Penry and Captain James Mitchell from CI2. We welcome Miss Patricia Porter, editor of the Swaffham Gazette, to the Report. Our stenographer is Mrs Ruth Tarrant. I would like to thank all those present for submitting written evidence."

North's voice was crisp, his manner decisive. "I also wish to greet Herr Rudy Brandt, the mayor of Pforzheim who is accompanied by *Museumsdirektor* Frideric Weller. In addition, I welcome Major Jim Rollings of the Royal Marines, Mr George Mulholland from the Foreign Office, Colonel Gregory Siegel from the Canadian armed forces, and Sir Selwyn Freeman from WATID."

North's dark eyes swept round the room. "I also have the sad duty to record the recent deaths of Major Eric Denby and Sergeant Gerry Scott, both formerly of the SAS. Although Major Denby and Sergeant Scott were part of the original conspiracy to rob the museum at Pforzheim, they came to me many years ago and confessed their part in the robbery. They were given free pardons in return for helping WATID and CI2 find the lost works of art. During the last eleven years they risked their lives to help us retrieve the stolen paintings. Without their efforts we would never have been able to return so many works of art to their original owners or heirs."

It was strange to hear my father's name in this impersonal place, but perhaps at last I would learn the truth about Pforzheim.

I wriggled back in my chair, easing my feet out of my shoes. North was assembling his papers meticulously on the table. The impression he gave was one of considerable authority.

"This consultation has three strands. The first concerns the fate of four Canadian and two English soldiers who died on the steps of the Pforzheim Museum on the 2nd of October in 1944."

Colonel Siegel nodded.

"The second strand concerns the theft of paintings and artefacts from the museum on the same day, and the third involves the reappearance of many stolen works."

North looked over his half-moon spectacles. "Captain Mitchell will first explain why Counter Intelligence 2 was set up in May 1938."

Mitchell spoke without notes. "CI2 was set up as an extra arm within the police force in 1938 to monitor enemy agents living in Great Britain, to trace their contacts and any cells they may have formed. We also set up units to supervise British people sympathetic to the Nazis.

"Among the many traumatised victims from the concentration camps who came to this country between 1945 and 1948 was a steady influx of fleeing Nazis and criminals disguised as refugees. There were also allied soldiers who had taken advantage of the often very unusual circumstances in which they found themselves in war. Some of those soldiers served with Major Denby in the raid on Pforzheim. CI2 has been closely involved in the retrieval of the stolen paintings and artefacts."

North nodded and Mitchell went back to his seat.

North closed a file on the table with a sharp slap that made us all sit up smartly. I was reminded of a judge setting out the case for the prosecution in a murder trial.

"Certain papers have come unexpectedly into our possession enabling us to go back to the tragic events of October 1944. They reveal, for the first time what happened to the six soldiers who died outside the museum."

The room was silent as he moved a piece of paper to one side. "The RAF had been supporting a ground force of special troops consisting of British and Canadian paratroopers who were being dropped on the outskirts of Pforzheim near the Museum."

A murmur ran through the room. I saw the colonel bend his head sharply as Rudy Brandt, the mayor of Pforzheim, whispered to him. Unperturbed, North sipped some water. When the room was quiet, he continued.

"Pforzheim is a small town in West Germany near the River Rhine. One of the reasons for the many raids on Pforzheim in 1944 and the beginning of 1945 lay in the importance of the manufacture of precision instruments for the German war effort. The instruments were made in small workshops, factories, and homes in Pforzheim. The museum which stands on the edge of the town had been holding an exhibition of art and artefacts from April 1943. Many of the works on display had been stolen from occupied countries in Europe and Russia. When the tide of war began to turn in the allies' favour in 1944, the exhibition was mothballed and stored in the cellars of the museum."

North sat back, his fingers locked together, his eyes moving over us.

"On Monday, 2 October 1944, the RAF began a series of raids over Pforzheim that lasted three days and nights using de Havilland Mosquito light bombers. Their task was to destroy factories and homes in the town producing precision instruments. At the same time, the Mosquitos were diverting attention from the main thrust of the day—the dropping of a special force of commandos onto fields below the museum. A report had reached Allied Intelligence that several factories had recently been built on the edge of the town in which arms and tanks were being made for use in the forthcoming German offensive in the Ardennes. The commandos' task was to blow up the factories and halt the production of arms. English and Canadian commandos had been specifically trained for this type of operation.

"However, unbeknownst to the Allies, a *Schutzkompanie,* part of a Light Infantry Division, had been brought back from the front to be rested on the low-lying fields on the outskirts of Pforzheim. The British and Canadian Special Force Unit successfully reached their objectives. They stormed the factories, killing all inside. According to Major Denby's report, from which I quote, 'delaying fuses were then set and we left the factories.'

"On the way back to the pick-up point, they were engaged in a fight with the detachment of German Light Infantry that had been hastily summoned to respond to the SAS attack. In the confusion and mêlée, there was considerable loss of life among the commandos, and Denby and his troop missed the assembly point and sought refuge in a nearby museum. Sometime later, the bombs exploded in the factories as the RAF was bombing the town.

"Also on that day, Herr Schmidt, the watchman at the museum, found the bodies of six Allied soldiers lying on the steps of the museum."

Matthau Schmidt acknowledged his name with a nod.

"Until very recently no-one knew what had happened to these men, for the bombing continued for three days, hampering a police investigation. In the ensuing chaos and general disorganisation the names and combat numbers, the dog-tags of the dead men, were not passed on to the proper authorities. On Wednesday the 4th of October the main police station suffered a direct hit. Now *this* is what has recently emerged."

The room rustled and I felt the tension rising in the spreading whispers. Beside me Madge moved irritably in her wheelchair tucking the rug round her legs. Mitchell was looking at Jane, who was fiddling with the clasp on her handbag. The Canadian officer, Siegel, was speaking in an undertone to Lambert

Weber the German police commissar. Why was I watching everyone closely again? I was breathing so shallowly I felt as if I were suspended in space.

Madge jogged my elbow. "Are you all right?"

I nodded and took a deep breath.

North continued, "In the years that followed the ending of the war, a great deal of rebuilding was done in Pforzheim, and a new police station was built where the old one had stood. Five years ago there were reports that the foundations were sinking in the cellar. When the cellar floor was dug up two more floors were revealed beneath. They had been crushed and driven under the cellar during the Mosquito attack in October 1944. When all the rubble had been cleared, hundreds of boxes filled with files and statements were found under the original floor. It has taken time for the German authorities to sift through the files, and only now has evidence emerged about what happened at the museum on that fateful day. We are grateful to the police and museum authorities who have passed this information on to us."

A nod to Kommissar Weber and the mayor of Pforzheim. "From the boxes we have, for the first time, lists of the objects that were stolen from the museum. And we have new information about the six dead men and how they died."

North straightened his back. For a moment his eyes rested on me. I braced myself for more revelations about my father, but his eyes moved on, his voice meticulous in retelling the facts.

"After the initial attack on the factories the action was carried over to the Rhine where the German Light Infantry Division had begun to encircle the Canadian troops. Only eight of Denby's men had survived the earlier attack. The tension placed on all the combatants was due in part to the RAF bombers sweeping across the skies and delivering their deadly cargo of bombs on to the town.

"When Major Denby's men reached the museum they found that the east wing had been almost destroyed. Major Denby and his men ran into the west wing, which was relatively intact. They found their way down into the cellar and while they were resting there they discovered major works of art by Monet, Picasso, van Gogh, and many others.

"Among the survivors of Denby's troop was a former Cambridge art undergraduate, Corporal Charlie Havilland. He instantly recognised the worth of the paintings and told Major Denby that a fortune was in their hands. Major Denby at once told his men to cut the paintings from their frames. Following

Havilland's advice the canvases were carefully rolled up and stored in the rucksacks that had formerly held the ammunition which had been placed in the factories. Major Denby has since told us that every man present, including himself, then stole artefacts for their own private use. Denby stole miniatures and rare medallions. Sergeant Scott took some beautifully decorated Russian knives. All the soldiers helped themselves liberally to other artefacts."

For the first time, North picked up some typewritten sheets on the table. "We can now confirm that the deaths of the six men on the steps of the museum were linked to the thefts from the west wing."

Colonel North's eyes, dark, inscrutable, met mine. "I have a witness statement here. It was given on the day of the raid by an eye-witness. That man is here today. Herr Matthau Schmidt served as a soldier in Ukraine and was subsequently invalided out of the *Wehrmacht*. I will now ask Sergeant Jenner and DS Penry to pass copies of his statement to everyone in the room. The original statement is in German with an English translation opposite. I will read the translation aloud and I would like you to follow it."

Statement by Obergefreiter Matthau Schmidt:

My name is Matthau Johann Schmidt. I was Obergefreiter Schmidt in the 2nd Panzer Army in Ukraine where I was wounded in the leg in late summer of 1941. When I left hospital I was fortunate to be given a job in my home town as day watchman at the Pforzheim Museum. Amongst my tasks was tidying up after visitors had left the building. I also had responsibility for putting out fires from the air raids. Finally I had to make sure that all was correct before handing over to the night watchman, Anton Klein, another former soldier.

Daybreak on Monday 2nd October 1944 was bitterly cold, and it began with the RAF dropping bombs on the town. I had difficulty in making my way from my home to the museum. I saw paratroopers landing and moving towards the new factories. Some paratroopers were captured soon after landing, but many were still free. On the way to the museum I suddenly found myself in the middle of fierce fighting between a section of one of our Infantry troops and the Allied commandos. I holed up in a bombed house. Eventually I reached the museum as our troops and the allied soldiers, still exchanging fire and mortars, moved down towards the Rhine.

The English bombers had destroyed the east wing of the museum and there were many fires. It was not long before I found Anton's body among the smouldering ruins. And all the time smoke was billowing everywhere, turning the sky black above the towering flames. The smell of burning ash was in my throat and lungs. I was fearful that I, too, would be found dead among the debris.

I was going up the steps of the west wing when I saw a group of ten English soldiers approaching. It was just before noon. I slipped behind a pillar and watched them smash their way into the west wing. One man was left on the steps as a guard. Then I saw four more soldiers approaching. At first I thought they were Americans. Then I recognised the Canadian uniform. I speak English and understood what was being said. As they came up to the museum steps one of the Canadians called out and asked the Englishman what he was doing there. Immediately the British soldier opened fire with his Sten gun.

The Canadian fell at once and two others with him collapsed, as the English soldier continued to fire his weapon. The fourth Canadian fired back, screaming and swearing as he hit the soldier in the chest, but before he died, the Englishman fired his weapon once more and the Canadian was silenced.

The eight men who had made their way into the museum came running out. One soldier knelt down and examined the dead Englishman, the others watched him in silence. Then they moved on to the Canadians. I could hear the English soldiers talking amongst themselves. Two of the Canadians had been badly injured but were still conscious. One of the Englishmen stood over the wounded men and shot both in the head, laughing crazily as he did so.

The officer in charge saw what happened. He ran up and struck the Englishman to the ground and shot him in the head with his Webley. Then the officer picked up the rucksacks of the two dead English soldiers and ordered his men to take the Canadians' rucksacks as well and fill them with artefacts from the museum. They ran back into the building and came out shortly after.

And then there was silence. The English soldiers had gone. I limped down the steps. I was looking at the dead soldiers when the arms factory nearby blew up. The noise of ammunition exploding was everywhere and flames were darting in all directions. The paratroopers must have used delay fuses. My home was near the factory and I ran to see if my family was safe.

Then the second factory exploded. It, too, must have been full of ammunition because it continued to throb with explosions throughout the next two days and nights. It was hell on earth as the roads became pathways of burning flames, and the rivers burned with toxic gas. My five-year old son ran screaming out of the house into my arms. I went inside the damaged building. My wife and younger *child were dead in the rubble. Only Heini survived the killing. He was wounded in the arm and I took him straight to the hospital which was still standing.*

The police have asked me to give a statement recording what happened at the Pforzheim museum on Monday 2ⁿᵈ October 1944. I gave this statement to them in the afternoon of the same day after reporting the deaths of the soldiers on the steps of the museum.

Matthau Schmidt, 2 October 1944, Pforzheim.

North looked up. "Herr Schmidt has kindly come here, with the mayor of Pforzheim, to hear the outcome of what happened at the museum and to answer any questions."

We looked at the old man with the tired-lined face. There were no questions. All I could hear were his words. *It was hell on earth.*

North put the statement to one side. "There are three more documents. The first is the German report, which states that the four dead Canadians had been shot with a Sten gun. The second report is a recent statement from Leutnant Gründer who gives information where the four Canadians and the two English soldiers are buried. He has asked us to pass this information on to their families, and this has been done. The third document contains the written testimony given by Mrs Paula James. We are indebted to her. Copies will now be given to you to read."

I watched Penry pass them round, I had mixed feelings. Jane turned and gave me a bitter glance. North waited a few moments and then went on.

"The third strand of this Report involves the work of CI2 and WATID in their task of investigating stolen paintings that have been resurfacing over the years. For example, during the war the Nazis seized paintings in Warsaw by Fallat and Linke. When these paintings turned up in London fifteen years later, CI2 became interested. Where had the paintings come from? Where had they been all this time? Works of art had been disappearing from museums, art galleries, and private collections all over Europe during and after the war.

"For a long time, the authorities had no idea who was responsible. However, the lists now given to us by the police in Pforzheim have been very helpful." He looked up. "In this third strand, I wish to thank Mrs James for finding the stolen miniature paintings, which, as I have already mentioned, will be returned to the Pforzheim Museum."

North then opened the second briefcase and held up a medallion with an Iron Cross in its centre. Penry stood up. "As you can see, the swastika is upright like the Iron Cross. The Cross itself is made of gold and decorated with diamonds and rubies. The word 'swastika' comes from Sanskrit." Penry paused, looking round. "It's actually a good-luck symbol. It only became a sinister sign when the Nazis turned it on its side. These medallions were a PR stunt. In 1943 the widows of German heroes were being presented with these medallions in a town hall in Berlin, but the hall was bombed and many of the widows perished in the flames. Only fifty of the medallions were later found amid the ruins."

I heard my mother's voice. *We are all victims in war.*

"The remaining medallions were packed up and sent to the Pforzheim Museum for safe keeping. They became part of the plunder stolen by Major Denby in October 1944. Apart from this one medallion that was found in Sergeant Scott's flat in Yarmouth, together with the Russian knives, no-one, until recently, knew what had happened to the other forty-nine medallions. However, we now know that Douglas Sellick paid Stan Parry a large sum for the medallions."

North went on. "A few months ago, the body of an ex-service man was found in a rotting boat in one of the Martham Pitts in Norfolk. The dead man was Stan Parry. He'd been stabbed to death. He was also present at the Pforzheim robbery. More remarkable was the discovery of a miniature portrait of Princess Victoria sewn into his clothing. We have to thank Mrs James and Sir Selwyn Freeman for this information, and for the retrieval of the remaining miniatures stolen by Major Denby at Pforzheim. An undercover officer who infiltrated a neo-Nazi group in Norwich led us to the rest of the medallions, which have now been returned to the museum."

He turned with a smile to *Museumsdirektor* Frideric Weller, who got to his feet, his beaming smile thanking everyone.

North gathered up his papers and passed them to Penry who put them into the large black cases before locking them. Finally, North thanked us for our patience and formally closed the meeting. We were free to leave the conference room. The ordeal was over.

"I'm going back to the States," Madge said, as I pushed her chair to the door. "What are you going to do, Paula?"

"Try to find a way of living my life. I just can't find the right way."

Madge stretched back and patted my hand. "Immerse yourself in a good job, that's my advice."

James and Selwyn were talking with the Pforzheim Museum's director and Lambert Weber. Quinn and Penry had joined the Royal Marine and the policeman with the beautiful Slavonic face. They were watching everyone leaving the room.

I pushed Madge into the lift and as Colonel North joined us, I saw Trish go down the stairs behind Mitchell and Freeman. We dropped down to the foyer. The door slid open and Trish waved as she walked past with the stenographer. Penry was near reception with Colonel Siegel. Selwyn and Mitchell were heading towards the tables near the bar. I saw Mitchell raise his hand to catch Colonel Siegel's attention.

A whiff of lavender wafted across the room, and my eyes were everywhere, watching everything and everyone.

I bent my head to hear what Madge was saying. She wanted to speak with Quinn. "He's supposed to be arranging transport for me to the airport."

Trish came up. "Good to see you getting about, Madge." She turned to me. "Come and join us for a meal, Paula. You too, Madge."

Madge said what she wanted was a drink. We went over to the bar in the foyer and Trish ordered two whiskies and a white wine for me.

"Hello, Mrs James, I hoped I'd catch you here!"

Mark Fisher stepped forward, a whisky in his hand.

"Who's this?" Madge snapped.

"Dr Mark Fisher, curator at a local museum," Trish said. "He knows a lot about art."

"You're here because of this Pforzheim business?"

"Indirectly, but later this evening, I'm giving a lecture on music and art." Fisher turned to me. "It's about the arts in the Renaissance and Baroque eras. I was hoping you'd stay and listen."

It sounded interesting, but then Quinn joined us. "Mrs Conway, you'll be going in a car with Colonel Siegel, Mrs Tarrant, Mr Holland and Colonel North. Enjoy your drink, you're leaving in ten minutes."

"My luggage?"

"Already in the car."

"You know, Ailie and Bette left Heathrow early this morning?"

Quinn nodded. "Mr Holland will go on to New York with you."

She looked at him, her eyes narrowing. "I need a guard?"

"Someone to help you," Quinn said suavely.

The lavender smell had dispersed. While Quinn was talking to Madge, I told Fisher I would stay for the lecture. "When does it start?"

"Eight-thirty." He pointed to a notice board on the wall near the bar. "You can read about it in the leaflet."

"I thought you would be at the meeting," I said.

"Colonel North didn't need me."

I looked through the leaflet and asked him which paintings he'd chosen to illustrate Vivaldi's four seasons.

An announcement came over the tannoy forming a background to our conversation:

Would Mr O'Hara please come to reception.

"I used some of Ricci's landscapes, and the sonnets, of course. What paintings would you use to help describe the Water Music?"

The same announcement swept the room again.

Would Mr O'Hara please come to reception.

I touched Fisher's arm. "That's Penry's voice."

Without waiting for his response, I walked over to reception, sensitive to everything happening round me. Madge was at a table finishing her drink with Trish. Mitchell had joined them. North was speaking to the stenographer who was nodding vigorously. Mulholland was at the bar with the three Germans and a tired-looking Selwyn. I watched Major Rollings walk briskly over to the revolving door and speak to the Marine and the police officer. They moved apart, positioning themselves, on guard, watching the room. A moment later, Quinn joined them.

The foyer was full of people moving round, some making their way to the lift or the stairs, others going over to the reception table. Families were sitting on the leather-covered settees and chairs in the centre of the foyer, others had congregated at the bar, and all the time there was a steady stream of people coming and going.

I scarcely noticed Fisher following me as I moved round the foyer. I took up a stand behind the greeny-brown settee where a father was reading to his two sons while his wife took a weeping toddler to the toilet. Four businessmen carrying briefcases were talking near the bar; newlyweds, the confetti still in their hair, were hastening across the room to the lift; a family of five, sitting on another settee, their luggage at their feet, were noisily waiting for a taxi. Once again, Penry's voice came over the tannoy: *Would Mr O'Hara come to reception, there is a message for him.*

A large group came hurrying through the revolving doors making their way across the foyer. One of the group, dressed casually in a blue open-neck shirt, jeans and dark blue jacket, turned suddenly and went back to the revolving doors just as I was walking over.

Quinn looked up as I approached, and Blue Shirt turned and passed me, before turning again and walking over to Reception. I frowned. I hadn't recognised the closely shaven greying hair and thick nose, but there was a hint of familiarity in the way he walked. I felt my hand busily sketching his shoulders and back.

"What's the matter?" Fisher touched my shoulder.

I looked up and he stepped back, his eyes widening. "Something's wrong." He gripped my arm. "What is it?"

"I…sort of recognised someone. It was the way he walked. A man in a blue shirt."

Quinn greeted Fisher. I wasn't surprised they knew each other. I saw Penry join the policeman at the revolving doors.

Fisher asked Quinn if he knew Blue Shirt.

"Why?"

"Mrs James thought she recognised the way he walked." He turned to me. "That's what you said?"

I nodded. "It looked familiar."

Quinn: "Who are you talking about?"

"He passed me a moment ago."

Trish came over, pushing Madge. "When's this car coming then?"

Fisher asked me to describe what I meant.

"It was the way he walked," I repeated helplessly.

"The way who walked?" asked Madge.

"The man in the blue shirt."

A glance flickered between Madge and Quinn. "Listen to the girl, Quinn. Now then, Paula, point him out to us!"

Trish looked round, puzzled. "Who are you talking about?"

Mitchell sauntered over, distracting me. "The car's been delayed. I've told Mrs Tarrant and the others. It'll be here at eight-thirty."

Madge nodded. "Good, good! Now this man, where is he?"

I thought I'd lost him among the people milling round the centre and reception. Then the crowd parted and he was walking straight towards us.

"Hello, I didn't recognise you!" I stepped forward with a smile, my hand outstretched. He took my hand, swinging me round hard, the muzzle of a Smith and Wesson against my temple, his arm pressed tightly against my throat.

Madge threw the tartan shawl onto the floor, but the bullets ripped into her before she could lift the revolver from her knee. There was no mistake this time. Madge was dead before her head fell back. Fisher dragged Trish down behind the wheelchair.

Moving quickly, the policeman locked the revolving glass door. The marine drew his weapon. Terror spread round the foyer like a fiery comet, as screams rose and people hid behind tables, chairs, or threw themselves on the floor.

The man in the blue shirt turned suddenly, dragging me round, and fired into the crowd near reception. I couldn't move in the grip he had locked round my neck and arm, but out of the corner of my eye, I saw the marine creeping round the edge of the room, his pistol steady in his hand.

North walked out into the middle of the foyer, alone, unarmed. "We were waiting for you, Hannagan. Or shall I call you O'Hara? Give up your weapon, there's no escape." He stepped closer. "Times have changed, O'Hara, there'll be peace in Ireland soon. Give up your weapon!"

I shuddered as the gun recoiled, and North dropped, the force of the bullets driving him across the wooden flooring. O'Hara fired again into the screaming group near the bar. Two lay still. Three tried to crawl away. More shots rang out, then they, too, lay still. I was waiting for the bullets to end my life. Perhaps the man in my nightmares had been Hannagan all the time.

"They won't let you get away," I croaked. He turned and fired as Fisher bent down and grasped the wheelchair from behind. Pressing his shoulder against the back, crouching and running, the dead woman's head bobbing grotesquely against the chair's wheel, Fisher propelled the wheelchair hard into O'Hara's legs and swept us both off our feet.

And all the time, O'Hara kept firing his revolver. The end came swiftly as Mitchell and Penry joined the policeman and marine and overpowered the man I had known as Mr Jolley the builder.

I'm lying on the floor.

A woman is groaning nearby.

There's blood on my legs.

Penry's head swims into view.

"The medics are here. Hold my hand, it'll help with the pain until they give you something."

I am back in my bedroom.

I call out to the woman groaning in the corner.

I tell her my legs are hurting.

Penry holds my hand.

"It's all right, they're giving you something to help with the pain."

Another voice. "Keep her still. I can't put a dressing on her legs if she keeps thrashing round."

A different voice. "Can't you stop that bloody groaning?"

"It's my mother," I moan. "She's groaning because the rose is bleeding all over her shoulder."

Or perhaps it's Amy. "The bullets ripped her blouse and the petals are falling like drops of blood."

I tell Penry anxiously that it might be Professor Baumgartner. "The knife is so deep in his chest he's coughing blood all over the flagstones."

Penry holds me tightly in his arms. "It's all right, lie still, they've nearly finished."

"But it can't be the professor," I explain patiently, "because a woman is groaning." I tell Penry I've been searching for the woman every night. "The man with the gun shot her. I've looked in every corner of the bedroom. I can hear her, she's always close by me, but I can't see her." I sip some water and shiver feverishly. "I reach out to touch her, but she's never there."

Later, I have some more water and feel better. I ask Penry if I'm going mad. "No madder than the rest of us," he says gently.

The injection helped with the pain and cleared away the curious fog in my mind. O'Hara was lying on a stretcher beside me. He had been wounded in the chest and legs, but the paramedic said he would survive. I begged Quinn to let me talk with O'Hara before we were both taken to hospital.

Quinn frowned, his face morose. "Five minutes!" he said finally.

"Why did they have to die?" I asked Mr Jolley. "And why did you let me live?"

He gave a twisted smile. "Years ago, I went to Yorkstone Cottage. I was looking round, getting the feel of the place. Your mother was too close to Enid. I had to find a way to stop her. I didn't think anyone was home, but I turned a corner and there you were, standing by a long lavender bush on your own. I'd say you were about four. A serious little girl, with a mop of blonde hair and dark blue eyes. Irish eyes. You were holding a glass of orange juice. 'You look tired,' you said. 'Have some magic orange and share my magic life and we'll walk together like giants across the world.'

"It was too tempting to refuse. I drank the orange and told you I felt just like a giant, and waved my hands about and stamped my feet. You laughed and gave me some magic fruitcake and held my hand to seal a giant's bond. I never forgot you. A little of your magic world touched me and soothed my pain. I could never rob you of your magic life."

I wish I'd known I had a magic life. "But why take all those other lives?"

He coughed, perspiration dripping from his face. "The buggers wouldn't give up. Quinn here, Mitchell, Denby, North, your mother, they never stopped searching. Marjorie was trying to break Enid down to betray me, and I began poisoning her, little by little, every time she came to the house. Enid knew nothing about it, but *I* knew Ackert's daughter would never let go. North laid the trap today. They knew I'd come. Sure, didn't I have to avenge Enid?"

He coughed again and blood trickled out of his mouth. The doctor moved closer. "Not yet," Quinn said. "I was in Belfast last week. I knew at once you'd set the bomb. Now then, there are things we have to know. Are you still in touch with your old unit?"

O'Hara's lips twisted. "I'm not talking of that, but it's sorry I am that Luighne Connacht has lost its last son." He lifted his head. "Sure, I'm glad I got North." His head dropped back. He was feverish, his lips shaking. "Denby got too close, but I wish I'd got you, Quinn, and bloody Mitchell."

They were the last words that Hannagan, or Ó hEaghra of an ancient Irish kingdom spoke, as he lay dying in convulsions.

"Poison *again*!" Quinn shouted. "Bloody poison! I should have known."

Quinn was beside himself. He had wanted Hannagan alive for the courts to hold him responsible for his crimes.

There was no-one to grieve for O'Hara. The world hated him for what he had done, but it's a lonely death when there are none to mourn your memory.

I had never felt uneasy with William Jolley, the builder. I had been much more alert to Enid's darker side.

Quinn sniffed. "I've spent all my life chasing villains, and Hannagan was the worst. He had no heart. He killed for his cause and went on killing." His mouth went down. "There are some criminals you can pardon, even like. Others you hunt down all your life."

But Hannagan had never forgotten the hand-clasp that had sealed our bond. And he had given me my life.

Thursday, 11th June 1981

The following day, Mitchell drove me down to The Rosary in Ealing to convalesce. "You can move into your new flat when you're ready. We'll hurry it along while you're staying with Aunt Gertrud."

My new flat was on the first floor. I told him about the courtyard I had created and the tool-shed I had hoped to use at Eversley Road. "In the new house, we all share the garden. It won't be the same."

"Maybe, but no-one will be shooting at you either." But Mitchell was not a gardener, the colours and shapes of plants did not fill him with happiness and ease. Mitchell had not understood.

While I was at The Rosary, DCI Quinn phoned. "A John Fellowes Greene is writing a biography about your mother. He wants to meet you. How do you feel about it?"

My reaction was immediate. "Tell him to wait at least three weeks, then I'll talk with him."

Quinn responded as usual with a grunt. "I'll tell him."

I stayed in The Rosary for two weeks and painted the nuns, with Mitchell posing as the gardener sweeping the steps while a smiling Trish presented a bouquet of mixed roses to Sister Gertrud.

I gave Gertrud an advance copy of the story she had liked—*Bobby and the Apricot Lady*. I told her the publishers wanted another story about Bobby. Gertrud was delighted.

At the inquest for Colonel North, Quinn was adamant that North had not planned an ambush for O'Hara. Mitchell supported him, but I knew Madge had been waiting for Hannagan with a gun under her rug.

Jane visited me in my new flat. She was bitter. "We've all suffered because of Werner."

She told me that Matthau Schmidt and Sir Selwyn Freeman had been among the dead in the foyer at Lansbury Hall.

End of June 1981

To the delight of Ailie and Bette, Peter Schiffer agreed to send the MJ Jeffries' paintings to Virginia to be shown at an exhibition in March. It would be mounted in memory of Madge Conway.

Two days after moving into my new flat, Mark Fisher visited me. He found me unresponsive. "Quinn warned me, he said you were difficult."

I offered him a mug of coffee. I was in another new kitchen. Savagely, I asked him why he'd come round.

He put the mug down. "We could make a good team fighting these bloody art fraudsters."

"But if I'm difficult—" I began.

He moved his hands angrily. "What I want is your knowledge. You grew up involved in art, you have an instinct for what is right or wrong. And you can draw. You're good at what you do. A lot of this job is about instinct as well as knowledge."

"Wherever I go, people get killed." I was bitter.

"That's all over, Quinn said so."

What did Quinn know? "I'll think about it." I was too tired to argue. I asked him what had happened to his lecture.

"Postponed until next week."

I tried to shrug off the apathy that had taken hold of me. "I always loved that period. A time of realism when artists communicated with people."

Fisher smiled, and I sketched the lines creasing the corners of his eyes. "OK, I'll let you do the lecture." He leaned forward. "Now, how about working with me?"

I liked the way his ears lay flat against his head and his hair waved as it touched his neck. "I need more time," I mumbled.

"I don't have time. I thought we were getting on well."

I was harsh. "That was before O'Hara."

"It's the O'Hara's and the scammers we're fighting, that's why I need you."

"It's too soon," I persisted.

"You're wrong, it's probably too late. It's becoming harder and harder to keep up with the fraudsters." Fisher got up and pulled his coat on, frustration in his long Norman face. "If you want the truth, I think you're a bloody difficult woman, but maybe, *because* of that, we could work well together." He pointed to my hand. "You're wearing an Odala ring. Did you know the Anglo-Saxons wore them? They were a sign of nobility. You've got a lot to live up to."

I said nothing. Fisher waited a moment, then flung his card on the table, walked out and banged the front door shut. I hadn't heard the door closing in my dreams for weeks now. Automatically, I got up and washed the cups under clear running water. I picked up the tea-towel. A bloody difficult woman, he'd said. That wasn't me, that was Marjorie Ackert.

Dad and Schiffer had called her a difficult woman, but they had loved her. Marjorie Ackert had been complicated. She had loved too much and hated too easily. The war had been a grey and bitter time for my mother. Other people's perceptions must have hurt her. Her faith had been her bedrock and had heightened the colours that glowed within her. But I wasn't like my mother, and though I had climbed Judd's ladder, in the end it was O'Hara who had brought me down.

My father had thought Hannagan was a danger to me. But Mr Jolley had been in my home, eating salmon and cucumber sandwiches, hanging pictures on the walls and talking pleasantries with his wife and me. I had liked William Jolley, yet he was the man who had murdered both my parents, and my blood ran cold when I thought of him talking and smiling with me.

The separate lives of parents. It had stayed in my mind. How can children understand the many layers that make up their parents' lives? I had thought my father was perfect, my mother brilliant, but their lives had been complex and disturbing and far removed from my childish memories.

Days and nights passed. There was no longer a woman groaning in the bedroom, or a man with a gun creeping out of the shadows and scaring me out of my wits. Penry had suggested the woman groaning in the room had been me all the time. I had laughed at him.

"No, listen to me," Penry said. "At night your brain is freed from the constraints of normality, and the weight of the terrors you suffered as a child is given free reign. No wonder you groaned as your mind lived through the shadow of the gunman firing at Amy, or through a knife twisting in the sun, or a rose

340

dripping blood on your mother's dress. You see, Paula, the shadows in the mind are just as tangible as reality."

Did I believe him? But, strangely, I hadn't heard the woman groaning since O'Hara died. One day, I thought as I dried the tea-things, I would like to wake up and find none of my life had happened. I would be someone else, someone who'd never seen violent death or had strange spiky moments when the sails of a windmill creaked in the misty night.

Without warning, I sank to my knees holding the tea-towel to my face. I let the tears fall unchecked, and in my inner mind, I saw Baumgartner step forward and my mother thrust the glistening knife deep into his chest. Hate had filled her bulging eyes.

Oh God, I didn't want to look like that, pushed to the edge of madness! Where did my mother begin and end in me? How could I live with these images burning in my brain? They coloured everything I did, everyone I met. I told myself I was a loose cannon spewing deadly metal wherever I went. Fisher should be glad I wanted nothing to do with him.

With a groan, I pulled myself up and ran fresh water over my face, again and again, to wash away the heavy scent of blue and purple lavender leaves.

The doorbell again! I dragged myself along to answer it. My legs were still hurting. I was hurting all over. All the terrible things that had happened had finally caught up with me.

Trish was on the doorstep. "God, what's wrong?"

Two whiskies later, I began to feel almost human. "I want to try life again," I told Trish, "but without the pain."

She looked at me quizzically. "Things happen round you, Paula, it's no good kidding yourself. Has Fisher been in touch?"

"He was here earlier. He called me a bloody difficult woman."

Trish's eyebrows rose. "Well, he's summed you up right! But did he offer you a job?"

"I didn't take it. It wouldn't be fair on him."

"Don't be silly, Paula, he knows what he's doing." She leaned forward. "It's you I'm thinking of. Why don't you write and illustrate your stories?"

I hear my mother's voice. "Well drawn, Liebchen." She's pointing to the willow trug full of daisies I've sketched. "You've controlled the lines as

341

beautifully as you've controlled the plot about the young woman and her clever dog."

She looks up, delight in her smiling sea-blue eyes. I sweep some daisies up and present them to her with a little knicks. "Now you curtsey!" We laugh together, and then she says, "We must find an agent."

Two days later, she was dead. I was suddenly grateful to my mother for her constant corrections, for her determination to make me see what was strong and what was wrong. I told Trish that Quinn had come round with a bottle of Chardonnay as a peace offering.

"He said he'd joined North's team in 1960 when my mum was about forty-five." I smiled fleetingly. "Most people were bowled over by her, but Quinn didn't like her."

Trish nodded. "Madge said Marjorie was intuitive. Quinn's a proper cop. He wouldn't have worked on her radar."

I didn't say anything to Trish, but Quinn had looked at me with a half-smile in his grey brown-flecked eyes. "I was overly influenced by Denby. He was so positive you had the Pforzheim miniatures. Penry thought Schiffer had them." He picked up his coat. "You're very like Marjorie, you know, clever, perceptive, beautiful, but I never felt the magic in her that I feel in you."

I was taken aback. "You never showed it."

"Policemen shouldn't fall in love with women they're investigating." And he had left.

A few minutes later, Penry had come in cheerfully. "Settling in all right? Good! Well, I thought you'd like some news. We've pulled in that representative you were always going on about."

"No! Tell me!"

"The rep was Mrs Irene Browne, Meg Farrell's assistant. She called herself Rowene Birne and she's spilt the beans. Meg Farrell knew nothing about it. When *The Auctioneers* threw your father and Scott out, they got a new leader, a young man without a conscience, Martin Spencer. He started *The Helpline*. He had no difficulty in finding criminals to work with him."

"James Mitchell told me. I can't believe I was in Dunham Village when it was all going on. Spencer should have used his gifts legally. He'd probably be a millionaire now."

Penry shook his head. "Not enough excitement. He's an evil young man."

"And Peter Linsey, what's happened to him?"

"He's going on trial. Mrs Conrad's recovering and wants to see you soon."

"Good! I'd like that." I hesitated. "I know it happened a long time ago, but do you know who shot Amy?"

"I thought you knew. Spencer told us. We were holding him responsible for Amy's death, but he was quick to point the finger. He said Charlie Havilland, a clever and unscrupulous art dealer, killed her. Havilland was convinced Amy had the miniatures. He hadn't been expecting her to have a weapon, and he shot her. Havilland told us you were there, but you hadn't seen him. He kept an eye on you all these years, just in case you remembered something."

I hadn't even known Havilland, yet he had taken the life of my mother's friend. I remembered talking to Corrie saying life wasn't fair, and she had replied cheerfully, "No, it bloody isn't!"

Penry had been kind to me. He had held me in his arms after Fisher brought O'Hara down, so I told him to search the pool at the Conrad's house.

"Oh?"

"Gillian once talked about the reflection of stars in the pool."

Penry frowned, hunching himself forward, doing a very good imitation of Quinn. "Why do you *always* know more than I do?"

I laughed with him.

Quinn returned the following day. The Pretoria Diamonds had been in the pool in plastic boxes. "A fortune was lying on the floor of the fishes' pond. Astonishing!"

"Will you advise Mrs Conrad to put them in a bank?"

"She's decided to use the diamonds to create bursaries for young artists and scientists."

"That's wonderful!" I was surprised she could show such good judgement.

Quinn got up to leave. "Denby won the MC in the war. A brave man and he cared about you. You should remember that."

When I told Trish about the diamonds, she said I should have jumped in the pool and got them for myself. "But seriously, Paula, either draw things or take Fisher's job. If you don't like working with him, you can move on. From what Quinn says, it's all over, all the things that were part of your mother's life, like Dieter Ackert and Pforzheim." She leaned back, smiling. "Think of it like this. Thirty is the new twenty. It's a clean slate. I'd give you a job myself, but you'll get a lot more out of working with Fisher. Or doing what you're really good at, sketching and writing."

I looked at Trish, at the thick hair pulled back from a low forehead, her dark brown eyes, well-formed mouth, determined chin and fair freckled skin. I wondered what lay hidden behind that smooth façade. Enid had warned me not to be so trusting.

We all have things to hide, my mother had said.

It's a clean slate, Trish had said.

Maybe, but everything that had happened had never been about me, it had always been about my mother. The past would always be there. I wished I could have cleansed away the hostility and malice my mother had suffered after Colonel North spread rumours about her during the war. North had never publicly cleared her name.

I toyed with Fisher's card. The willow trug had sparked a memory. A ten-year-old girl making a daisy-chain bracelet, watching Franz drawing her mother into a passionate embrace.

"Come with me," he says.

"And Paula?" my mother asks.

"No, just you and me."

I was suddenly overcome with gratitude, because she had chosen to keep me with her.

I thought of the child, Jane, listening to Aunt Niamh's enchanting tales of Red Knights in Irish castles. How could she have known that ten years later her father would be hanged in Mountjoy Gaol?

In my pocket were the two rings I had taken out of the attic of Lintwhite Villa, the Eif ring and my mother's diamond ring. *Carry truth and humanity throughout your life.* Mum had protected the Pforzheim miniatures because she truly believed the purpose of art was to serve mankind, and she had painted *Wild Marjoram* as a shield, not knowing that her murderer and her daughter had already sealed their magic bond.

I put Fisher's card down as Trish's voice penetrated my thoughts. "Do you think your mother was right to hide the miniatures?"

I gestured irritably. "I don't want to talk about it."

Trish leaned back. "I'm sorry, I didn't mean to upset you."

What *did* she mean?

"Articles!" Trish said explosively.

"*What?*"

"You promised me some articles!" A long time ago. "You said you'd write down the Tim Harvey story."

I couldn't do that, not yet, but perhaps it would spur me on to write. The thought began to take hold. "I can't write about the scam and the Retirement Homes because of the trial, but I could write about summer holidays in Acle when I was a child. I'll start tomorrow."

Trish smiled. "Tomorrow sounds good!"

She poured out another whisky and we sat and drank to an uncertain future.

The End